THE 49TH GOLDEN AGE OF SCIENCE FICTION MEGAPACK®

NELSON S. BOND

THE 49TH GOLDEN AGE OF SCIENCE FICTION MEGAPACK®
NELSON S. BOND

WILDSIDE PRESS

CONTENTS

TROUBLE ON TYCHO

Originally published in *Planet Stories*, March 1943.

The audiophone buzzed thrice—one long, followed by two shorts—and Isobar Jones pressed the stud activating its glowing scanner-disc.

"Hummm?" he said absent-mindedly.

The selenoplate glowed faintly, and the image of the Dome Commander appeared.

"Report ready, Jones?"

"Almost," acknowledged Isobar gloomily. "It prob'ly ain't right, though. How anybody can be expected to get *anything* right on this dagnabbed hunk o' green cheese—"

"Send it up," interrupted Colonel Eagan, "as soon as you can. Sparks is making Terra contact now. That is all."

"That ain't all!" declared Isobar indignantly. "How about my bag—?"

It *was all*, so far as the D.C. was concerned. Isobar was talking to himself. The plate dulled. Isobar said, "Nuts!" and returned to his duties. He jotted neat ditto marks under the word "Clear" which, six months ago, he had placed beneath the column headed: *Cond. of Obs*. He noted the proper figures under the headings *Sun Spots*: *Max Freq.—Min. Freq.*; then he sketched careful curves in blue and red ink upon the Mercator projection of Earth which was his daily work sheet.

This done, he drew a clean sheet of paper out of his desk drawer, frowned thoughtfully at the tabulated results of his observations, and began writing.

"*Weather forecast for Terra*," he wrote, his pen making scratching sounds.

The audiophone rasped again. Isobar jabbed the stud and answered without looking.

"O.Q.," he said wearily. "O.Q. I told you it would be ready in a couple o' minutes. Keep your pants on!"

"I—er—I beg your pardon, Isobar?" queried a mild voice.

Isobar started. His sallow cheeks achieved a sickly salmon hue. He blinked nervously.

"Oh, jumpin' jimminy!" he gulped. "*You*, Miss Sally! Golly—'scuse me! I didn't realize—"

The Dome Commander's niece giggled.

"That's all right, Isobar. I just called to ask you about the weather in Oceania Sector 4B next week. I've got a swimming date at Waikiki, but I won't make the shuttle unless the weather's going to be nice."

"It is," promised Isobar. "It'll be swell all weekend, Miss Sally. Fine sunshiny weather. You can go."

"That's wonderful. Thanks so much, Isobar."

"Don't mention it, ma'am," said Isobar, and returned to his work.

South America. Africa. Asia. Pan-Europa. Swiftly he outlined the meteorological prospects for each sector. He enjoyed this part of his job. As he wrote forecasts for each area, in his mind's eye he saw himself enjoying such pastimes as each geographical division's terrain rendered possible.

* * * *

If home is where the heart is, Horatio Jones—known better as "Isobar" to his associates at the Experimental Dome on Luna—was a long, long way from home. His lean, gangling frame was immured, and had been for six tedious Earth months, beneath the *impervite* hemisphere of Lunar III—that frontier outpost which served as a rocket refueling station, teleradio transmission point and meteorological base.

"Six solid months! Six sad, dreary months!" thought Isobar, "Locked up in an airtight Dome like—like a goldfish in a glass bowl!" Sunlight? Oh, sure! But filtered through ultraviolet wave-traps so it could not burn, it left the skin pale and lustreless and clammy as the belly of a toad. Fresh air? Pooh! Nothing but that everlasting sickening, scented, reoxygenated stuff gushing from atmo-conditioning units.

Excitement? Adventure? The romance he had been led to expect when he signed on for frontier service? Bah! Only a weary, monotonous, routine existence.

"A pain!" declared Isobar Jones. "That's what it is; a pain in the stummick. Not even allowed to—Yeah?"

It was Sparks, audioing from the Dome's transmission turret. He said, "Hyah, Jonesy! How comes with the report?"

"Done," said Isobar. "I was just gettin' the sheets together for you."

"O.Q. But just bring *it*. Nothing else."

Isobar bridled.

"I don't know what you're talkin' about."

"Oh, no? Well, I'm talking about that squawk-filled doodlesack of yours, sonny boy. Don't bring that bag-full of noise up here with you."

Isobar said defiantly, "It ain't a doodlesack. It's a bagpipe. And I guess I can play it if I want to—"

"Not," said Sparks emphatically, "in *my* cubby! I've got sensitive eardrums. Well, stir your stumps! I've got to get the report rolling quick today. Big doings up here."

"Yeah? What?"

"Well, it's Roberts and Brown—"

"What about 'em?"

"They've gone Outside to make foundation repairs."

"Lucky stiffs!" commented Isobar ruefully.

"Lucky, no. Stiffs, maybe—if they should meet any Grannies. Well, scoot along. I'm on the ether in four point sixteen minutes."

"Be right up," promised Isobar, and, sheets in hand, he ambled from his cloistered cell toward the central section of the Dome.

He didn't leave Sparks' turret after the sheets were delivered. Instead, he hung around, fidgeting so obtrusively that Riley finally turned to him in sheer exasperation.

"Sweet snakes of Saturn, Jonesy, what's the trouble? Bugs in your britches?"

Isobar said, "H-huh? Oh, you mean—Oh, thanks, no! I just thought mebbe you wouldn't mind if I—well—er—"

"I get it!" Sparks grinned. "Want to play peekaboo while the contact's open, eh? Well, O.Q. Watch the birdie!"

He twisted dials, adjusted verniers, fingered a host of incomprehensible keys. Current hummed and howled. Then a plate before him cleared, and the voice of the Earth operator came in, enunciating with painstaking clarity:

"Earth answering Luna. Earth answering Luna's call. Can you hear me, Luna? Can you hear—?"

"I can not only hear you," snorted Riley, "I can see you and smell you, as well. Stop hamming it, stupid! You're lousing up the earth!"

The now-visible face of the Earth radioman drew into a grimace of displeasure.

"Oh, it's *you*? Funny man, eh? Funny man Riley?"

"Sure," said Riley agreeably. "I'm a scream. Four-alarm Riley, the cosmic comedian—didn't you know? Flick on your dictacoder, oyster-puss; here's the weather report." He read it. "'*Weather forecast for Terra, week of May 15-21—*'"

"Ask him," whispered Isobar eagerly. "Sparks, don't forget to ask him!"

Riley motioned for silence, but nodded. He finished the weather report, entered the Dome Commander's log upon the Home Office records, and dictated a short entry from the Luna Biological Commission. Then:

"That is all," he concluded.

"O.Q.," verified the other radioman. Isobar writhed anxiously, prodded Riley's shoulder.

"Ask him, Sparks! Go on ask him!"

"Oh, cut jets, will you?" snapped Sparks. The Terra operator looked startled.

"How's that? I didn't say a word—"

"Don't be a dope," said Sparks, "you dope! I wasn't talking to you. I'm entertaining a visitor, a refugee from a cuckoo clock. Look, do me a favor, chum? Can you twist your mike around so it's pointing out a window?"

"What? Why—why, yes, but—"

"Without buts," said Sparks grumpily. "Yours not to reason why; yours but to do or don't. Will you do it?"

"Well, sure. But I don't understand—" The silver platter which had mirrored the radioman's face clouded as the Earth operator twirled the inconoscope. Walls and desks of an ordinary broadcasting office spun briefly into view; then the plate reflected a glimpse of an Earthly landscape. Soft blue sky warmed by an atmosphere-shielded sun ... green trees firmly rooted in still-greener grass ... flowers ... birds ... people....

"Enough?" asked Sparks.

Isobar Jones awakened from his trance, eyes dulling. Reluctantly he nodded. Riley stared at him strangely, almost gently. To the other radioman, "O.Q., pal," he said. "Cut!"

"Cut!" agreed the other. The plate blanked out.

"Thanks, Sparks," said Isobar.

"Nothing," shrugged Riley "*He twisted* the mike; not me. But—how come you always want to take a squint at Earth when the circuit's open, Jonesy? Homesick?"

"Sort of," admitted Isobar guiltily.

"Well, hell, aren't we all? But we can't leave here for another six months at least. Not till our tricks are up. I should think it'd only make you feel worse to see Earth."

"It ain't Earth I'm homesick for," explained Isobar. "It's—well, it's the things that go with it. I mean things like grass and flowers and trees."

Sparks grinned; a mirthless, lopsided grin.

"We've got *them* right here on Luna. Go look out the tower window, Jonesy. The Dome's nestled smack in the middle of the prettiest, greenest little valley you ever saw."

"I know," complained Isobar. "And that's what makes it even worse. All that pretty, soft, green stuff Outside—and we ain't allowed to go out in it. Sometimes I get so mad I'd like to—"

"To," interrupted a crisp voice, "what?"

Isobar spun, flushing; his eyes dropped before those of Dome Commander Eagan. He squirmed.

"N-nothing, sir. I was only saying—"

"I heard you, Jones. And please let me hear no more of such talk, sir! It is strictly forbidden for anyone to go Outside except in cases of absolute necessity. Such labor as caused Patrolmen Brown and Roberts to go, for example—"

"Any word from them yet, sir?" asked Sparks eagerly.

"Not yet. But we're expecting them to return at any minute now. Jones! Where are *you* going?"

"Why—why, just back to my quarters, sir."

"That's what I thought. And what did you plan to do there?"

Isobar said stubbornly, "Well, I sort of figured I'd amuse myself for a while—"

"I thought that, too. And with *what*, pray, Jones?"

"With the only dratted thing," said Isobar, suddenly petulant, "that gives me any fun around this dagnabbed place! With my bagpipe."

Commander Eagan said, "You'd better find some new way of amusing yourself, Jones. Have you read General Order 17?"

Isobar said, "I seen it. But if you think—"

"It says," stated Eagan deliberately, "'*In order that work or rest periods of the Dome's staff may not be disturbed, it is hereby ordered that the playing or practicing of all or any musical instruments must be discontinued immediately. By order of the Dome Commander,*' That means you, Jones!"

"But, dingbust it!" keened Isobar, "it don't disturb nobody for me to play my bagpipes! I know these lunks around here don't appreciate good music, so I always go in my office and lock the door after me—"

"But the Dome," pointed out Commander Eagan, "has an air-conditioning system which can't be shut off. The ungodly moans of your—er—so-called musical instrument can be heard through the entire structure."

He suddenly seemed to gain stature.

"No, Jones, this order is final! You cannot disrupt our entire organization for your own—er—amusement."

"But—" said Isobar.

"No!"

Isobar wriggled desperately. Life on Luna was sorry enough already. If now they took from him the last remaining solace he had, the last amusement which lightened his moments of freedom—

"Look, Commander!" he pleaded, "I tell you what I'll do. I won't bother nobody. I'll go Outside and play it—"

"Outside!" Eagan stared at him incredulously. "Are you mad? How about the Grannies?"

Isobar knew all about the Grannies. The only mobile form of life found by space-questing man on Earth's satellite, their name was an abbreviation of the descriptive one applied to them by the first Lunar explorers: Granitebacks. This was no exaggeration; if anything, it was an understatement. For the Grannies, though possessed of certain low intelligence, had quickly proven themselves a deadly, unyielding and implacable foe.

Worse yet, they were an enemy almost indestructible! No man had ever yet brought to Earth laboratories the carcass of a Grannie; science was completely baffled in its endeavors to explain the composition of Graniteback physiology—but it was known, from bitter experience, that the carapace or exoskeleton of the Grannies was formed of something harder than steel, diamond, or battleplate! This flesh could be penetrated by no weapon known to man; neither by steel nor flame, by electronic nor ionic wave, nor by the lethal, newly discovered atomo-needle dispenser.

All this Isobar knew about the Grannies. Yet:

"They ain't been any Grannies seen around the Dome," he said, "for a 'coon's age. Anyhow, if I seen any comin', I could run right back inside—"

"No!" said Commander Eagan flatly. "Absolutely, *no*! I have no time for such nonsense. You know the orders—obey them! And now, gentlemen, good afternoon!"

He left. Sparks turned to Isobar, grinning.

"Well," he said, "one man's fish—hey, Jonesy? Too bad you can't play your doodlesack any more, but frankly, I'm just as glad. Of all the awful screeching wails—"

But Isobar Jones, generally mild and gentle, was now in a perfect fury. His pale eyes blazed, he stomped his foot on the floor, and from his lips poured a stream of such angry invective that Riley looked startled. Words that, to Isobar, were the utter dregs of violent profanity.

"Oh, dagnab it!" fumed Isobar Jones. "Oh, tarnation and dingbust! Oh—*fiddlesticks*!"

CHAPTER II

"And so," chuckled Riley, "he left, bubbling like a kettle on a red-hot oven. But, boy! was he ever mad! Just about ready to bust, he was."

Some minutes had passed since Isobar had left; Riley was talking to Dr. Loesch, head of the Dome's Physics Research Division. The older man nodded commiseratingly.

"It is funny, yes," he agreed, "but at the same time it is not altogether amusing. I feel sorry for him. He is a very unhappy man, our poor Isobar."

"Yeah, I know," said Riley, "but, hell, we all get a little bit homesick now and then. He ought to learn to—"

"Excuse me, my boy," interrupted the aged physicist, his voice gentle, "it is not mere homesickness that troubles our friend. It is something deeper, much more vital and serious. It is what my people call: *weltschmertz*. There is no accurate translation in English. It means 'world sickness,' or better, 'world weariness'—something like that but intensified a thousandfold.

"It is a deeply-rooted mental condition, sometimes a dangerous frame of mind. Under its grip, men do wild things. Hating the world on which they find themselves, they rebel in curious ways. Suicide ... mad acts of valor ... deeds of cunning or knavery...."

"You mean," demanded Sparks anxiously, "Isobar ain't got all his buttons?"

"Not that exactly. He is perfectly sane. But he is in a dark morass of despair. He may try *anything* to retrieve his lost happiness, rid his soul of its dark oppression. His world-sickness is like a crying hunger—By the way, where is he now?"

"Below, I guess. In his quarters."

"Ah, good! Perhaps he is sleeping. Let us hope so. In slumber he will find peace and forgetfulness."

But Dr. Loesch would have been far less sanguine had some power the "giftie gi'en" him of watching Isobar Jones at that moment.

Isobar was not asleep. Far from it. Wide awake and very much astir, he was acting in a singularly sinister role: that of a slinking, furtive culprit.

Returning to his private cubicle after his conversation with Dome Commander Eagan, he had stalked straightway to the cabinet wherein was encased his precious set of bagpipes. These he had taken from their pegs, gazed upon defiantly, and fondled with almost parental affection.

"So I can't play you, huh?" he muttered darkly. "It disturbs the peace o' the dingfounded, dumblasted Dome staff, does it? Well, we'll *see* about that!"

And tucking the bag under his arm, he had cautiously slipped from the room, down little-used corridors, and now he stood before the huge *impervite* gates which were the entrance to the Dome and the doorway to Outside.

On all save those occasions when a spacecraft landed in the cradle adjacent the gateway, these portals were doubly locked and barred. But today they had been unbolted that the two maintenance men might venture out. And since it was quite possible that Brown and Roberts might have to get inside in a hurry, their bolts remained drawn. Sole guardian of the entrance was a very bored Junior Patrolman.

Up to this worthy strode Isobar Jones, confident and assured, exuding an aura of propriety.

"Very well, Wilkins," he said. "I'll take over now. You may go to the meeting."

Wilkins looked at him bewilderedly.

"Huh? Whuzzat, Mr. Jones?"

Isobar's eyebrows arched.

"You mean you haven't been notified?"

"Notified of *what*?"

"Why, the general council of all Patrolmen! Weren't you told that I would take your place here while you reported to G.H.Q.?"

"I ain't," puzzled Wilkins, "heard nothing about it. Maybe I ought to call the office, maybe?"

And he moved the wall-audio. But Isobar said swiftly. "That—er—won't be necessary, Wilkins. My orders were plain enough. Now, you just run along. I'll watch this entrance for you."

"We-e-ell," said Wilkins, "if you say so. Orders is orders. But keep a sharp eye out, Mister Jones, in case Roberts and Brown should come back sudden-like."

"I will," promised Isobar, "don't worry."

* * * *

Wilkins moved away. Isobar waited until the Patrolman was completely out of sight. Then swiftly he pulled open the massive gate, slipped through, and closed it behind him.

A flood of warmth, exhilarating after the constantly regulated temperature of the Dome, descended upon him. Fresh air, thin, but fragrant with the scent of growing things, made his pulses stir with joyous abandon. He was Outside! He was Outside, in good sunlight, at last! After six long and dreary months!

Raptly, blissfully, all thought of caution tossed to the gentle breezes that ruffled his sparse hair, Isobar Jones stepped forward into the lunar valley....

How long he wandered thus, carefree and utterly content, he could not afterward say. It seemed like minutes; it must have been longer. He only knew that the grass was green beneath his feet, the trees were a lacy network through which warm sunlight filtered benevolently, the chirrupings of small insects and the rustling whisper of the breezes formed a tiny symphony of happiness through which he moved as one charmed.

It did not occur to him that he had wandered too far from the Dome's entrance until, strolling through an enchanting flower-decked glade, he was startled to hear—off to his right—the sharp, explosive bark of a Haemholtz ray pistol.

He whirled, staring about him wildly, and discovered that though his meandering had kept him near the Dome, he had unconsciously followed its hemispherical perimeter to a point nearly two miles from the Gateway.

By the placement of ports and windows, Isobar was able to judge his location perfectly; he was opposite that portion of the structure which housed Sparks' radio turret.

And the shooting? That could only be—

He did not have to name its reason, even to himself. For at that moment, there came racing around the curve of the Dome a pair of figures, Patrolmen clad in fatigue drab. Roberts and Brown. Roberts was staggering, one foot dragged awkwardly as he ran; Brown's left arm, bloodstained from shoulder to elbow, hung limply at his side, but in his good right fist he held a spitting Haemholtz with which he tried to cover his comrade's sluggish retreat.

And behind these two, grim, grey, gaunt figures that moved with astonishing speed despite their massive bulk, came three ... six ... a dozen of those lunarites whom all men feared. The Grannies!

CHAPTER III

Simultaneously with his recognition of the pair, Joe Roberts saw him. A gasp of relief escaped the wounded man.

"Jones! Thank the Lord! Then you picked up our cry for help? Quick, man—where is it? Theres not a moment to waste!"

"W-where," faltered Isobar feebly, "is *what*?"

"The tank, of course! Didn't you hear our telecast? We can't possibly make it back to the gate without an armored car. My foot's broken, and—" Roberts stopped suddenly, an abrupt horror in his eyes. "You don't have one! You're here *alone*! Then you didn't pick up our call? But, why—?"

"Never mind that," snapped Isobar, "now!" Placid by nature, he could move when urgency drove. His quick mind saw the immediateness of their peril. Unarmed, he could not help the Patrolmen fight a delaying action against their foes, nor could he hasten their retreat. Anyway, weapons were useless, and time was of the essence. There was but one temporary way of staving off disaster. "Over here ... this tree! Quick! Up you go! Give him a lift, Brown—There! That's the stuff!"

He was the last to scramble up the gnarled bole to a tentative leafy sanctuary. He had barely gained the security of the lowermost bough when a thundering crash resounded, the sturdy trunk trembled beneath his clutch. Stony claws gouged yellow parallels in the bark scant inches beneath one kicking foot, then the Granny fell back with a thud. The Graniteback was *not* a climber. It was far too ungainly, much too weighty for that.

Roberts said weakly, "Th-thanks, Jonesy! That was a close call."

"That goes for me, too, Jonesy," added Brown from an upper bough. "But I'm afraid you just delayed matters. This tree's O.Q. as long as it lasts, but—" He stared down upon the gathering knot of Grannies unhappily—"it's not going to last long with that bunch of superdreadnaughts working out on it! Hold tight, fellows! Here they come!"

For the Grannies, who had huddled for a moment as if in telepathic consultation, now joined forces, turned, and as one body charged headlong toward the tree. The unified force of their attack was like the shattering impact of a battering ram. Bark rasped and gritted beneath the besieged men's hands, dry leaves and twigs pelted about them in a tiny rain, tormented fibrous sinews groaned as the aged forest monarch shuddered in agony.

Desperately they clung to their perches. Though the great tree bent, it did not break. But when it stopped trembling, it was canted drunkenly to one side, and the erstwhile solid earth about its base was broken and cracked—revealing fleshy tentacles uprooted from ancient moorings!

Brown stared at this evidence of the Grannies' power with terror-fascinated eyes. His voice was none too firm.

"Lord! Piledrivers! A couple more like that—"

Isobar nodded. He knew what falling into the clutch of the Grannies meant. He had once seen the grisly aftermath of a Graniteback feast. Even now their adversaries had drawn back for a second attack. A sudden idea struck him. A straw of hope at which he grasped feverishly.

"You telecast a message to the Dome? Help should be on the way by now. If we can just hold out—"

But Roberts shook his head.

"We sent a message, Jonesy, but I don't think it got through. I've just been looking at my portable. It seems to be busted. Happened when they first attacked us, I guess. I tripped and fell on it."

Isobar's last hope flickered out.

"Then I—I guess it won't be long now," he mourned. "If we could have only got a message through, they would have sent out an armored car to pick us up. But as it is—"

Brown's shrug displayed a bravado he did not feel.

"Well, that's the way it goes. We knew what we were risking when we volunteered to come Outside. This damn moon! It'll never be worth a plugged credit until men find some way to fight those murderous stones-on-legs!"

Roberts said, "That's right. But what are *you* doing out here, Isobar? And why, for Pete's sake, the bagpipes?"

"Oh—the pipes?" Isobar flushed painfully. He had almost forgotten his original reason for adventuring Outside, had quite forgotten his instrument, and was now rather amazed to discover that somehow throughout all the excitement he had held onto it. "Why, I just happened to—Oh! *the pipes!*"

"Hold on!" roared Roberts. His warning came just in time. Once more, the three tree-sitters shook like dried peas in a pod as their leafy refuge trembled before the locomotive onslaught of the lunar beasts. This time the already-exposed roots strained and lifted, several snapped; when the Grannies again withdrew, complacently unaware that the "lethal ray" of Brown's Haemholtz was wasting itself upon their adamant hides in futile fury, the tree was bent at a precarious angle.

Brown sobbed, not with fear but with impotent anger, and in a gesture of enraged desperation, hurled his now-empty weapon at the retreating Grannies.

"No good! Not a damn bit of good! Oh, if there was only some way of fighting those filthy things—"

But Isobar Jones had a one-track mind. "The pipes!" he cried again, excitedly. "That's the answer!" And he drew the instrument into playing position, bag cuddled beneath one arm-pit, drones stiffly erect over his shoulder, blow-pipe at his lips. His cheeks puffed, his breath expelled. The giant lung swelled, the chaunter emitted its distinctive, fearsome, "*Kaa-aa-o-o-o-oro-oong!*"

Roberts moaned.

"Oh, Lord! A guy can't even die in peace!"

And Brown stared at him hopelessly.

"It's no use, Isobar. You trying to scare them off? They have no sense of hearing. That's been proven—"

Isobar took his lips from the reed to explain.

"It's not that. I'm trying to rouse the boys in the Dome. We're right opposite the atmosphere-conditioning-unit. See that grilled duct over there? That's an inhalation-vent. The portable transmitter's out of order, and our voices ain't strong enough to carry into the Dome—but the sound of these pipes is! And Commander Eagan told me just a short while ago that the sound of the pipes carries all over the building!

"If they hear this, they'll get mad because I'm disobeyin' orders. They'll start lookin' for me. If they can't find me inside, maybe they'll look Outside. See that window? That's Sparks' turret. If we can make him look out here—"

"*Stop talking!*" roared Roberts. "Stop talking, guy, and start blowing! I think you've got something there. Anyhow, it's our last hope. *Blow!*"

"And quick!" appended Brown. "For here they come!"

He meant the Grannies. Again they were huddling for attack, once more, a solid phalanx of indestructible, granite flesh, they were smashing down upon the tree.

"*Haa-a-roong!*" blew Isobar Jones.

CHAPTER IV

And—even he could not have foreseen the astounding results of his piping! What happened next was as astonishing as it was incomprehensible. For as the pipes, filled now and primed to burst into whatever substitute for melody they were prodded into, wailed into action—the Grannies' rush came to an abrupt halt!

As one, they stopped cold in their tracks and turned dull, colorless, questioning eyes upward into the tree whence came this weird and vibrant droning!

So stunned with surprise was Isobar that his grip on the pipes relaxed, his lips almost slipped from the reed. But Brown's delighted bellow lifted his paralysis.

"Sacred rings of Saturn-look! They *like* it! Keep playing, Jonesy! Play, boy, like you never played before!"

And Roberts roared, above the skirling of the *piobaireachd* into which Isobar had instinctively swung, "Music hath charms to soothe the savage beast! Then we were wrong. They *can* hear, after all! See that? They're lying down to listen—like so many lambs! Keep playing, Isobar! For once in my life I'm glad to hear that lovely, wonderful music!"

Isobar needed no urging. He, too, had noted how the Grannies' attack had stopped, how every last one of the gaunt grey beasts had suddenly, quietly, almost happily, dropped to its haunches at the base of the tree.

There was no doubt about it; the Grannies *liked* this music. Eyes raptly fixed, unblinking, unwavering, they froze into postures of gentle beatitude. One stirred once, dangerously, as for a moment Isobar paused to catch his breath, but Isobar hastily lipped the blow-pipe with redoubled eagerness, and the Granny relapsed into quietude.

Followed then what, under somewhat different circumstances, should have been a piper's dream. For Isobar had an audience which would not— and in two cases *dared* not—allow him to stop playing. And to this audience he played over and over again his entire repertoire. Marches, flings, dances—the stirring *Rhoderik Dhu* and the lilting *Lassies O'Skye*, the mournful *Coghiegh nha Shie* whose keening is like the sound of a sobbing nation.

The Cock o' the North, he played, and *Mironton* ... *Wee Flow'r o' Dee* and *MacArthur's March* ... *La Cucuracha* and—

And his lungs were parched, his lips dry as swabs of cotton. Blood pounded through his temples, throbbing in time to the drone of the chaunter, and a dark mist gathered before his eyes. He tore the blow-pipe from his lips, gasped.

"Keep playing!" came the dim, distant howl of Johnny Brown. "Just a few minutes longer, Jonesy! Relief is on the way. Sparks saw us from his turret window five minutes ago!"

And Isobar played on. How, or what, he did not know. The memory of those next few minutes was never afterward clear in his mind. All he knew was that above the skirling drone of his pipes there came another sound, the metallic clanking of a man-made machine ... an armored tank, sent from the Dome to rescue the beleaguered trio.

He was conscious, then, of a friendly voice shouting words of encouragement, of Joe Roberts calling a warning to those below.

"Careful, boys! Drive the tank right up beneath us so we can hop in and get out of here! Watch the Grannies—they'll be after us the minute Isobar stops playing!"

Then the answer from below. The fantastic answer in Sparks' familiar voice. The answer that caused the bagpipes to slip from Isobar's fingers as Isobar Jones passed out in a dead faint:

"After you? Those Grannies? Hell's howling acres—*those Grannies are stone dead*!"

* * * *

Afterward, Isobar Jones said weakly, "But—dead? I don't understand. Was it the sound-waves that killed them?"

Commander Eagan said, "No! Grannies absolutely cannot hear. That is one thing we do know about them—though we will soon know a great deal more, now that our biologists have a dozen carcasses to dissect, thanks to you. But Grannies have no auditory apparatus."

"But then—what?" puzzled Isobar. "It couldn't be vibration, because our Patrolmen tried shootin' 'em with the vibro-ray pistol, and nothin' never happened—"

"Nevertheless," said Dr. Loesch quietly, "it *was* vibration which killed them, Isobar. That is, of course, only my conjecture, but I believe subsequent study will prove I am correct.

"It was the effect of *dual*, or disharmonic vibration. You see, the vibro-ray pistol expels an ultrasonic wave which disrupts molecular construction sensitive to a single harmonic. The Grannies' composition is more complex. It required the impact of two different wave-lengths, impinging on their nerve centers at the same moment, to destroy them."

"And the bagpipe—" said Isobar with slowly dawning comprehension—"emits two distinct tones at the same time!"

The full meaning of his words flashed upon Isobar. He turned to Commander Eagan, sallow cheeks glowing with new color.

"Then—then what means we've licked our problem!" he cried. "We've found a weapon that'll kill the Grannies, and it won't be necessary to live inside Domes no more! Now we can move out into the open and live like human beings!"

"Absolutely true!" agreed the Commander. "But *you* will not be living Outside, Jones. Not right away, anyway."

"H-uh? W-hat do you mean, Commander?"

"I mean," said Eagan sternly, "that regardless of results, you are still guilty of flagrant disobedience to orders! That, as Commander of this outpost, I cannot tolerate. You are hereby sentenced to thirty days confinement to quarters!"

"But—" stammered Isobar—"but tarnation golly—"

"In the course of which time," continued Commander Eagan imperturbably, "you will serve as Instructor for every man in the Dome—at double salary!"

"You can't *do* me like this!" wailed Isobar. "Jinky-wallopers, I won't— Huh? What's 'at? Instructor? Instructor in *what*?"

"In the—er—art," said Eagan, "of bagpipe playing. If we are to rid Luna of the Grannies, we must all learn how to perform on that—er—lethal weapon. And, Jones, I think I can truthfully say that this punishment hurts me more than it hurts you!"

SHADRACH

Originally published in *Planet Stories,* Fall 1941.

CHAPTER I

The man at the end of the bar was very drunk. That was not, in itself, unusual. Xuerl's Cosmobar, dangling like a leech on the drab outskirts of Mars Central, did not cater to a select clientele. It was not noted for its culture or gentility; it was famed from one end of the System to another as a place where a hard-fisted, full-pursed spaceman, newly in from the mines or out from Earth, could get a weapon or a wench, a bottle or a battle, any or all with equal celerity. And at an instant's notice.

But the man at the end of the bar was very drunk. So drunk, indeed, that he seemed neither to notice nor to be concerned about the actions of his comrades. And they, Chip Warren thought as he watched the bleary man pour yet another jigger of green from a malevolently gleaming bottle of lisk, were a particularly evil-looking and ill-assorted lot. Even for a dive like this.

"A Venusian," he mused, "a greenie, a runt—and an Earthman. Like bugs in a rug...."

"Trink?" piped a thin, reedy voice at Chip's elbow. "Trink, ssor?"

Chip shook his head in reply to the Martian barman's query. Damned chrysanthemum! he thought. Damned squeaking, upright chrysanthemum! He would never, so long as he lived, get used to hearing English speech emanating from the curled petals that served as a Redlander's head. Martians tried to look like Earthlings. They braced their soft, pallid bodies in steel uprights, they underwent serious and probably painful operations to give themselves a humanoid appearance, but they still looked—and always would to Chip—like ungainly flowers of madness.

"No," he said. "Not just now, thanks. Later." He returned his gaze to the group at the end of the bar. A new member had joined the quartet. Another Earthman. Warren's eyes became more speculative as the newcomer drew the Jovian aside, queried him briefly, then moved to the drunken man's shoulder.

"Trink?" piped the persistent voice of the barman.

"Blast jets!" said Chip curtly. "I'll order when I get damn good and—hey!"

The gasp broke unbidden from his lips. In the din and confusion of Xuerl's Cosmobar it went unnoticed, even as had gone unnoticed by everyone else the momentary byplay he had glimpsed.

As the newcomer slipped his arm about the drunken man's shoulder, the first Earthman, turning suddenly, dropped from his hand to the floor a previously concealed something. A silvery, glistening, round something that hit the floor—and bounced!

Four figures reacted immediately, violently, eagerly. The Venusian, the Uranian, the Jovian—like four minds with but a single thought they formed a wall of flesh around the drunken one. The other Earthman's hand leaped out greedily to catch the bouncing blob on the rebound. But in vain. The drunk had retrieved the object, shoved it into a pocket.

But Chip Warren knew what the object was. It was a ball of ekalastron!

Ekalastron! Most recently discovered, rarest, and most precious of all metals known to man! A metal so unique that up to the time of its discovery there had been no place for it in man's supposedly "complete" periodic table.

A metal that, defying man's previous deliberations on the habits of metals, supplied man with the most valuable servant he had ever known. A metal so light that a child could carry enough in one hand to coat the entire hull of a space-cruiser—yet so adamant that a gossamer film of it would deflect the impact of a meteoride or the battering crush of a rotor-gun shell! A metal strong enough to grind diamonds to powder—but so resilient that, when molded and properly treated, it would bounce like a rubber ball!

In all the wide universe, hungry mankind had found less than two tons of this vitally precious new metal. An ounce was worth a prince's ransom; so jealously was each gram weighed, guarded and distributed that the U.S.C.—Universal Science Council—could account for every known ounce of it. Yet here, in the noisy bar of Mars' most infamous refuge for scoundrels, a drunken miner toyed with a chunk the size of a billiard ball!

If Chip Warren's attention had previously been attracted by the oddly-assorted quintet, it was riveted now. Fierce curiosity hunched him forward. Abandoning all shame at eavesdropping, he strained eyes and ears upon the group.

It was well that he did so. Otherwise he would not have seen the sober Earthman's gesture to the bartender, the bartender's furtive acquiescence, the tentacular hand opening a colorless phial, pouring its contents into the miner's bottle of lisk. There would have been no one to protect the drunken man from the drug that would swiftly have left him at the mercy of his companions.

But Chip was watching. And moving on raw instinct, without a thought for the consequences, he surged forward. His arm brushed the surprised Uranian aside, his hand thrust just in time to sweep the doped drink from the miner's lips. Glass shattered on the floor, singing a shrill song. Chip's challenging voice echoed its brittle crispness.

"Hold course a minute, buckoes!" he ordered. "What in space goes on around here?"

Chip thought afterward that never in his life had he ever looked upon such stark, forbidding coldness as that which, in the next moment, flamed upon him from the eyes of the newly arrived Earthman.

Everything about the man was cold, bitter and bleak as the hostile depths of space. His eyes were glacier-gray, his lips thin and bloodless as hoarfrost; the hand he shoved forward to grip Chip's wrist in steely grasp was like ice.

The coldness of death was in his voice, although he spoke with infinite quietude.

"I might ask the same of you, sailor." The man had raven-black hair save where, from a widow's peak, one single swatch of pure white sprang startlingly to lie like a stream of ice between dark banks. "By what right do you intrude on a private party?"

Chip shook the man's hand from his wrist. His eyes parried with hot defiance the stranger's frigid calm.

"By the right of any man," he growled, "to see fair play! I saw—"

"A moment, sailor!" The man's voice was like a low note struck in warning. "Before you tell what you saw, you might like to know who I am. My name is Blaze Amborg."

"I don't give a portside blast," snarled Chip, "if your name is Lucifer himself. I saw—"

"You haven't been out here long, have you, sailor? Well—that's your misfortune, I fear. Torth!"

He inclined his head gently toward the giant Venusian. The big man rolled forward. His hamlike paws reached for Chip. But fast as he moved, Chip moved faster still; in the split of a second his hand had found his belt. The dull lights of the Cosmobar glinted sallowly on metal that prodded Amborg's middle.

"So that's the way it is, eh?" gritted Chip. "Your bullies do your fighting for you? Well, maybe you're right. I haven't been out here long. But where I come from, men do their own scrapping. Now—tell these scum of yours to keep their distance, or by the Seven Sacred Stars, I'll let ether through you!"

A man could not tell by studying Amborg's features if his lips were white with fear or what. But the ice in his eyes was deeper, more shadowy. And he said, "Back, Torth!"

"That's better!" approved Chip. "And now—come out of it, you!" The drunken man had finally slipped out of the picture. Blissfully unaware of what was going on about him, his head had slumped to the bar. He was asleep, lips loosely agape, breath coming in sodden grunts. Chip grasped the nape of his neck, shook him roughly. "Pull yourself together!" he commanded. "We're getting out of here!"

The man came to with a start, stared at Chip Warren blearily. "W-whuz-zup? Whuzzmatter? Don' shake me like that, ole boy. All pals t'gether. All good ole pals...."

His head dropped forward again, and Chip sighed. It was like kicking a pup, he thought, but it had to be done. His rousing slap jarred the drunk to grieved awareness.

"Hey! Don' do that! We're pals, ain't we? All—"

"I wouldn't know about that," snorted Chip. "But I do know these other 'pals' of yours are getting ready to dig you for that—that stuff in your pocket."

That did it. The warning drove its way through the miner's stupor. His head jerked up, his eyes widened, and a hand clawed at his pocket.

"What? My ekalastron? The filthy thieves—!"

His loud voice carried throughout the room clearly. Too clearly. For with a sudden fear, Chip could feel a tension tighten through the hard habitues of the bar. Nervous scrapings of feet, the frou-frou of suddenly intense voices. "Ekalastron! Eka—"

For a moment, Chip's guard relaxed. He twisted his head to survey a new and potent danger. And as he did so, a sharp cry burst from Amborg's lips. "Raat 'Aran! Torth!"

Chip whirled back to face immediate trouble. Shapes were plunging down upon him. He wheeled, slipped, tumbled to one side even as the scorching burst of a needle gun seared a hissing path past his shoulder. Someone behind screamed a high, thin scream that died in a choked gurgle....

Then all was madness! The magic word "ekalastron" had wakened the riches-lust of the mob; now the presence of death had roused its blood-lust. In the space of a moment's time, a score of guns were drawn and wildly flaming as the throng charged the bar.

Chip only lived in that moment because he lay helplessly asprawl upon the floor. The hobnailed boots of miners kicked and trampled him, thick bodies struggled, cursed and groaned above him. Once as he tried to scramble to his feet his hand slipped nauseatingly in a pool of freshly spilled and steaming blood.

He was aware that somewhere in the howling mob that fought, not knowing why, and fighting died, the glacier-eyed Amborg strained for sight of him. But the tide of conflict, sweeping over and about them, separated them.

There came a reedy cry in the voice of the Martian barman; the lights went out suddenly, and the room was alive and spiteful with the flames of criss-crossing fire-needles. A questing hand found Chip's throat in the darkness, fingers tightened. But in a flash of fire, Chip saw the figure atop him suddenly crumple, steel clattered aimlessly beside him as his assailant choked and died. Thus close to him walked mad, unreasoning Death.

But he was on his feet again, now, and armed! Chip forced his way toward that spot at the bar where last he had glimpsed the drunken miner. No figure stood there, but his feet stumbled against a yielding body. He stooped—then he blinked as the lights suddenly flared on again.

He looked upon a frightful scene of carnage. Where men had fought, a dozen bodies lay upon the floor like broken things; elsewhere about the room a dozen struggling piles of life, human and humanoid, white, coral and green, Earthborn and spawn of a dozen globes, still fought their purposeless battle. And at the far side of the room—

Amborg!

But Amborg had seen him first. Even as he raised his needle-gun, Chip realized the dousing of the lights, the sudden return of them, had been a trick of Amborg's to gain advantage. The other man had the drop on him ... even now his hand was tightening on the press.

And then, miraculously—

"Hold!" cried a thunderous voice. "'Stay now thine hand from the sword, yea, loose not thine arrow from the bow—else by My might shall I crush thee to the dust, truly My lightnings shall wither thee with fire!' Thus saith my Lord God which is Jehovah!"

A vast, awed silence fell suddenly upon the room, a paralysis seized all forms and held them motionless. Amborg stayed his finger. All eyes sought the doorway. And there, covering the whole of the Cosmobar with the ugliest but most efficient looking piece of private ordnance Chip had seen in his life, stood a man. A tall, gangling scarecrow garbed in rusty black; a lean-jawed, hawk-eyed man with tumbling locks of silver and blazing eyes.

A whisper arose from men's lips. A whisper at once respectful and—fearful.

"It's Salvation! Salvation Smith!"

For a long, dramatic moment the ol man stood there in the doorway; then, satisfied that all motion had stopped, he stepped forward into the room. Chip knew, now, who—and what—he was. "Salvation" Smith, sin-driving missionary of the Wastelands, was a legendary, almost fabulous, figure of the Martian scene.

A devoutly religious man with the heart and soul of a pioneer, he had taken upon himself the mission of carrying to the savage outland tribes the story of the God he worshipped. That this God was Him of the Old Testament, a God of wrath and vengeance, fire and flame, was evidenced by those methods Salvation sometimes employed to make his message acceptable to uncivilized breasts. In addition to being the most pious man on Mars, Salvation was also reputed to be the best shot!

Earth's softhanded ecclesiastics did not altogether approve of their wayward missionary's reputation, but had to concede that he, working unaided and alone, had done more to bring the light to Mars than the rest of their emissaries as a group.

Thus Salvation Smith, who stared now at the corpses on the floor and muttered beneath his breath a prayer so hot and violent as to be almost blasphemous.

There came a shrill bleat, and Xuerl, proprietor of the infamous Cosmobar, minced across the floor, grotesque in the rigid habiliments that lent him a humanoid shape.

"Sssalvation," he pleaded, "Thisss wasss none of my doing, sssir! I have kept the peace, as I promisssed—"

"Silence!" roared the old man, and frowned. "Your foul den is a stench in the nostrils of Heaven. I am tiring swiftly of your iniquitous ways, Xuerl! One day I—shall—who started this, anyway?" he demanded.

"Thisss man!" Xuerl pointed a quavering tentacle at Chip. Salvation gazed at the young man sternly.

"You are new around here. What is your name?"

"Chip Warren. I'm just out from Earth a week or so ago. Free-lance prospector. But—but I didn't start this, sir. I merely interfered when that man and his thugs tried to steal a ball of ekalastron from this dead miner—"

Chip paused suddenly, staring at the drunken miner.

"But he's still alive! I thought—"

Salvation was at his side in an instant. They both kneeled beside the miner, whose eyes had flickered open. He was no longer influenced by drink. His eyes were clear with prevision of a longer flight than he had ever known. For a moment he struggled for breath. There was recognition in his feeble tones.

"S-salvation—"

"Peace, my son. We will take you to a hospital."

"N-never mind that, Padre. It's too late. But the ekalastron—"

"You stole it, my son? You wish to confess?"

"N-no, Padre! Not stolen. I found it. A mine—" His breath was coming in tiny, tortured gasps; he spoke more swiftly as if aware that he must tell his secret ere silence claim him. "Danger ... on Titania! The caves ... natives ... and the furnace of flame ... beware!"

"But he survived!" Chip burst in. "He got some and returned. Ask him how, Padre!"

The miner's head moved slightly as if to signify he understood the query, but even as his lips moved to frame an answer, a swift, cold shadow frosted his eyes with glaze. A moment later his breath stopped. Then it shuddered back as with a violent effort the dying man dragged himself back from death itself. A convulsion shook him. He cried weakly the single word:

"Shadrach!"

Then a blood-specked spume gushed from his lips and he lay still. "May the Lord have mercy on his soul!" begged Salvation Smith. He pushed Chip gently away, fumbled at the dead man's clothing, arranging it more neatly, then rose.

"He is gone," he told the spellbound assembly. "He is gone, bearing with him to the world beyond the secret for which you jackals strove. Thus be it, O Lord God of Hosts!"

But one man did not accept this as final. That man was Blaze Amborg who, bolstered now by his hard-bitten group of outlaws, strode forward belligerently.

"Not so fast, psalm-singer! He and I were partners. Anything he had belongs to me now!" He bent over and with a jerk disarranged the clothing Salvation had smoothed. "And by the Comet, I'm going to have it—" His hands moved with deft assurance, then with tense, hardening suspicion. "It's gone!" He wheeled to face Chip. "You stole it! You—"

But the old missionary barred his rush with a steel forearm. "Slowly, my friend! What is gone?"

"The ball of ekalastron! It's worth a fortune, and it's mine! This snoopy young thief—"

Salvation turned to Chip sternly. "Well, young man—is this true? Did you steal it? If so—"

"I didn't. I swear I didn't!"

"He was bending over Jenkins," Amborg raged, "when the lights went on. He's got it! Let me at him!"

"There has been sufficient violence!" snapped Salvation Smith. He turned to Chip. "Young man, I order you to let your accuser search you. If you are truly innocent, you will not demur. If you refuse—" He shifted his rifle from one horny palm to another significantly. "Justice shall prevail!"

"Very well!" said Chip. He submitted himself to Amborg's triumphant search. His flesh ran cold at the feel of the man's icy fingers, and a dull resentment suffused him—but he got his reward in the look of bafflement that grew on Amborg's face as it became clear that the missing sphere was not on his person. "Are you satisfied now?" he demanded.

Amborg's normally pale face was whiter still with impotent fury; his eyes flamed with hatred. "It's not on you," he admitted. "But I know you took it. You've hidden it somewhere. I'm not through with you yet, sailor! I'll have that metal or—"

"There will be no 'or'!" proclaimed Salvation Smith stridently. "The lad has passed the test and proven himself guiltless; the case is closed. He will walk from this place unharmed—in my company! 'The true man shall suffer no hurt, neither shall the righteous fail.' Come, my son!"

And he lifted his gun. Blaze Amborg's lips thinned to a hard, white line. But he made no reckless move as the two men stalked silently from the room....

CHAPTER II

The Martian night was clear and cold. Its thin air was sweetly welcome to Chip's nostrils. When they gained the street outside, Salvation spoke to him suddenly. "Where is your ship, my son?"

"Ship, sir?" queried Warren. "But why—?"

"Don't waste time!" snapped the old man. "We're in grave danger. Blaze Amborg is a man of violence. In a few minutes he'll figure out what happened to the ekalastron and be out looking for us."

Chip stared at him. "The ekalastron? But what did happen to it? It disappeared—"

"Into," grunted Salvation, "my pocket! While I was arranging Jenkins' clothing. 'He who taketh in the cause of righteousness hath done the will of the Lord!' Amborg is an evil, wilful man. He would have used the ekalastron for his own wicked purposes. In our hands, all mankind shall profit of its beneficence. But, come! Where?"

"C-churchill Field," stammered Chip. "Dock 31, Bin A. T-this way, Padre."

They moved at quickened stride through the darkened streets. As they neared the cradles wherein lay the vessels of a thousand diverse ports, Salvation questioned Chip still further.

"What type of ship is it, lad?"

"Not a very new one, sir. A Challenger 7-jet, four berth explorer. But in good shape. My friend and I managed to get it cheap, reconditioned it—"

"Then you have a companion?"

"Yes, Padre. Syd Palmer. He's waiting aboard. We had planned to lift gravs tomorrow for a prospecting tour of the planetoids. I visited the Cosmobar because I thought I might run into some old space-dodger who would give me a tip on a lode-rock—"

"And you ran into," said the missionary, "something which may turn out to be the greatest discovery ever made by man. Murder ... thievery ... wealth ... is this the ship?"

They had stopped before one of the smaller cradles. Chip pressed a signal button, a buzzer responded, there came from within the familiar wheeze of an air-lock generator.

"This is it, sir. Please step in. 'Lo, Syd. This is Doctor—Mister—"

"Call me 'Salvation'," said the old man. "I'm used to it. Palmer, I take it you're the chief engineer of this jaloppy?"

Syd Palmer was short and chubby; his hair was a tow colored bristle that stood up like a cock's-comb when he was excited or annoyed. It stood up now, and his pale blue eyes danced with tiny, indignant sparks.

"I'm the engineer of this ship!"

"Call it what you will," grunted Salvation. "Is it fast?"

Palmer grinned. "Puh-lenty! I've hepped the hypos to super-max. The Chickadee can outrun anything its size in space, and a lot of bigger ones, besides!"

"Good! And have you got clearance papers?"

"Why, yes, but—"

"Excellent: 'Verily, He taketh care of His own nor faileth them in time of need.'" Salvation nodded to Warren. "We'll lift gravs," he said, "immediately!"

Palmer stared at him, then at his companion.

"What is this, Chip? Old boy off his jets?"

"Far from it," said Chip seriously. "Can't explain everything now, Syd; time's too short. But you like a good, old-fashioned fight, don't you?"

"Fight? Sa-a-ay, now—"

"Then warm the hypos," ordered Chip, "while I plot a course. We're lifting gravs immediately—for Titania."

During the long days that followed, there was time and to spare in which to clarify the situation to Syd. When he heard of Chip's adventure at the Cosmobar, his pale eyes gleamed and fists less chubby than they appeared tightened at his sides. "Wish I'd been there—" he muttered. Salvation glared at him and snorted, "'Verily they are fools who do not rejoice that they have escaped woe!'"

And when Chip showed him the ball of ekalastron—

"Glory be!" exclaimed Syd. "There's enough to dip a whole battle unit in that one ball! What are we going to Titania for? Why not fly this to Earth immediately and let the Council know—"

"Because Amborg knows," replied Chip grimly, "that this came from Titania. He was nearby when Jenkins said so in his dying breath. That was probably the secret Amborg's thugs had been trying to probe from the miner all night. I have a hunch that Amborg is out there somewhere right now!"

He nodded toward the quartzite view-pane. Outside lay space—the long, dreary reaches of space between Mars and Uranus. But it didn't look like space. Not like space as navigators a short ten years ago had known it, an eternal pall of blackness spangled with the livid dots of a myriad stars.

This was a blotched, striped, crazy-quilt of color. Crimson, ochre, emerald—all the hues of the rainbow merged into a faery, magic loveliness. This was space as seen when Man traveled at the terrific speed attainable only through the use of the recently developed V-I unit, velocity intensifier, invented by that mad genius of the spaceways, Lancelot Biggs of the lugger, Saturn.

Five years ago, in the year 2210, the fastest craft in the ether had had a top speed of approximately 200,000 miles per hour. Now almost every ship was equipped with the V-I adapter that gave it a flight-potential limited only by the critical velocity of light. Where once it would have required almost ten months to reach Titania, second satellite of far Uranus, the trio could now expect to gain their destination, traveling at a speed of more than 650,000,000 mph., in something less than half that many days!

"I have a hunch," repeated Chip, "that Amborg and his crew are somewhere out there right now, speeding, as we are, to Titania. Of course we can't tell. We're not equipped with a magno-tector, and we couldn't see them unless by sheer chance they should approach within our visibility parellax. But when we get to Titania and slow down, we must go on the alert. Salvation has told me about Amborg. He's a hard, brilliant man with a dangerously criminal mind. Let him find Jenkins' ore-deposit and the Federation of Planets would pay through the nose for his discovery. Jenkins said there was a whole mine of ekalastron. With that at his disposal, Amborg could make himself a robber baron. An Emperor of the outlaw world."

"Which is why," Salvation offered gravely, "we must get there before he does. Lay claim to the deposit, somehow secure its safety against the arrival of I.P.S. troops. Can we but find the mine, soldiers will come in jigtime from New Oslo on Uranus. But—"

Syd nodded.

"I see. But we couldn't walk into the garrison and hand them a line about a 'mine' of ekalastron. They'd shove us into the nearest looney-bin. And I wouldn't blame them a bit. If I didn't know Chip Warren like I know my own lovely pan—but suppose we meet Amborg?"

"'The Lord,'" said Salvation, "'is my strength and my salvation. In His hands do I place my guidance.'" His lean hands flexed powerfully. "We destroy them," he said gently, "like the rats they are...."

Thus four days sped by in plan and conjecture. And on the fifth day Syd

Palmer cut the velocity-intensifiers to normal, and a scant thousand miles beneath them, so accurate had been Chip's astrogation, gleamed the silvery mote which was Titania, second child of the mother planet, Uranus.

"Well done, my son!" approved Salvation. "The best landcast I've ever seen!"

Palmer was less exuberant. He stared at Titania, scratched his yellow crest morbidly.

"A damn snowball!" he mourned. "A damned snowball, eight hundred miles in diameter! Sweet crimes of Beelzebub, Chip, how do you ever expect to find a pinpoint of a mine on that huge hunk of ice? It will take us ages!"

"We'll cruise at low elevation," said Chip, "until we see something. There must be a dark spot showing against that sheen of white somewhere. Jenkins spoke of caverns and natives and flame. We have plenty of supplies—look out!"

He leaped even as he shouted. Leaped to the panels and jammed the full strength of his six foot plus frame to a deflecting lever. The control room of the Chickadee whirled giddily as the little ship spun into a crazy spiral; Palmer yelped, skidding helplessly across the floor. Salvation let loose a roar and clung ardently to a stanchion, his silvery locks whipping straight out from his head with the force of the drive.

Chip threw himself into the bucket-shaped pilot's-chair, gained possession of the controls. An instant later, the Chickadee was tossing through the maddest gyrations Chip could devise. Fore, loft and jet, with hypos throbbing, the little craft was blasting, shaking, quivering like a leaf in a cyclone.

And above the tumult of racing hypos came the sound of Syd's voice: "What is it, Chip? Amborg?"

Chip nodded tightly, his hands gripping the control levers, his eyes glued to the perilens through which he saw the enemy craft. A larger ship, with a red fang darting from its prow, slashing viciously at the bobbing Chickadee. "It's Blaze Amborg, all right! And he means business! He's got an Ingermann ray-rotor on that crate of his; he's trying to burn us clean out of the ether!"

Chip Warren and Syd Palmer were the co-owners of the Chickadee; it was Chip whose alertness had saved them in that first, terrifying moment, Chip it was who still held the controls. But it was Salvation Smith who usurped the mastership during the crisis.

"Hell's flaming damnation!" he cried, and there rang in his voice a rage above weak need of profanity. "Lend now Thy servant strength, O Lord, to smite these sons of Hurkan!" He whirled on Palmer, snarling. "Break out bulgers for us in case they should pierce the hull! Chip, son, do the controls answer well? Good! Keep dodging. Swing aft; the beam can't nip you there! You've armament aboard this heap?"

Syd, tugging three spacesuits from the store-closet, puffed over his shoulder, "Only a low-cycle heat-gun. There! Under that tarp. Press the green stud to clear the nose from the hull-plates. It's retractable—"

"You're telling me," bellowed Salvation, "how to rig a cannon? I was teethed on a lanyard, praise be to Jehovah!" He had the tarpaulin off in a jiffy, the fore-irons open, and shot an experimental burst from the small weapon. He smiled. "Good! But you've got to get closer to him, Chip; this thing is only effective at short range."

Chip said dubiously, "I don't know, Padre. Perhaps we should cut and run for it. If that beam hits us—"

"Are we mice," bellowed Salvation, "or men? You've got to get closer! The Lord is our right hand. 'Surely the evil shall fail, yea, the way of the transgressor shall perish!'" He loosed another blast from the small gun, breathed a sigh of satisfaction. "Aaah! that's better! Closer!"

"You're the skipper!" decided Chip suddenly. A jab of the finger, the stern-jets crackled and the Chickadee cut suddenly to starboard, swinging straight toward the craft of Blaze Amborg.

So unexpected was the move that it caught the enemy gunner napping. For an instant he had a clear target before him. But he had not been expecting such luck, and before he could center his sights on the Chickadee, the smaller vessel was streaking down upon and over his own.

And Salvation Smith's voice shouted triumph through the room. "'Vengeance is mine, saith the Lord!'" he intoned, "'I shall repay!'" His hand jerked the release-stud.

And as though the metal skin of the enemy boat were tinfoil held above a flame, there appeared suddenly upon its hull a leprous spot of black, from the curling edges of which silvery alloy sloughed off in rolling, sluggish waves. From within the ship small motes poured forth, sucked out by the frigid vacuum of space to explode and die frightfully; sore, raw, pressured clots of matter that had been men. The other ship reeled for a moment like a stricken hart, then crumpled upon itself, a wildly spinning boomerang of death.

"You got 'em!" squealed Syd Palmer from his vantage spot at the per-ilens. "Got 'em all, Padre! No—there goes a life-skiff from the wreck!" His voice rose in sharp fear. "Omigod! Swing out, Chip! Swing—"

But Chip had seen the new danger as quickly as his comrade. Here was peril beyond Amborg's fondest devising. As the stricken ship, folding upon itself, spun aimlessly in space, its forejet wheeled like a flaming spiral— and from the prow still flamed the withering, crimson ray now untended by living hands!

Like a gigantic scythe it flailed the ether, swinging a huge curve directly toward the Chickadee. Vainly Chip jammed the studs before him, striving to escape above, below or beyond that sword of doom.

There came the ear-splitting crash of impact, metal screamed thin agony, rending itself to shreds somewhere aft; the Chickadee shuddered like a pole-felled steer under its mortal wound.

Instinct shot Chip's hands to the lock-stud which sealed the control chamber airtight from the rest of the ship; that action alone spared them for a few minutes. But each of them knew the ship was doomed to crash. Syd croaked, "Here! The bulgers! Get in them—quick!"

Split seconds later, they were three grotesque figures huddled before the control board, staring through quartzite globular headpanes at Chip's last, frenzied efforts to break the fall of the Chickadee. The studs beneath his fingers were unresponsive as the inarticulate phalanges of a broken limb. In vain and desperately he struggled to gain a modicum of control over the falling craft, now firmly gripped by Titania's gravitational field. They had fallen into the high atmosphere of the little globe, now; thin winds howled and bansheed about their sharded hull, and the walls of the room began to heat.

The aft jets were dead, the anti-gravs broken, helpless. There remained but one possible way in which to keep them from being crushed to bits. A prow landing, braked by the fore jets. It was dangerous, but—

"There!" cried Syd. "Look there, Chip! Below us!"

Chip risked a brief glance, saw that the smooth and icy surface of Titania was broken by a long, ragged swatch of black. Ironic laughter curled the corners of his tight-set lips. What a quirk of fate that here, with death but a hair's-breadth removed, they should unwittingly find that for which under happier circumstances they might have sought endlessly and in vain. The promised spot of habitation on the bleak little moon of Uranus.

"I'm fore-jetting!" he crisped. "Stand by for—a fadeout!"

Salvation's hand was on his shoulder, reassuringly, somehow warm despite its casement of rubberoid fabric. "Be of strong heart, my son," he said simply, "He who watcheth the fall of the smallest sparrow, He shall not fail His own in their hour of need."

Then Chip pressed the necessary, the only remaining responsive keys. And the control room trembled like a hurt thing, seemed to stop stock-still in space, shake itself for a moment—then plunge on. Forejets flamed blast upon roaring blast. Chip felt the gravitational force seem to lessen as the flares beat stubbornly against the adamant breast of the globe below. Drop ... stagger ... drop again ... the shocking concussion of brakes ... then a swift, dizzy, headlong fall....

Wild winds howled, and the din of metals tortured beyond endurance slashed at Chip's eardrums. He was aware of the last cry of Syd Palmer, his life-long friend. "Luck, Chip, old pal—!" And the remembered ghost of Salvation's promise. "He shall not fail His own—"

Then a horrendous crash jarred his head back on the seat. A smashing veil of crimson settled before his eyes ... then there was darkness. And silence.

He felt some mad conceit that this was death ... that the restless fingers of the gray unalive plucked at his arm, bidding him rise and stir forward toward he knew not what.

Then suddenly he was awake, alive, and conscious—and it was not death, but life; fingers did tug at him, but they were the figures of—

"Greenies!" cried Chip. "Hands off, you! Or—"

The green complexioned native growled some guttural comment, moved closer rather than away, and pinioned Chip's arms to his sides. Chip saw, now, that the Chickadee, though battered and broken beyond hope of repair, had miraculously grounded without destroying them all. For Syd was stirring, and Salvation, too, but each of them was surrounded by green natives, as was Chip. These creatures, the nearest approach to Man's physiology that had ever been found in the System, were tall and rugged, masterfully built. They were equipped with native lariats or bolas; these they whipped cuttingly about their captives.

Chip strained lashed fingers toward the heat-pistol in his belt. But Salvation, seeing his motion, stopped him.

"No, lad! Relax! Don't make a hostile move!"

Chip growled, "No damned greenie is going to make a trussed duck out of me. If I can reach this gun—"

"If you value your life," said Salvation, "and your welfare, keep your hands quiet and your wits active! These creatures aren't Uranians. They're Titanians. An offspring of the parent race, but as savage and untamed as beasts. I don't know what they plan to do with us. I have heard they are a strange, mystical race; their tribal rites and taboos are many and—dangerous! Our only chance is to be quiet, try to reason with them, convince them we are not foes but friends—"

All three were securely tied, now, save for their legs. The tallest Titanian, evidently the group chieftain, grunted a word of command. Strong arms prodded Chip and his fellows forward, out of the broken Chickadee, into the bleak landscape of Titania.

They had crashed in the dark spot Chip had viewed from above. They discovered, now, that this spot was dark because—incredibly—here the thick, icy blanket had been stripped away to discover the raw and rocky core of the Uranian moon.

Black rocks thrust jagged spires skyward, mountains of stone girdled this one clear space on the whole of Titania; greater wonder still, gnarled and stunted trees, lichens of hardiest verdure, eked a precarious existence from the grudging soil.

And here the natives had—a village. One coarser, cruder, than the village of the meanest of Earth's savages, but a village nonetheless. Slab dwellings dabbed with thick black clay, a central structure, larger than the rest, something that looked like a market—or community gathering-spot.

Chip's wonderment had made him impervious at first to such trivia as personal comfort and discomfort. He found now, though, that he was cold. By dint of much effort, he managed to squirm a hand to his belt-studs, operate the tiny needle that increased the warmth of his space-suit.

Almost immediately there came a howl from the green native maintaining a vigilant grip on Chip's arm; the fellow leaped away, bellowing angry, guttural speech at his leader.

And Salvation spun to Chip swiftly.

"Chip—turn down that heat, boy!"

"B-but—" stammered Chip.

"Quickly!"

Chip obeyed. It was well he did so, for the leader was moving toward him menacingly. With a cautious finger he touched Chip's suit. Then, apparently mollified to discover it satisfactorily cold, he snarled a word or two and the little party moved on.

Chip stared at the old missionary.

"But, why?" he demanded. "What did I do wrong? I don't get it. I was freezing, and—"

"Then you've got to freeze," said Salvation Smith, "and like it. Until we can escape from these creatures. Do you have any idea how cold it is here on Titania, my boy?"

Chip said, "Why, plenty cold, I suppose—"

"About minus 380° Fahrenheit!" said Smith. "That's all. Uranians and Titanians may look like Earthmen, lad, but they're built entirely different. They are not children of the Sun, as we are. Their bodies are so constituted as to be able to stand extremes of frigidity that would quick-freeze us like salmon. Sluggish basal metabolism, dermal, rather than pneumonic respiration—these enable them to endure what to us appear the impossible living conditions of a world on which mercury and gallium are adamant solids, liquid hydrogen forms seas, and the snow is carbon dioxide. When you turned on the heating unit of your bulger you subjected that native's hand to what was to him a burning, unendurable heat!"

Chip nodded.

"I see. That makes sense. But—but there must be some warmth around here? A cleared patch—"

"I haven't yet decided whether this patch was cleared by heat or labor," said Salvation. "If we can make them believe we are friends, I may learn. I can sling their talk a little. It's not unlike the Uranian language. But—"

He stopped, and his voice rose to a shout. "Behold! Thou hast delivered mine enemy into mine hands, O Lord; Thou hast brought the wicked even unto judgment!"

And Chip, following his gaze, saw a second party of Titanians approaching the central gathering place from the opposite direction. These natives held captive, even as he and Salvation and Syd were held, an ill-assorted foursome in spacemen's bulgers. A giant Venusian, a greenie, a dwarfed Jovian and an Earthman!

"Amborg!" yelled Chip. "Blaze Amborg and his crew! They got away on that life-skiff, but they were caught when they landed! Padre—"

It had not occurred to him that the arms of Amborg and his men would not be, like their own, lashed securely. Thus it came as a heart-stopping shock to hear Amborg's cry ring in their ears, a sharp cry of command— then suddenly there flamed from the sidearms of the other captive group the withering blasts of heat-guns!

CHAPER III

Chip Warren had bitterly resented the close guard with which the Titanians had surrounded him and his comrades; he had reason, now, to be grateful for that very protection. Otherwise his dreams of space adventure would have ended suddenly and terribly in that moment.

As it was, the foremost wall of Titanians took the brunt of Amborg's vicious attack. They screamed as pencils of crimson scorched the life from their unprotected bodies, screamed and died horribly, falling in blackened piles that whimpered futilely for an instant and were still.

Chip had never known a moment of such dreadful impotence as this. Arms lashed to his sides, his own weapon as securely removed from his grasp as if it no longer existed, there was nothing he could do but attempt to evade the flame of the lethal guns.

With a choking cry to his mates, he threw himself forward; his knees struck rocky ground, grit slashed his unprotected headpane as he fell, and for an instant he feared the impact might shatter the quartzite, exposing him to the deadly, ammoniac atmosphere of Uranus' second moon.

Then he was entrenched behind the still-smouldering bodies of the slain Titanians, watching the speed of their fellows' reprisal.

And it was speedy. Salvation had spoke truly when he said these creatures were savage and untamed as beasts. Reckless of their own lives, green-casted features snarling, they swooped down on the treacherous quartet. In the split of a second they had seized them, bound them, removed their weapons.

But Chip and his companions suffered the same fate as their adversaries. The Titanians stripped them of their sidearms, as they had taken those of Amborg's men. Ungentle hands herded them into one of the nearby hovels, and there, as two guards held the single doorway, they were deserted.

Salvation groaned his rage and discomfiture.

"A judgment on that beast in man's flesh!" he proclaimed. "He has destroyed us all! Had I been given an opportunity to talk with their chief, quietly, peaceably, this matter might have been settled with no harm done to anyone. But as it is—" He shook his head.

Syd said, "What do you think they'll do next?"

"Whatever it is," said Chip tightly, "I've got an idea it isn't going to be pleasant. They're gathering; hear their footsteps and voices? And there's something like the beat of a tom-tom—" He stared at Salvation speculatively. "Padre—torture?"

Salvation stroked his long, lean jaw. "I hope not, my son. But—I don't know. They are savages, and I have heard they place much faith in rites and ceremonies. But we will learn soon. Meanwhile, keep faith with Him who watches us all."

They learned sooner than they dared expect. Whatever else might lay in store for them, they were at least spared the agony of waiting. The Titanian preparations took but little time. Within scant hours after their incarceration, the three Earthmen were once again dragged from their prison to meet their judgment and their fate.

That some form of ritual was in progress was immediately apparent. From hillside, rock, cranny and hovel had come the Titanians; there were more of them than Chip would have believed could subsist in this hostile environment. A solid phalanx of them walled the avenue up which they were led. As they walked, the Titanians chanted a slow and ominous threnody. There was a dirgelike quality to the chant; despite the surface courage with which Chip bolstered himself he felt the chill of nervous apprehension upon him. Palmer must have felt the same way. He edged closer to Chip, spoke from the corner of his mouth in a tone that belied the forced gaiety of his words.

"Swell end to our trip, pal. Piece de resistance for a gang of green choristers!"

Salvation overheard him. "We have not yet come to the end of our journey," he said. "The line stretches up the side of yonder hill. To those caves." He lifted his voice sonorously, drawing curious stares from the green-skinned Titanian guards. "I shall lift up mine eyes unto the hills," he cried, "whence cometh my strength and my salvation—"

"Caves!" Sudden memory flashed back upon Chip Warren. "Jenkins said something about caves, Padre, remember? Caves and flame—"

"There's Amborg," interrupted Syd. His plump face was tightly pale behind his globular mask. "I don't care so much about checking out," he said, "but I wish I could get my hands on that rat just for a minute before—"

His words dwindled into silence. It was, Chip believed, an impressed silence. For they had reached the foot of the hill, now, and were climbing between two chanting rows of natives toward a huge, ornate, altarlike structure placed before the largest of the cave-mouths.

The dirge rose and soared, filling their ears with numbing fear; they moved upward inexorably, monotonously, almost mechanically. And finally they stood before the high altar.

Chip saw, then, what he would never have credited if it had been told him by another; what he could not have believed had he not seen it with his own eyes. He saw into the cave-mouth—and what he viewed there was so incredible that it brought a gasp unbidden to his lips.

This cave, deepset in the mouths of icy Titania—this cave, which by all laws of nature, of logic and reason, should be a dank, forbidding gateway to frightful cold—was bright-gleaming with orange, crimson, ochre tongues of flame! Within it, high-rising to the very lofted vaults, roared a staggering, tremendous holocaust of fire!

* * * *

And beyond the altar was a precipice overlooking a sunken vale. This vale, like the interior of the cave, was shimmering like the plains of Abaddon with coruscating fingers, sheets, spires of red.

He was aware that he had gasped, for he detected a similar gasp from Syd, and he heard Salvation Smith say a single, incredulous word. "Sheol!" Then the chieftain, or high priest—Chip did not know which—spoke from the altar. Shortly he spoke, but with strident emphasis, jabbing his fingers at the two groups of captives in turn.

"What is he saying?" demanded Chip.

Salvation interpreted hastily. "We have violated their land. We have been brought to the Place of Destruction to meet judgment for our crime. The test of fire will prove our guilt—" Then he raised his voice, spoke to the Titanian ruler.

The outland ruler heard him through, then answered. Salvation turned to Chip and Syd. "I told him," he explained, "that we were friends, come in amity. That we intended them no harm or offense—"

"And what did he say?"

"He said," relayed Salvation grudgingly, "that they were forced to distrust us because our 'companions' were men of sin and violence—"

"Companions!" interjected Syd angrily.

"—and he said, also, that he realized we might be gods. He says there are two types of white creatures, those who are mortals and evil, and those who are Masters of Fire. We must be tested to see which we are."

"Two types?" cried Chip. "Masters of Fire? Padre, what does he mean?"

Salvation shrugged helplessly. "I don't know. But wait—he is talking again."

This time the green chieftain's speech was longer, more dramatic. He postured, gestured; once he strode to the edge of his raised platform and pointed majestically down into the chasm below. Then, concluding his words with a tone of finality, he folded his arms across his chest.

Chip noticed that a few rods away Amborg's Uranian companion was interpreting his decision to Blaze. Salvation performed the same function.

"He says," explained Salvation, "we must walk into this cave of fearful flame. It leads through burning corridors to the valley below. In that valley is the life-skiff which brought Amborg and his men here. If we are good men, gods, and guiltless, the flame will not destroy us. There was one not long ago who walked unscathed through the fires, he says. That man was surely a god."

"Jenkins!" broke in Chip. "It must have been—"

Salvation nodded. "That is what I thought, too, my son. But—but how? How could Jenkins survive the flames?" And he stared sombrely, questioningly, at the sheet of ruddy fire filling the cave from base to arch. He shook himself. "Well—that is a problem we must solve, and soon. For the ceremony has begun. Amborg!" he cried.

The dark man turned. Chip saw that his face was set in granite lines. Nearest to the cavern mouth, his men were being prodded toward the awful test they must endure.

Even in this critical moment, Salvation was the man of god. "Amborg," he said, "you have been ever an evil man, living and thinking the thoughts of Satan. But there is yet time for you to repent and confess your sins. As a fellow man, I loathe and despise you. But as His emissary, I offer you even in this hour of trial the peace that surpasseth all human understanding—"

Amborg laughed at him. His voice crackled harshly, metallically, in the audio-phones of Chip's space-helmet.

"Save that stuff for the suckers, old man. You and your pals are just worried because we get first chance to go down into the valley. Well— you'd better worry! There's a rotor-gun mounted in that life-skiff. If we hadn't all been jarred cold when we landed, we'd have given these greenies a sweet greeting. We're going to lift the ship out of that ditch and bring it back over here. Save your prayers; you'll need them when we come over!"

Salvation reminded him stonily, "The flames—"

"Flames be damned! Superstitious poppycock! Spacesuits will protect us from heat or cold alike. Well—come on!"

He gestured his mates to him. The wailing chant of the Titanian natives increased in tone and volume as the four outlaws left their guards and boldly strode the last few rods up the hill, past the dais—and into the roaring hell-mouth of the cave!

And as they entered, Chip Warren knew a swift sinking of heart. His apprehensions had been unfounded, Amborg's claim that the lethal power of the flame was "superstitious poppycock" was true. The spacesuits were adequate protection, and in short moments, Amborg would be soaring back across the plateau, the jets of his rotor-gun spewing death and destruction upon them all....

Then, "My God!" gasped Syd Palmer, his voice awed.

Chip looked, and shuddered to see, the last judgment of Blaze Amborg and his men. A scant dozen yards they strode into the cavern. Vast spirals of fire played about them, but they did not falter. Their suits, ingeniously woven of metal, rubber, asbesto-quartz, defied the combustive powers of fire. But despite this—one of the figures staggered. The stunted Jovian was first to succumb. He had just pitched forward to his face when the second figure reeled. Raat 'Aran, the Uranian. He reeled and clutched at the tall Venusian, Torth—but the Venusian, too, had dropped to his knees; his hands clawed frenziedly at his breast.

Then the mysterious death struck Amborg. His voice rang out in a piercing scream; Chip saw him stare wildly at the three now-motionless bodies of his comrades, whirl, race back toward the safety of the hillside.

But he never reached it. He had taken no more than a dozen strides when he fell. A moment his incoherent cries babbled sickening delirium into his watchers' ear-phones....

Then all was still, save for the inexorable chanting of the natives. And the grave, judicial voice of the Titanian on the altar.

"They have been tested in the flame," interpreted Salvation Smith soberly, "and found guilty. Now it is our turn...."

Chip Warren was not a religious man. He lived by a simple code: do good and keep your sidearms primed. But now there faced him the inevitable finality of death; he felt an urge to meet that last, great mystery in comfort. He turned to his friends gravely.

"Now," he said, "it is our turn. So I guess this is goodbye, Syd. And Padre—it might help if you could say a few words for us ... just something...."

"So be it, my son!" said Salvation, understandingly. He lifted his head; his fine old eyes sought the murky gray skies of Titania, so different from the sweet blue Earthly skies for which all space-farers' hearts yearned when their journey's end was reached.

"If this be the way," he said quietly, "thy servants must depart, then so be it, O Lord. Yet even now in extremis we do not forget Thee and Thy might. We remember even yet—" He looked at the flaming cave-mouth toward which they must in a moment walk. "Even yet we remember a fellowship like ours who met and defied the dread embrace of fire.

"'And in those days,'" he said, "'there were three children of Israel which the king Nebuchadnezzar ordered to be cast without raiment into the fiery furnace. And their names were Shadrach, Meshach and Abednego—'"

"Shadrach!" cried Chip. There was no intentional irreverence in his interruption. Understanding had burst upon him so suddenly that the words hurtled from his lips.

"Peace, my son!" counseled the old man. "Let not your heart be troubled—"

"It's not! We're all right, Padre! If my hunch is right—and it must be! Look, they are bidding us walk into the caves. We haven't a moment to spare. Hurry, get off your spacesuits!"

There was biting cold upon Chip Warren's limbs and body as he cast the limp shell of his bulger behind him. But as he neared the cavern's mouth, the cold grew less intense. Less intense! That in itself was final, convincing proof he had been right! He was barely two yards from the writhing gouts of flame now. Were that the true fire it appeared to be, its searing blasts would already be parching his skin to black flakes—

But it was not! It was merely—pleasantly warm!

"I was right!" he cried exultantly. "Syd ... Padre! Come on in!" His voice was almost hysterical with relief as he stepped gingerly over the prostrate bodies of those who had gone into the fiery furnace garbed in suits of metallic substance. "Come on in—the fire's fine!"

And together the three new Children of Israel walked unharmed into the fiery furnace of Titania....

The corridors led, as the Titanian chieftain said, downward, winding, through the hill to the vale below, where rested Amborg's navigable lifeskiff. The small cruiser in which they were to fly to neighboring Uranus, there find aid and eager ears into which to pour their story.

And it did not surprise Chip Warren in the least to discover, about halfway down the flickering tunnel, a ledge of brightly gleaming ore that was resilient to the touch but broke the keen edge of the knife with which Chip attempted to scratch it.

"Ekalastron!" he cried. "See—a whole mountain of it! Not just a mine; a mountain! Enough to fill Man's needs for centuries!"

Syd's eyes, behind the quartzite globe, were big as saucers. He gulped, "C-chip—are you sure we're alive? Do you think maybe we died back there in the first cave, maybe? And this is all some wild illusion—?"

"It is not illusion," proclaimed Salvation serenely. "I understand, now, what Chip divined in time to save us from a dreadful fate." And he looked at the young man affectionately. "Radiation was what killed the others, my boy?"

Chip nodded. "Must have been, Padre. The 'flames' were not true flames at all. Not as we Earthlings, children of a warm Sun, masters of combustive fire, understand flame. Different elements have different combustive temperatures. On bitter-cold Uranus and Titania, the kindling point of certain rare gases is necessarily in ratio to the outer cold. The kindling point of the gases in this tunnel is a temperature which—though fiery-hot and deadly to the Titanians—is only pleasantly warm to us!"

"So Amborg," continued Syd, "walked into the flaming tunnel wearing a space-suit—"

"A metallic space-suit," reminded Chip, "which was a transmitter for certain lethal radiations inherent to this 'cold heat.' Blaze Amborg did not die of flame. He died of—electrocution."

Then a strange thought struck him and he turned suddenly to Salvation Smith. "Padre—?"

"Yes, my son?"

"The story you started to tell. The one that gave me my inspiration. About Shadrach. I wonder if some time long ago in the past, that legend may not have sprung from an adventure such as ours?"

Salvation smiled and shook his head.

"That is not mine to say, my boy, not yet thine to question. Perhaps some day the truth shall be known to you and me. But meanwhile—"

But meanwhile, the life-skiff was theirs for the taking. This was no question to long plague Chip Warren or any other space-adventurer, before whom stretched a whole, wide universe of wonder.

THE LORELEI DEATH

Originally published in *Planet Stories*, Winter 1941.

CHAPTER I

Chip Warren stood before an oblong of glass set into one wall of the spaceship *Chickadee II*, stared at what he saw reflected therefrom—and frowned. He didn't like it. Not a bit! It was too—too—

He turned away angrily, ripped the offending article from about his neck, and chose another necktie from the rack. This one was brighter, gaudier, much more in keeping with the gaiety of his mood. He emitted a grunt of satisfaction, spun from the mirror to face his two companions triumphantly.

"There! How do you like *that*?"

Syd Palmer, short and chubby, tow-headed and liquid-blue of eye, always languid save when engaged in the solution of some engineering problem concerned with the space vessel he mothered like a brooding hen, moaned insultingly and forced a shudder.

"Sunspots! Novae! Flying comets! And he wears 'em around his neck!"

"You," Chip told him serenely, "have no appreciation of beauty. What do *you* think of it, Padre?"

"Salvation" Smith, a tall, gangling scarecrow garbed in rusty black, a lean-jawed, hawkeyed man with tumbled locks of silver framing his weathered cheeks like a halo, concealed his grin poorly. "Well, my boy," he admitted, "there is *some* Biblical precedent for your—ahem!—clamorous raiment. 'So Joseph made for himself a coat which was of many colors—'"

"Both of you," declared Chip, "give me a pain in the pants! Stick-in-the-muds! Here we are in port for the first time in months, cargo-bins loaded to the gunwales with enough ekalastron to make us rich for life—and you sit here like a pair of stuffed owls!

"Well, not me! I'm going to take a night off, throw myself a party the likes of which was never seen around these parts. Put a candle in the window, chilluns, 'cause li'l' Chip won't be home till the wee, sma' hours!"

Syd chuckled.

"O.Q., big shot. But don't get too cozy with any of those joy-joint entertainers. Remember what happened to poor old Dougal MacNeer!"

Salvation said soberly, "Syd's just fooling, my boy. But I *would* be careful if I were you. We're in the Belt, you know. The forces of law and order do not always govern these wild outposts of civilization as well as might be hoped. The planetoids are dens of iniquity, violent and unheeding the words of Him who rules all—"

The old man's lips etched a straight line, reminding Chip that Salvation Smith was not one of those milk-and-water missionaries who espoused the principle of "turning the other cheek" to evildoers. Salvation was not the ordained emissary of any church. A devoutly religious man with the heart of an adventurer, he had taken upon himself the mission of carrying to outland tribes the story of the God he worshipped.

That his God was the fierce Yahveh of the Old Testament, a God of anger and retribution, was made evident by the methods Salvation sometimes employed in winning his converts. For not only was Salvation acknowledged the most pious man in space; he was also conceded to be the best hand with a gun!

Now Chip gave quiet answer. "I know, Padre: I'll be careful. Well, Syd—sure you won't change your mind and come along?"

"No can do, chum. The spaceport repair crew's still smearing this jalopy with ek. Got to stay and watch 'em."

"O.Q. I'm off alone, then. See you later!"

And, whistling, Chip Warren stepped through the lock of the *Chickadee* onto the soil of the asteroid Danae.

* * * *

Danae was, thought Chip as he strolled along briskly toward the town beyond the spaceport, a most presentable hunk of rock. Nice *lucentite* Dome ... good atmo ... a fine artificial grav system based on Terra normal. It seemed to be a popular little fueling-stop, too, for its cradle-bins were laden with vessels from every planet in the System, and as he gained the main drag he found himself rubbing shoulders with citizens of every known world. Lumbering, albino Venusians, petal-headed Martians, Jovian runts, greenies from far Uranus, Earthman—all were here.

Quite a likely place, he thought happily, to chuck a brawl. A brilliantly gleaming xenon sign before him welcomed visitors to:

XU'UL'S SOLAREST
*Barroom—Casino—Dancing*100—Lovely Hostesses—100

He entered, and was immediately deluged by a bevy of

charm-gals vying for the privilege of: (1) helping him beat the roulette wheel; (2) helping him drink the house dry, and/or (3) separating him as swiftly as possible from the credits in his money belt.

Chip shook them off, gently but firmly. He wanted a good time, true; but he wanted it solo. The main cabaret was too crowded; he passed through it and another equally blatant room wherein twoscore Venusians were straining the structure with a native "sing-stomp," and ended up finally, with a sigh of relief, in a small, dimly-lighted private bar unfrequented by anyone save a bored and listless Martian bartender.

The chrysanthemum-pated son of the desertland roused himself as Chip entered, rustled his petals and piped a ready greeting.

"Welcoom, ssirr! Trrink, pleasse?"

This was more like it! Chip grinned.

"Scotch," he said. "*Old Spaceman.* And let's have a new bottle, Curly. None of that doctored swill."

"Of courrsse, ssirr!" piped the bar-keep aggrievedly. He pushed a bottle across the mahogany; Chip flipped a golden credit-token back at him.

"Tell me when I've guzzled this, and I'll start work on another." He took a deep, appreciative sniff. "And don't let any of those dizzy dolls in here," he ordered. "I've got a lot of back drinking to catch up on, and I don't want to be disturbed—*Hey!*"

In his alarm, he almost dropped the bottle. For the door suddenly burst open, and in its frame loomed a figure in Space Patrol blues. A finger pointed in Chip's direction and a bull-o'-Bashan voice roared:

"*Stop!* Bartender—grab that man! He's a desperate criminal, wanted on four planets for murder!"

Shock momentarily immobilized Chip. Not so the bartender. He was, it seemed, an ardent pacifist. With a bleat of panic fear he scampered from his post, his metallic stilts clattering off in the distance. Chip's accuser moved forward from the shadows; dim light illumined his features. And—

"*Johnny!*" Chip's voice lifted in a note of jubilant surprise. "Johnny Haldane—you old scoundrel! Where in the void did *you* drop from?"

The S.S.P. man chuckled and returned Chip's greeting with a bone-grinding handclasp.

"I might ask the same of you, chum! Lord, it's been ages since we've crossed 'jectory! When I saw you meandering across the Casino, you could have knocked me down with a jetblast! What's new? Is old Syd still with you?"

"We're still shipmates. But he's back at the spaceport. The jerry-crew is plating our crate with ek, and—"

"Ek! Plating a private cruiser!" Haldane stared at him in astonishment, then whistled. "Sweet Sacred Stars, you must be filthy with credits to be able to coat an entire ship with ekalastron!"

"You," boasted Chip, "ain't heard nothing yet!" And he told him how they had discovered an entire mountain of the previous new element, No. 97 in the periodic table, on frigid Titania, satellite of far Uranus. "It was touch-and-go for a while," he admitted, "whether we'd be the luckiest three guys in space—or the deadest! But we passed through the flaming caverns like old Shadrach in the Bible—remember?—and here we are!" [1]

Haldane was exuberant. "A mountain of ekalastron!" he gloated. "That's the greatest contribution to spaceflight since Biggs' velocity-intensifier!" It was no overstatement. "Element No. 97 was a metal so light that a man could carry in one hand enough to coat the entire hull of a battleship—yet so adamant that a gossamer film of it would deflect a meteor! A metal strong enough to crush diamonds to ash—but so resilient that, when properly treated, it would rebound like rubber! What are you going to do with it, Chip? Put it on the open market?"

Warren shook his head.

"Not exactly. We talked it over carefully—Syd and Salvation and I— and we decided there are some space-rats to whom it shouldn't be made available. Privateers and outlaws, you know. So we turned control of the mines over to the Space Patrol at Uranus, and visiphoned the Earth authorities we were bringing in one cargo—"

"Visiphoned!" interrupted Haldane sharply. "Did you say visiphoned?"

"Why—why, yes."

"From where?"

"Oh, just before we reached the Belt. We don't have a very strong transmitter, you know. Sa-a-ay, what's all the excitement, pal? Did we do something that was wrong?"

Haldane frowned worriedly. "I don't know, Chip. It wasn't anything *wrong*, but what you did was damned dangerous. For if your message was intercepted, you may have played into the very hands of—the Lorelei!"

Chip stared at his friend bewilderedly for a moment. Then he grinned. "Hey—I must be getting slightly whacky in my old age. I stand here with an unopened bottle in my hands and hear things! For a minute I thought you said 'Lorelei.' The Lorelei, my space-cop friend, is a myth. An old Teutonic myth about a beautiful damsel who sits out in the middle of a sea on a treacherous rock, combing her golden locks, warbling and luring her fascinated admirers to destruction."

He grunted. "A dirty trick, if you ask me. Catch a snort of this alleged Scotch, pal, and I'll torture your eardrums with the whole, sad story." He

1   "Shadrach," *Planet Stories*, Fall, 1941.

started to sing. "'*Ich weiss nicht was soll es bedeuten—*'"

The Patrolman laid a hand on his arm, silenced him.

"It's not funny, Chip. You've described the Lorelei exactly. That's how she got her name. An incredibly beautiful woman who wantonly lures space-mariners to their death.

"The only difference is that her 'rock' is an asteroid somewhere in the Belt—and she does not sing, she calls! She began exercising her vicious appeal about two months ago, Earth reckoning. Since then, no less than a dozen spacecraft—freighters, liners, even one Patrolship—have fallen prey to her wiles. Their crews have been brutally murdered, their cargos stolen."

"Wait a minute!" interrupted Chip shrewdly. "How do you know about her if the crews have been murdered?"

"She has a habit of locking the controls," explained Haldane, "and setting ravaged ships adrift. Apparently there is no room on her hideout—wherever it is—for empty hulks. One of these ships was salvaged by a courageous cabin-boy who hid from the Lorelei and her pirate band beneath a closetful of soiled linens in the laundry. He described her. His description goes perfectly with less accurate glimpses seen over the visiphones of several score spacecraft!"

Chip said soberly, "So it's no joke, eh, pal? Sorry I popped off. I thought you were pulling my leg. Where do *I* come into this mess, though?"

"Ekalastron!" grunted Johnny succinctly. "A jackpot prize for any corsair! And you *advertised* a cargo of it over the etherwaves! The Lorelei will be waiting for you with her tongue hanging out. The only thing for you to do, kid, is go back to Jupiter or Io as fast as you can get there. Make the Patrol give you a convoy—"

A sudden light danced in Chip Warren's eyes. It was a light Syd Palmer would have groaned to see—for it usually presaged trouble. It was a bright, hard, reckless light.

"Hold your jets, Johnny!" drawled Chip. "Aren't you forgetting one thing? In a couple more hours, I can face the Lorelei and her whole mob—and be damned to them! She can't touch the *Chickadee*, because it's being plated right now!"

Haldane snapped his fingers in quick remembrance.

"By thunder, you're right! Her shells will ricochet off the *Chickadee's* hull like hail off a tin roof. Chip, are you in any hurry to reach Earth? I thought not. What do you say we go after the Lorelei *together*! I'll swear you in as a Deputy Patrolman; we'll take the *Chickadee* and—"

"It's a deal!" declared Chip promptly. "You got any idea where this Lorelei's hangout is?"

"That's why I'm here on Danae. I got a tip that one of the Lorelei's men put in here for supplies. I hoped maybe I could single him out somehow, follow him when he jetted for his base, and in that way—*Chip! Look out!"*

Haldane shouted and moved at the same time. His arm lashed out wildly, thrusting, smashing Chip to the floor in a sprawling heap. The as-yet unopened bottle was now violently opened; it splintered into a thousand shards against a wall.

Bruised and shaken, Chip lifted his head to see what had caused Johnny's alarm. Even as he did so, the dull gloom of the bar was blazoned with searing effulgence. A lancet of flame leaped from the dark, rearward doorway, burst in Johnny Haldane's face!

The Patrolman cried once, a choking cry that died in a mewling whimper. His unused pistol slipped from slackening fingers, and he sagged to the floor. Again crimson lightning laced the shadows; Haldane's body jerked, and the air was raw with the hot, sickening stench of charred flesh.

With an instinct born of bitter years, Chip had come to his knees behind the shelter of the mahogany bar. But now his own flame-pistol was in his hand, and a dreadful rage was mingled with the agony in his heart. Reckless of results, he sprang to his feet, gun spewing livid death into the shadows.

His blast found a mark. For an instant flame haloed a human face drawn in inhuman pain. A heavy, sultry, bestial face, already puckered with one long, ugly scar that ran from right temple to jawbone, now newly scarred with the red brand of Chip's marksmanship.

Then, before Chip could fire again, came the rasp of pounding footsteps. The man turned and fled. Chip bent over his fallen friend, seeking, with hands that did not even feel the heat, fluttering life beneath still smoldering cloth.

He felt—nothing. Johnny was dead.

A snarl of sheer animal rage burst from Chip's lips. Someone would pay for this; pay dearly! Help was coming now. He himself would lead the hue-and-cry that would track a foul murderer to his lair. He spun as the footsteps drew nearer.

"Hurry!" he cried. "This way! Follow me—"

In a bound, he hurdled the bar, lingered at the door only long enough to let the others mark his course. For they had burst into the room, now, a full score of them. Excited, hard-bitten dogs of space, quick-triggered and willing. Once more he cried for help.

"After him! Come on! He—"

And then—disaster struck! For a reedy voice broke from the van of the mob. The voice of the Martian bartender.

"That's him!" he piped sibilantly. "That's the man! He's a desperate criminal, wanted on four planets for murder! The Patrolman came to arrest him—*and now he's murdered the Spacie!"*

CHAPTER II

The stunning injustice of that accusation came close to costing Chip Warren his life. For a split second he stood motionless in the doorway, gaping lips forming denial. Words which were never to be uttered, for suddenly a raw-boned miner wrenched a Moeller from its holster, leveled and fired.

The hot tongue of death licked hungrily at the young spaceman's cheek, scorched air crackled in his eardrums. Now was no time to squander in vain argument. Chip ducked, spun, and hurled himself through the doorway. There still remained one hope. That he might catch the real murderer, and in that way clear himself....

But the door led to a small, deserted vestibule, and it to an alleyway behind Xu'ul's Solarest. Viewing that maze of byways and passages, Chip knew his hope was futile. There remained but one thing to do. Get out of here. But quick!

It was no hard task. The labyrinth swallowed him as it had engulfed the scarred killer; in a few minutes even the footsteps of his pursuers could no longer be heard. And Chip worked his cautious way back to the spaceport, and to the bin wherein was cradled the *Chickadee.*

Syd Palmer looked up in surprise as Chip let himself in the electro-lock. The chubby engineer gasped, "Salvation, look what the cat drug in! His high-flying Nibs! What's the matter, Chip? Night-life too much for you?"

"Never mind that now!" panted Chip. "Is this tin can ready to roll? Warm the hypos. We're lifting gravs—"

Palmer said anxiously, "Now, wait a minute! The men haven't quite finished plating the hull, Chip!"

"Can't help that! We've got important business. In a very few minutes—*Ahh!* There he goes now!" Chip had gone to the *perilens* the moment he entered the ship; now he saw in its reflector that which he had expected. The gushing orange spume of a spaceship roaring from its cradle. "Hurry, Syd!"

There were a lot of things Syd Palmer wanted to ask. He wanted to know *who* went *where*; he was bursting with curiosity about the "important business" which had brought his pal back from town in such a rush; his keen eye also had detected a needle-gun burn on Chip's coat-sleeve. But he was too good a companion to waste time now on such trivia.

"O.Q.," he snapped. "It's your pigeon!"

And he disappeared. They heard his voice calling to the workmen, the scuff of equipment being disengaged from the *Chickadee's* hull, the thin, high whine of warming hypatomics. Salvation looked at Warren quizzically.

"It smells," he ventured gently, "like trouble."

"It is trouble," Chip told him. "Plenty trouble!"

"In that case—" said the old man mildly—"I guess I'd better get the rotor stripped for action." He stepped to the gunnery turret, dropped the fore-irons and stripped their weapon for action. "'Be ye men of peace,'" he intoned, "'but gird firmly thy loins for righteous battle!' Thus saith the Lord God which is Jehovah. Selah!"

Then came Syd's cry from the depths of the hyporoom.

"All set, Chip! Lift gravs!"

Warren's finger found a stud. And with a gusty roar the *Chickadee* rocketed into space on a pillar of flame.

* * * *

Two hours later, Chip was still following the bright pinpoint of scarlet which marked the course of his quarry.

In the time that had elapsed since their take-off, he had told his friends the whole story. When he told about the Lorelei, Salvation Smith's seamy old features screwed up in a perplexed grimace. "A woman pirate in the Belt, son? I find it hard to believe. Yet—" And when he described the death of Johnny Haldane, anger smoldered in the missionary's eyes, and Syd Palmer's hands knotted into tight, white fists. Said Syd, "A man with a scar, eh? Well, we'll catch him sooner or later. And when we do—" His tone boded no good to the man who had slain an old and loved friend.

"As a matter of fact," offered Salvation, "we've got him now. Any time you say the word, Chip. We're faster than he is. We can close in on him in five minutes."

"I know," nodded Warren grimly. "But we won't do it—yet. I'm borrowing a bit of Johnny's strategy. I've been plotting his course. As soon as I'm sure of his destination, we'll take care of *him*. But our first and most vital problem is to locate the Lorelei's hideaway."

Syd said, "That's all right with me, chum. I like a good scrap as much as the next guy. Better, maybe. But this isn't our concern, strictly speaking. What we ought to do is report this matter to the Space Patrol, let them take care of it."

Salvation shook his head.

"That's where you're mistaken, Sydney. This is very much our concern. So much so, in fact, that we dare not make port again until it's cleared up. I think you have forgotten that it is not the scar-faced man who is wanted for the killing of Haldane—but Chip!"

"B-but—" gasped Palmer—"b-but that's ridiculous! Chip and Johnny were old buddies. Lifelong friends!"

"Nevertheless, the circumstantial evidence indicates Chip's guilt.

Twenty men saw him standing over Johnny's dead body, with a flame-pistol in his hand. And the barkeep heard Johnny 'arrest' Chip and accuse him of murder!"

Chip said ruefully, "That's right, Syd. It was only a joke, but it backfired. The bartender thought Johnny meant it. He scooted out of there like a bat out of Hades. I'm in it up to my neck unless we can bring back evidence that Scarface actually did the killing. And that may not be so easy."

He stirred restlessly. "But we'll cross that bridge when we come to it. Right now our job is to keep this rat in sight. We've gone farther already than I expected we would." He turned to the old preacher. "Where do you think we're going, Padre? Out of the Belt entirely?"

"I've been wondering that myself, son. I don't know for sure, of course, but it looks to me as if we're going for the Bog. If so, you'd better keep a weather-eye peeled."

"The Bog!" Chip had never penetrated the planetoids so deeply before, but he knew of the Bog by hearsay. All men did. A treacherous region of tightly packed asteroids, a mad and whirling scramble of the gigantic rocks which, aeons ago, had been a planet. Few spacemen dared penetrate the Bog. Of those who did dare, few returned to tell the tale. "The Bog! Say! I'd *better* keep a sharp lookout!"

He turned to the *perilens* once more, fastened an eye to its lens. And then—

"Syd!" he cried. "Salvation! Look! She—she—!"

He pressed the plunger that transferred the *perilens* image to the central viewscreen. And as he did so, a phantom filled the area which should have revealed yawning space, gay with the spangles of a myriad glowing orbs. The vision of an unbelievably beautiful girl, the golden-crowned embodiment of a man's fondest dreaming, eyes wide with an indistinguishable emotion, arms stretched wide in mute appeal.

And from the throats of all came simultaneous recognition.

"The Lorelei!"

At the same moment came a plea from the enchantress of space through a second medium. For no reason anyone could explain, the ship's *telaudio* wakened to life; over it came to their ears the actual words of the girl:

"Help! Oh, help! Can anyone hear me? Help—"

Even though he knew this to be only a ruse, a deliberate, dastardly trap set for the unwary, Chip Warren's pulse leaped in hot response to that desperate plea. Even with the warning of Johnny Haldane fresh in his memory, some gallantry deep within him spurred him to the aid of this lovely vision. Here was a woman a man could live for, fight for, *die* for! A woman like no other in the universe.

Then common sense came to his rescue. He wrenched his gaze from the tempting shadow, cried: "Kill that wavelength! Tune the lens on another beam, Syd!"

Palmer, bedazzled but obedient, spun the dial of the *perilens*. Despite his vastly improved science Man had never yet succeeded in devising a transparent medium through which to view the void wherein he soared; the *perilens* was a device which translated impinging light-waves into a picture of that which lay outside the ship's hull. When or where electrical disturbances existed in space, its frequency could be changed for greater clarity. This was what Syd now attempted.

But to no avail! For it mattered not which cycle he tuned to—the image persisted. Still on the viewscreen that pleading figure beckoned piteously. And still the cabin rang to the prayers of that heart-tugging voice:

"Help! Oh, help! Can anyone hear me? Help—"

Gone, now, was any fascination that thrilling vision might previously have held for Chip Warren. Understanding of their plight dawned coldly upon him, and his brow became dark with anger.

"We're blanketed! Flying blind! Salvation, radio a general alarm! Syd, jazz the hypos to max. Shift trajectory to fourteen-oh-three North and loft ... fire No. 3 jet...."

He had hurled himself into the bucket-shaped pilot's seat; now his fingers played the controls like those of a mad organist. The *Chickadee* groaned from prow to stern, trembled like a tortured thing as he thrust it into a rising spiral.

It was a desperate chance he was taking. Increasing his speed thus, it was certain he would be spotted by the man he had been following; the flaming jets of the *Chickadee* must form a crimson arch against black space visible for hundreds—thousands!—of miles. Nor was there any way of knowing what lay in the path Chip thus blindly chose. Titanic death might loom on every side. But they had to fight clear of this spot of blindness, clear their instruments....

And then it came! A jarring concussion that smashed against the prow of the *Chickadee* like a battering ram. Chip flew headlong out of his bucket to spreadeagle on the heaving iron floor. He heard, above the grinding plaint of shattered steel the bellowing prayer of Salvation Smith:

"We've crashed! 'Into Thy hands, O Lord of old—'"

Then Syd's angry cry, "Crashed, hell! He's smashed us with a tractor-blast!"

Chip stared at his companion numbly.

"But—but that's impossible! We're plated with ek! A tractor-cannon couldn't hurt us—"

"Half-plated!" howled Syd savagely. "And those damn fools started working from the stern of the *Chickadee*! We're vulnerable up front, and

that's where he got us! In a minute this can will be leaking like a sieve. I'll get out bulgers. Hold 'er to her course, Chip!"

He dove for the lockers wherein were hung the space-suits, tore them hastily from their hangers. Chip again spun the *perilens* vernier. No good! No space ... no stars ... just a beautiful phantom crying them to certain doom. By now he was aware that from a dozen sprung plates air was seeping, but he fought down despair. While there remained hope, a man had to keep on fighting.

He scrambled back into the bucket-seat, experimented with controls that answered sluggishly. Salvation had sprung to the rotor-gun, was now angrily jerking its lanyard, lacing the void with death-dealing bursts that had no mark. The old man's eyes were brands of fire, his white hair clung wetly to his forehead. His rage was terrible to behold.

"'Yes, truly shall I destroy them!'" he cried, "'who loose their stealth upon me like a thief from the night—'"

Then suddenly there came a second and more frightful blow. The straining *Chickadee* stopped as though pole-axed by a gigantic fist. Stopped and shuddered and screamed in metal agony. This time inertia flung Chip headlong, helpless, into the control racks. Brazen studs took the impact of his body; crushing pain banded about his temples, and a red wetness ran into his eyes, blurring and blinding him, burning.

For an instant there flamed before him a universe of incandescent stars, weaving, shimmering, merging. The vision of a woman whose hair was a golden glory....

After that—nothing!

CHAPTER III

From a billion miles away, from a bourne unguessable thousands of light-years distant, came the faint, far whisper of a voice. Nearer and nearer it came, and ever faster, till it throbbed upon Chip's eardrums with booming savagery.

"—coming to, now. Good! We'll soon find out—"

Chip opened his eyes, too dazed, at first, to understand the situation in which he found himself. Gone was the familiar control-turret of the *Chickadee*, gone the bulger into which he had so hastily clambered. He lay on the parched, rocky soil of a—a something. A planetoid, perhaps. And he was surrounded by a motley crew of strangers: scum of all the planets that circle the Sun....

Then recollection flooded back upon him, sudden and complete. The chase ... the call of the fateful Lorelei ... the crash! New strength, born of anger, surged through him. He lifted his head.

"My—my companions?" he demanded weakly.

The leader of those who encircled him, a mighty hulk of a man, massive of shoulder and thigh, black-haired, with an unshaven blue jaw, raven-bright eyes and a jutting, aquiline nose like the beak of a hawk, loosed a satisfied grunt.

"Ah! Back to normal, eh, sailor? Damn near time!"

Climbing to his feet sent a swift wave of giddiness through Chip—but he managed it. He fought down the vertigo which threatened to overwhelm him, and confronted the big man boldly.

"What," he stormed, "is the meaning of this?"

The giant stared at him for a moment, his jaw slack. Then his raven-bright eyes glittered; he slapped a trunklike thigh and guffawed in boisterous mirth.

"Hear that?" he roared to his companions. "Quite a guy, ain't he? 'What's the meanin' o' this?' he asks! Game little fightin' cock, hey?" Then he sobered abruptly, and a grim light replaced the amusement in his eyes. Here was not a man to be trifled with, Chip realized. His tone assumed a biting edge. "The meanin' is, my bucko," he answered mirthlessly, "that you've run afoul o' your last reef. Unless you have a sane head on your shoulders, and you're willing to talk fast and straight!"

"Talk?"

"Don't stall. We've already unloaded your bins. We found it. And a nice haul, too. Thanks for lettin' us know it was on the way." The burly one chuckled coarsely. "We'd have took it, anyway, but you helped matters out by comin' to us."

Johnny Haldane had been right, then. Chip remembered his friend's ominous warning. "—if your message was intercepted, you may have played into the hands of—" He said slowly, "Then you *are* the Lorelei's men?"

"The who? Never mind that, bucko, just talk. That ekalastron—where did it come from?"

And it occurred to Warren suddenly that although the big man *did* hold the whip hand, he was still not in possession of the most important secret of all! While the location of the ekalastron mine remained a secret, a deadlock existed.

"And if I won't tell—?" he countered shrewdly.

"Why, then, sailor—" The pirate leader's hamlike fists tightened, and a cold light glinted in his eyes—"why, then I guess maybe I'll have to beat it out o' you!"

He took a step forward. Chip, still unsteady on his feet, but feeling his strength renew itself with each passing moment, braced for rough encounter. But the moment of contest was not yet. For even as the big man's companions drew back, grinning evilly, to form a ring about the pair, rose a familiar voice from behind Chip.

"*Hold!* 'Stay now the hand of wrath, yea, shalt thou restrain even thine arm raised in striking lest His vengeance smite thee into dust!'"

A look of swift, incredulous dismay, sweeping across the giant's face, vanished in an expression of unholy glee.

"Salvation!" he exclaimed exultantly. "It's Salvation Smith! So we meet again!"

The circle parted, admitting newcomers. Syd and the old missionary and the pirates who had dragged them from the broken *Chickadee*. Chip thought that never before had he been so glad to lay eyes on his two comrades. Events had followed so swiftly that he had had no time to feel concern for them, but it was a relief to find them alive and unharmed.

Nor had the crash sapped either of his valor. Syd's face was stubbornly determined, and Salvation breathed raging defiance. He glanced once at Chip, as if to assure himself the young spaceman was uninjured, then turned to their captor.

"Aye, Salvation Smith!" he thundered. "And how came you to this new rat's nest, Blacky Jordan?"

Blacky Jordan! The name touched the fringes of Chip Warren's memory, tugged there fretfully. Then came recollection. Of course! Blacky Jordan had been the chief lieutenant of Balder Sorenson ... the only one of Sorenson's space-preying gang to escape when Lt. Russ Bartlett of the Solar Postal Department had smashed the mail-robbers off Eros two years ago!

The filthiest kind of a scoundrel, Blacky Jordan. A treacherous, back-stabbing murderer who found no methods too low to achieve the results he desired. Chip understood, now, why only one small, frightened boy had ever returned to tell of the Lorelei's gang.

But—the Lorelei? Where was she? And in what way had Jordan earned the allegiance of a girl like—

He snapped out of it abruptly. For Jordan's chunky frame had stiffened, his raven-bright eyes narrowed to meager slits, and he was moving forward, hands half-clenched at his sides in an anticipatory hunger. His voice was low and hard.

"Salvation Smith! The psalm-singin' dog who ran me out of Mars Central! I always said some day I'd get even for that! Well, now's the time!"

And suddenly he lunged, hands clawing for the older man's throat. But they never found their mark. For, swiftly as he moved, Chip Warren moved faster still. A step forward, a foot outthrust, an arm upraised, spinning the man....

"*So!*" bellowed Jordan. "So you're still lookin' for trouble, bucko? O.Q. I'll take care o' that mealy-mouthed space-parson later!"

He turned on Chip viciously; the blow he directed at the smaller man's head would have felled an ox. But Chip was no ox. He was like a panther as he gave with the blow, bobbed, weaved in underneath Jordan's flailing arm, and came up with both fists driving like pistons.

A right to the heart, a short, jabbing left into the mid-section, dropping the bigger man's guard—then a crashing right to the jaw! And—

Jordan went down!

But not yet had Chip Warren fully recovered from the effects of his recent shock. His blows had the power to hurt and sting, but they lacked their accustomed effectiveness.

Scarcely had he touched the ground than Blacky Jordan was up again, his beefy face a red mask of rage, his voice a roaring thunder. Like an unleashed behemoth he hurled himself upon his slighter antagonist, bulling Chip back by sheer bulk, smashing down Chip's guard with sledge-hammer blows.

Even so, Chip gave more than he took. Even as he retreated, his fists continued to dance in for stinging slashes at the other man's face, heart, wind. And had the locale of their meeting been a sporting ring, even yet he might have emerged the victor. But there was little sporting spirit in those who watched.

The foot of a pirate gangster slipped between Chip's legs, tripping him. As he stumbled backward, off balance, the tentacular paw of a Martian whipped about his shielding arm. He was completely at the mercy of the charging Jordan. Mercy was a word the black-haired one did not know. With a bellow of triumph, he smashed both fists, left, right, left again, into Chip's unprotected face. The blows throbbed home like burning rivets. A dizzy nausea assailed Chip; he felt the rocky soil springing up to meet him.

And now it was Syd who, angered beyond discretion, would have leaped forward to take up his friend's fight. But he could not. A dozen arms locked him in a vise of flesh; he was held motionless, straining futilely, as Jordan transferred his attentions to Salvation Smith.

This was no battle at all. Given a gun, the old war-horse was a match for any man in the System. But age had taken its toll of his strength; Jordan's first spite-filled punch smashed down his feeble defenses. In no time at all he was on the ground, stunned, bruised, shaken, unable to defend himself even against the lashing kicks of the pirate's boots. And as he drained the dregs of his vengeance, Blacky Jordan laughed.

"I've waited a long time for this, Salvation Smith!" he gloated. "You kicked me out of Mars; now it's my turn—"

With deliberate savagery he raised his thick, lead-soled boot, buried it in the old man's side. And again. And yet again. Salvation moaned and tried to rise, failed. Chip Warren, shaking off the dark clouds that had blinded him, got to his knees uncertainly, managed one lurching step toward the pirate. And then—

"*For shame!*" A voice that must be born of delirium. A voice lilting-clear as crystal, golden as dawn, valiant and proud as a banner flying. "You—you monster! I always knew you were a cur, Blacky Jordan, but I didn't know you'd stoop to *this*—"

And through the circle burst a figure Chip knew ... the figure of a girl with the face of an angel. But an avenging angel now, with her halo of golden hair cascading about her shoulders, her warm, ripe lips tightset with scorn and anger. Like a dancing gleam she raced between Jordan and his victim; her white hand raised once and descending stingingly upon the pirate's cheek ... then, with a little cry of sympathy, she was on her knees beside Salvation Smith.

It was—the girl of the lens! The Lorelei!

CHAPTER IV

What happened then was not in any wise comprehensible to Chip Warren.

Had Blacky Jordan turned viciously on the latecomer, striking her down as brutally as he had Chip and Salvation—that would have been understandable. Or had he meekly begged forgiveness—that, too, Chip could have understood. For the girl was—had to be!—either one of two things. Servant or mistress of the pirate chieftain.

But Jordan did neither of these things. Instead, he fingered his cheek where it flamed dull scarlet against brown, and his eyes were cloudy pools of anger and some contrasting emotion Chip could not name. His fingers twitched, his mouth worked. Then something like a shrug stirred his shoulders; he turned to his silently watching followers.

"Well—what are you standin' around here for? You got work to do, ain't you? Well, get goin', then!"

With obedient alacrity the mob dispersed. Chip had his first clear, unobstructed view of the terrain upon which the *Chickadee* had crashed. He saw that his guess had been a good one. It was an asteroid. And judging by the swift dip of the horizon, the visible arch of the distant landscape, a rather small one. Barely a mile in diameter. A mere sliver in the colossal débris of the Belt.

But, then, whence came its gravity? Though he wore no bulger he felt comfortably secure on this tiny fragment of matter. And how did a floating rock of this size maintain an atmosphere of Earth normal?

These were perplexing questions, but there was no opportunity now to solve them. For the girl had helped Salvation to his feet, had lent him a shoulder in support, and now was moving away. Jordan glared at her pettishly.

"An' just where do you think you're goin'?"

The Lorelei's gaze did not meet his, it passed clear through him as if he did not exist. Her voice was icy cold.

"Stand aside, please! I'm taking him below."

And again Blacky Jordan backed down! As before, his manner toward the girl was baffling. It was peremptory, yet at the same time conciliatory; at once truculent and submissive! He gave in with a graceless shrug.

"Oh, all right! Take 'em *all* below. I can't waste any more time on 'em right now. But I'll see 'em again later. Especially *you*—" He jerked his head toward Salvation, then stared thoughtfully at Chip—"and you, too, bucko. Yeah. Me and you is goin' to have a nice little talk later on."

And he stalked away. Hope flared in Chip that now he might find a chance to improve their lot. Not one of the men was guarding them. Only this girl, and she was preoccupied with Salvation—

But—his hope was vain. No gaoler needs guard prisoners immured on a desert isle. Their weapons had been stripped from them, their ship was a tangled heap of wreckage. And there was no other space vessel in sight.

Chip looked at Syd. Palmer's shake of the head confessed an equal bewilderment. Perhaps the answer to this mad situation lay where the girl led. The two spacemen followed.

* * * *

Their way took them into a tunnel which sloped for a few hundred yards into the earth, then debouched into a small cavern. Into the far wall of this was set a grilled gateway which, when opened by the girl, revealed—an elevator. Into this she helped Salvation. Chip and Syd, delayed by the same doubt, held back. The girl, noting their hesitation, addressed them directly for the first time.

"This way," she said. "Come on! Quickly!"

Chip said suspiciously, "Just a minute, sister. How do we know this isn't a trick of some kind—"

Her eyes flamed electric-blue, and her voice cracked like a whip.

"Don't be a fool! Get in here—and hurry! When he thinks it over he may change his mind. We're getting away with murder!"

It didn't make sense, but there was nothing to gain by lingering here. The two entered the conveyance, the girl pressed a button and concealed motors whined as they began to descend swiftly. But the last word was still Chip's.

"That's just what you *have* been getting away with," he acknowledged grimly, "but you're nearing the end of your rope now—Lorelei!"

In the semidarkness, the girl's eyes were pools of liquid surprise.

"Getting away with—end of—I don't understand?"

"Murder!" gritted Chip. "Murder and piracy. A dozen spacecraft within the past two months, scuttled and every man of their crews done to death. But your siren-song won't tempt many more, Lorelei. The Space Patrol is on to your alluring little trap. You may finish *us* off, but the battle fleet will find you eventually, and when it does—"

He didn't finish his prophecy, for the elevator came to rest; the door opened. And peering in at them, hurrying forward to greet them and take the sagging weight of the aged missionary from the girl's arm, was a white-haired old man.

"Alison!" he cried. "You're back safely! Thank the Lord! You shouldn't have gone above. It's dangerous, child, dangerous to mingle with such scoundrels! Who are these—?"

And then the girl did a surprising thing. A particularly surprising thing, inasmuch as a few minutes ago, facing Blacky Jordan like a golden Valkyr, her boldness had won from Chip Warren a grudging admiration. She fled to the old man's side, buried her face in his shoulder and cried:

"Daddy—this piracy, this murder and bloodshed—these men think *I* am part of it!"

The old man said, "Now, now, dear!" soothingly, and glared reproof at his visitors. "There must be some mistake—" And to the others he suggested, "Gentlemen, will you come with me? We must get to the bottom of this."

Their journey this time was short. Through one door to a series of warm, well-lighted chambers. But stupefying. Because here, at what Chip realized must be the very core of the tiny planetoid, had been carved from solid rock quarters that matched, in efficiency and luxury, any elaborate dwelling on the face of a civilized planet!

Comfortable living chambers were here, furnished in excellent taste. And through the doorways leading to adjacent rooms Chip glimpsed white-tiled compartments wherein were visible rows upon rows of beakers and flasks, retorts, motor-units, experimental apparatus. Laboratories, beautifully arranged and maintained! He stared at his host in astonishment.

"How—?" he stammered. "Who—?"

"Will you be seated, gentlemen?" suggested the older man. "There! Now, let us get to the root of this frightful affair. You accused my daughter of implication—?"

Chip said, "We—we had ample reason to, sir. First let me introduce myself and my friends. I am Chip Warren ... this is my friend and shipmate, Syd Palmer ... and this is Salvation Smith...."

"Salvation Smith! Not really? I've heard of you, Padre," said the old man. "You were engaged in bringing spiritual light to the Martian outlanders at about the time I was supplying Mars with a more—er—mechanical type—"

Salvation lifted his head suddenly.

"Grayland Blaine! Dr. Grayland Blaine. The greatest astrophysicist in the System!"

"Thank you, Padre. You flatter me. And this is my daughter, Alison. But now—to business. You were saying—?"

"Tell him, Chip," bade Salvation. "I don't know how Dr. Blaine and his daughter got involved with Blacky Jordan. But I know one thing—that they're as innocent of any wrongdoing as any pair alive."

Chip needed no second invitation. A great gladness was upon him that the girl now listening to his words was not what he had feared and believed. Eagerly he embarked on his story, told them everything from the moment of his meeting Haldane to the moment Alison Blaine had so fortuitously appeared in time to save Salvation.

But if his spirits were high, those of his listeners seemed to sink lower with each word. When he had finished, a gloom hung heavily upon Dr. Blaine's brow. He looked at his daughter and sighed.

"It is worse than we feared and suspected, my dear. They *are* using my inventions, but not for the benefit to mankind I intended. Instead, they have distorted them to their own foul purposes. And we are helpless to stop them!"

"Your—your inventions?" repeated Syd Palmer.

Dr. Blaine nodded somberly. "Yes. You say you saw Alison's face in your *perilens*? And heard her voice calling for help?"

"On every cycle! That was the amazing part. Every wavelength carried her image, and her voice came through in spite of the fact that the audio was not turned on."

"But naturally," assented the old man. "That is the principle on which it operates. I call it the 'omniwave.' It is a new method of superimposing sound and light waves on receptors in such a way that they can be transmitted through any medium over a series of overlapping wavelengths ranging from 30 kilocycles down to 4,000 Angstrom units. It requires only a supersensitive iconoscope of my own devising, coupled with radiant-projectors—"

"It blanketed," Chip told him, "every instrument on our ship. We tried to tune it out so we could see where we were going, but it was impossible. The result was we were easy prey for Jordan's gang. They clamped a tractor on us, crashed us on this asteroid. Only thing I don't understand," he frowned, "is how we managed to get within their range. I was blind-flying, true. But I forejetted the *Chickadee* to avoid the possibility of ramming any asteroid—"

Again Dr. Blaine shook his head.

"You would have had a hard time avoiding this one, my boy. Because, you see, it was not sitting stationary. It was moving toward you."

"Moving toward—Oh, no, Doctor! Impossible. The asteroids follow a clockwise course about the Sun!"

"Not this one," denied the old man. "Because this is no ordinary asteroid, Warren. This whole rock, this mass of matter in space—is a navigable spaceship!"

Salvation's jaw dropped open. He said in hallowed tones, "'Surely the Lord worketh in wondrous ways His marvels to unfold!' You said—a spaceship, Dr. Blaine?"

Blaine's shoulders drooped dispiritedly.

"Yes. This is the great invention on which I have labored in secret for years. The invention which I had hoped would prove a glorious boon to man. The construction of that one type of space-voyager which could be destroyed by only a most devastating catastrophe.

"As you all know well, the major hazard of spaceflight is that the craft employed, however strongly constructed, is ever but a mote as compared with those hurtling celestial bodies it may chance to meet in space. Thus the efforts of science have ever been to cut down the collision risk. The Moran deflector ... the permalloy hood ... the automatic warp ... these are a few of the devices used. With some success, yes; but—there are failures, too. Each year more than a hundred ships crash headlong, or are crashed into by rogue asteroids, meteor swarms, bits of cosmic débris of mountainous size.

"Patrol lightships have been placed in those locations recognized to be most dangerous to space travel. But you know that the toll taken by relentless Nature on these gallant ships is terrible.

"I therefore dreamed that Man might build a gigantic lightship from a solid asteroid! A rock so large that no tiny meteor could damage it, one of sufficient mass to repel the advance of rogue asteroids. To the accomplishment of this I bent my efforts. You are within the result."

"You mean," Chip demanded, "this entire planetoid is equipped with rockets? It can fly itself?"

"Exactly. With an atomblast my laborers hollowed out living quarters, control chambers. At one-eighth mile intervals jets have been installed in the asteroid. These are fed from the central explosion chamber. In addition, gravity and atmosphere of Earth normal constant are maintained, when the planetoid is at rest, by means of energy-warp accumulators."

The old man sighed. "It was a fond dream. But just as it neared fruition, came tragedy. Blacky Jordan's pirate gang, by sheer chance, landed on the *Aurora*—the name of my cosmic craft. Trusting fool that I am, I made them welcome, took them into my refuge and proudly displayed its mechanism."

Chip nodded.

"I can guess the rest. They took over. Since then they've held you prisoners here, and used this as their base. And the image of Alison—"

"A recording," explained Blaine, "made when she attempted, vainly, to call for help. Jordan was clever enough to realize its value. Now whenever he sights a craft which he wishes to ravage, he tempts it within range by playing the visual record. When the unwary ship is drawn near enough, it finds itself blanketed, as you were. And Jordan then smashes the *Aurora* into the hapless vessel."

Salvation ventured, "And your laborers? Dead?"

"All of them. Jordan follows the ancient principle of all unprincipled rogues. 'Dead men tell no tales.' The only reason Alison and I are still alive is that he fears he may some day need my knowledge. And Alison—"

The girl spoke for herself. Softly enough, but her eyes were brittle and challenging. "Alison lives because the brutish fool fancies himself as a Don Juan."

It was a complete giveaway that this simple statement should strike the spark of Chip's anger more vehemently than any other. His brow darkened, and he came to his feet with a roar.

"What! You mean that he actually dares—"

"Steady, son!" That was Salvation Smith. Age might have taken its toll on the missionary's strength, but not his recuperative powers. The old man seemed to have completely recovered from the effects of the beating he had taken a short while before. There was even the thin ghost of a smile upon his lips.

"The young lady seems to be quite capable of taking care of herself. Our job, as I see it, is to wrest control of the *Aurora* from Blacky Jordan and his gang. Dr. Blaine, surely you must have some plan?"

Dr. Blaine shook his head miserably. "I fear not. I built the *Aurora*; I know every nook and cranny of her. But it does me no good. Jordan is complete master of the vital working parts of the asteroid. Alison and I are virtual prisoners in this one, harmless compartment, separated by tons of solid rock from the machine chambers. If we could regain control of those rooms, of course—"

"Well," demanded Chip belligerently, "why can't we? There are five of us now. Together we should be able to force our way into—"

"Into," Dr. Blaine told him morbidly, "an early grave. You underestimate Jordan's savagery, Warren. Alison and I have lived on sufferance only. You and your companions have continued to exist only because you have a secret he would give much to possess. Let us make one hostile move, and he will have no compunctions whatsoever against destroying us all. And he has both the men and the weapons with which to do it."

"Nevertheless," gritted Chip, "there must be *some* way. And by the Seven Sacred Stars—"

"Shhh!" hissed Syd warningly. "Someone outside!"

True, the hum of the elevator had sounded and ceased. Now the latch clicked, and one of Jordan's men stared at them suspiciously from the doorway. His eyes swept the group, singled out Chip Warren.

"You," he said. "Come along. The chief wants to see you."

CHAPTER V

As Dr. Blaine had said, the apartment in which he and Alison had been isolated was far removed from the vital power-rooms of the *Aurora*. Chip's guide prodded him surlily into the elevator, to the surface, across a quarter mile of ore-reddened rock, then down into a similar shaft. But this time as they descended in an elevator Chip could hear an incessant humming murmur betraying the presence of nearby, tremendous hypatomic motors.

Stepping from the cage he stood in a corridor upon which opened a number of doors clearly marked POWER ROOM, STORAGE, SUPPLIES. But it was through an unmarked doorway his captor motioned him. Chip found himself in a huge, luxuriously appointed control-turret, at the plot-desk of which lounged Blacky Jordan. Another man, back turned to Chip, was studying the dial controls.

Jordan nodded to Chip's guide. "O.Q., you can beat it now. Well, Phipps—is this the guy?"

"Phipps" turned, and at the sight of him an unforgotten flame of hatred rekindled in Warren's heart. For the man's face was newly swathed in bandages, but by the apish droop of his shoulders, the malignant gleam that darted from his tiny deepset eyes, by the cicatriced twist of his partly covered lips, Chip knew him. It was Scarface, the eavesdropper of Xu'ul's Solarest, murderer of Johnny Haldane, the living bait by which they had been lured into this trap.

Chip's breath panted from his lips in a tiny explosion of rage. He took two swift paces forward, then stopped, staring into the ugly maw of Jordan's leveled Moeller.

"Hold it, bucko," drawled Jordan. "Don't start nothin' you can't finish. Grab a seat, there, and calm down." Then, as Chip sank impotently into the designated chair, "There, that's better. No reason we three can't be chummy, is there? Like bugs in a rug." He chuckled and turned again to Phipps. "Then it *is* him, huh?"

Scarface nodded, his voice muffled beneath layers of bandage. "It's him, Chief. A whole mountain of ekalastron, he said. Only I didn't hear him say where. And after that the Spacie was going to swear him in as a deputy, and they was going to come hunting for us—"

"Yeah, I know. Only he got a sort of a surprise when he done it. Didn't you, sailor?"

Chip said in a voice that he struggled to keep level. "The game's not played yet, Jordan. I've still got a hand to draw to."

"Sure," grinned the pirate chieftain, "but you got yours to get, and I've already got mine. Aces full. Now look here, bucko—" He bent forward, and his voice assumed a wheedling tone—"They ain't no sense in us two scrapping. We got off on the wrong foot together, that's all's the trouble with us. You ain't got nothin' against me, and I ain't got nothin' against you. To tell the truth, I kinda *like* you. You got guts. I got respect for anybody that'll stand up and swap punches even when the deck's stacked against him. Now, you strike me as being a right sensible guy. I've got a little proposition to make you—"

He paused, and Chip's eyes narrowed as every nerve in his body quivered with raw dislike. But he capped the rising flood within him. It was wisdom in this crisis to test every opening which presented itself.

"Go on," said Chip. "I'm listening."

"Good! Now, you just made the biggest discovery any man in space ever made. A mountain of ekalastron. Right?"

"I'm not saying," parried Chip. "But if I did?"

"Oh, you *did*, bucko! Well, listen. Here's the proposition. I got a nice little organization here. Fifty good men. Maybe they ain't the cream o' society—" Jordan chuckled—"but they're as good fightin' men as ever lifted gravs.

"I've also got, thanks to Doc Blaine's dopiness, the biggest, toughest, hardest-to-lick spaceship that ever fired a jet. It can stand up against any cruiser in the fleet. Matter of fact, the only thing that keeps us from becomin' the most powerful pirate organization in Space is the Patrol. The *Aurora* could fight off one, two, maybe as much as a half dozen of their battle ships—but you know how Spacies are. When they get all hot and bothered about something, they don't mess around with small-time stuff. They call out the whole damn fleet. And I'm frank in admittin', bucko, that's why we've had to hide out so far, concealin' ourselves in the Bog like we was just an ordinary asteroid."

"So?" said Chip.

"So how's about you and me throwin' in together? You tell me where this here mine of ekalastron is. We'll fly out there and work it and get enough ek to armor-plate this whole damn asteroid."

"This whole—!" Warren started. What proposition he had expected from the outlaw he did not know, but certainly it was nothing so magnificently fantastic as this. And yet—his brow cudgeled. Was it so fantastic, after all? Every chemist knew that element No. 97 was one of the most malleable of all metals. A thousand tons of it, girdling the *Aurora* to a thickness of only a cobweb veil, would undoubtedly convert the asteroid into an impregnable battleship, a superdreadnaught that could defy the combined assault of every Patrolship in the void!

* * * *

Blacky Jordan was staring at him eagerly. "Well, how about it, bucko? It's a good idea, ain't it?"

Chip said tentatively, "It's an—idea, all right. But how about me, Jordan? What do *I* get out of this?"

The burly one slapped his thigh delightedly. "Now you're beginning to talk like a man, bucko! That's the sort of thing I like to hear. What do you get out of this? I'll tell you. I already said I kinda like you, didn't I? Well—I like you enough that I'd like to see you become my Number One man. Throw in with me and you'll be the big boss around here ... next to Blacky Jordan, o' course. Together we'll be an unbeatable combination."

"And the others? The Blaines and Syd Palmer and Salvation?"

"The Blaines will stay with us. You never can tell when we're going to need the old man's brains again. And the girl—well—" Jordan grinned—"She's a bit of a hellcat, but I been workin' on her, and she'll come around in time. I got plans for that girl, bucko. Who knows, maybe one of these days she may listen to reason and throw in with us? And then you and me and her will be a trio. As for Palmer—you can do whatever you want. If he'll play ball, O.Q. If he won't, we'll land him safe on some outpost. He don't know enough to do us any harm, and by the time he finds his way back to civilization we'll have what we want."

"And Salvation?"

Blacky Jordan's good humor vanished. A dark light glittered in his eyes. "Well, now, I hope we ain't goin' to have no trouble about that, bucko. But I got an old score to settle with Salvation Smith. Only—only, maybe if you're willin' to be agreeable, I'll even go so far as to meet you halfway on *that*, too. Well, what do you say?"

Chip knew what he wanted to say. The answer had trembled on his tongue from the moment the outlaw started speaking. Only a violent effort of will-power had kept him from surging to his feet, hurling his fist into the pirate's face. But that way, he realized, lay madness. So far Blacky Jordan had been astonishingly conciliatory. But Chip knew, as did the pirate, that if this peaceful means of gaining his end were unavailing, Jordan had at his disposal other means of learning the secret he desired.

Chip was bolstered, too, by one bit of knowledge Blacky Jordan did not possess: that the ekalastron mine was *already* occupied by a strongly armed corps of the Uranus Space Control. But it would not do to reveal this now. Neither would it do to pledge false allegiance nor proffer blunt refusal. The only other alternative was to stall for time. This Chip did. He stroked his jaw thoughtfully.

"This is pretty sudden," he hesitated. "I hardly know what to say, Jordan. Could I have a little while to think it over?"

Jordan rose from his desk with the toothy grin of one who sees his plan already half accomplished.

"Sure, bucko! Take all the time you want. Take a half an hour if you like. I got a few things to do, anyhow. I'll just roll along and take care of them. You stay here and make up your mind. And, Phipps—you stay here and keep an eye on Mr. Warren," Jordan grinned. "Not that I don't trust you, you understand, bucko. You and me's going to be buddies. But you might want to play double sol, or somethin'. Well—see you later!" And with a wide anticipatory grin on his lips, the big man lumbered from the room.

But barely had he disappeared than happened that which was most stunning of all which had befallen Chip Warren. Phipps, with an agility surprising in one so apishly squat, scurried across the room, and listened until the whine of the elevator advised him the coast was clear. Then he spun to Chip.

"Listen, Warren," he husked, "I gotta talk fast; are you for his plan or ain't you?"

Warren stared at the man in numb astonishment. "Why, I—I—" he faltered. "What are you getting at?"

"Because if you're for his plan *and him*," hurried Scarface, "I'm through talking. But if you're for his plan and *against* him, maybe you and I can do a little private business."

"Private business?" Chip was still puzzled.

"Private business?"

"Strictly *ongtree-new*," grinned Phipps evilly, "I don't mind telling you, Warren, I'm fed up with the way I been kicked around by Blacky Jordan. I'm supposed to be his right hand man, but I'm one of those right hands that never knows what the left hand's doing. I run all the risks, like going into civilization for supplies and taking care of that space-cop, for instance, and Jordan gets all the gravy. Not only that, but he'd rat on me in a minute if it would put one bean in his soup. Like he just done a few minutes ago; talking about making you his chief partner when I've been his buddy and done his dirty work for years.

"Well, I'm sick of it, see? And I'm pulling out. What I want to know is—if I take care of Blacky Jordan, can you and me make a dicker like the one he propositioned you on?"

CHAPTER VI

Chip stared at the man with a sort of sick distaste in his mouth. He did not like Blacky Jordan. The outlaw was coarse, brutal, bestial. But it had to be said to Jordan's credit that his villainy was at least open and aboveboard; not such treacherous, skulking infamy as this.

Chip said contemptuously, "Aren't you taking an awful chance, Phipps? Suppose I were to tell Jordan about this proposition of yours?"

Phipps' leer was the more vicious because it marred only the visible half of his face.

"I ain't taking no chance, Warren. 'Cause if you're agreeable, I'll set the wheels moving. I've got *my* followers, too. There won't be no Blacky Jordan to worry about. If you *ain't* agreeable, well—" He patted the Moeller holster at his side with a sinister sort of affection—"I can always tell Blacky you tried to escape, you know."

Chip Warren could restrain himself no longer. For fifteen minutes he had held his ever-fiery emotions in check. Now his lips spat venomous loathing. "Why, you—you rat!" he growled. "You filthy, contemptible cur! I'd as soon form a partnership with a Venusian marsh-snake! Oh! So *that's* your game!"

He cried aloud in swift alarm as Scarface, stung by his scathing refusal, reached for his Moeller. Like a striking serpent the squat man's hands darted to his holster, but Chip, too, was in motion, and even more swiftly. The young spaceman left his feet in a diving tackle; his shoulder smashed Phipps' knees bruisingly, his clawing hand locked around the pirate's straining wrist.

They hit the floor with a crash, struggled there silently, writhing like octopi locked in deadly embrace. Phipps brought his knee up hard into Warren's groin, shaking Chip with a sudden, violent nausea. But still Chip clung desperately to the other man's wrist. The adrenalin of emotion pumping through his veins broomed away his weakness; he lashed out again and yet again for his antagonist's chin, putting every ounce of power behind his blows.

But somehow Phipps' hand managed to to wriggle free. In that second, death menaced Chip with flaming certainty. An instant more and the world he knew would have dissolved forever in coruscant oblivion. But once more, with desperate savagery, his fist sought his antagonist ... and this time found its mark! A sledge of pain shattered Chip's knuckles. He heard a rasping grate of bone as the scarred one's jaw collapsed. A gust of withering heat scorched past his shoulder, and Phipps flew backward across the room. His head hit the angle of a metal cabinet. There came the sickening crunch of yielding bone. Phipps' body shuddered once—and lay still.

Chip pulled himself to his feet, heart pounding with furious triumph. Then suddenly the light of battle died from his eyes, and a look of horror took its place as he realized what he had done. Never in this world would he convince Blacky Jordan that Phipps' own treachery had brought about his death. The pirate's retribution for this deed would be swift and violent.

The fat was in the fire now. Somehow he must warn his friends. Chip spun, stared avidly at the controls about him, found the one he sought: a telaudio unit. There was not time to single out the key which would give him a private line to Dr. Blaine's quarters. He depressed the all-circuit plunger, cried desperately, "Dr. Blaine! Salvation! Can you hear me?"

An answer came back instantly in Syd's voice. "We hear you, Chip. What's up?"

"Find some way to defend yourselves! And hurry! I've just fought Scarface and killed him, and the heat's on!"

"The—the *what*?"

"The heat's on, I said! They'll be after us in no time. *There!*" An ominous, all-too-familiar whining sound came dimly to Chip's ears. "I hear him now. Jordan's coming back. Wait a minute!"

He leaped to Phipps' body, snatched the Moeller from the dead man's hand, then sprang to the door, locked it. It was a feeble defense, he knew, but it offered him at least a moment of respite. Came the grate of Jordan's feet in the corridor outside, then a hammering on the door, and the pirate's querulous roar.

"Hey, what's going on in there? Phipps! Open up!"

And then—a miracle occurred. For when Chip deserted the control panel, he had released the telaudio key. And theoretically all communication between himself and his friends was broken. But now sounded a high, singing note in the air, a note that took on cadence, a cadence forming itself into words, words that were the excited voice of Syd Palmer!

"Chip, boy! Can you hear me? You all right! The heat *is* on! *That's the answer!* For God's sake, find a bulger, quick! Climb into it!"

There were cabinets in the room. To these Chip Warren raced, tearing at their handles with avid fingers, wrenching them open with violent disregard for whatever precious manuscripts, intricate and valuable apparatus, tumbled out to mingle in damaged heterogeneity on the floor. In the fourth cabinet he found that which he sought, a quartzofabricoid bulger.

Into this he flung himself, keeping a wary eye upon the door, about whose lock was already glowing a smoky circle of scarlet as Blacky Jordan, belatedly realizing there was something amiss, melted the lock with his Moeller. With a final *zzzp!* Chip closed the seam of his space suit, with a final twist of the hand screwed into place its transparent helmet. Thus, like some bloated and grotesque denizen of ocean depths, Moeller leveled and ready, he stood waiting to meet Blacky Jordan in their third, and this time necessarily final, encounter.

But Blacky Jordan never stepped into that room! The door never opened. What happened outside Chip Warren did not know nor could he guess, but that it was something fearful and beyond belief he could tell by the cry which in that moment ripped from the outlaw's throat.

"Oh, Lord! Fire! I'm on fire!"

And suddenly the clamor of his footsteps beat *away* from the door, down the hallway! Chip heard the big man hurl himself into the elevator, heard the spiraling whine of the lift rising. Wondering, yet cautious, he stepped to the door, eased it open. His hearing had not beguiled him. The corridor was empty and the elevator gone. Even as he stood there, dazed and uncomprehending, that eerie voice from nowhere again smote his ears. This time the cadence resolved itself into the reverberant tones of Salvation Smith, roaring in throaty triumph.

"Lo, with Thy lightnings Thou hast destroyed them, O Lord! Chip, lad—you hear me? The hour of retribution has come! They cower like craven lice on the flesh of the sphere that hid them. Go to the control panel, boy; press the studs numbered 1 and 12. Haste, while we have them at our mercy!"

Obediently Chip sprang to the board, plunged the studs Salvation had named. As he did so, the steady hum of the hypatomic deepened. There came the ponderous *thud!* of a rocket jet exploding. Then another. Then almost at once the first again.

The floor beneath him shook, throbbed, trembled. Chip was conscious of a curious lightness, a sense of whirling giddiness that he recognized almost immediately. He had experienced the sensation once before when a spaceship in which he had been a passenger was thrown into axial revolution by the titanic tug of Jupiter. Clinging for support to whatever offered itself, he moved with difficulty to the room's vision-plates, opened the circuit that revealed the exterior of the *Aurora*, and—what he saw brought a cry to his lips. A cry in which was mingled triumph and awe and almost a certain horror-stricken, involuntary pity.

His depression of studs 1 and 12, firing-jets at opposite poles of the *Aurora*, had spun the tiny planetoid into axial rotation. It was whirling, now, like a gigantic top in the void. And from its surface, no longer held captive by the feeble artificial gravity, were hurtling the bodies of those whom a moment before had so proudly and confidently strode the asteroid's surface!

Chip saw one sight which would haunt him forever. Blacky Jordan emerging from the surface tunnel ... being whisked from the bosom of the *Aurora* as if by an invisible hand ... drawn violently to his vacuum tomb. For the split second there was an expression of terrible, uncomprehending fear on the pirate's face—then there was neither face nor pirate. Just the black, inexorable depths of space, studded with the myriad planetoid shards which formed the Bog.

* * * *

Afterward Chip Warren said to Dr. Blaine, "I'm afraid Doctor, that if we're ever to set foot again in any civilized port, you must take us there. After the *Aurora* stopped revolving I went top-side to look for the *Chickadee*. I thought we might be able to repair it. But it's gone, just like Blacky Jordan and his crew. Everything on the surface of the planetoid was whisked away."

Dr. Blaine said, "I intend to do just that, Chip. As a matter of fact, Syd is already plotting our course. But I hope that after we've landed you, that won't be the last we'll ever see of you. Alison and I owe you an undying debt of gratitude. Had it not been for you—"

"You were magnificent!" breathed the girl. And looking at her, finding with an incredulous surprise a look in her eyes which more than echoed her father's wish, Chip knew Dr. Blaine would not, indeed, easily avoid seeing more of him. For he had heard the Lorelei's call and found it sweet.

Salvation, intercepting the look that passed between them, laughed. Flushing, Chip took refuge in denial of Dr. Blaine's claim. "Thank you, sir, but I'm afraid you overestimate our part in besting Jordan. Or at least *my* part. All *I* did was press the plunger. I wouldn't have known to do that if you folks hadn't told me. And I *still* don't understand what caused Jordan and all of the rest of his men who were below ground to race for the surface of the asteroid."

Dr. Blaine said, "That was Sydney's idea." But Syd contradicted him peremptorily. "Nope! I'm a great one for passing the buck. Oh, I thought of the means, maybe. But it was Chip who gave me the idea."

"Me?"

"Uh-huh. When you shouted 'the heat's on!' Remember? We four had been down here cudgeling our brains for some way to get the draw on Blacky Jordan, but we overlooked a hell of an obvious trick until you mentioned *heat*. Then all of a sudden Doc Blaine and I saw the answer at the same time. Fortunately he had an omniwave unit there in his laboratory and that did the trick. See?"

"No," confessed Chip frankly. "I don't."

"Well, it's really very simple. Doc Blaine told us the omniwave transmitted every length of radiation from 30 kilos down to 4000 Angstroms. In other words, everything from long radio waves down to visible light rays."

"So?" said Chip.

"So, dopey-puss," said Syd amiably, "of course, that includes the *infra-red rays*. Heat waves. Waves that have the power to speed up molecular velocity in bodies. Or—" He grunted satisfaction—"hot enough to create a raging fever in any human being on the asteroid who wasn't dressed in a spacesuit!

"Well, right away I asked Doc Blaine how he'd taken care of that problem in distributing his omniwave radiation, and he said he had always used a cutout to eliminate that danger. So we just quietly removed the cutout, and turned on the omniwave full force, and—" Syd shrugged—"burnt those babies to a crisp! They didn't even know what ailed them! All they knew was that they were as hot as boiled potatoes, and wanted to get outside where they could cool off. The rest of us, dressed in bulgers, were O.Q."

"And," said Chip, "when they got outside we revolved the *Aurora*, and—"

"*Finis!*" agreed Syd cheerfully, "and a good day's work, too, if you ask me. Incidentally, Chip, while we're on the subject—"

Syd was a very talkative guy. He would have undoubtedly continued this harangue for a couple more hours. But at that moment his eyes happened to intercept another glance passing between Alison Blaine and Chip Warren. It was a glance that meant things. It was a glance that meant that maybe some day in the not-too-far-distant future the Lorelei might yet lure, but not necessarily to destruction, a mariner who had flown thousands of miles across space to answer her call.

Syd coughed uncomfortably. "Say," he suggested, "Doc ... Salvation ... what do you say we go down to the control-turret and plot our course a little more carefully? We wouldn't want to make any mistakes, you know. This is a mighty valuable invention we're flying—"

Syd was a very talkative guy. But, thought Chip Warren, sometimes he talked good ideas....

BEYOND LIGHT

Originally published in *Planet Stories*, Winter 1940.

They stood in the *Orestes'* tiny observation turret, Mallory's defiant arm still tight about the slim and lovely girl, just exactly as bull-voiced Captain Lane had found them. The shimmering reflection of the planet Venus, only a few thousand miles ahead, bathed the trim, hard-jawed man and the softly pretty girl in a gentle glow, but it failed to soothe the grizzled space ship skipper.

"What in hell does this mean?"

Mallory, remembering an old forgotten saying—something about a soft answer turning aside wrath—spoke rapidly. "Sorry if we gave you a shock, sir," he said. "But your daughter and I are engaged."

Few medical men would have guaranteed Space Captain Jonathan Lane a long life at that moment. His usually ruddy face was a violent mauve-scarlet, his eyes hot pin-points of anger, his lean, hard body was atremble with emotion.

"Engaged. *Engaged!*" He made a convulsive motion. "Did you say engaged? To this inane young fool. You're talking nonsense. Go to your cabin, girl."

Dorothy Lane sighed and looked hopefully up at Mallory.

Tim Mallory had forgotten his old and wise quotation.

"Why not engaged," he snapped. "What have you got against me?"

"What," growled Captain Lane. "He asks me *what*!"

He had a reason; one which he shared with all fond parents who have ever seen a beloved child slipping from their arms—jealousy. Jealousy and grief. Now his mind pounced on a substitute for the true reasons that he would not—could not—name.

"Well, for one thing," he said curtly, "you're not a spaceman. You're nothing but a blasted Earthlubber!"

Mallory grinned.

"You can hardly call me an Earthlubber, Captain. I spent two years on Luna, three on Mars; I'll be five or more on Venus—"

"Pah! Luna ... Mars ... Venus ... you're still a groundhog. I'll not see my girl married to a money-grubbing businessman, Mallory."

"Tim's not a businessman," broke in Dorothy Lane. "He's an engineer." And anyone seeing her young fury would have smiled to note how much alike she was to her bucko, space captain father.

"Engineer! Nonsense! Only an astrogation engineer deserves that title. He's a—a—What is it you do? Build ice-boxes?"

"I'm a calorimetrical engineer," Mallory answered stiffly. "My main job is the designing and installation of air-conditioning plants where they are needed. On airless Luna, the cold Martian deserts, here on Venus. The simple truth is—"

"The simple truth is," stated the skipper savagely, "that you're a groundhog and a damned poor son-in-law for a spaceman. You being what you are, and Dorothy being what she is, I say the hell with you, Mr. Mallory! Perhaps I can't prevent your marriage. But there's one thing I can do—and that is wash my hands of the two of you!"

He watched them, searching for signs of indecision in their eyes. He found, instead—and with a sense of sickening dread—only sorrow. Sorrow and pity and regret. And Tim Mallory said quietly, "I'm sorry, sir, that you feel that way about it."

Lane turned to his daughter.

"Dorothy?" he said hoarsely.

"I'm sorry, too." Her voice was gentle but determined. "Tim is right. We—" Then her eyes widened; sudden panic lighted them, and her hand flew to her lips in a gesture of fear. "Something's wrong! Venus! The ship—!"

* * * *

Captain Lane did not need her warning. His space-trained body had recognized disaster a split-second before. His legs had felt the smooth flooring beneath him lurch and sway. His eyes had glimpsed, through the spaceport, the sudden looming of the silver disc toward which they had been gliding easily but now were plunging at headlong, breakneck speed. His ears howled with the clamor of monstrous winds that clutched with vibrant fingers the falling *Orestes*.

In a flash he spun and fought his way up a sharply tilting deck to the wall audio, thrust at its button, bawled a query. The mate's voice, shrill with terror, answered:

"The Dixie-rod, sir! It's jammed! We're trying to get it free, but it's locked! We're out of control—"

"Up rockets!" roared Lane. "Up rockets and blast!"

"They're cut, sir! The hypo's cold. We'll have to 'bandon ship—."

Abandon ship! Tim Mallory did not need Dorothy's sudden gasp to tell him what that meant to the trio caught in the observation turret. Earthlubber he might be, but he knew enough about the construction of space craft to realize that there were no auxiliary safety-sleds anchored to this section of the *Orestes*.

Venus was no longer a beaming platter of silver in the distance. They had burst through its eternal blanket of cloud, now; The world below was no longer a sphere, it was a huge saucer of green, swelling ominously with each flashing second. Tempests screamed about them, and the screaming was the triumphant cry of hungry death.

No ships. No time to seek escape. Life, which had but recently become a precious thing to Tim Mallory, was but a matter of minutes.

He saw the agony of indecision on Captain Jonathan Lane's face, heard, as in a dream, the skipper delivering the only possible order.

"Very well, Carter! 'Bandon ship!'"

And the pilot's hectic query, "But where are you?"

"Never mind that. Cut loose, you fool!"

"No, Captain! You're below. I can't let you die. I'll keep trying—"

"'Bandon ship, Carter! It's an order!"

And the faint, thin answer, "Aye, sir!" Silence.

Tim turned to Dorothy, and from somewhere summoned the ghost of a smile. His arms went out to her, and as one in a dream she moved toward him. There was, at least, this. They could die together.

And then Captain Lane was between them, bellowing, commanding, pushing them apart.

"Avast, you two! This is no time for play-acting. Mallory, jerk down those hammocks. Tumble in and strap yourselves tight! It's a chance in a billion, but—"

Tim swung into motion. The old man was right. It was a slim chance, but—a chance! To strap themselves into the pneumatic hammocks used by passengers at times of acceleration, hope that by some miracle the *Orestes* would not be crushed into a metal pancake when they crashed, pray that it might land on a slope, or some yielding substance.

It was a breathless moment and a mad one. Frenzied winds and the groan of scorching metal, the thick panting of Captain Lane as he strapped himself into a hammock between Tim and Dorothy, Dorothy's voice, "Tim, dear—" And his own reply, "Hold tight, youngster!"

Then heat increasing, heat like a massive fist upon his breast, hot beads of sweat, salt-tasting on his lips, an ear-splitting tumult of sound from somewhere.... A swift, terrifying glimpse of solid earth rushing up to meet them.... The last, wrenching shudder of the *Orestes* as it plunged giddily groundward. Heat ... pain ... flame ... suffocation....

Then darkness.

Out of the darkness, light. Out of the sultriness, a thin, cool finger of breeze. Out of the silence of death, life!

Tim Mallory opened his eyes. And a thick, wordless cry of thanksgiving burst from his lips as he stared about him. The impossible had happened!

The ship had crashed. Its control-room was a fused and twisted heap of wreckage smoldering in the giant crater it had plowed. But somehow the observation turret, offset in a streamlined vane of the *Orestes*, had escaped destruction.

Great rents gaped where once girders had welded together sturdy *permalloy* sheets, purposeless shards lay strewn about, even the hammocks had been wrenched from their strong moorings, but he and his companions still lived!

Even as Tim fought to loose the straps that circled him, Captain Lane groaned, stirred, opened his eyes. Dully, then with wakening recollection. And his first word—

"Dorothy?"

"Safe," said Mallory. "She's safe. We're all safe. I don't know how. We must bear charmed lives." He bent over the girl, loosened her straps, chafed her wrists gently. Her eyes opened, and the image of that last moment of panic was still mirrored in their depths. "Tim!" she cried. "Are we—Where's Daddy?"

"Easy, sugar!" soothed Tim. "He's here. It's all over. We pulled through. It was a miracle."

He said it gratefully. But Captain Lane corrected him. The safety of his daughter assured, the old spacedog's next thought had been for his ship. He had walked forward, studied the crumpled ruin of the control-room. Now he said, "Not a miracle, Mallory. A sacrifice. It was Carter. He didn't bail out with the others. He must have stayed on in the control-room, fighting that jammed Dixie-rod. It must have come clean at the last moment, slowing the ship, or we wouldn't be here. But it was too late, then, for him to get away—"

His voice was sad, but there was a sort of pride in it, too. Dorothy began to cry softly. Captain Lane's hand came to his forehead in brief, farewell salute to a gallant man. Then he rejoined the others. "It was the first time," he said, "he ever disobeyed my orders."

Tim said nothing. There was nothing he could say. But for the first time he realized why Captain Lane, why all spacemen, felt as they did about their calling. Because the men who wore space-blues were of this breed.

For a long moment there was silence. Then the old man stirred brusquely.

"Well, we'd better get going."

"Going?" Tim stared about him. It was a far from reassuring scene that met his eyes. They had landed in the midst of wild and desolate country, on a plateau midway between sprawling marshlands below and craggy, cloud-created hills above. The shock of the crash must have stunned into silence all wild-life temporarily, for upon awakening, Tim had been dimly conscious of a vast, reverberant quietude.

But now the small, secret things were creeping back to gaze on the smoking monster that had died in their midst; small squeals and snarls and chirrupings bespoke an infinitude of watchers. The hour was just before dawn; the eastward horizon was tinged with pearl. "Going?" Tim repeated. "But where are we?"

Captain Jonathan looked at him somberly. "In the Badlands," he said. "And the term is not a loose one; they *are* bad lands, Mallory." He pointed the hour hand of his wrist-watch at the pale mist of rising sunlight. "I don't know exactly where we are, or how far from civilization, but it's far enough."

Tim said determinedly, "Then we'd better pack up, eh? Hit the trail?"

The skipper laughed scornfully. "What trail? We'd be committing suicide by heading into those marshes, those hills, or those jungles. Our only chance of survival is to stay close to the *Orestes*. Five of the sailors bailed out, you'll remember. In safety-sleds. We've got to hope one or more of them will reach Venus City, start a rescue party out after us."

"But you said 'get going'?"

"To work, I meant. We're going to need protection from the sun." Again Captain Lane glanced at the sky, this time a little anxiously. "I know this country. After that sun gets up, it will be a bake-oven. A seething cauldron of heat. Damp, muggy heat. Steam from the marshes below, the raw, blinding heat blazing down from the rocks above. This is Venus, Mallory—" He laughed shortly; but there was no mirth in his laughter. "This isn't an air-conditioned home on Earth. Come along!"

Silently, Tim followed him. They picked their way through the tangled wreckage of the *Orestes*, stopping from time to time to salvage such bits of equipment as Lane felt might be of use. Flashlights, side-arms, vacuteens of clear, cold water, packets of emergency rations. Through chamber after shattered chamber they moved, Captain Lane leading the way. Tim and Dorothy following mutely behind. Everywhere it was the same. Broken walls, bent and twisted girders, great rents in what had once been a sturdy spacecraft.

And finally Lane gave up.

"It's no use," he said. "There's no protection in this battered hulk.

Shading ourselves in one of these open cells would be like taking refuge in a broiler."

"Then what can we do, Daddy?"

"There's only one thing to do. Break out bulgers. They're thermostatically controlled. We'll keep cooler in space-suits than anything else. Mallory, you remember where they were?"

"Yes, sir!" Tim went after the space-suits, grateful for a chance to contribute in some way to their common good. The storeroom in which the bulgers had been locked was no longer burglar-proof; one wall had been sheared away in the crash as if cleft with a gigantic ax. He clambered into the compartment, broke out three bulgers, gathered up spare oxytainers for each of them.

He had just finished lugging the equipment out of the storeroom, sweating from the exertion of lifting three heavy space-suits beneath a sun which was now glowing brazenly in an ochre, misted sky, when a sharp cry startled him.

"Daddy! Behind you!" It was Dorothy who screamed the warning. And then, "Tim! *Tim!*"

"Coming!" roared Mallory. He was scarcely conscious of the weight of the bulgers now. In a flash he was plunging toward the source of the cry, tugging at the needle-gun in his belt. But before he had taken a dozen steps—

"Never mind, Mallory!" roared Captain Lane. "Stay where you are! Back, you filthy—!" There came the sharp, characteristic hiss of a flashing needle-gun, the *plowp!* of some unguessable, fleshy thing exploding into atoms. "Stay where you are! We'll come to you. Quick, Dorothy!"

Then their footsteps pounding toward him, Dorothy rounding a bend of the ship, white-faced and flying, Captain Lane on her heels, covering their retreat with his gun. As Mallory sprang to join them Lane flashed him a swift glance and tossed curt words of explanation.

"Proto-balls! Giant, filthy amoebae. Pure proteid matter. *Aaah!* Scorched that one! Damned needle-guns won't stop 'em, though. Just slows 'em down. Only thing'll kill 'em is an acid-spray. We've got to get out of here!"

"But where, Daddy?"

"Got those bulgers, Mallory? Climb into 'em. And hurry. Saw caves in the mountainside up there. They won't enter caves. Need sunlight. *Look out!*"

Again that sharp, explosive hiss. Mallory leaped back, feeling the brief, furtive brush of something foreign across the toe of his boot. The attacking proto-balls were of all sizes; they ranged from huge, oily-glistening, foul-odored spheres to tiny globules the size of a baseball. One of the latter size had rolled swiftly toward him; for a second, before Captain Lane's gun splashed flame upon it, it had come in contact with Mallory's foot. Where it had touched was now a patch of crumbling gray that had been leather!

"Eat anything!" rasped Lane. "Didn't touch you, eh, Mallory? Good. Start backing away. And get into the bulgers. Move!"

Mallory climbed swiftly into his space-suit. Its weight disappeared as he touched the grav control button; the heat which had begun to oppress him fled, too, when he closed the face-port. He touched Lane's shoulder, thrust the remaining bulger at him.

"I'll hold them while you get into it!"

And he did. It was an unequal battle, though. The proto-balls were the next thing to imperishable. The needle-gun could not destroy them, it only slowed them down. An occasional perfect bull's-eye shot, striking a vulnerable spot, would burst a proto-ball into a thousand pieces—but when that happened, each of the pieces, amoeba-like, curled instantly into a tiny daughter proto-ball and surged forward again.

Yet there must have been some elementary nervous-system in these creatures, for while it could not kill them, still they seemed to fear the flaming ray of the needle-gun. And it was to this fear that the trio of Earthlings owed their existence during those next hectic minutes while they stumbled, ever backward and upward, giving ground steadily, toward the cave-mouth Captain Lane had pointed out on the hillside.

Tim did not even know the cave was near. Shoulder to shoulder with the old space-captain, he maintained a rear-guard defense against the proto-balls, gun flaming without cessation, his eyes aching from the strain of constant watchfulness against an unexpected flank attack. And then—

And then, suddenly, incredibly, a shadow fell under his stumbling feet; at that line of division between glowing sun and somber shade the proto-balls stopped, quivering and oozing viscous droplets of slime, hesitated, and turned away.

Lane's roar was gleeful. "Good work, young fellow! We made it!"

They were safe in the black harbor of the cave.

* * * *

When he turned to stare into the depths beyond him, at first he could see nothing but a great orange ball, which was his photo-image of the dazzling sunlight whence they had fled. Then tortured nerves surrendered to the soothing dark and he could see that they stood at the mouth of not a cave but a great, many-corridored cavern that stretched—for all Mallory could tell—clear down into the murky bowels of Venus.

Jonathan Lane was loudly exuberant.

"This is fine!" he declared. "We owe those grease-balls a vote of thanks.

This is an ideal refuge. Shady and cool and safe—and look! We can even see the ship from the heights, here! If anyone—I mean, *when* they come to rescue us, we can signal them."

Mallory hoped the slip had passed unnoticed by Dorothy. "*If* anyone—" the skipper had started to say. Which meant that he, too, had misgivings as to the likelihood of rescue. But that was a question Mallory would not press. He hurdled the awkward moment with a swift response.

"We'll have to have something to signal with, sir. Our bulger audios won't operate that far, will they? We'll have to build a fire, or at least have one ready to be kindled when they arrive."

"Right," agreed the skipper. "But we can't gather wood until those protos have gone away. We'll take care of that later. Meanwhile—" He glanced into the jetty depths beyond them. "It will be some hours before we can expect to get relief. Time to waste. Why not amuse ourselves by exploring this cave?"

"Explo—" began Tim. It was a childish idea. One *so* ridiculous, in fact, that it was on the tip of Mallory's tongue to make caustic rejoinder to Lane's suggestion. But even as the comment trembled on his lips, his eyes met those of the captain—and in Lane's shrewd, pleading glance, Tim found a reason and an answer for this subterfuge.

Lane feared that very thing which he, himself, had dreaded. This cave might be their refuge for a long, long time!

There might be no rescue party. If so, and since a trek across the Badlands was suicidal, their only chance for ultimate salvation was to find a place where they could live. This cave was such a place. If it had water, and if it were undenizened by wild beasts; if in it, or near it, they could find food....

He hoped his voice was not too suspiciously hearty.

"Great idea!" he agreed. "Splendid. It should be a lot of fun. What do you say, Dorothy?"

Dorothy looked from her lover to her father, back to her lover again. And her voice was grave and fearless.

"I say," she said quietly, "you are the two finest men who ever lived. But you're not fooling me for a moment. I know very well why we must explore this cave. And I say, let's start!" There came swift lightness and heart-warming humor to her tone. "After all, if a gal has to keep house in a place like this, she ought to know how many rooms it has!"

Tim looked at her long and gravely. And then,

"You," he said, "are swell. Once I called you wonderful. I didn't really know—then."

"Wonderful?" snorted Captain Lane. "Of course she is! She's my daughter, isn't she? Well, come along!"

Grinning, Tim fell in behind him. And into Stygian darkness, preceded by a yellow circle from the flashlight of the *Orestes'* skipper, moved the marooned trio.

* * * *

The main cave opened out as they picked their path forward; the walls pressed back, the ceiling lofted, until they were standing in a huge, arched chamber almost two hundred feet wide and half as high. This amphitheater debouched into a half dozen or more smaller corridors or openings; for a moment Captain Lane stood considering these silently, then he nodded toward that on their extreme left.

"Might as well go at it in orderly fashion. We'll try that one first. No, wait a minute!" He halted Tim, who had pressed obediently toward the corridor-mouth. "Try not to be a groundhog all your life, Mallory! You should know better than to stroll aimlessly around a place like this. A confounded labyrinth, that's what it is! If we got lost down here, we might spend the rest of our natural lives trying to find a way out."

He slipped his needle-gun from his bulger belt, let its scorching ray play for an instant on the rocky floor of the cavern. Hot rock bubbled, and a fresh, new groove shone sharply in the shape of an arrow.

"Every time we make a turn we'll do this. Then we can retrace our steps." Lane smiled sarcastically. "But a hot-and-cold engineer wouldn't think of a thing like that, I suppose?"

Tim made no reply. But he reproached himself secretly for not having considered this necessity; it did not make him feel much better that Dorothy, standing beside him, pressed his arm in mute encouragement.

The corridor was a short one, opening into another cavern like that which they had just quitted. Similar, but not quite the same. For as Lane played his light about the walls of this inner, deeper, chamber, all three adventurers gasped with the impact of sudden, breathtaking beauty. The ebon walls, warmed by the light, flashed into a glittering, scintilliscent miracle of loveliness; a galaxy of twinkling stars seemed to appear from nowhere and hang in dark space burning and gleaming.

"It—it's magnificent!" breathed the girl. "What is it, Daddy? Jewels? It looks like the fabulous caves of Ali Baba."

It was Tim who supplied the answer. "They're not jewels. Just nitre crystals protruding through a coating of black oxide of manganese. I've seen the same thing on Earth—in the Mammoth Cave of Kentucky."

And they moved on. Deeper and yet deeper into the Lethean depths, pausing from time to time to char a signpost for their retreat. Miracles without wonder they saw. Domes huge enough to house a spaceship, stalactites lowering like great, rough fangs from ceilings lost in dizzy heights, twin growths springing, oftimes without apparent reason, from the cavern floor—stalactites formed by centuries of slow lime dripping from the roof. And gigantic columns, hoariest monsters of all, columns of strange, iridescent beauty.

Once they passed a pit so deep, so dark, that even the skipper's probing beam could not penetrate its majestic depths. From somewhere far below came the whispering surge of churned water; in the light of the flash there seemed to hover above the rim of this chasm a faint, white, wraithly film. Lane frowned, unscrewed his face-port for an instant, sniffed, and hastily ducked back into the bulger.

"Ammonia," he said. "I thought as much. Keep your bulger-ports closed. Venus caves aren't Earth caves. Queer things here. No telling what we'll bump into."

He didn't mention the all-too-obvious fact that so far they had not "bumped into" that thing which they sought. A fuel supply, a water supply, signs of an underground grotto wherein might be found food. Nor had their winding way at any time moved them toward the surface, toward a possible second exit from the caverns. Their movement was ever down, deeper into the bowels of this weird, faery wonderland.

* * * *

Once, for a heart-stopping moment, they thought they had found their desire. Rounding a bend, they came upon a cavern alive with color; towering vines and trees laden with great clusters of grapes; bushes aflower with myriads of gorgeous buds. Dorothy sprang forward with a cry of joy—but when she touched one of the mock roses it shattered to fine, white, powdery snow; upon investigation the trees, the vines and "grapes" turned out to be of the same, perishable nature.

And Tim remembered their name. "Oulopholites," he said. "Sulphate of magnesia and gypsum. Mother Nature *does* repeat herself, you see. She uses the same forms, but these are lifeless mimicry." And he looked at his watch. "Guess we'd better turn back, eh, skipper? We've been two hours on the prowl, and there doesn't seem to be anything in this direction. Shall we go back and try another corridor?"

Lane nodded slowly.

"I suppose so. But—Oh, while we're this far, we might as well peek into that next cavern. Won't take but a minute. And if there's nothing there—"

The words died on his lips. As he spoke them, they had moved through a short archway; the yellow circle of his flashlight had swung about a cavern larger than any in which they had yet stood. The floor of this cavern sloped sharply downward, narrowing into a funnel. And at the end of that funnel....

"Great gods of space!" whispered Captain Lane, awestruck. "Am I crazy? Do you see what I see?"

For that upon which his lightbeam had ended, the incredible structure from which its glow was now reflecting in shimmering clarity, was—*a massive door of bronze*! Golden in sheen, strong and secure, obviously the work of intelligent craftsmen, it met their wondering stares with bland imperturbability.

And Tim gave a great shout.

"A door! Venusians! We're all right now. Food and rest ... they'll tell us how to get back to civilization...."

And then—

"Quiet!" rasped Captain Lane. His flashlight beam faded abruptly, darkness closed in about them like a shroud. But only for an instant. Because a new effulgence lit the scene. The massive door was slowly swinging open—and from its widening groove came a pallid, greenish glow. Like some monstrous, hungry mouth the door opened wider and yet wider. Dim shapes were shadows behind it, vague at first, dark and sinister....

And then, out of the ghoulish semi-gloom, suddenly two figures stood limned in stark relief. But they were not the figures of Earthmen, neither were they fat, friendly shapes of Venusians. They were tall, lean creatures, thin-faced and hungry-fanged, garbed with what appeared to be huge mantles covering them from their shoulder-blades to the tips of their long, prehensile fingers!

Two wobbling, awkward steps they took from the now completely opened door; for an instant Tim heard the shrill, piping chatter of their speech—then their "mantles" spread and became huge, jointed wings on which they soared straight across the cavern toward the spellbound trio!

Captain Lane's cry was thick with horror.

"Good God, Mallory! Shoot, and shoot quick! We've found the gates of hell. They're the bat-men—the Vampires of Venus!"

Even as he spoke, he was tugging his own needle-gun from its holster; now its fiery beam lanced squarely at the foremost of the two attackers. Nor was Tim Mallory slow in heeding. His weapon was out in one swift movement; its beam slashed a hole in the gloom as it sought one of the silently winging creatures above.

But they might as well have taken aim at a will-o'-the-wisp. The dim glow from beyond the open door illumined only a portion of the cavern; the heights above were a well of jet, against which the crepuscular creatures were all but invisible. Again and again the two heat-beams stabbed black shadows, once Tim thought he heard a brief, whimpering cry, but no winged creature, charred in death, hurtled from the eyrie point of vantage. Only the sound of great wings beating persisted—and once an ebon shape flung itself from an ebon shadow to rake sharp claws gratingly across Tim's bulger helmet. It had glided away again, mockingly, before he could spin to flame a shot after it.

Then Lane's free arm was thrusting at him. Lane's voice was sharp, incisive.

"Out of here! Dorothy first! Maybe there are just two of these devils— *Ooow!* Damn your rotten hide!"

He had turned to speak over his shoulder. In that moment of inattention, one of the bat-men had rocketed down upon him, slashed viciously at his gun-arm with clawed hands. Metal clattered on rock; Captain Lane went swiftly after the lost gun, groping for it blindly, down on his knees.

Tim had taken a backward step; now he moved forward again to cover the frenzied fumbling of the older man. His eyes were suddenly dazzled as Lane, desperate, used his flash to search for the weapon. And the skipper groaned.

"It's gone! It fell down that fissure! Mallory—quick! Do you have another gun? They're closing in—"

Beads of cold sweat had suddenly sprung out on Tim Mallory's forehead. Not only did he *not* have another gun—but the one he now held was about to become useless! A dim shape wheeled above him; he pressed the trigger, but no red flame leaped from the muzzle. Just a spluttering, ochre ray that simmered into nothingness a few feet above his head!

The gun's charge was practically exhausted. Battle with the proto-balls ... the constant drainage of raying their route-turns ... these had done it! There were fresh capsules in his ammunition kit, but in the length of time required to recharge the gun....

"A minute!" he cried. "Fight 'em off a minute! I have to—"

And he reached for a new capsule. But the skipper, misunderstanding, impatient, turned peril into disaster with his next, impetuous move.

"Don't stand there like an idiot, you Earthlubber!" he howled. "Here— give that to me!"

And he jerked the useless weapon from Tim's hand!

For a stark instant, Tim was wrenched in a vise of indecision. To fight the winged demons without a weapon was madness. Wisdom lay in hurrying back to the ship, equipping themselves with new guns. But—but Lane had said these bat-men were vampires. The Vampires of Venus, he had said. And Tim had heard stories ... the word "vampire" meant the same in any language, on any planet.

But there was Dorothy to consider, too. He groaned aloud. His instinct bade him plunge forward, weaponless or not; common sense advised the other course.

And then, in a split-second, the decision became no longer his to make.

For as if the victory of the first two bat-men had determined the action of the entire clan, out of the bronze gateway flooded a veritable host of the sickening winged creatures!

Then a battering-ram smashed him crushingly and he choked, gasped, felt the weakness of oblivion well over him like a turgid, engulfing cloud. He was conscious of raking talons that gripped his armpits, of sudden, swift and dizzy flight ... of a vast, aching chaos that rocked with hungry, inhuman mirth.

* * * *

Captain Lane's voice was an aeon away, but it came closer. It said, "—be all right now. You must have been in a hell of a fight, boy!"

And Dorothy was beside him, too. There were tears in her eyes, but she shook them away and tried to smile as Tim pushed himself up on one elbow. Tim's head was one big ache, and his body was bruised and sore from the buffeting of the bat-men's hard wings. He looked about him dazedly.

"Wh-here are we?"

The room was a low-ceilinged, square one. It had but one door, a bronze one similar in design, but smaller, than the gateway that had led to the city of the Vampires. Elsewhere the walls were hewn from solid rock.

"Where are we?" he repeated. He started to unscrew his face port, but the skipper stayed his hand.

"Don't, Mallory! We tried that. It's impossible. The air's so ammoniated it would kill you. From that."

He pointed to a trough-like depression in the room. A curious arrangement. Probably for purposes of sanitation. Liquid ammonia, or something akin, entered the trough from a gushing tube set low in one wall, transversed the room, and exited through a second circular duct. These were the only openings in the chamber, save for—Tim glanced up, noticed several round holes. He studied these curiously. Lane answered his unspoken query.

"Yes, that's right. Ventilation. These devils may be inhuman in form but they're clever. They've built this underground city, equipped it with heat, light, ventilated it to maintain circulation—"

There was something wrong there. Tim frowned.

"Ventilation? Yet you say that stream is ammoniated enough to kill a man. Then how do they live?"

"They're not men," replied Lane bitterly. "They're vampires. Heaven knows how they can breathe this atmosphere, but they can. The ingenious, murdering..."

* * * *

He didn't complete the sentence. For at that instant there came the scrape of movement outside their dungeon door. The door swung open. A bat-man entered. His hooked claw signalled them to come forth. Tim glanced at the older man. Lane shrugged resignedly.

"There's nothing else to do. Maybe we can strike a bargain with them. Our freedom for something they want."

But there was no hope in his voice. Tim threw an arm about Dorothy's shoulders. They followed their guide out of the room. There a cordon of other bat-creatures circled them, and Tim, for the first time, got an opportunity to see his captors at close range.

They weren't much to look at. They were such stuff as nightmares are made of. Tall, angular, covered from head to toe with a stiff, glossy pelt of fur. Their faces were lean and hard and predatory; their teeth sharp and protruding. Their wings were definitely chiropteric; the wing-membranes spanned from their shoulders to their claws, falling loosely away when not in use, and were anchored to stiff, horny knobs at clavicle and heel.

They walked now, guarding their captives, but it was apparent that flight was their usual method of locomotion. Anything else would be awkward, for their knees bent backward as did the knees of their diminutive Earthly prototype.

They turned, at last, into a huge chamber. And before them, perched obscenely on a platform elaborately laid with jewels and tapestries, was the overlord of the Harpies.

* * * *

No man, by the wildest stretch of the imagination, could have considered any of the vampires attractive. But of all they had seen, this monster was the most repugnant. It was not only that his frame was tauter, skinnier, than that of his fellows; it was not that his furry body was raw and chafed, as if from ancient, unhealed sores; it was not only that his pendulous nose-leaf perpetually snuffled, pulsed, above a red-lipped, vicious mouth. It was the unclean aura of evil about him that made Tim feel dirty. As though by merely looking on this thing he had profaned himself in some strange, inexplicable fashion.

Dorothy felt it, too. She choked once, turned her face away. And Captain Lane growled a disgusted curse.

"Lord, what a filthy beast! Mallory, I wouldn't mind dying if I could get one shot at that pot-bellied horror first!"

He did not expect—none of them could have expected—that which happened then. There came a high, simpering parody of laughter from the thing on the dais before them. And the words in their own tongue—

"But you cannot, Man! For here *I* am the Master!"

Lane's jaw dropped; his eyes widened. Tim Mallory felt the small hairs at the nape of his neck tighten coldly. The bat-thing could speak! Was speaking again, its cruel little mouth pulled into a grimace remotely resembling a grin.

"You are surprised that I speak your language? Ah, that is amusing. But you are just the first of many who will soon discover how foolish it was to underestimate the intellect of our ancient race.

"With fire and flame you forced us to the caverns, Man-thing. But we are old and wise. We built our cities here, warmed them against the dreadful damp and cold. Soon we shall burst forth in all our might. And when we do—"

He stopped abruptly; the tensing of his claws told the rest more eloquently than words. He rapped a command to one of the guards.

"Take off their garments! I would see what prizes have stumbled into our refuge!"

Obediently, the bat-creature shambled forward; his talons fumbled at Captain Lane's face-port. Tim cried out, "No! Don't let him! The atmosphere—"

The vampire overlord grinned at him cunningly.

"Fear not, Earthman. The air in this chamber will not harm you. We have other plans—" His wet, red tongue licked his lips.

Then Lane's headpiece was removed, and his bulger was stripped from him. A dazed expression swept across his forehead. He said, "Mallory—it—it's *hot* in here! And the air is breatheable!"

But by that time, Tim, too, had been removed of his space-suit; he, too, had felt the sultry, oppressive heat of the cavern. It was incredible but true. The vampires had found a way to make their underground city warm as the surface from which men had hunted them. That then—it came to Tim with sudden, startling clarity—that was why—

The overlord was speaking again. His tone was one of gratification.

"The men will do. We shall feast well tonight—*very* well! The woman—" He gazed at Dorothy speculatively. "I wonder?" he mused in a half whisper. "I wonder if there is not a better way of undermining Earthmen than just crushing them? A new race to people Venus? A race combining our ancient, noble blood and that of these pale creatures?" His eyes fastened on Dorothy's suddenly flaming loveliness. "That is a matter I must consider.

"That will do!" He motioned to his followers even as Tim, white of lip and riotous with rage, took a forward step. "Allow them to don their clumsy air-suits again; take them back to their dungeon. We shall bring them forth again when the time is ripe."

Strong claws clutched Mallory, staying him. Short minutes later, surrounded by their guards, they were once more on their way to the nether prison.

It was a grim-faced Captain Lane who paced the floor of their dungeon. There was anger in his eyes, and outrage, too. But beneath those surface emotions was a deeper one—fear! The dreadful, haunting fear of a power-less man, caught in a trap beyond his utmost devising.

"If there were only something we could do!" he raged savagely. "But we're weaponless—helpless—we can't even die fighting, like strong men. I'd rather we had all died in the *Orestes* than that this should happen. You and I, Mallory, a feast for such foul things. Dorothy—"

He stopped, shaken, sickened. Dorothy's face was pale, but her voice was even.

"There is one thing he overlooked, Daddy. We still have the privilege of dying cleanly. Together. We can take off our suits. Here. Before they come for us."

Lane nodded. He knew what death by asphyxiation meant; he had seen men die in Earth's lethal chambers. But anything, even that, was better than meek surrender to the overlord's mad, lustful plan.

"Yes, Dorothy. That is the only way left to us." He thought for a moment. "There is no use delaying. But before we—we *go*, there is one thing I must say—" And he looked at his daughter and her lover in turn. "I was wrong in forbidding your marriage. You're a *man*, Mallory. It's too bad I had to learn that under such circumstances. But I want you to know—at the end—that if things had turned out differently, I—I'd change my mind."

Tim said quietly, "Thank you, sir." But his thoughts were only half upon the older man's admission. There was a tiny something scratching at the back of his mind. Something that had occurred to him, dimly, in the hot chamber above. He couldn't quite place his finger on it, but—

"I still find it in me to wish," said Captain Lane, "that you had been a spaceman. But there's no use talking about that now. What might have been is past. There remains only time to acknowledge past faults, and then—and then—"

He faltered. And Dorothy took up the weighty burden of speech.

"Shall we ... do it now?"

Her hands lifted to the pane of her helmet. For an instant they hesitated, then began to turn. And then—

"*Stop!*" cried Tim. He struck her hands away, spun swiftly to the older man. "Don't do it, Skipper! I've got it! Got it at last!"

Lane stared at him dazedly. "Wh-what do you mean?"

Tim's sudden laughter was almost hysterically triumphant. "I mean that this is one time a 'groundhog engineer' knows more than a spaceman. There's no time to explain now, but quick!—you have some gun-capsules, haven't you?"

"Y-yes, but—"

"Give them to me! All you have. And hurry!"

* * * *

As he spoke, he was emptying his own capacious ammunition pouch. Capsule after capsule poured from it, until he had an overflowing double handful. With frenzied haste he broke the safety-tip off the first, tossed the cartridge into the stream that ran through their prison. As it struck, it hissed faintly; bubbles began to rise from the fluid, and a thin, steamy film of vapor rose whitely.

"Do that to all of them. Toss them in there! I'm right! I know I am. I *have* to be!"

Bewilderedly, Captain Lane and Dorothy began doing as he ordered. A dozen, a score, twoscore of the heat-gun cartridges were untipped, thrown into the coursing stream. The white film became a cloud, a fog, a thick, dense blanket about them, through which they could barely see each other. And still Tim's voice cried, "More! Faster! All of them!"

Then the last capsule had been tossed into the fluid, and their only contact with each other was by speech and the sense of touch. They were engulfed in rolling billows of white; vapor that frosted their view-panes, screened the world from view.

For half an hour they stood there waiting, turn with a thousand mingled doubts. Until, at last—

"I can't stand it any longer, Tim!" cried Dorothy. "What is it? What do we do? What is this wild plan?"

The vapor had thinned a trifle. And through gray mists, she saw a form loom before her. It was Tim's shape, and his hand stretched out to her. His voice was tense.

"Now—" he said. "Now we walk from our prison!"

And he flung open the door.

"Careful!" cried Captain Lane. "The guards, son! 'Ware the Harpy guards!"

But no guards sprang forward to bar their passage. There were guards, a dozen of them. But not a single one of them moved.

And Dorothy, wiping a sudden veil of hoar-frost from her view-pane, saw them and gasped.

"Dead!" she cried. "Tim—they're all dead!"

Tim shook his head.

"Not dead, darling. Just—sleeping! And now let's hurry. Before they waken again!"

* * * *

When they had reached the uppermost corridor of the caverns, they paused for a moment's rest. It was then that Captain Lane found time for the question that had plagued him.

"You were right, Tim. They were sleeping. I could see that overlord's nose-leaf quivering with slow breath just before I shot him. But—but what caused it? Anesthetic? I don't understand."

"No," grinned Tim, "it was not an anesthetic. It was a simple matter of remembering a biological trait of bats, and applying a little technical knowledge. The knowledge—" He could not resist the dig. "The special knowledge of what you called a 'hot-and-cold' expert. Refrigeration!

"Bats are hibernating creatures. And hibernation is not merely a matter of custom, tradition, desire to sleep—it is a physical reflex which cannot be avoided when the conditions are made suitable.

"Bats, like many other hibernating mammals, are automatically forced into slumber when the temperature drops below 46°F. Knowing this, and realizing that was the reason the Harpies—bat-like in form and habit—kept their underground chambers superheated I applied an elemental principle of refrigeration to cool their city below that point!"

Dorothy said, "The—the ammonia—?"

"Exactly. The set-up was perfect. Our apparatus was, perforce, crude, but we had all the elements of a refrigerating unit. Ammoniated water, running in a constant stream, capsules of condensed and concentrated heat from our needle-guns—a small room which was connected, by ventilating ducts, with the rest of the underground city.

"The principle of the absorption process depends on the fact that vapors of low boiling point are readily absorbed in water and can be separated again by the application of heat. At 60°F, water will absorb about 760 times its own volume of ammonia vapor, and this produces evaporation, which, in turn, gives off vapor at a low temperature, thereby becoming a refrigerator abstracting heat from any surrounding body. In this case—the rooms above!

"It—" Tim grinned. "It's as simple as that!"

Captain Lane groaned.

"Simple!" he echoed weakly. "The man says 'simple'! I don't understand a word of it, but—it worked, son! And that's the pay-off."

"No, sir," said Tim promptly.

"What? What's that?"

"The pay-off," persisted Tim, "comes later. When we get back to civilization. You said something about removing your objections to our marriage, remember?"

Captain Jonathan growled and stood up. "Confound it, do you think of everything? Well—all right, then. I'm a man of my word. But when we get back to civilization may be a long time yet."

"I can wait," grinned Tim. "But I've got a feeling I won't have to wait long. Maybe I'm psychic all of a sudden. I don't know. But somehow I've got a hunch that when we get to the cave-mouth, we're going to find a rescue party waiting for us up there. I just *feel* that way."

"Humph!" snorted Lane. "You're a dreamer, lad! A blasted, wishful dreamer!"

But it was a good dream. For the hunch was right.

CAPTAIN CHAOS

Originally published in *Planet Stories*, Summer 1942.

We picked up our new cook on Phobos. Not Phoebus or Phoebe; I mean Phobos, Mars' inner moon. Our regular victual mangler came down with acute indigestion—tasted some of his own cooking, no doubt—when we were just one blast of a jet-tube out of Sand City spaceport. But since we were rocketing under sealed orders, we couldn't turn back.

So we laid the *Leo* down on Phobos' tiny cradle-field and bundled our ailing grub-hurler off to a hospital, and the skipper said to me, "Mister Dugan," he said, "go out and find us a cook!"

"Aye, sir!" I said, and went.

Only it wasn't that easy. In those days, Phobos had only a handful of settlers, and most of them had good-paying jobs. Besides, we were at war with the Outer Planets, and no man in his right senses wanted to sign for a single-trip jump on a rickety old patrolship bound for nobody-knew-where. And, of course, cooks are dime-a-dozen when you don't need one, but when you've got to locate one in a hurry they're as difficult to find as petticoats in a nudist camp.

I tried the restaurants and the employment agencies, but it was no dice. I tried the hotels and the tourist homes and even one or two of the cleaner-looking joy-joints. Again I drew a blank. So, getting desperate, I audioed a plaintive appeal to the wealthy Phobosian colonists, asking that one of the more patriotic sons-of-riches donate a chef's services to the good old I.P.S., but my only response was a loud silence.

So I went back to the ship. I said, "Sorry, sir. We're up against it. I can't seem to find a cook on the whole darned satellite."

The skipper scowled at me from under a corduroy brow and fumed, "But we've got to have a cook, Dugan! We can't go on without one!"

"In a pinch," I told him, "*I* might be able to boil a few pies, or scramble us a steak or something, Skipper."

"Thanks, Dugan, but that won't do. On this trip the men must be fed regularly and well. Makeshift meals are O.Q. on an ordinary run, but when you're running the blockade—"

He stopped abruptly. But too late; I had caught his slip of the tongue.

I stared at him. I said, "The blockade, sir? Then you've read our orders?"

The Old Man nodded soberly.

"Yes. You might as well know, Lieutenant. Everyone will be told as soon as the *Leo* lifts gravs again. My orders were to be opened four hours after leaving Sand City. I read them a few minutes ago.

"We are to attempt to run the Outer Planets Alliance blockade at any spot which reconnaisance determines as favorable. Our objective is Jupiter's fourth satellite, Callisto. The Solar Federation Intelligence Department has learned of a loyalist uprising on that moon. It is reported that Callisto is weary of the war, with a little prompting will secede from the Alliance and return to the Federation.

"If this is true, it means we have at last found the foothold we have been seeking; a salient within easy striking distance of Jupiter, capital of the Alliance government. Our task is to verify the rumor and, if it be true, make a treaty with the Callistans."

I said, "Sweet howling stars—some assignment, sir! A chance to end this terrible war ... form a permanent union of the entire Solar family ... bring about a new age of prosperity and happiness."

"If," Cap O'Hara reminded me, "we succeed. But it's a tough job. We can't expect to win through the enemy cordon unless our men are in top physical condition. And that means a sound, regular diet. So we must find a cook, or—"

"The search," interrupted an oddly high-pitched, but not unpleasant voice, "is over. Where's the galley?"

I whirled, and so did the Old Man. Facing us was an outlandish little figure; a slim, trim, natty little Earthman not more than five-foot-two in height; a smooth-cheeked young fellow swaddled in a spaceman's uniform at least three sizes too large. Into the holster of his harness was thrust a Haemholtz ray-pistol big enough to burn an army, and in his right hand he brandished a huge, gleaming carving-knife. He frowned at us impatiently.

"Well," he repeated impatiently, "where is it?"

The Old Man stared.

"W-who," he demanded dazedly, "might you be?"

"I might be," retorted the little stranger, "lots of people. But I came here to be your new cook."

O'Hara said, "The new—What's your name, mister?"

"Andy," replied the newcomer. "Andy Laney."

The Old Man's lip curled speculatively. "Well, Andy Laney," he said, "you don't look like much of a cook to *me*."

But the little mugg just returned the Old Man's gaze coolly. "Which makes it even," he retorted. "*You* don't look like much of a skipper to *me*. Do I get the job, or don't I?"

The captain's grin faded, and his jowls turned pink. I stepped forward hastily. I said, "Excuse me, sir, shall I handle this?" Then, because the skipper was still struggling for words: "You," I said to the little fellow, "are a cook?"

"One of the best!" he claimed complacently.

"You're willing to sign for a blind journey?"

"Would I be here," he countered, "if I weren't?"

"And you have your space certificate?"

"I—" began the youngster.

"Smart Aleck!" That was the Old Man, exploding into coherence at last. "Rat-tailed, clever-cracking little smart Aleck! Don't look like much of a skipper, eh? Well, my fine young rooster—"

I said quickly, "If you don't mind, sir, this is no time to worry over trifles. 'Any port in a storm,' you know. And if this young man *can* cook—"

The skipper's color subsided. So did he, grumbling. "Well, perhaps you're right, Dugan. All right, Slops, you're hired. The galley's on the second level, port side. Mess in three quarters of an hour. Get going! Dugan, call McMurtrie and tell him we lift gravs immediately—*Slops!* What are you doing at that table?"

For the little fellow had sidled across the control-room and now, eyes gleaming inquisitively, was peering at our trajectory charts. At the skipper's roar he glanced up at us eagerly.

"Vesta!" he piped in that curiously high-pitched and mellow voice. "Loft trajectory for Vesta! Then we're trying to run the Alliance blockade, Captain?"

"None of your business!" bellowed O'Hara in tones of thunderous outrage. "Get below instantly, or by the lavendar lakes of Luna I'll—"

"If I were you," interrupted our diminutive new chef thoughtfully, "I'd try to broach the blockade off Iris rather than Vesta. For one thing, their patrol line will be thinner there; for another, you can come in through the Meteor Bog, using it as a cover."

"*Mr. Dugan!*"

The Old Man's voice had an ominous ring to it, one I had seldom heard. I sprang to attention and saluted smartly. "Aye, sir?"

"Take this—this culinary tactician out of my sight before I forget I'm an officer and a gentleman. And tell him that when I want advice I'll come down to the galley for it!"

A hurt look crept into the youngster's eyes. Slowly he turned and followed me from the turret, down the ramp, and into the pan-lined cubicle which was his proper headquarters. When I was turning to leave he said apologetically, "I didn't mean any harm, Mr. Dugan. I was just trying to help."

"You must learn not to speak out of turn, youngster," I told him sternly. "The Old Man's one of the smartest space navigators who ever lifted gravs. He doesn't need the advice or suggestions of a cook."

"But I was raised in the Belt," said the little chap plaintively. "I know the Bog like a book. And I was right; our safest course *is* by way of Iris."

Well, there you are! You try to be nice to someone, and what happens? He tees off on you. I got a little sore I guess. Anyhow, I told the little squirt off, but definitely.

"Now, listen!" I said bluntly. "You volunteered for the job. Now you've got to take what comes with it: orders! From now on, suppose you take care of the cooking and let the rest of us worry about the ship—Captain Slops!"

And I left, banging the door behind me hard.

* * * *

So we hit the spaceways for Vesta, and after a while the Old Man called up the crew and told them our destination, and if you think they were scared or nervous or anything like that, why, you just don't know spacemen. From oil-soaked old Jock McMurtrie, the Chief Engineer, all the way down the line to Willy, our cabin-boy, the *Leo's* complement was as thrilled as a sub-deb at an Academy hop.

John Wainwright, our First Officer, licked his chops like a fox in a hen-house and said, "The blockade! Oboyoboy! Maybe we'll tangle with one of the Alliance ships, hey?"

Blinky Todd, an ordinary with highest rating, said with a sort of macabre satisfaction, "I hopes we *do* meet up with 'em, that's whut I does, sir! Never did have no love for them dirty, skulkin' Outlanders, that's whut I didn't!"

And one of the black-gang blasters, a taciturn chap, said nothing—but the grim set of his jaw and the purposeful way he spat on his callused paws were mutely eloquent.

Only one member of the crew was absent from the conclave. Our new Slops. He was busy preparing midday mess, it seems, because scarcely had the skipper finished talking than the audio hummed and a cheerful call rose from the galley:

"Soup's on! Come and get it!"

Which we did. And whatever failings "Captain Slops" might have, he had not exaggerated when he called himself one of the best cooks in space. That meal, children, was a meal! When it comes to victuals I can destroy better than describe, but there was stuff and things and such-like, all smothered in gravy and so on, and huge quantities of this and that and the other thing, all of them unbelievably dee-luscious!

Beyond a doubt it was the finest feast we of the *Leo* had enjoyed in a 'coon's age. Even the Old Man admitted that as, leaning back from the table, he patted the pleasant bulge due south of his belt buckle. He rang the bell that summoned Slops from the galley, and the little fellow came bustling in apprehensively.

"Was everything all right, sir?" he asked.

"Not only all right, Slops," wheezed Captain O'Hara, "but perfect! Accept my congratulations on a superb meal, my boy. Did you find everything O.Q. in the galley?"

"Captain Slops" blushed like a stereo-struck school-gal, and fidgeted from one foot to another.

"Oh, thank you, sir! Thank you very much. Yes, the galley was in fine order. That is—" He hesitated—"there is one little thing, sir."

"So? Well, speak up, son, what is it? I'll get it fixed for you right away." The Old Man smiled archly. "Must have everything shipshape for a tip-top chef, what?"

The young hash-slinger still hesitated bashfully.

"But it's such a *little* thing, sir, I almost hate to bother you with it."

"No trouble at all. Just say the word."

"Well, sir," confessed Slops reluctantly, "I need an incinerator in the galley. The garbage-disposal system in there now is old-fashioned, inconvenient and unsanitary. You see, I have to carry the waste down two levels to the rocket-chamber in order to expel it."

The skipper's brow creased.

"I'm sorry, Slops," he said, "but I don't see how we can do anything about that. Not just now, at any rate. That job requires equipment we don't have aboard. After this jump is over I'll see what I can do."

"Oh, I realize we don't have the regular equipment," said Slops shyly, "but I've figured out a way to get the same effect with equipment we do have. There's an old Nolan heat-cannon rusting in the storeroom. If that could be installed by the galley vent, I could use it as an incinerator."

I said, "Hold everything, Slops! You can't do that! It's against regulations. Code 44, Section xvi, says, 'Fixed armament shall be placed only in gunnery embrasures insulated against the repercussions of firing charges, re-radiation, or other hazards accruent to heavy ordnance.'"

Our little chef's face fell. "Now, that's too bad," he said discouragedly. "I was planning a special banquet for tomorrow, with roast marsh-duck and all the fixings, pinberry pie—but, oh, well!—if I have no incinerator—"

The skipper's eyes bulged, and he drooled like a pup at a barbeque. He was a bit of a sybarite, was Captain David O'Hara; if there was anything he dearly loved to exercise his molars on it was Venusian marsh-duck topped with a dessert of Martian pinberry pie. He said:

"We-e-ell, now, Mr. Dugan, let's not be too technical. After all, that rule was put in the book only to prevent persons which shouldn't ought to do so from having control of ordnance. But that isn't what Slops wants the cannon for, is it, son? So I don't see any harm in rigging up the old Nolan in the galley for incineration purposes. Did you say *all* the fixings, Slops?"

Maybe I was mistaken, but for a moment I suspected I caught a queer glint in our little chef's eyes; it might have been gratitude, or, on the other hand, it might have been self-satisfaction. Whatever it was it passed quickly, and Captain Slops' soft voice was smooth as silk when he said:

"Yes, Captain, all the fixings. I'll start cooking the meal as soon as the new incinerator is installed."

* * * *

So that was that. During the night watch two men of the crew lugged the ancient Nolan heat cannon from stores and I went below to check. I found young Slops bent over the old cannon, giving it a strenuous and thorough cleaning. The way he was oiling and scrubbing at that antique reminded me of an apprentice gunner coddling his first charge.

I must have startled him, entering unexpectedly as I did, for when I said, "Hi, there!" he jumped two feet and let loose a sissy little piping squeal. Then, crimson-faced with embarrassment, he said, "Oh, h-hello, Lieutenant. I was just getting my new incinerator shipshape. Looks O.Q., eh?"

"If you ask me," I said, "it looks downright lethal. The Old Man must be off his gravs to let a young chuckle-head like you handle that toy."

"But I'm only going to use it," he said plaintively, "to dispose of garbage."

"Well, don't dump your cans when there are any ships within range," I warned him glumly, "or there'll be a mess of human scraps littering up the void. That gun may be a museum piece, but it still packs a wallop."

"Yes, sir," said Slops meekly. "I'll be careful how I use it, sir."

I had finished my inspection, and I sniggered as his words reminded me of a joke I'd heard at a spacemans' smoker.

"Speaking of being careful, did you hear the giggler about the old maid at the Martian baths? Well, it seems this perennial spinster wandered, by accident, into the men's shower room and met up with a brawny young prospector—"

Captain Slops said, "Er—excuse me, Lieutenant, but I have to get this marsh-duck stuffed."

"Plenty of time, Slops. Wait till you hear this; it will kill you. The old maid got flustered and said, 'Oh, I'm sorry! I must be in the wrong compartment—'"

"If you don't mind, Mr. Dugan," interrupted the cook loudly, "I'm awfully busy. I don't have any time for—"

"The prospector looked her over carefully for a couple of seconds; then answered, 'That's O.Q. by me, sister. I won't—'"

"I—I've got to go now, Lieutenant," shouted Slops. "Just remembered something I've got to get from stores." And without even waiting to hear the wallop at the end of my tale he fled from the galley, very pink and flustered.

So there was one for the log-book! Not only did our emergency chef lack a sense of humor, but the little punk was bashful, as well! Still, it was no skin off my nose if Slops wanted to miss the funniest yarn of a decade. I shrugged and went back to the control turret.

* * * *

All that, to make an elongated story brief, happened on the first day out of Mars. As any schoolchild knows, it's a full hundred million from the desert planet to the asteroid belt. In those days, there was no such device as a Velocity-Intensifier unit, and the *Leo*, even though she was then considered a reasonably fast little patroller, muddled along at a mere 400,000 m.p.h. Which meant it would take us at least ten days, perhaps more, to reach that disputed region of space around Vesta, where the Federation outposts were sparse and the Alliance block began.

That period of jetting was a mingled joy and pain in the britches. Captain Slops was responsible for both.

For one thing, as I've hinted before, he was a bit of a panty-waist. It wasn't so much the squeaky voice or the effeminate gestures he cut loose with from time to time. One of the roughest, toughest scoundrels who ever cut a throat on Venus was "High G" Gordon, who talked like a boy soprano, and the meanest pirate who ever highjacked a freighter was "Runt" Hake— who wore diamond ear-rings and gold fingernail polish!

But it was Slops' general attitude that isolated him from the command and crew. In addition to being a most awful prude, he was a kill-joy. When just for a lark we begged him to boil us a pot of spaghetti, so we could pour a cold worm's nest into Rick Bramble's bed, he shuddered and refused.

"Certainly not!" he piped indignantly. "You must be out of your minds! I never heard of such a disgusting trick! Of course, I won't be a party to it. Worms—Ugh!"

"Yeah!" snorted Johnny Wainwright disdainfully, "And *ugh!* to you, too. Come on, Joe, let's get out of here before we give Slops bad dreams and goose-flesh!"

Nor was hypersensitiveness Slops' worst failing. If he was squeamish about off-color jokes and such stuff, he had no compunctions whatsoever against sticking his nose in where it didn't belong.

He was an inveterate prowler. He snooped everywhere and anywhere from ballast-bins to bunk-rooms. He quizzed the Chief about engine-room practices, the gunner's mate on problems of ballistics, even the cabin-boy on matters of supplies and distribution of same. He was not only an asker; he was a teller, as well. More than once during the next nine days he forced on the skipper the same gratuitous advice which before had enraged the Old Man. By sheer perseverance he earned the title I had tagged him with: "Captain Slops."

I was willing to give him another title, too—Captain Chaos. God knows he created enough of it!

"It's a mistake to broach the blockade at Vesta," he argued over and over again.

"O.Q., Slops," the skipper would nod agreeably, with his mouth full of some temper-softening tidbit, "you're right and I'm wrong, as you usually are. But I'm in command of the *Leo*, and you ain't. Now, run along like a good lad and bring me some more of this salad."

So ten days passed, and it was on the morning of the eleventh day out of Sand City that we ran into trouble with a capital trub. I remember that morning well, because I was in the mess-hall having breakfast with Cap O'Hara, and Slops was playing another variation on the old familiar theme.

"I glanced at the chart this morning, sir," he began as he minced in with a platterful of golden flapjacks and an ewer of Vermont maple syrup, "and I see we are but an hour or two off Vesta. I am very much afraid this is our last chance to change course—"

"And for that," chuckled the Old Man, "Hooray! Pass them pancakes, son. Maybe now you'll stop shooting off about how we ought to of gone by way of Iris. Mmmm! Good!"

"Thank you, sir," said Slops mechanically. "But you realize there is extreme danger of encountering enemy ships?"

"Keep your pants on, Slops!"

"Eh?" The chef looked startled. "Beg pardon, sir?"

"I said keep your pants on. Sure, I know. And I've took precautions. There's a double watch on duty, and men at every gun. If we do meet up with an Alliance craft, it'll be just too bad for them!"

"Yes, sirree!" The Old Man grinned comfortably. "I almost hope we do bump into one. After we burn it out of the void we'll have clear sailing all the way to Callisto."

"But—but if there should be more than one, sir?"

"Don't be ridiculous, my boy. Why should there be?"

"Well, for one thing," wrangled our pint-sized cook, "because rich eka-lastron deposits were recently discovered on Vesta. For another, because Vesta's orbit is now going into aphelion stage, which will favor a concentration of raiders."

The skipper choked, spluttered, and disgorged a bite of half-masticated pancake.

"Eka—Great balls of fire! Are you sure?"

"Of course, I'm sure. I told you days ago that I was born and raised in the Belt, Captain."

"I know. But why didn't you tell me about Vesta before? I mean about the ekalastron deposits?"

"Why—why, because—" said Slops. "Because—"

"Don't give me lady-logic, you dope!" roared the Old Man, an enraged lion now, his breakfast completely forgotten. "Give me a sensible answer! If you'd told me *that* instead of just yipping and yapping about how via Iris was a nicer route I'd have listened to you! As it is, we're blasting smack-dab into the face of danger. And us on the most vital mission of the whole ding-busted war!"

He was out of his seat, bustling to the audio, buzzing Lieutenant Wainwright on the bridge.

"Johnny—that you? Listen, change traj quick! Set a new course through the Belt by way of Iris and the Bog, and hurry up, because—"

What reason he planned to give I do not know, for he never finished that sentence. At that moment the *Leo* rattled like a Model AA spacesled in an ionic storm, rolled, quivered and slewed like a drunk on a freshly-waxed floor. The motion needed no explanation; it was unmistakeable to any spacer who has ever hopped the blue. Our ship had been gripped, and was now securely locked, in the clutch of a tractor beam!

* * * *

What happened next was everything at once. Officers Wainwright and Bramble were in the turret, and they were both good sailors. They knew their duties and how to perform them. An instant after the *Leo* had been assaulted, the ship bucked and slithered again, this time with the repercussions of our own ordnance. Over the audio, which Sparks had hastily converted into an all-way, inter-ship communicating unit, came a jumble of voices. A call for Captain O'Hara to "Come to the bridge, sir!" ... the harsh query of Chief McMurtrie, "Tractor beams on stern and prow, sir. Shall I attempt to break them?" ... and a thunderous *groooom!* from the fore-gunnery port as a crew went into action ... a plaintive little shriek from somebody ... maybe from Slops himself....

Then on an ultra-wave carrier, drowning local noises beneath waves of sheer volume, came English words spoken with a foreign intonation. The voice of the Alliance commander.

"Ahoy the *Leo*! Calling the captain of the *Leo*!"

O'Hara, his great fists knotted at his sides, called back, "O'Hara of the *Leo* answering. What do you want?"

"Stand by to admit a boarding party, Captain. It is futile to resist. You are surrounded by six armed craft, and your vessel is locked in our tensiles. Any further effort to make combat will bring about your immediate destruction!"

From the bridge, topside, snarled Johnny Wainwright, "The hell with 'em, Skipper! Let's fight it out!" And elsewhere on the *Leo* angry voices echoed the same defi. Never in my life had I felt such a heart-warming love for and pride in my companions as at that tense moment. But the Old Man shook his head, and his eyes were glistening.

"It's no use," he moaned strickenly, more to himself than to me. "I can't sacrifice brave men in a useless cause, Dugan. I've got to—" He faced the audio squarely. To the enemy commander he said, "Very good, sir! In accordance with the Rules of War, I surrender into your hands!"

The firing ceased, and a stillness like that of death blanketed the *Leo*.

It was then that Andy Laney, who had lingered in the galley doorway like a frozen figuring, broke into babbling incredulous speech.

"You—you're giving up like this?" he bleated. "Is this all you're going to do?"

The Old Man just looked at him, saying never a word, but that glance would have blistered the hide off a Mercurian steelback. I'm more impetuous. I turned on the little idiot vituperatively.

"Shut up, you fool! Don't you realize there's not a thing we can do but surrender? Dead, we're of no earthly use to anyone. Alive, there is always a chance one of us may get away, bring help. We have a mission to fulfil, an important one. Corpses can't run errands."

"But—but if they take us prisoners," he questioned fearfully, "what will they do with us?"

"A concentration camp somewhere. Perhaps on Vesta."

"And the *Leo*?"

"Who knows? Maybe they'll send it to Jupiter with a prize crew in command."

"That's what I thought. But they mustn't be allowed to do that. We're marked with the Federation tricolor!"

A sharp retort trembled on the tip of my tongue, but I never uttered it. Indeed, I swallowed it as comprehension dawned. There came to me the beginnings of respect for little Andy Laney's wisdom. He had been right about the danger of the Vesta route, as we had learned to our cost; now he was right on this other score.

The skipper got it, too. His jaw dropped. He said, "Heaven help us, it's the truth! To reach Jupiter you've got to pass Callisto. If the Callistans saw a Federation vessel, they'd send out an emissary to greet it. Our secret would be discovered, Callisto occupied by the enemy...."

I think he would have turned, then, and given orders to continue the fight even though it meant suicide for all of us. But it was too late. Already our lock had opened to the attackers; down the metal ramp we now heard the crisp cadence of invading footsteps. The door swung open, and the Alliance commandant stood smiling triumphantly before us.

* * * *

There are soldiers and soldiers. Fighting men, as a rule, are pretty decent guys at the core. Having experienced danger, violence and the crawling horror of death themselves, they know the meaning of mercy. They respect their foes, and extend a fine magnanimity in the moment of victory.

Lieutenant-Colonel Ras Thuul, commander of the Third Outer Planets' Alliance Flotilla, was not this type of enemy. Half-breed spawn of a Jovian tribal priestess and a renegade Earthman, he retained the worst characteristics bequeathed by each of his parents.

From his father he had inherited height—he towered a full head above the squat, gnarled Jovian "runts" he led—and a festering hatred of the planet Earth. From his priestess mother he had suckled the milk of sadistic savagery which typified Jovian civilization before space-spanning Earthlings carried enlightenment to the far-flung sisterhood of the Sun.

His first words demonstrated clearly how slender was the mercy we might expect at his hands. To Captain O'Hara he said coldly, bluntly, rudely, "Your sidearms, Captain!" Then as the Old Man silently proffered his personal weapons: "You will walk before me, sir, on a tour of inspection. You might advise your men I hold you as hostage. One hostile move from any source means your death."

The skipper's reply was richly disdainful.

"I have surrendered myself to you under the Rules of War, Colonel. This play-acting is childish and altogether unnecessary."

Ras Thuul's swarthy cheeks sallowed; he took a swift step forward and, before one could guess his intention, slapped the Old Man viciously across the mouth with his gauntlet. The heavy, asbestos-lined space-glove cut and bruised; a thin trickle of blood split the skipper's lips.

"One in your position," snarled the invader, "should learn not to insult his betters! Now, lead the way, Captain. There is much to be done, and no time to waste."

Thus began our painful journey through the conquered *Leo*. As Ras Thuul had said, there was much to be done by his forces—nor had they delayed in getting about their task. A laboring crew was busily engaged in stripping the food-stuffs from our supply bins, other workmen were dismantling all hypo and radio equipment, verifying our belief that the O.P.A. was desperately in need of such material. Grim-faced Jovians had herded our marksmen from the gun embrasures, and were quickly dismantling every piece of ordnance the *Leo* boasted.

From room to room we went, from passage to sector to cabin. Nothing escaped the eagle eye of our foeman. By word and sign he designated to his henchmen those items which were to be removed, those which were to be destroyed. Only in the control-room was everything left untouched. It was here that Ras Thuul volunteered the explanation which proved the depths of his infamy. With a grin of sheer savagery he explained:

"I find it needless to waste energy in smashing this equipment, Captain. I am sure the rocky fragments of the Bog will do that most efficiently."

The Old Man stared at him uncomprehendingly.

"You—you mean you're going to wreck the *Leo* in the Bog? Just turn it loose and let the grindstone smash it?"

Ras Thuul shrugged. "It is the easiest way."

"But—" puzzled the skipper confusedly—"how about us? I mean, are you going to take us aboard your ship, or do we get camped on one of the asteroids, or—"

The half-breed shrugged negligently. "Why, Captain, you wouldn't want to desert your ship? I've always heard you Earthmen made it a point of honor to stand by your decks. Of course I would not think of forbidding you this signal honor."

The skipper's face turned white, but it was not fear that drained his cheeks of color; it was righteous rage. His words exploded like a fused hypatomic.

"*What!* You *dare* do a thing like this, Colonel! You accepted my surrender under military covenant—"

"That will do, Captain!" rapped Ras Thuul. "It will do you no good to prate of technicalities. I acknowledge but one rule of war—destroy your enemy! When this vessel has been stripped of its fuel and supplies, I shall turn it loose in the Bog. What happens then to it—or you—is none of my concern. Your pleas are vain, sir!

"And now, have we seen the entire ship?"

It was his selection of the word "pleas" that ended the Old Man's protestations. O'Hara needed no microscope to read our adversary's character; he knew that Ras Thuul would enjoy nothing more than listening to pleas for mercy. If we had to die, we could at least die like men. His jaw clamped forever on argument.

"We have," he said. "We are now where we started."

* * * *

And so we were, back in the Officers' Mess. A half hour ago our troubles had begun here; now they threatened to end abruptly and, for us, horribly.

But the half-breed's eyes had narrowed. A liar and dastard himself, he had a liar's distrust for everyone else. He nodded toward the closed door on the farther wall.

"We haven't been in there. Where does that lead?"

I said caustically, "No, and there's one mouse-trap you haven't crawled into yet, too. What's the matter? Got a tapeworm? That's just the kitchen."

It sounds right daring now that I see it in writing, but it was pure braggadocio. I figured my number was up, and a few healthy insults wouldn't make me die any deader. But our captor paid no attention. Prodding Captain O'Hara before him, he pushed into the galley.

Of course Captain Slops was on duty. The little guy was a study in technicolor; sort of pink around the eyebrows, white around the lips, and green around the gills. But I had to hand it to him, he was a game little fighting cock. Never a cringe for the Jovian commander, who brushed by him to peer about the cookhouse, and though the runt warriors had taken his massive old Haemholtz when they stripped us all, I saw he had a very large, and a very sharp, cleaver hanging not too far from his grasp.

Naturally, there wasn't anything for our foe to find in the galley. But he went through all the motions, just the same. Squinted in the stove, the refrigerator, the vegetable bins. And finally—

"Ah, ha!" rasped he. "What have we here? A cannon! So, Captain O'Hara—a concealed weapon, eh? Sergeant—"

He wheeled to one of his subalterns. But Andy Laney stepped forward awkwardly.

"It—er—it's not really a cannon, sir," he piped. "If you'll just open the breech, sir, you'll see—Oh! *Do* be careful, sir! Oh, my goodness!"

Because Lieutenant-Colonel Ras Thuul had hurled open the breech, and the incinerator-cannon was full—or had been a moment before. Now it was half empty, and the accumulation of slops and refuse as yet unincinerated had dumped backwards all over him!

It was the one bright spot in an otherwise dull day. Thuul howled and bellowed, and that was a mistake because his mouth opened. Then he spluttered. And gagged. And coughed. And backed, slipping and sliding on cold gravy, away from the incinerator. He wasn't the impressive figure he had been ten minutes ago. Coffee-grounds mottled his gold tunic, and lima beans tangled coyly with his once-gleaming epaulets. Potato-peelings draped gracefully from his ears, and the exotic odor of a slightly antique egg exuded from his shirt-front.

Well, what would *you* do? Even if you knew your life was in danger, what would you do at such a moment?

The same as we did, of course. We laughed. The Old Man and I, we burst out in a guffaw and rocked till we almost split our surcingles. And Slops laughed, too, in that piping little squeal of his, though even through his laughter he was gasping spasmodically, "I—I tried to warn you, sir. I'm *so* sorry! But you see it's only a garbage incinerator."

But he who laughs last, laughs last. And if our foe had been despicable before, he was a raging fury now. He did not even stop to scrape the last clinging turnip-top from his jacket. He spun to his subordinates and screamed, "Come! We are finished here! Back to our ship! I'll show these Earthmen one does not insult a Jovian commander with impunity!"

And his face a thundercloud of wrath, he dashed from the galley. We heard him calling his men, heard them exiting through the airlock, and then—silence again.

* * * *

It was then, his paroxysms of mirth stifled by sober recollection, that the Old Man turned and said, "Well, it was fun while it lasted. But it's all over now, Dugan. Call the men together. This is the last act, and we might as well all face it together."

But before I could leave the room, Slops clutched my arm with fingers tense and hot as live wires.

"No, Joey! Don't go! I need your help. And yours, Skipper! Hurry! We haven't a minute to lose!"

I stared at the Old Man and he at me. "H-huh?" said the two of us. "Help? Help for what?"

"Oh, don't *talk* so much!" bleated Andy. "*Work!* Get this garbage out of here—like this!"

And recklessly he plunged both arms into the channel of the incinerator, recklessly hurled it about the previously immaculate floor of the galley. As he worked, he panted: "An incinerator, yes ... but ... it was a good cannon ... in its ... day. It will still work. I cleaned ... and oiled it ... and connected it to the charger. *It still shoots!*"

Shoots! That was all we had to hear. We fell all over ourselves trying to get an armload of that goo. I never thought I'd live to see the day I'd go fond and blissful over a gallon of boiled noodles, but that's just what happened. I dug in, and so did the skipper. In less time than I've taken to tell it, we had that incinerator-cannon empty, swabbed out and ready for use as a cannon-incinerator.

Then the captain clapped a hand to his forehead.

"Omigawd—I clean forgot! The firing-plate! There ain't no vision-field for this gun!"

"Oh, yes there is!" cried Captain Slops. "Over your head, there—the galley-vent. I—I removed the atmosphere-duct and installed a vision-field. Use the crossed wires for a target centering device."

I flung open the vent. As he had said, the vent had been converted into a perfect firing-plate. There before me, a fat and gladsome target, was the largest of the enemy ships which had captured us, the flagship of Ras Thuul's fleet. As I watched, I saw the commander and his boarding party re-enter their own craft.

I said grimly, "Well, it's six against one. They'll blast us out of space, but by the purple gods of Pluto, we'll take at least one of them with us. This thing is connected?"

And I reached for the trigger. But once again Slops held my hand.

"No, Joey! There's a fighting chance we can get *all* of them. Wait till they cut the tractor beams and we're free of them. Then turn the cannon *upward* toward the Belt—"

"Upward?" I repeated dazedly. It didn't make sense. I glanced outside to make sure. Here was the situation. The planetoid Vesta lay about a mile or so below us. Larger than most of the meteoric and planetesimal fragments that comprise the Belt, its orbit was irregular. The smaller hunks of rock—and of course when you talk about "smaller" asteroids that means shards ranging anywhere from a yard to several miles in diameter, with weights ranging from a hundred pounds to twice that many thousands of tons—were whirling and swirling *above* our ships in a tight, lethal little huddle. That, of course, was the *melee* into which Ras Thuul planned to plunge us after he cut his tractor beams.

* * * *

Surprisingly, it was O'Hara who seconded Andy Laney.

"Do what he says, Joe. I don't know exactly what he has in mind, but it's his pigeon. He's steered us right this far; we might as well go whole-hog."

"Thank you, Captain!" said Slops gratefully. And as he spoke the words, the *Leo* rocked violently. With gathering speed we began to move away from our erstwhile captors, their tractor beams now released. Upward we surged toward the web-work of flailing missiles that spelled pure destruction.

"Now, Joey!" almost screamed Slops. "Aim the cannon at the rubble. Hold it firm. Full strength!"

And I did. I yanked the controls over to full power and aimed the heat gun straight into the heart of the rubble. The radiation was invisible, of course. Our enemies couldn't know we had an operative weapon. I held it for seconds which dragged like centuries. Nearer we were hurtling toward doom, nearer and nearer.

I cried, "Nothing's happening, Skipper! We're going to crash in a minute. I might as well turn the gun on one of their ships—"

"*Hold it!*" shrieked Captain Slops. "It's working as I hoped. Hold it steady, Joey!"

And now, returning my gaze to the target, I saw what he meant. Something strange and weird was happening—not to us or to the enemy spacecraft, but to the Bog itself! Like a huge, churning kettle it was seething, rolling, boiling! And even as I cried aloud my astonishment, one of the tinier bits of matter plummeted *down* from the overhanging canopy of death to rattle against the hull of Ras Thuul's flagship.

Then another ... and another ... and then a large piece. A hunk of rock which must have weighed half a ton. It struck one of the Jovian vessels like a sledgehammer, and a huge gap split in the spaceship's seams. There came signs of frenzied activity from aboard the enemy boat; fire spurted from stern-jets as engineers hurriedly warmed their rockets.

We saw two warships, desperately trying to get under way, ram each other head on. Three more were crushed, beaten shapeless, by the tons of stony metal that smashed their very girders. The last, Ras Thuul's flagship, met its doom most horribly. It was caught as in a vise between two mountainous boulders which rolled tangentially over it. When they separated, all that remained of a once proud ship was a flattened, lacerated shred of tortured steel.

It was then, and then only, that Slops said to me:

"That's all, Joey. You can turn it off now." There was something akin to sadness in his voice. I understood. I didn't feel any too good myself, watching those Jovians, foes though they were, die so frightfully. "Captain O'Hara, if we can repair the damage done by the marauders, we can now go on to Callisto and complete our mission. I—What's the matter, Captain?"

Cap O'Hara was glaring at his little finger irately.

"Matter? Why, confound it, I cut myself on that tin can. Look at this!"

He thrust before our noses a pudgy paw, the pinky of which was leaking very feebly. I chuckled. Not so Slops; he loosed one horrified gasp, and—

"Blood!" he screamed. "Oh, gracious, I simply can't *stand* the sight of blood! *Oooooohh!*"

His face went suddenly white. And—just like that!—Captain Slops fainted dead away!

The skipper said, "Well, I'll be damned!" Dazed, he knelt beside the little fellow, fumbled at his jacket collar. "Ain't that the funniest you ever saw, Dugan? Sees six ships scuttled without batting an eye-lash, and passes out at seeing a pinprick! Aw, well, it's probably shock more than anything else. I'll unloose his shirt, give him a little air—"

I said, "He's the queerest guy I ever met. But he's a *man*, Skipper."

Then a funny thing happened. The Skipper, strangely scarlet of face, rose suddenly from Andy's side. He croaked, "You—you wouldn't like to lay a little bet on that, Dugan?"

"Huh?" I said. "On what? I don't understand—"

The Old Man moaned softly.

"Neither do I, Dugan. But you were wrong! Slops, here, ain't no man at all, and never was! He—*he's a girl!*"

* * * *

Well, looking back on it now I can see how we should have realized it from the beginning. Sure, Captain Slops was a girl! That high, mellow voice ... the oversized uniform coat ... that prudishness which was not prudishness at all, but understandable modesty.

Later, as we were streaking the spaceways toward our Callisto rendezvous, the *Leo* completely repaired, we demanded and received an explanation. I might add that in female togs the pint-sized chef looked just the right size, and a hundred percent O.Q.

"I didn't exactly lie about my name," she explained. "It *is* 'Andy Laney'—only you spell it a bit differently. I am really 'Ann Delaney.' My father was a spaceman, so was my grandfather and my great-grandfather. Daddy was always sorry he had a daughter instead of a son. He wanted to see the old tradition of a 'Delaney in space' go on. But you thick-headed males have rules against allowing women to take to the spaceways except as passengers, so there was nothing I could do."

"You," I told her admiringly, "did all right."

"More than all right!" acknowledged the Skipper. "If it hadn't been for you—Don't worry, Miss Delaney. I'll see that the proper authorities hear all about this. Only—" A crease puckered his forehead—"There's something I ain't yet puzzled out. How come you ordered Mr. Dugan to shoot not at, but above the ships? At the Bog? And how come the rocks came tumbling down thataway?"

"Why," smiled Ann Delaney shyly, "it was really very simple. Heat, Captain."

"Heat?"

"Of course. As any student of thermodynamics knows, heat has a definite attractive force, varying directly as the difference in temperature. Space, being a vacuum, lacks heat entirely. Its temperature is that of Absolute Zero. Our gun emitted a heat-force equivalent to that of ten solar degrees. Thus the radiation we discharged at the bitter cold fragments of rock and ore comprising the Bog created a sort of passageway, an attractive channel down which the detritus was drawn. To state the problem more simply: have you ever watched a pot of beans boil? A seething whirlpool is created; the beans seek the heat."

"By golly!" said O'Hara. "I think you got something there, Miss Delaney. Why—why, that's terrific! That gives us a brand-new combat technique for locations where there are small cosmic bodies. Wait till the War Department hears it!"

But Ann Delaney just sniffed.

"New?" she repeated disdainfully. "New? Why, every woman cook knows that, Captain!"

You'll find the rest in the history books. Callisto *did* sign a pact with us ... the Federation *did* open a new front almost within spitting distance of Jupiter....

We've got a better universe to live in now. For one thing, there's peace throughout the Solar System. Because of Ann Delaney, the government changed its ruling about women in space; you'll find 'em everywhere, nowadays, doing everything and anything men do.

But I'm glad to say Ann isn't one of those void-vampires any more. She and I—oh, sure! We're married now. I couldn't let a swell cook like her get away, could I?

COLOSSUS OF CHAOS

Originally published in *Planet Stories*, Winter 1942.

PROLOGUE

Out of the darkness It came. Out of the grim, bleak, frore, incalculable depths of outer space, into the empire of light and warmth ... and life.

It was like nothing known to Man. It was round, but not quite round; It was hard, but not altogether hard; It was cold, but not cold with the terrible, utter iciness of things which come from Beyond. It was in motion but It did not move of Its own volition, for It was quiescent, insensate. It let Itself be carried by the vagrant and unpredictable whims of a kinetic universe, confident that in a day ... or a century ... or a thousand, thousand centuries ... the fitful fingers of chance would find for It a bourne, a resting-place.

Out of the night It came ... the endless, inpenetrable night which spans the void between star and star. Out of one cosmos into another; out of oblivion into waking horror.

No eye beheld Its coming. None saw Its faint, thin, cool iridescence; no voice lifted to challenge Its arrival on the sixth satellite of the sixth solar planet. It dropped to earth unwatched, rolled a brief, sluggish way, then rested in a deep, soft, sandy pit.

A gray hoar-frost rimed Its surface as the warmth of a friendly orb dispelled the frightful chill of space; a pale mist rose from Its petroid carapace and trembled into the air like a wan and restless ghost.

It had found a home, a lair, a birthing-place. With a slow, ecstatic, burrowing motion It dug Itself still deeper into the nourishing sands. It had arrived. It grew....

CHAPTER I

"A dangerous place," said the heavy man with ominous deliberation. "A most dangerous place!" He raised his glass to his nostrils, passed it back and forth appreciatively, and rolled a single drop of the liqueur upon his tongue. A smile creased his full, red lips. "Excellent, my dear Captain!" he approved. "A most superior brandy. Allow me to congratulate you. Domrémy-Thol '98, I should judge?"

Captain Burke, skipper of the IPS space-cruiser *Gaea*, basked in the sunshine of his passenger's approbation.

He swirled the liquor in his frosted glass, glanced about the table with a self-satisfied complacency that was almost ludicrous. Then he nodded his head slowly, acknowledging the compliment bestowed upon his judgment in selecting the after-dinned liquor.

"Allow me," he corrected, "to congratulate you, sir, on a truly magnificent palate. You have named the exact vine and season. But ... danger? You spoke of danger?"

The connoisseur glanced at the young lady across the table and permitted his eyebrows to arch significantly.

"Perhaps it would be better to abandon the subject," he suggested. "After all, I do not wish to cause Miss Graham undue alarm—"

The girl laughed. She did not seem, noted young Dr. Roswell, occupant of another seat at the captain's table, the least bit perturbed by Grossman's shadowy hint of menace. On the contrary, her already vivid features assumed new color at the scent of danger. Her gray-green eyes brightened, a flush highlighted the natural golden beauty of her cheeks; she bent forward interestedly.

"Please, Mister Grossman ... don't stop because of me. I want to learn everything I can about Titan. It's going to be my home from now on, you know. I'll learn sooner or later."

"Ye-e-es," acknowledged the heavy man grudgingly, "I suppose that is true. Your father is Commandant of the Space Patrol post at New Boston, isn't he? Hasn't *he* warned you of the dangers you face in coming to live with him?"

Again the girl laughed.

"Hardly! You see, he doesn't know I'm coming. He'd have conniption fits if he knew I were aboard the *Gaea*. He's a lamb, really, but terribly old-fashioned. 'Women belong on Earth,' you know ... that sort of thing. He thinks I'm safe in a Terra boarding-school right now. If he *dreamed* I were less than an hour off Titan—well, I'm afraid he'd be pale violet with anger."

"And," reproved Grossman sternly, "rightly so. Your father is a wise man. Titan is no place for a girl of gentle breeding. It is a vile and treacherous pest-hole. It should never have been opened to Earth colonists!"

Rockingham Roswell coughed gently. The young savant was taller than any man present, and but for the conservative cut of his clothing might have looked his true weight, but he carried himself in such a way as to seem more fragile than he really was. His lean, close-shaven cheeks were pale, and his tow-colored hair was meticulously plastered to his scalp. He wore thick-lensed, tortoise-shell glasses which he removed and polished nervously as he spoke.

"In ... er ... in that case, Mister Grossman, it strikes me as a bit odd that you should ... er ... have established business headquarters on the satellite."

Grossman glanced sharply at the slender man, snapped impatiently, "A business man cannot always pick and choose his locations, Doctor Roswell. He must follow the path of empire as it leads. Since there are Earthmen on Titan, someone must serve them. It is an obligation which cannot be refused—"

"Er ... quite!" acknowledged Roswell confusedly. "Job of work to be done ... noble noble sacrifice ... the white man's burden ... all that sort of rot ... what?"

Unaccountably, Grossman flushed. "If you are trying to imply, sir," he fumed, "that I have any ulterior motive in establishing a trading post on Titan—"

"Oh, gracious, no! Nothing of the sort. I wouldn't presume to question your ... er ... business acumen, Factor. I'm hardly the type, what?" Roswell smiled a faint, thin, apologetic smile. "I mean I ... er ... I really don't know much about this sort of thing ... if you know what I mean...."

Captain Burke stared at the younger man impatiently. A spaceman toughened in the crucible of action, he had little patience with such learned young fops as this passenger. His words were polite, as befitted the skipper of a luxury liner, but his tone was brushed with acid.

"If you don't mind, Doctor Roswell, Factor Grossman was about to tell us something about the hazards of Titan. Well, Mister Grossman?"

Grossman took another appreciative sip of his brandy, set down the tulip-glass, and steepled his fingers.

"Well, the perils of Titan fall into several classes. Geographic, physiological and racial. In the first place, it is a satellite approximately the size of Earth's moon ... large enough to sustain life, but small enough to be influenced by the perturbations not only of its massive primary, which lies a scant seven hundred and sixty thousand miles away, but also by the attractive forces of the Ring and Saturn's eight *other* satellites.

"Evidence of this is the peculiarity interwoven orbit trajectories of Titan and its nearest sister, Hyperion, which sometimes approach each other perilously close. Were Titan a sphere of pumaceous formation, like Luna, it would long since have burst into a million fragments under the impact of these conflicting forces. Fortunately, it is of a basaltic nature, and consequently reasonably stable.

"More immediately hazardous are what might be called the physiological dangers of Titan. These are multifold. To begin with, there is the so-called 'water' of the orb—"

"I've read about that," nodded Captain Burke gravely. "Not water at all, but—"

"But a deadly corrosive acid," finished the speaker, "yes! Happily, the 'seas' of Titan do not cover such a share of the planet's surface as do those of Earth; if they did, no life—either flora or fauna—would ever have developed upon the little world."

His heavy shoulders shivered.

"Still ... imagine frothing, tide-swept lakes as large as Lake Erie or Victoria Nyanza splashing endlessly at shores until inch by inch and foot by foot those beaches are eroded, rotted, eaten away by the action of the fluid they contain! These are the 'oceans' of Titan. There are four of them, fed by subterranean sources we have not yet discovered. One day they will have completely devoured the parent planet, and Titan will cease to be."

"But that day, of course," interposed the girl, "is a long way off. Is this the only physiological danger?"

"There is one even *more* dreadful. The T-radiation."

"T-radiation? What is that?"

Grossman smiled mirthlessly.

"Were I able to tell you, I should be a greater physicist than any who have so far visited Titan. Dozens of the wisest have come, probed, pondered, analyzed ... and left Titan none the wiser for their efforts. Frankly, they do not know! The very name 'T-radiation' is an admission of their failure. It is simply an abbreviation for 'Titan-radiation.' It is an electromagnetic or radioactive emanation lethal to humans ... that is all they know about it."

Young Dr. Roswell wiped his spectacles carefully and interrupted, "But ... er ... but surely, Factor, these physicists were able to determine the wavelength of the radiation? Did that not tell them—?"

Grossman said bluntly, almost rudely, "The radiation lies in the Hertzian range, Doctor Roswell. Does that knowledge help you any? Perhaps now *you* can tell us why these rays are deadly?"

Roswell flushed and faltered into silence. The girl glanced curiously at Grossman.

"Hertzian range, Factor?"

"Electrical waves ranging between 1 m. and 1/10 c.m. in length, Miss Graham. Their place is between the so-called 'short waves' of radio transmission and the infra-red or heat waves. Their existence has been known, theoretically, for at least two hundred years. But man has never been able to find a reason, a place, or use for them. Nor have they been found to occur freely in nature elsewhere than on Titan."

"And," asked Captain Burke, "you say these waves are deadly to humans? But how, then, have our colonists managed to win and maintain a foothold—"

"I should have said," admitted Grossman, "the waves are deadly to *unshielded* humans. Lead sheathing protects the wearer from harm; consequently men in bulgers are quite safe. And one of the first acts of the Solar Space Patrolmen, upon reaching Titan, was to project a series of leaden highways or avenues between the cities of the satellite. Upon these, and *only* upon these, may Earthmen travel unprotected by bulgers. To stray from one of these roadbeds means exposure to the T-radiation. And that, in turn, means death!"

Rockingham Roswell shuddered delicately. "Beastly!" he murmured. "Deuced unpleasant sort of place, what? But, I say ... how about the natives? How did they manage to survive before our countrymen built those jolly old lead roadways?"

Grossman pursed his lips impatiently at the affected young scholar.

"They, Doctor Roswell," he said scornfully, "are immune to the T-radiation. Certainly you are acquainted with the principles of selective breeding?"

"Selective—oh, yes! Survival of the fittest ... all that fiddle-di-diddle? You mean the present Titanians *are* the present Titanians simply because they adapted their physiques to the surroundings, eh? Why, rather! That's clear enough. Still, if they can stand the radiation, I don't see why other humans—"

"Other *humans*!" Grossman laughed curtly. "My dear Doctor, it is obvious you have never seen a Titanian. Human, indeed! Why, it is the dissimilarity between the Titanians and ourselves which led me to name racial divergence as among the hazards of life on Titan.

"The creatures who rule Titan look less like humans than like those monsters deranged and alcoholic patients see in their dreams. For some reason—possibly because of this mysterious T-radiation—the denizens of the world have never bred true. Consequently, there is no way of foretelling what the child of any two parents may resemble ... though one almost certain guess is that it will resemble neither parent.

"Bilateral symmetry is about the only constant human attribute to be found amongst the Titanians. That and a more or less rudimentary intelligence ... an instinct which is more akin to animal cunning than to intellect.

"Some Titanians walk erect on their hind legs. Some crawl on all fours or squirm on their bellies. Some resemble the humanoid races of our planet, or Mars, or Venus. Others look like obscene jungle beasts, ghouls, fabulous monsters.

"I have seen Titanians whose leprous flesh covered bones have no counterpart in the human skeleton ... others with no faces at all, as we know the meaning of the word ... others who grope blindly along on tactile tentacles, 'seeing' with foot-long tongues, 'hearing' through their fingertips.

"Some there are who look like gigantic, crimson ants; others inch their way along the streets like hideous, mangled slugs; while yet again—astonishingly—you may chance upon a Titanian not only similar in appearance to Earthmen, but as clever and quick in thought as any terrestrial."

Grossman paused, nodding significantly. "These," he said, "are the most dangerous of all."

"And—" breathed Lynn Graham—"the nature of this danger, Mister Grossman? Attack, perhaps?"

"Attack!" The trading-post factor laughed brusquely, harshly. "A mild word for it. Extermination! The Titanians hate interlopers on their world—*particularly* Earthmen—with a smoldering, implacable hatred inconceivable to a civilized mind. Had they their will, they would hunt down every Earthman and slaughter him with the most horrible tortures their warped and twisted minds can devise.

"Your father, Miss Graham—" Grossman bent forward across the table to lend emphasis to his warning—"maintains a post on Titan by sufferance only. Because the natives have not the strength nor the weapons with which to rebel. But if ever the day dawns when they find such strength or weapons—" Grossman drew a deep breath and shook his head—"Then ... Lord help all like us who dwell on Titan!"

CHAPTER II

It had arrived. It had found a birthing-place. It grew. There in the lone, lorn silence, in the thawing warmth of the nourishing sands. It spawned according to its nature.

It made no sound save that of a thin, dry grating as Its shell-like covering stirred against the sides of the pit. But a change had come upon Its carapace. Its one-time stony surface now was mottled with yolky cloud; Its one-time opaque walls were now translucent with a jelly-like shimmering. And from within the egg came the bruit of liquid movement. Slow, groping movement of Life that would be free. Amorphous hands scraped and slithered at softening, yielding walls. A single flake chipped and fell away from the gigantic shell. Another followed it. Another ... and another.

A native of the planet, random-roaming, chanced upon the pit. His nostrils quivered with the scent of food. With greedy stealth he moved upon his prey.

And then:

And then the native witnessed the phenomenon. Wide-eyed with wonder he beheld the monstrous sight ... the ultimate emergence of the Thing!

In his dull, brutelike brain there dawned a dreadful fear. A fear ... and a great hope! On trembling limbs he fell back from the pit, all thoughts of food forgotten, turned and scampered to the city whence he had come.

Meanwhile, the sprawling, raw and new-fledged Thing lay gasping in the sunlight, sucking strength from the depths of the nourishing soil. It was born. It grew....

CHAPTER III

A strained silence followed the factor's final words. A silence during which Lynn Graham's troubled gaze swept the table, searching reassurance—finding none—in the eyes of her dinner companions. A silence during which Dr. Rockingham Roswell fidgeted uneasily, removed his glasses, breathed upon them, polished them, and replaced them for the hundredth time.

It was Captain Burke who finally broke the spell. He cleared his throat and rose.

"Well, I must be getting along to the bridge. We'll be at New Boston space-port in a matter of minutes now. I suggest that you go to your staterooms, see that your luggage is in order, and prepare to disembark."

Dr. Roswell said hesitantly, "Er ... Captain ... just a moment. When ... er ... how soon does the *Gaea* return to Earth?"

"Return to Earth! But—" Captain Burke turned a blank, uncomprehending stare upon his questioner—"but you have not yet set foot on Titan!"

Dr. Roswell shuffled uncomfortably.

"I ... er ... I quite realize that, Captain. But I ... er ... have been reconsidering. In view of Mister Grossman's revelations, I ... er ... am not altogether certain it would be wise to pursue my investigations...."

The space skipper's broad, flat features contracted into a grimace of disdain. Despite his company's instructions to maintain at all times a respectful mien toward passengers, he permitted contempt to echo in his voice.

"You don't mean to say you are *afraid*, Doctor Roswell!"

The young man's cheeks flushed. He said, "I ... er ... should not put it quite that way, sir. However, I prefer not to expose myself to needless risks. The work I had intended to do on Titan is not sufficiently important to warrant—"

Grossman chuckled. The girl, Lynn Graham, looked at the embarrassed pedant almost pityingly. Captain Burke said, "I am afraid, Doctor Roswell, it will not be possible to return to Earth immediately. The *Gaea* is not returning to Earth."

"Not returning—"

"No. We are going on to Uranus to leave a cargo of food and medical supplies there. We will, however, stop back at Titan in three Solar Constant weeks. If—" The skipper's voice was openly ironic—"if you can endure the rigors of the satellite for that length of time, we will be glad to pick you up on our return trip."

"I ... er ... I suppose it would not be possible for me to ride with you to Uranus?"

"I'm sorry," said Burke decidedly. "The Uranus post is a military zone forbidden to civilian tourists. I cannot take you there."

"Then in that case," shrugged Roswell, "I must stay. But you *will* stop for me?"

"I'll stop for you. Meanwhile, you had better make arrangements to stay somewhere where you will be quite safe." Captain Burke's patience was quite exhausted. "Miss Graham can, perhaps, prevail upon her father to allow you to remain at the Space Patrol base."

The young doctor turned to the girl eagerly.

"Can you, Miss Graham? I would be *most* grateful—"

Lynn Graham nodded, her icy politeness more devastating than forthright scorn.

"Yes, Doctor Roswell, I am reasonably sure you can make such arrangements. I will ask Daddy as soon as we land. And now, gentlemen, if you will excuse me—"

She rose and left the dining-hall. Grossman, still chuckling, followed her example. He stopped at the doorway.

"Sorry I upset you, Roswell. But cheer up! Three weeks will pass swiftly. You'll be all right on Titan if you keep your eye peeled and carry your Haemholtz at all times."

But his reassurance proved to be just the opposite. For the savant's lower jaw dropped; he quavered, "Haemholtz! Gracious ... you mean I should carry a ray-pistol! Oh, mercy! I couldn't *think* of doing such a thing!"

And with a little bleat of dismay, he turned and ran toward his stateroom. The two men in the dining-hall watched him disappear. Then Grossman laughed aloud, and Captain Burke snorted.

"The younger generation! If that's the kind of men Earth is breeding nowadays, Lord help us all!"

* * * *

Dr. Rockingham Roswell pattered down the long, metal corridors of the *Gaea* to his A-deck suite. He fumbled near-sightedly at the vibro-lock and stumbled into his compartment. But once inside, the door securely bolted behind him, a change came over him. A change which would have astonished those who had a few moments before been amused at his timidity.

He removed his spectacles, casing them and thrusting them into an inside pocket. He then removed his coat. Oddly enough, rid of that close-ly-tailored garment, his shoulders looked considerably broader, his chest inches deeper. He drew a deep breath ... much the same sort of breath as a sponge diver draws when he emerges from the hampering depths of the sea to the more accustomed world above ... and called a name.

"Bud?"

A figure appeared from the plushy wallows of a divan, waved at the young professor companionably.

"Hi, Rocky! Beginnin' to wonder when you was comin' back. We're halfway to the cradle. What's the good word?"

"The good word," grinned his informant, "is that I've paved the way. Miss Graham is going to ask her father to let us stay at the Patrol base."

"Huh?" Mulligan looked baffled. "What's good about *that*? We could've stayed at the Patrol Base anyway. All you had to do was tell Colo-nel Graham who you were—"

His superior officer groaned in mock despair.

"Sometimes I wonder if that cranium of yours is good for anything but a hair-garden! Don't you see, Bud, that the whole scheme depends on our being *invited* to become guests at the Patrol base? Of course, we could present our credentials, walk directly from the *Gaea* to headquarters. But it would be a cold tip-off to Grossman that we are S.I.D. men.

"As it is, he hasn't got the faintest idea that 'Doctor Rockingham Ro-swell' and his 'valet' are members of the Solar Investigation Department. He thinks I'm a very badly rattled pedagogue, and you're a mealy-mouthed nonentity. And that is exactly what we want him to believe—until we get the goods on him."

"Then he *is* our man?"

"I'm practically certain of it now. He's as nervous as a cat. Flared up the moment I questioned his reasons for living on Titan. As factor of the New Boston trading-post he is in an ideal situation to stir up trouble amongst the Titanians. And that's precisely what he has been doing. We don't know exactly why—yet!—but it's quite clear that for some reason of his own he wants all Earthmen save himself to leave Titan."

"Gold, maybe?" suggested Bud. "Oil? *Ekalastron?*"

"No-o-o, I don't think so. The mineralogists would have detected the presence of any of those when they surveyed Titan. His reason is something deeper than that—Say! Wait a minute! I wonder if it possibly—?"

"Yeah?"

"No, I'm crazy! It couldn't be that. I happened to think of that T-radi-ation. But I don't believe even Grossman is enough of a scientist to have discovered what it is or how it can be used—if at all. Well, anyhow—"

"Anyhow, we're in at the Base. And Grossman doesn't suspect us. That's part of the job. So—the next move?"

"We circulate. We move around and ask questions and snoop and pry and investigate."

Mulligan grinned.

"In the good old Rocky Russell tradition, eh?"

"Who?"

"Rocky Russell, I said. Don't tell me you've forgot your real name, chum?"

Rocky Russell reached into an inside pocket, brought forth a pair of thick-lensed spectacles, hooked them over his ears. His voice lifted to a high, gentle, hesitant whine.

"Oh, mercy me!" he simpered. "Forgotten my ... er ... real name? But, of course not! I am Doctor Rockingham Roswell. And you are my valet, Ambrose."

Bud groaned.

"Gawd! All the names in creation, and I've got to be called 'Ambrose'!"

"So you're a doctor?" asked Colonel Graham. "That's fine. We can use another doctor on this post. Glad to have you stay with us, Doctor Roswell."

Several hours had passed since the *Gaea's* landing on Titan. In that time, much had happened. Dr. Roswell and his "man" had made their adieux to a scornful Captain Burke and a highly amused Factor Grossman, removed their baggage from the cruiser, and accompanied Lynn Graham to the S.S.P. base a few miles outside the Titanian city of New Boston.

There they had witnessed the surprise meeting of the Commandant and his daughter. Lynn Graham had rightly guessed her father's reaction upon seeing her. She had erred in only one minor detail. She had expected him to turn "pale violet" with anger. The color he *actually* achieved was some-where in the apoplectic spectrum between dull scarlet and turkey red.

His outraged bellows, replete with invocations to the deities of a dozen worlds and highly censorable, were audible for a good half mile. But even-tually—when Lynn had pointed out that: (1) she could not return to the *Gaea*; (2) she didn't want to return to the *Gaea*, and (3) that she had no intention of returning to the *Gaea* even if she could—he calmed down a trifle. And in his brusque kiss of greeting was an affection hardly in keeping with the violence of his protestations.

It was then that Lynn had introduced Dr. Roswell and his valet, explain-ing their desire to stay at the base. Confused and bewildered, the comman-dant had agreed. And now the quartet were gathered in the colonel's private quarters. The colonel, in his own crisp way, was trying to be friendly.

"A doctor," he repeated. "That's good. We need the services of a good doctor around here."

Rocky smiled feebly.

"I ... er ... I'm afraid you don't understand, sir. I'm not an M.D., you know. I'm an ... er ... D.M."

"D.M.?" repeated Graham wonderingly. "What's that?"

"A Doctor," explained Rocky, "of Mythology. It's an archeological degree, rather than a medical one. I'm what ... er ... might be called a research student. I gather folk tales and ancient legends, study them, analyze them, and attempt to determine their underlying meanings." He beamed happily from behind his thick-lensed glasses. "A most fascinating hobby," he said. "Oh, goodness, yes ... *most* fascinating!"

Colonel Graham stared at him incredulously.

"Legends! Folk tales! But why on earth—?"

Red of face, he spluttered into silence. Lynn tried to bridge the awkward moment.

"What Daddy means, Doctor Roswell, is—why do you hunt down these ancient fables? Does your work have any practical value?"

Rocky's eyebrows arched as if the query caused him a physical pain.

"Practical value! My dear young lady, of course not! It is purely a labor of love. Knowledge for the sake of pure knowledge. Er ... *scientia gratia scientiarum*, you know ... that sort of thing. Of course—" He shrugged— "once in a while the research of my learned colleagues does contribute a share to the understanding of man's more mundane pursuits, but such occasions are, I hasten to assure you, quite incidental—"

Colonel Graham had recovered his composure.

"Mythology, eh? Well, what sort of legends interest you, Doctor? Fairy tales? Ghost stories?"

"Well—no," said Rocky pedantically. "The tales of greatest interest are those of fabulous monsters ... incredible beings endowed with fantastic powers or attributes. Such may be found in the mythologies of any race or clan. Not only on Earth, but on all the planets have we heard such stories. It is our delight to track down these tales and unearth the germ of underlying truth which created them."

"You mean," queried the girl, "that behind each folk tale lies a true cause or event or—or creature?"

"Exactly. For instance—well, let me see—you are familiar with the Earthly legend of the phoenix, aren't you?"

"The bird which was supposed to have had a life-span of a thousand years, at the end of which time it threw itself into a blazing pyre, from the ashes of which it was reborn?"

"That," nodded Dr. Rocky, "is the legend. Quoted as you have told it, it made no sense to Earthmen for thousands of years. Until, in fact, the year

1987 A.D., when the first Martian expedition visited the desert planet. The members of this expedition were amazed to discover a *rara avis* upon Mars impervious to extremes of both heat and cold. A bird with an astonishing life-span in excess of a thousand Earthly years. In short ... the archetype of the fabled phoenix!"

Colonel Graham looked interested in spite of himself.

"By Gad, that's right! The *tulalaroo* bird. Doesn't mind heat or cold, either one. Nests in ice or red-hot coals! That's rather interesting, Doctor. Any more such examples?"

"Scores! There is the fabled unicorn ... a one-horned gazelle-like animal certainly not indigenous to Terra, yet it found its place in the 'unnatural natural history' of not one but a dozen races. Whence originated this record of a single horned creature we could not guess .. until we discovered such a beast on Venus.

"The fabulous 'salamander' turned out to be a common asbestos-like lizard of Mercury. Aqueous Venus solved for us the problems of the mermaid, the sea serpent and the undine. On mighty Jupiter mythologists encountered the fire-breathing saurian which gave rise to the 'dragon' myth—"

"But, Doctor Roswell!" gasped the girl, "what does this mean? That once upon a time, countless centuries ago, beasts of this sort roamed Earth? Or—?"

Rocky shook his head soberly.

"We do not know, Miss Graham. There are a number of equally valid possibilities. One is that which you have mentioned ... that Earth was once host to all the types of animal life now to be found on its sister planets. Another is that aeons ago Earthmen—or the intellectual rulers of one of the other planets—knew the secret of spacetravel. The factual records of places visited, strange sights seen, would in the musty passage of time become mythology.

"Still another possibility—"

"Yes?"

"Well, it is ... er ... a theory recently advanced by an erudite scholar, but it has elements of fantasy which make it almost incredible. You are ... er ... familiar with the theories of Svante Arrhenius?"

Lynn frowned. "I remember the name faintly. Didn't he claim life traveled through the ether?"

"Yes. He put forward, the concept that the life-germ is universally diffused, constantly emitted from all habitable worlds in the form of spores which traverse space for years or ages, the majority being ultimately destroyed by the flame of some blazing star, but some few finding a resting-place on bodies which have reached the habitable stage.

"My colleague has carried this theory a step forward, suggesting it is not only the fundamental life-germ which thus travels ... but also individual and distinctive life-forms! He has suggested that from each and every world in every galaxy, occasionally there set forth into the void the spores or eggs of every highly developed life-form.

"Most of these never reach their destinations. Some do. And when these do, unwilling worlds play host to beasts of nightmare mien."

CHAPTER IV

A babble from the street lifted Humboldt Grossman's eyes from shrewd perusal of his ledgers. He frowned, rose to investigate the tumult, then stood stock-still in his tracks, startled as the door of his private chamber burst open.

A stunted troll with four, gnarled, dangling arms—a native Titanian—served as spokesman for the excited group.

"A marvel, Master!" he jabbered. "Behold, a marvel! It was found by one of us in the sand-pits north of the city, captured and brought to you immediately. See, O Master, its height, its bulk, its strength."

He stood aside and into the room a score of tugging natives hauled a bound and helpless creature.

Bound and helpless creature?

Bound ... yes. With yards upon yards of tightly laced metal cord which even now stretched taut over bulging sinews. Helpless ... perhaps. It stood quietly, struggling not, but in its very quiescence Factor Grossman found a swift, disturbing menace. It was still as flood-waters are still, ere, angered, they burst with fury the puny dams constraining them. It was motionless as powerful machines are motionless before, spurred to deed, they ravage all before them.

A creature it was. But such a creature. Humanoid in form ... male ... but dull of eye as a brain-fogged idiot. It was seven feet tall and half as broad of shoulder, heavy of thigh and iron-strong of bicep. A Hercules, an Atlas of a man.

Grossman stared at it strangely. Then he turned to his native visitors.

"It is a marvel, yes. A great man. But what has it to do with me?"

The spokesman cringed forward hopefully.

"It has power, O Master. You promised us vengeance and freedom when we found you one with strength to fight our cause."

Grossman's thick face mottled with disdain. "Fool!" he spat. "Do you call this creature power enough to wage a war? One halfwit giant against a well-armed garrison of humans? Take it away. This is not the power I asked for!"

The Titanian inched another step forward. "Wait, O Master!" he advised. "Wait and see what we have seen! For not yet do you understand. He is still growing!"

Grossman stared, his tiny, pig-like eyes bewildered.

"Growing? This giant—growing?"

"*Yes, Master. He is as yet a babe! This monster is less than two hours old....*"

CHAPTER V

The gunner said, "This yere now four-headed animule jest sorta wriggled its fur, like, an' presto! all of a sudden it ain't no beast a-tall, but a bird! Yessirree, jest as sure as I'm tellin' the gospel truth, it turned smack into a purple bird with six green wings an' a lavender tail—"

He stopped and aimed an accurate stream of Venusian *mekel*-juice at a hapless insect. The insect floundered helplessly. So did Rocky Russell—inwardly—with his desire to laugh out loud. But he restrained himself, nodding his head sagely as he jotted a transcript of the old trooper's narrative in his little black notebook.

At his side, Lynn Graham protested, "Oh, Gunner, but *really*! I mean you must be mistaken! Animals simply don't turn into birds and fly away—"

"This un did!" swore Gunner solemnly. "Hope to drop dead in my—I mean, cross my heart! An' that ain't all the curious sights I seen in my life, neither. If the Puffessor would like to hear another little story—"

"I'm sure," said Rocky primly, "it would be most interesting. But I hate to trouble you—"

"No trouble, Puffessor. No trouble a-tall. 'Course my throat is gettin' a mite dry-like from talkin' so much. I might could use a sip o' water ... or mebbe a drap o' likker to sorta loosen my tongue—"

Rocky dug deep, and a coin passed between him and his informant. "Please allow me, Gunner. And many thanks. We'll have another little chat soon. I'm afraid I must be running along now, though."

Followed by his two companions, he climbed from the pill-box embrasure in which he had been interviewing the not-too-reliable old Patrolman.

* * * *

Two days had passed since "Dr. Roswell" and his aide had taken up residence in the Base. In that time, Rocky had wandered much, talked much, and learned much. Slowly he was beginning to gather that accumulation of facts which, he hoped and believed, would ultimately bring the weight of the Law to bear on Factor Humboldt Grossman.

Exactly what Grossman's racket was, he *still* didn't know. But from various and sundry sources he had heard tales of the fat man's greed and cunning, his autocratic domination over a number of the lower-class Titanians. In his own small way, and to those rebels he had gathered about him, Humboldt Grossman was emperor of New Boston. It remained to be proven whether or not he could extend his control to embrace the whole of the satellite.

Emerging from the sunken gunnery pit, the trio found themselves upon one of the metal highways which criss-crossed the little world.

To their left lay the squat, grim rows of structures which comprised Fort Beausejour, the Solar Space Patrol base on Titan. Barracks, administration and ordnance headquarters, messhalls, dumps and depots mingled in gray heterogeneity behind a strong defense-in-depth calculated to withstand months of siege or any known form of military attack.

To their right, several miles distant at the far end of the highway, lay the city of New Boston. It was a strange city, a curious commingling of ancient and modern, savage and cultured, alien and civilized. It boasted two tremendous skyscrapers of ultramodern design constructed by Earth colonists, but about and around these, clustered like mud-daubers' nests, clung rows upon rows, thousands upon countless thousands, of tiny, dingy, one-story hovels ... the dwellings of the natives.

It was into this city Rocky Russell's investigations now led him. He glanced at his wrist chronometer.

"Bless my soul! Very nearly time for my appointment with Factor Grossman. You are sure we can use a roller, Miss Graham?"

"Positive," answered the girl cheerfully. "I asked Daddy yesterday. You wait here; I'll get it and come back."

She moved away, giving the two S.I.D. men their first moment of privacy in hours. Bud Mulligan sighed and fumbled for a cigarette.

"So we're really gonna get to see Grossman at last? Good! How'd he sound when you audioed him for an interview?"

"Friendly enough," answered Rocky. "He said he was very busy, but he'd be glad to give me a few minutes."

"Did he know what you wanted?"

Rocky grinned a slow, lopsided grin. "Everybody on Titan knows by now," he drawled, "that there's a myth-chasing crackpot roaming loose. I'm Public Joke No. One. Which suits me just fine."

"Yeah," snorted Bud disgustedly, "but when this job's done, I'm gonna backtrack and do a little plain and fancy nose-punchin'! Like that old spacerat we talked to a few minutes ago—did you ever hear such lyin' in your life? A bird with purple wings an'—"

"Cheer up!" chuckled Rocky. "Gunner thought he was giving me the runaround, and for a generally unimaginative old codger he didn't do such a bad job of yarn spinning. He'd be surprised to learn, though, that his wild story is not half so fantastic as some of the honest tales I've heard since I began this masquerade."

Bud nodded grudgingly.

"That's true enough. An', boy, I really got to hand it to you. You talk that Doctor-o'-Mythology patter like you really *was* one. Sometimes you sound like you really believed in it yourself!"

"And the funny part of it is," said Rocky, "I almost *do*! As for talking the patter ... well, no wonder! I studied comparative mythologies for three solid months under the best experts in the field before I undertook this job, Bud. I know more about hamadryads and demigods and winged horses than old man Bulfinch himself! Well—" He nodded significantly, and his voice lifted to the high-pitched tones of "Dr. Rockingham Roswell"—"here comes Lynn. Off we go!"

Bud shot a swift, appraising glance at him. "Oh-ho! So it's 'Lynn', now, eh?"

Fortunately, Rocky Russell did not have time to concoct an alibi for that slip of the tongue. Because the roller was drawing up beside them, Lynn was motioning them in. And in a few minutes they were on their way to New Boston.

* * * *

"You understand," said Factor Grossman, "I have never *seen* this creature myself, Dr. Roswell. I am merely repeating the description given me by some of my friends."

Rocky nodded, busily jotting in his ubiquitous black notebook the facts just told him by the fat man. "A furry animal," he repeated, "with the netherparts of a horse and the torso of a human. Two curly black horns ... cloven hoofs ... is occasionally glimpsed in damp, woodland dells ... excellent!"

He looked up, smiling. "Very interesting, sir. You have perhaps already noted the similarity between this ... er ... thing and the 'Centaur' of Greek mythology? Amazing, isn't it, that we should find the same ... er ... legendary monster on two worlds separated by so many millions of miles? Well, we must organize an expedition to search for this creature. Now, have you any other fables to add to my little collection?"

He poised his pencil expectantly, his eyes vaguely eager and excited.

"We-e-ell, let me see—" Grossman stroked a sleek, fleshy jaw—"I heard one the other day about—Yes? What is it, Grushl?"

A Titanian had pressed open the door of the factor's private office. He glanced at the guests nervously.

"If you please, sir—the Thing-that-Grows! It has broken its—"

"*That will do!*" Grossman's voice crackled like the snap of a bulldozer's whip. He rose hastily, bowed apology to his visitors. "If you will excuse me a moment—"

He strode to the door, propelled his underling out of sight and hearing. The three guests stared after him in astonishment.

"Well!" exclaimed Lynn Graham. "Whatever came over him so quickly? Why, he turned positively pale!"

"You're telling me?" grunted Bud. "He looked like he seen his grandmother's ghost ... or his own. What did that guy say? 'Thing-that-Grows'? What would *that* be? And what would it break?"

"Shhh!" warned Rocky. "He's coming back.... Ah, there Factor! Everything all right?"

* * * *

Grossman had been gone but a few seconds, but in that time a change had come over him. His eyes were dark with ... Rocky could not tell just what. Excitement? Or fear? A thin film of perspiration overspread his cheeks, his forehead, his upper lip. He tried to put reassurance into his voice, but the effort didn't quite jell.

"Quite all right, Doctor. A little trouble with ... with a small horticultural experiment we are conducting. But I'm afraid I must ask you to leave now. I have work to do."

Rocky said, "If I ... er ... can be of any help—?"

"No. Thank you very much, but this is work of an ... er ... experimental nature. Company business, you know." The Factor bustled them to the door. "We will meet again. Good afternoon."

And almost before they had stammered their confused farewells, he had waved to them and lumbered off.

"Well!" said Lynn. "I must say that's the quickest brush-off I ever got ... if not the smoothest."

"Horticultural experiment," mused Rocky. "Mmm-hmmm! It's possible, of course, but ... I wonder. Bud ... er ... I mean, Ambrose—"

"Yeah?" said Ambrose.

"I think I'll stay here in New Boston for a few more hours. I'd like to ... er ... study the native quarters. Perhaps you would be kind enough to escort Miss Graham back to the Fort?"

"Certainly," nodded Bud. "A pleasure. But—"

Lynn Graham had been staring from one to the other of the two men querulously. Now she declared herself. "Oh, no!" she stated flatly. "You don't get rid of *me* so easily as all that. Doctor Roswell—just what's going on here?"

Rocky fumbled for his glasses.

"Er ... going on, Miss Graham? I don't understand—"

"Neither do I—which is just why I'm asking. First Grossman goes into a mild panic; now you two are acting like the masked strangers in Act Two. Not to mention the fact—" the girl pointed out shrewdly—"that for a few minutes you quite forgot to talk like a college professor ... and addressed your alleged 'valet' as 'Bud'—"

Rocky did remove his glasses. But this time he did not breathe on them, wipe them, and replace them as was the habit of "Dr. Roswell." Instead, he shoved them out of sight, and grinned at the girl. When he spoke it was in his natural voice.

"All right, Miss Lynn," he said, "you win. I pulled a boner. Now I might as well come clean. I am not Doctor Rockingham Roswell at all. My name is Russell ... Rocky Russell ... and I'm here on Titan to—"

But not at that moment did he tell Lynn Graham who he was, and his purpose on the satellite. For suddenly he paused in midsentence, his jaw dropping open, and his eyes widening to match.

"Lord!" he gasped. "Look ... look at *that!*"

The others, too, had turned to determine the origin of the rumbling sound. Now they saw it. A tremendous motor-roller trundling down the main thoroughfare of New Boston. A heavy roller bearing a ponderous burden ... a single, gigantic item. The appearance and purpose of this item was unmistakable, but its size....

"Manacles!" croaked Bud. "But ... but who ever heard of manacles that size! *That Thing is twenty feet in circumference!*"

CHAPTER VI

Humboldt Grossman entered the cavern cautiously. It was dark in there, but not altogether dark. The ever-present luminescence of the chamber walls lent an eerie glow by which could be seen the giant figure huddled at the far end. There had been bonds upon the wrists and ankles of this figure, but now the frayed ends of snapped hawsers dangled loosely as the creature pawed fretfully at adamant walls and ceiling.

At sight of the monster, Grossman faltered, stunned. To the Titanian behind him he choked hoarsely, "He—he still grows!"

"Yes, Master. Already he must crouch to avoid being crushed by the cavern's roof. Each hour he grows faster. In a day ... half a day ... perhaps less ... he will die in here if we do not let him out."

Grossman smiled. It was not a pleasant smile.

"Have no fear. Before that time, he will be outside—under my control!" He stepped forward into the cave. The creature's eyes turned questioningly toward this tiny mote of life which dared approach him thus, stretched forth a hand to crush the annoying insect. But from a curiously-shapen tube in the insect's claw leaped a lancet of flame. A gout of red agony that scorched and blistered his palm. The giant howled and pulled his hand away. Grossman smiled. Good! Who holds an adversary in fear of pain possesses a slave. Now, if only the creature were telepathic—"You!" he thought, his thought directed and intensified by the menavisal unit in his helmet, "have you intelligence? Can you understand me?"

The giant's answer came back sluggishly.

"*I can ... understand.*"

"That is well. Then listen to me, and mark well my words. I am Master here. Do you acknowledge that?"

The creature stirred restlessly. "Master? I accept no Master. I am Master of mine own will."

Grossman pressed the grip of his Haemholtz. A flash of livid lightning seared the subterranean chamber. Grossman challenged, "You defy the Master of the fire-that-bites?"

The giant cringed against the farthest wall. "Nay!" he conceded. "You are Master. I am your servant."

"It is well you understand. For there is work to be done. When it is accomplished, then you will be freed. Hear now, huge one, what is expected of you...."

CHAPTER VII

"Manacles!" repeated Rocky Russell, "Manacles twenty feet in circumference! But that—that's impossible! Handcuffs for a normal six-foot man measure about six *inches* in circumference. Twenty foot manacles would be used on someone *two hundred and forty feet tall*!"

"Always assuming of course," Lynn pointed out, "that these gyves are to be used on a *man*. Which isn't very likely. Much more possible that they were constructed for some beast ... some tremendous animal—"

"True," admitted Rocky. "But even so—imagine the size of that animal! Well, that settles it. Bud, I want you to take Miss Graham back to the fort immediately."

"And you?"

"I'm going to follow that roller."

"But there may be danger—"

"There undoubtedly *is* danger," replied Rocky grimly, "directed at the Patrol ... perhaps the whole of Titan. Those manacles are somehow associated with Grossman's secret. I've got to learn how. You can help best by racing back to Beausejour and warning Colonel Graham to be on guard against any eventuality. Keep your portable vocoder tuned to our private wave-length. If and when I learn anything important I'll send it on to you. O.Q.?"

Bud shrugged helplessly.

"You're the boss. But I'd rather stay here with you and—"

"Get going! Oh—when you reach the Base, take off the lid. Tell Colonel Graham who we are."

"And if it's not too much trouble," interrupted Lynn Graham, "would you mind telling me *now*?"

Rocky grinned at her, for the last time using Dr. Roswell's high whine, "Oh, mercy, Miss Graham, you mustn't be impatient. Ambrose will tell you as you ride."

"*Ambrose!*" fumed Bud. "Ambrose be damned—!" But he was talking to empty space. Rocky had already disappeared down the avenue after the gyve-laden roller.

Fortunately the roller, groaning under its ponderous burden, was not moving very fast. Rocky, though on foot, was able to keep it within sight without too obviously appearing to be following it. In the character of Dr. Rockingham Roswell, already known and amusing to the Titanians, he dawdled through the city five hundred yards or so in the wake of the burdened vehicle.

Through business streets he followed it, where eyes turned to follow its passage and furtive Titanians whispered to each other behind concealing palms, and—as the squalid little shops thinned out—into the suburban residential districts ... finally quite out of the city proper.

Out here it was practically impossible to follow the truck without being noticed. Once the city's artificial foliage was left behind, the landscape of Titan's countryside stretched stark and severe so far as the eye could see ... its drab, sandy monotony broken only by an occasional dune, its dull sameness embellished only by the silvery span of roadbed upon which humans must travel to live on Titan.

By dropping far behind the roller, Rocky was able to keep it in sight for a little while longer. But then his efforts came suddenly to naught as the driver of the truck—a Titanian—swerved completely off the lead highway and began rolling across the barren desert toward a hummock outlined on the horizon some miles distant.

* * * *

Lacking a bulger, Rocky was stopped cold. No way to follow, now. But he waited and watched a while longer to assure himself that the swollen rise of ground *was* the roller's destination, then strolled back into New Boston.

Here he sought the privacy of a 'fresher, and called Bud on the vocoder. Mulligan answered immediately.

"Yeah, Rocky? Everything all right?"

"Everything's all *wrong*! The confounded roller left the highway and plowed across the gray-and-nasty. Having no desire to be cooked into frizzled beef, I gave up the chase."

"That's tough, Chief. What do we do now?"

"I," said Rocky, "stay right here. You load a couple of bulgers in a roller and come charging back here as fast as you can. I *still* want to find out what Grossman's hiding in those hills that needs to be tied up with twenty-foot bands of forged steel."

"O.Q." said Bud. "Sit tight. I'll pick you up in three shakes."

"Make it two!"

"One," chuckled Bud. "I'm practically on my way now."

He was as good as his word. Rocky had only finished one cigarette when a blue S.S.P. roller came tearing up the highway from Fort Beausejour. Bud jumped out, bulger-clad and carrying a second protective suit for his comrade.

"Here you are, pal. Where do we go from here?"

"Out of town on the east highway. I'll show you. A hill rising out of— Hey, wait a minute! Who's driving this crate?"

Bud looked embarrassed.

"Oh—she is!"

"She?"

"Miss Graham. She—"

"—refused," chimed in Lynn Graham, "to be left out of it. Indeed I did. Captain Russell, you ought to be ashamed of yourself, deceiving us the way you did. When the Sergeant, here, told me who you *really* were, and what you were doing here, I almost *died* with excitement! And to think that you, a Captain in the S.I.D., pretended to be a mythologist! It's the funniest thing—"

"Miss Graham," interrupted Rocky impatiently, "there is nothing at all amusing about the job we are engaged in. It is, moreover, no work in which a girl should be involved. You would oblige me by returning to the Fort on the first transport bus—"

"Oh, no! This is a Patrol roller, and I requisitioned it in my own name. Either I drive it or—" Stubbornly—"or it doesn't roll!"

"Very well, then. You may take us as far as the desert path. But there we leave you. And now, let's get going. We have wasted enough time as it is."

Rocky motioned Bud into the roller. A few seconds later they were speeding noiselessly out on the highway toward the spot where Rocky had seen the truck leave the road.

* * * *

Russell had been keeping an eye on his chronometer for the past little while, estimating the number of daylight minutes left to him. On this little satellite there was no such thing as dusk or twilight. At ninety million miles from Sol, there was little enough sunlight. Titan's main radiance came not from the Sun, but from its own parent planet which, a huge, shining platter in the sky, gathered up and reflected to its tiny satellite the thin illumination from afar ... for all the world like a gigantic, reflecting mirror.

Titan revolved on its axis in fifteen hours, twenty-three minutes. Almost the whole of its day period had elapsed now. Shortly....

Yes, even as he studied out the problem, night came suddenly and completely to this part of Titan. It descended instantaneously, snuffing out the light as a finger presses the wick of a candle. Only the stars remained, glowing white in the rich, jet vastness of outer space.

The girl reached toward the dashboard instinctively, but Rocky's hand clasped about her wrist.

"No! Don't!"

"But—but I was only going to turn on the lights."

"I know. But you mustn't. We're getting very close to the spot now. Can you see to drive without them?"

"Why, I—I guess so," said Lynn dubiously. She was surprised, herself, to learn that she could. "Why, yes! The road stands out like a dark ribbon against the sands on either side. Isn't that strange?"

"Not so strange at that," grunted Rocky. "I'm beginning to get an idea about the mysterious T-radiation of this planet. I may be completely wrong, of course, but so far my theory fits all the facts I've observed. There's something I would like to know, though. Grossman told us the soil killed humans. I wonder *how* they die?"

"I can answer that. Daddy told me the first day I was here. He was warning me against ever leaving the shielded areas ... the Fort, the city, the roads. He said that if they wander onto the soil of Titan without protection, humans just shrivel up and crumble into dust like—like mummies!"

"Like mummies, eh!" grunted Rocky. He sounded quite well satisfied. "Mmm-hmm! Then *that* fits, too. Yes, I think I'm beginning to understand a lot of things ... including the reason Factor Grossman would like to rid this little world of all competitors—"

"Well, don't keep secrets!" snapped Bud. "We'd like to know, too. What's it all about?"

"No time now. There's the hill out yonder. Pull up here, Miss Lynn. Here's where we leave you."

Lynn stopped the roller obediently. But as Bud and Rocky climbed out she asked, "What do you want me to do now? Can't I come with you?"

"No. You turn the roller around and wait here. We have no idea what we're going to buck up against. We may have to retreat—suddenly. If so, I'll fire three blasts on my Haemholtz. Two short, one long. If you see that signal, get ready to start moving. We'll come on the double-quick. But if we're being pursued too closely to make it—"

"Yes?"

"Then don't wait for us!" ordered Rocky.

"Head for the Base and bring the Patrolmen. Understand?"

"All but one thing," complained the girl. "Why not send for a platoon of Patrolmen right now? Why wait until it is too late?"

"Because," explained Rocky patiently, "despite our suspicions, we have as yet no actual *proof* that the factor is involved in anything shady. The Patrol is an organization sworn to maintain the Law, not to violate it, riding roughshod over the rights and privileges of citizens.

"When we are certain—as I fully expect we shall be shortly—that Grossman is implicated in some illegal scheme *then* we can call in the Patrol. But until that time—"

"Until that time," broke in an oily, taunting voice, "you will play the part of quixotic fools, eh, my dear Doctor? But has it never occurred to you that by the time you get the proof you want ... it may be too late to summon help?"

Rocky whirled, as did his two companions. From the side of the road, where they had lain in dark concealment behind a low escarpment, rose a circle of shadowy figures. The largest of these, a heavy man looming even greater in his protective bulger, approached them. In his left hand he held a flash; its rays glinted upon still another instrument in his right hand ... the tube of a Haemholtz burner held steadily upon them. All recognized the newcomer's voice at once.

"*Grossman!*"

CHAPTER VIII

In the gloom, Grossman's features could not be seen behind the quartzite view-pane of his bulger, but by the thick satisfaction in his voice, Rocky could guess the complacent smirk lingering on his over-red lips.

"Yes, my friends," he acknowledged, "Grossman. This is somewhat of a reversal, no? The one you came to apprehend has captured you. My dear Doctor Roswell, did you consider me a perfect fool? Did you not know the driver of my roller would report to me that you had followed him to this spot?"

Rocky said levelly, "Not 'Doctor Roswell,' Grossman. My name is Russell. Captain Russell of the S.I.D. And it is my duty to advise you that you stand self-convicted of armed assault upon the persons of legal officers engaged in the performance of their duties. Anything you say may later be used against you."

Grossman laughed.

"My soul, Captain, you *are* a cool one! Not the same man at all as the learned doctor who was afraid of firearms! It is too bad you have blundered into this situation. I rather admire your effrontery. We could have been friends, I think."

"The question," said Rocky dryly, "is open to argument."

Lynn Graham bridled, "This is all very high-handed, Mister Grossman, and very mysterious. What is all this talk of 'capturing' someone? What do you intend to do with us?"

Grossman said soothingly, "Have no fear, Miss Graham, you will come to no harm. But I fear that for the present I shall be compelled to take you into—well, shall we call it, 'protective custody'? You see, I have—ah—*certain plans*. It would not do for these plans to be overthrown at the final moment. Therefore, I must request you to be my guests until I have succeeded in gaining my objective—"

"Which is," interrupted Rocky harshly, "complete control of Titan?"

"Exactly, Captain Russell."

"And its wealth."

"And its—" Grossman stopped abruptly, the tone of his voice altering. "Ah! Then you know?"

"Enough," said Russell. "Enough to warn you, Grossman, that it won't work. This isn't the first time, you know, that an individual has tried to discard interplanetary law and seize control of some rich plum. The penal colonies are full of ambitious men like yourself who thought they could defy the Space Control. But it won't work, Grossman. No man, or group of men, wields sufficient power to defeat the forces of justice and order—"

Grossman chuckled again, this time delightedly.

"You know a little, Captain—yes. But not enough! Titan will be mine—and soon!—because I have found an ally powerful enough to win me my demands. You doubt? Very well, you shall see for yourself. Come!"

He spun to his little coterie of followers, snapped commands in the strange, guttural tongue of Titan. The oddly assorted creatures, some humanoid in form, some frighteningly animalistic, formed a rough guard about Rocky and Bud. Grossman hesitated before Lynn.

"You have no protective suit? That is unfortunate. It would, of course, be fatal for you to accompany us across the sands without one. Yet I cannot permit you to go free—Grushl!"

"Yes, Master?"

"Take the girl to my office building in the city and keep her there until I come. She must not escape, nor may she communicate with any other humans. You understand?"

"Yes, Master."

"Very well. Take her away. And now, gentlemen, if you are quite ready—Forward, march!"

The Titanians behind Bud and Rocky prodded. Helpless in the face of vastly superior odds, the two S.I.D. men stumbled forward off the highway and across the rough desert, toward the hill dully gleaming a short distance away.

* * * *

Seated at the controls of the tiny roller, Lynn Graham was thinking furiously as she drove. Obviously there was no chance of escaping so long as that flabby-fleshed parody of manhood crouched behind her with a Haemholtz leveled on the small of her back. Yet somehow she must get away ... get to the Fort and bring the Patrol....

Guile, that was her only chance. Take advantage of the slow-thinking Titanian's inferior mentality. She turned and smiled back over her shoulder.

"Have you ever been to the Patrol Base before?" she asked pleasantly.

Grushl answered mechanically, "Yes. Many times—" Then the implication of her words penetrated his brute brain. "Before? But we are not going to the Patrol Base."

"Maybe," retorted Lynn airily, "*you're* not, but *I* am. Just as fast as this roller will carry me."

Grushl's heavy brows gathered in perplexity.

"But, no! You are to drive to the office building, there await the Master."

Lynn laughed. "What nonsense! So long as I am the driver of this roller, I will take it where I wish."

"Then," said Grushl thoughtfully, "I will be forced to shoot you. You must not escape."

"But you can't do that," Lynn pointed out shrewdly. "Factor Grossman said nothing about shooting me. He ordered that I was to be kept safely until he came."

"Yes," pondered the Titanian, "that is true. But I see no other way to—"

"I am afraid you will have to let me drive to Fort Beausejour. So long as I am driving, there is nothing you can do to prevent me taking the roller where I wish."

Grushl, who had been wrestling laboriously with the problem, now suddenly saw the light. His deepset eyes brightened. "Oh, no! There is another way!" he cried triumphantly. "*I* will drive the roller!"

"B-but—" cried Lynn.

"That is the solution. Stop the roller. You and I will change places. I will drive; you will move back here."

Obediently, Lynn drew the car to a halt, slipped from the driver's cubicle as the Titanian moved from the rear seat to take her place. Grushl smiled at her complacently. "You see?" he boasted. "It is really very simple. Now I can stop the roller wherever I wish. The Master will be obeyed." He reached for the controls laying his Haemholtz on the cushion beside him as he did so. That was what Lynn had been waiting for. In one sudden motion she leaned forward, scooped up the weapon.

"Sorry, Grushl!" she cried. "But it's you or me—"

She slashed the tube down hard upon the Titanian's scalp. Grushl groaned once, heavily—and sagged. His hands, falling away, dragged at the steering control-stick. In an instant the car jerked into convulsive motion, charged toward the edge of the road.

Lynn screamed and tugged at the door beside her. In a moment more she would have been carried out across the deadly sands without a shield of any sort. But just as the roller left the road, the girl threw herself through the door ... fell sprawling on the edge of the roadbed.

The roller bounced out fifty ... a hundred ... two hundred yards into the desert-land ... then stalled. It lay there, a dark form dimly outlined against the thin iridescence of the soil, a silent vehicle bearing a single, unconscious occupant.

Lynn Graham stared at it dolefully for a few moments. Then, because there was no use crying over spilt milk—or lost means of transportation—she turned and hurried toward the city as quickly as possible ... afoot.

* * * *

As they approached the hill in the darkness, the two S.I.D. men were aware of much activity going on around them. They heard the cries of foremen, the grunts of laborers, the chuff-chuff of old-fashioned combustion engines, and the high, shrill whining of a single highpowered atomotor.

Rocky glanced at the New Boston factor inquisitively.

"Mining, Grossman—already?"

Grossman chuckled.

"Mining, yes. But not for what you think. Before we mine for wealth, we must mine for power."

"Mine for power?"

"You shall see in a moment what I mean." Grossman motioned one of his native aides to him. "Ho, there! He is secure? The mighty one is shackled as I commanded?"

"Yes, O Master. He is bound wrist and ankle."

"Good! And the excavation?"

"Proceeds on schedule, Master. By dawn it should be finished."

"That is well. For if he still grows—"

"He does, O Master!"

"—dawn will be none too soon. The cavern will no longer hold him."

Bud whispered to his friend and superior, "Say, what goes on here? What are they talking about?"

"If I'm not greatly mistaken," answered Rocky, "the thing for which those manacles were made."

Verification of his guess came almost immediately. Again their guards prodded them forward, and behind Grossman they entered a passageway dipping into the side of the hill. Through an ancient tunnel, damp and malodorous, they marched, debouching finally into a gigantic cavern ... a huge bubble of emptiness blown into the solid rock in some forgotten geologic age of change.

And there at last before them stood....

No ... it did not stand. There was no longer room for it to stand upright in an underground cavern whose roof was but three hundred feet high. It crouched. It knelt upon all fours like a great, mute beast; knelt and stared with dumbly questioning eyes at the tiny motes now entering its lair to look upon it.

It had been secured, as the Titanian had said, with great metal manacles, from the welded joints of which stretched mighty chains so huge that a man might walk upright through a single loop. Its wrists were also gyved, and a length of chain swung between the two.

But it made no effort to fight these bonds. It just crouched there in the strange semi-gloom, watching with pale-gleaming eyes the movements of its self-proclaimed Master.

Subconsciously Rocky Russell had been expecting just some such revelation as this. Even so, it was one case where realization of an idea far surpassed speculation. A gasp of sheer astonishment wrenched itself from his lips; he stared at the giant with shocked incredulity.

"Colossus!" he choked. "Lord—the Colossus himself, come to life! Grossman, where did you find this—?"

Grossman smiled urbanely.

"Not a bad name for him, Captain. Your brief period of masquerade as a mythologist apparently left some impression on you. Colossus—yes! But this time no brainless monster of brass. A living creature, intelligent and obedient to my commands. You, there!" He turned and addressed his slave, again utilizing the menavisal unit. "You know your orders? You know what must be done?"

The creature had telepathic power commensurate with its bulk. The mental answer came rolling into the brains of the Earthmen with almost audible force.

"*I know my orders. I know what must be done.*"

"And who is Master? Whose will must be obeyed?"

This, thought Rocky with swift distaste, was sheer braggadocio, and typical of Grossman. It was not necessary to bludgeon a servile answer out of the gigantic captive. He had already proven his point.

But if the question had been intended to elicit a humble deference, it failed in its purpose. For the Colossus did not answer. Instead, it continued to stare down at its accoster mutely, speculatively. Almost, thought Rocky, defiantly.

"Well?" repeated Grossman. "Who is Master here?"

And this time, whipping a tube from his holster, he accompanied the question with a rapier-like lash of fire that swept across the Colossus' hurriedly upraised palm. For at sight of the gun, at the crackle of the heat-beam, the giant had begun to stammer a hasty answer—

"*You, O Master! You are Master! You—*"

And then, as suddenly as it had begun—it stopped! And over its features spread a strange, strained look. What that expression meant, Rocky could not guess. It seemed to mirror surprise. Vast, pleased surprise. The giant lifted the palm across which Grossman's ray had swept and studied it with sluggish interest. It drew a finger of its other hand across what should be a badly burned piece of flesh ... and began smiling. It was an evil smile. There was no mirth in it. Just grim, savage exultation. And determination!

Then deliberately it reached forward—and attempted to grasp Grossman!

This time it was the Factor who fell back hurriedly. A cry burst from his lips, he pointed the Haemholtz at the giant and coldly, murderously, turned its ray to the maximum concentration. The air of the confined quarters seethed and crackled with blistering heat as the livid flame blasted its way to its target.

But the Colossus ... *laughed*!

It was the first time human ears had ever heard a sound from that inhuman throat. Nor did those who heard it ever want to hear it again. From those great, gaping lips towering yards above them peeled a deep-pitched torrent like the simultaneous rolling of a thousand summer thunders. It was a sound to batter, blast and deafen the eardrums. Were it not for the bulgers in which they were clad, the Earthen would in that moment have been stricken with instantaneous deafness. As it was, Rocky's ears rang fearsomely with the vibrations of the Colossus' laughter, muted, as the sound was, through his helmet diaphragm.

And Grossman's flame ... meant nothing. The Colossus ignored it as if it were a dancing sunbeam briefly flickering across his flesh. Again he stretched forth an avid, clutching hand....

Grossman screamed aloud in panic fear ... and ran! Into the narrow tunnel he darted, where that mighty hand could not follow and close about him. Through the tunnel, out and up from the depths of the underground cavern. Behind him ran the unguarded duo he had called his captives.

At the mouth of the tunnel, attracted by the tumult, were gathered a knot of Titanians. To these Grossman panted swift commands.

"The mouth of the tunnel ... close and block it immediately. The Colossus has gone mad. And the excavation, stop working on it!"

"But, Master ... it is almost finished!"

"All the worse! Fill it in again. He must not break free. He will destroy us all!" Grossman turned to Rocky and pawed at him beseechingly. "Russell, call the Base! Tell the Colonel to send men here ... guns! This creature—"

Russell said sternly, "Rather sudden change of heart, Grossman. A few short minutes ago the Colossus was your ally, the aide through whose efforts you were going to force the Patrol off Titan and gain sole possession for yourself."

"That doesn't matter now. I was ambitious ... yes. I had dreams of being a king, an emperor. You know why, Russell. You are a clever man. You guessed the reason for the T-radiation. But I did not dream, when the egg was hatched two days ago, that its occupant would continue to grow ... and *grow* ... and GROW!" Grossman's voice rose hysterically. "It is a madness from space, come to kill us all. I thought at first I could use It, bend It to my will. It was afraid of flame. But now It has grown too large, Its flesh too thick, to mind such puny weapons. It is strong, Russell ... inconceivably strong. It is practically invulnerable—"

Bud said, "But what you're doing ought to hold it in check. If you bury it alive ... don't feed it..."

"Feed it!" Grossman laughed mirthlessly. "It doesn't *need* feeding! Don't you understand ... it has never been fed a mouthful in its life!"

"Never been—!" Rocky stared at the shaking Factor. "But—but do you realize what that means? It does not eat—yet it continues to grow. From *somewhere* it must be deriving the nourishment to gorge its cells. From somewhere—"

"Rocky!" Bud's voice interrupted him suddenly. It was a voice cracked with terror and strain. "Rocky—quick! We've got to get out of here! Look! The earth! Quaking—"

His warning was superfluous. All present had experienced the trembling at the same time, a violent, insistent rocking of the soil beneath their feet. Now gaunt Titanians, panic-stricken, were fleeing in all directions. Grossman had stumbled and fallen to his knees. Rocky bent over him, lifted him by main force and howled into his ear,

"A roller, Grossman! You must have a private roller somewhere around here! Where is it?"

"O-over there!" The Factor pointed uncertainly at a gray bulk dim in the gloom.

"Then come on!" snapped Rocky. "We've got to get to New Boston!"

"N-new Boston? The city? But—but why? We want to get to the Patrol Base—"

"New Boston," Rocky grated, "first. That's where you sent Lynn Graham—remember? Gad! I didn't think he could do it! But he is! Start this roller, Grossman, and let's get out of here—quick! Look! The Colossus—"

The others stared, and a little whimper escaped Grossman's slack lips as he saw the final act of the drama which had begun with the trembling of the earth beneath them.

The thin iridescence of the hillside was seamed and cracked with a myriad of tiny black veins. The whole hummock quivered and trembled as though stricken with some petrologic ague. And then, suddenly, with a crash like that of rolling doom, the whole crown of the hill seemed to erupt explosively before them. Gigantic boulders ripped loose from ancient bedrock and raced wildly down tattered slopes. A myriad tiny fragments burst skyward, sifted down as a hail of deadly debris. There came the rending, tearing, grating sound of stone grinding against stone ... cacophonous background for the cries of maddened Titanians, the screech of roller motors roaring into action, the moans of injured and dying natives. Then—

Then Colossus burst from the womb of the hampering earth! Rose to stand upright in the prison he had outgrown. He shook himself, and detritus scattered about the terrified watchers. He raised a great palm, and with demoniac deliberation brought it squarely down upon a tiny band of huddled and terrified natives. When he lifted his palm again ... it dripped redly!

Rocky thrust the fumbling Grossman from the controls. "Move over! Let me at the stick—"

In a flash he had started the roller's motor, sent the speedster tearing headlong and recklessly across the broken desert flooring. Not a moment too soon. For the Colossus, having once shed blood, now swung into a literal orgy of savage destruction. Like a huge, brainless automaton he flailed the hillside about him clean of every moving thing ... beating with gigantic, steel-hard fists at anything and everything he saw, until that thing lay like a flattened pulp upon the ground.

And all the while horrendous laughter peeled incessantly from his contorted lips. Laughter which carried to New Boston, miles away; even to the Patrol Base beyond the city. Laughter which struck terror into the hearts of listeners who did not know as yet—happily!—whence it came, or the awful fate which lay in store for them.

For Colossus wearied, now, of lingering in his pit. He placed a palm on either side of the chasm he had opened for his escape, and vaulted easily to the surface. The enormous manacles with which his captors had hoped to hold him dangled uselessly. The ground shuddered beneath him. Where his feet met earth they forced depressions. Colossus was drawing sustenance, now, at ever-increasing speed from the soil which fed his odd, unnatural appetite. Already he was taller than New Boston's highest building. More than a quarter mile he towered into the air. And still he grew....

CHAPTER IX

Lynn Graham, plodding at long and weary last into the outskirts of the city, wondered again—with the vague, dull incuriosity which was the only emotion of which her exhausted brain was capable—what had been the meaning of those sounds she had heard from the desert wastes behind her a few hours ago.

It was all very mysterious ... mysterious and alarming. First had come the wails. Not wails, really, but dreadful, ear-splitting howls like the bellowing of some monstrous beast. Then out of the darkness behind her had come hurtling a small roller. A madly ricocheting vehicle without lights. She had attempted to signal the driver ... but in vain. As well try to hitch a ride on a runaway comet as on that speeding car.

And now? Now she was entering a city which ought to be asleep, but, instead, was seething with furious activity. Lights shone from the windows of buildings, shacks, stores. Crowds congregated at corners, huddled groups of frightened figures that looked astonishingly like mobs of refugees.

It was as though a mass-panic had seized the entire city. Earthmen gathered their families fearfully about them; Titanians scurried, slithered, hobbled in every direction in helter-skelter confusion. Vainly Lynn accosted passers-by in search of an explanation. Her queries were met with terror-numbed stares, with mumbles, with incomprehensible mouthings.

"We heard.... Danger approaching.... Someone said.... Must leave the city.... They told us.... Giant beast.... Death...."

Despairing of ever learning the truth from such informants, Lynn fought her way to a public audio booth. After a longer-than-usual wait, her call was put through. Over the selenoplate she stared into the worried eyes of her father.

A prayer of relief and gratitude escaped the Colonel as he recognized his caller.

"Lynn! Thank the Lord you're safe! I've been worried sick about you. And so has that young doctor—"

"Rocky? You mean he and Bud escaped? They're with you at the base?"

"Roswell—I mean *Russell*—is. Mulligan has gone out with the Fleet on scout patrol."

"F-fleet?" stammered Lynn. "Scout patrol? Daddy—what *is* this all about? I seem to be the only person on this world who doesn't know what's wrong—"

A voice at the other end of the wire said politely, "May I, sir?"—and Colonel Graham's face faded back to be replaced by the grave, sharp-lined features of the young S.I.D. captain. "Lynn—" he began, and even in that tense moment Lynn Graham found time to wonder that he had dropped all pretense of formality—"Lynn, we are all in the gravest peril. Colossus has broken loose!"

"Co-colossus?"

"The *Thing* for which those manacles were forged. It turned out to be a giant humanoid. Bud and I saw it. It was more than a thousand feet tall when it escaped Grossman. Now it has more than doubled that height!"

Lynn gasped.

"But—but where is it?"

"After it broke from its underground cell it headed west. For almost seven hours it has been roaming the planet wildly and at will. It completely destroyed the mining-town of Hawesbury and the villages of Placer and Dry Ditch."

"But aren't we doing anything to stop it? It must be destroyed—"

"Three flights are out looking for it. Two haven't been able to contact it at all ... the third is unreported. We fear that flight ... found it!" Russell's voice was more sober than ever. "Lynn ... our weapons seem to be useless against it. Its skin is incredibly tough, hard, resistant. Heat does not bother it, and our heaviest HE shells are like pebbles upon a hippo's hide."

"But there must be *some* way—"

"There has *got* to be some way," nodded Russell, "for if we don't find it ... and soon ... Titan will be a dead world, peopled by a single, monstrous entity. Now—" He abandoned explanations for a more immediate problem—"you stand tight. I'm coming to New Boston to get you."

"Oh, that's not necessary. I'll hire a transport."

"There's no such thing. The road between here and the city is and has been thronged with refugees for hours. I don't believe there's a commercial roller left in the city. Because, you see—"

"Yes?" pressed Lynn as he hesitated.

"Never mind. I'll be right there for you."

"You were going to tell me something, Rocky. What?"

"Well," said Rocky reluctantly, "I guess you'd better know. According to the seismograph, Colossus has almost completed his circumambulation of Titan ... and is on his way back toward New Boston. You must be very,

very careful. And now, good-bye! See you later!"

The circuit faded, and he was gone. Lynn stood for a moment thinking swiftly. Then she decided. Better to *do* something than to just sit waiting ... waiting ... waiting ... in a city gone mad with fear. She would start toward the Base *now*, meet Rocky on the way.

Having made her decision, she turned quickly and took her place in the jostling throng pressing southward....

* * * *

Rocky, moving north on the New Boston safeway, as he wormed his roller through the ever-thickening mass of panicky Titanians and terrified Earth colonists rushing to the safety of the Base was once again—for perhaps the hundredth time—trying to grasp that elusive half-thought which had lurked in the back of his brain ever since Colossus had broken free.

Something Grossman had said—Grossman who now cowered in a Patrol cell, far from the haughty, autocratic figure he had pretended to be—had brushed a spark in Rocky's mind. But now that spark had dulled, and Rocky could not recapture it. It had something to do with Colossus ... it suggested some means of combating....

"*Damnation!*"

The hordes of refugees had been parting like a flesh sea before him ever since he left the Fort gates. But now the numbers were becoming so great that he could not move the roller through them except at a crawl. He realized this, and gave up the unequal struggle. He called an Earthman to him.

"Here, you—can you drive a roller?"

"Yes, indeed, sir!"

"Then take this back to Colonel Graham at the Fort. Tell him Captain Russell is going ahead on foot."

The colonist stared at him strikingly. "You—do you mean you're going back toward the city, sir? But you can't do that! It—it's suicide. They say a huge monster, ten miles tall, is coming to smash the city to pieces—"

Rocky said tightly, "Never mind that now. You give my message to the Commandant—*understand*?" And he climbed from the car and forced his way against the tide, northward on foot.

It was as he was pressing along that he thought of Bud Mulligan, who had gone out with "B" flight in an effort to find and destroy—or at least delay—Colossus. Thinking of Bud reminded him that they wore on their persons the means of constant communication. The chances were greatly against Bud's being on the beam, but it was worth a try. He took the miniature vocoder from his breast pocket and activated it on the secret S.I.D. wave-length. Vastly to his surprise, he got an immediate reply.

"O.Q., chief! Where in Tophet have you been? I've been buzzing you for the past hour and a half!"

Rocky signaled back, "Where are you, Bud?"

"Look north," ordered Bud, "and east ... about thirty thousand elevation. If you see five black dots in the sky, they ain't asterisks—they're us. Flight B, keeping an eye on the Mountain that Walks Like a Man."

"Then he—he's in sight?"

"How can you miss him? He's bigger than the landscape. Can't you see him yet?"

"No."

"Well, I'm afraid you will. He's heading your way now. Keep an eye on the horizon and—"

A sudden roar rose from the throngs swarming the safeway. It was a roar of fear, but deeper even than the note of fear was that of awe. Rocky, looking up from his vocoder swiftly, beheld two things simultaneously. First—the dawn of a new day. Saturn-rise, breaking swiftly, suddenly, over the horizon, brooming all shadows in its path immediately. And the second phenomenon—

* * * *

Colossus! Colossus rising over the horizon ... a head, then mighty neck, broad shoulders, naked torso ... rising from the other side of the world like a vast, bestial nightmare. A tremendous Colossus whose head was so far above the veiled cloudlets of Titan that from time to time he was forced to bob and weave in order to avoid collision with the "rogues," those tiny bits of cosmic debris escaped from Saturn's Ring which besprinkle space in the neighborhood of the girdled planet.

"Rocky!" Bud was chattering on the vocoder. "Rocky, what's the matter. CX, Rocky Russell. CX, Rocky Russell.... Are you all right, Rocky?"

Rocky answered slowly, "I'm all right, Bud. But I just saw him. We all just saw him. He—he's tremendous!"

"You're telling me? See them manacles? He's grown so big they've split in half ... right up the back! They look like the only reason they're hanging on is because they're imbedded in his flesh! And his height.... Whew! The navigator here just shot an estimate! Over six thousand feet, Rocky! Colossus is more than a mile high!"

Rocky said, "Keep on the beam, Bud, and don't mind if I don't answer you immediately. I'm fighting my way north on the safeway, hunting for Lynn. She's in New Boston—"

"New Boston!" Bud's voice was horror-stricken. "My Lord, no! She mustn't be, Rocky! That's where he's heading for right now. He can see it ... he's got a glint in his eye ... a blood-lust.... Oh, great gods of space.... Rocky!"

The voice died in a tiny wail.

Russell needed no explanation of his agonized words. For he, too, saw the climax of that frightful action. Colossus had climbed completely over the horizon, now. There was no doubt he had spotted the city. He seemed fascinated by its twin towers. Like a destructive child experimenting with some new toy he leaned over, gripped the spire of the nearest between a massive thumb and forefinger ... and snapped it off!

From the shard of stone and metal wherein a few desperate fugitives had taken refuge dropped tiny motes, tumbling hundreds of feet to certain, dreadful doom! Rocky could not hear their screams ... but he could imagine them. One of those black fragments *might* have been ... *could* have been....

He shook his head doggedly. No! He must not think of such things! Lynn still lived. *Must* live!

Then another sound burst so close to him that for a moment his tense nerves shrieked in agony. A mighty hissing roar ... the explosive blast of a rotor-gun going into action. Glancing to his right he found himself beside the very gun-embrasure wherein yesterday—("*Lord, only yesterday? Not a hundred thousand centuries ago?*")—a jovial gunner had told "Dr. Rockingham Roswell" fabulously genial tales of monstrous beasts. Could either of them have guessed that today....

"Gunner!" he cried.

The old warrior glanced up, identified him amongst the hordes of refugees. "Oh, you, Puffessor! Come on! I'm short-handed here. Crew didn't make it afore the attack. If you're still lookin' for fab'lus monsters, here's y'r chance to git some fust-hand experience—"

Rocky needed no second invitation. A terrible rage was upon him, now. Futile to attempt to any longer buck the mob to New Boston still more than three miles away. If Lynn had been in the city, neither he nor any man could help her now. The only thing he could do was ... avenge her....

He dropped into the pit, and swung instantly into action. "What do you need here? Oh—short a prime-loader, eh? All right, Gunner—" He spun toward the charge-rheo, jazzed its fill to max, slammed home the breech of the rotor, snapped, "O.Q. Charge set!"

"Range," said Gunner mechanically, "*Fire!*" The beam blasted away. Then, and only then, did the old fighter seem to realize what had happened. His leathery old face crinkled, and he stared at Rocky in bewilderment. "Hey, wait a minute! What's goin' on here? Puffessor, where did *you* ever learn to prime-load a Mallory rotor?"

"The same place," grunted Rocky, "you saw a purple bird with six green wings and a lavender tail! Stop loafing! Let's give that beast another bellyful. Charge set!"

"Range," said Gunner automatically, "*Fire!*" A slow grin overspread his face. "Comets! Looks like I pulled the wrong guy's leg, hey?"

* * * *

But not long did Rocky work with the gun-crew. Came another buzz from Milligan, aloft. And this time the S.I.D. sergeant's news was worse than ever before.

"It's no good, Rocky. Neither the groundfire nor our aerial blasts are having any effect on him. Heat-beams don't even make his muscles twitch, and as for physical ordnance—the shells don't even penetrate his hide."

Rocky cried, "But there has to be some way to stop him, Bud! He's practically on top of New Boston now. After that, he'll turn on the Patrol Base—"

"And crush us all out," conceded Bud dolefully, "like a bad kid stamping out an ant-heap. That's all we are to him. Just so many ants. No, there's only one way left. The Flight Leader has decided we've got to use ourselves as human shells, Rocky. Bullets won't harm him, but if we can smash these ships into some vulnerable spot ... his eyes ... perhaps we can kill him before we ... we...."

"*Wait!*" cried Rocky. "*Ants! That's it!* Not *ants*—but *Antaeus*! Bud, listen carefully! Those craft are equipped with repulsor beams?"

"Why—why, yes, but—"

"Then contact your Flight Leader immediately. Tell him these are orders. As an S.I.D. agent it is your privilege to take over any command in case of urgency. I want the three ships of your flight to turn on their repulsor beams to maximum strength—and bear down on the Colossus!"

"B—but, Rocky—"

"Do as I say!"

"Y—yeah, sure. But if they don't lift him?"

"Don't be an ass! Repulsors are used to move asteroids from tradelanes, aren't they? Colossus is huge, but no bigger than thousands of asteroids! They'll lift him off the face of this world!"

"And—and then?"

"Then we shall see," said Rocky grimly, "if I have saved us, or just given us a few minutes' grace. If I'm wrong, he'll fight his way free as soon as the repulsors wear down. But if I'm right—"

"Well?"

"I've got to be right! And now—get going!"

"Y—yessir!" gulped Bud obediently, and disconnected to contact the Flight Commander of the spacevessels.

Thus it was that a few moments later, as Rocky and Gunner lay in their pit watching hopefully, as the unceasing throngs continued to block the safeway, casting fearful looks back over their shoulders as they fled from one doomed place to another, that the five ships gathered together momentarily ... then separated ... then converged on the Colossus in a narrow V—their prows invisibly pouring repulsor radiation at the gigantic creature.

The reaction of Colossus was the only thing which assured Rocky his plan was being carried out. For the repulsor radiation was colorless. But as the ships neared Colossus, he bent, momentarily, at the middle as if he had suffered a surprise thrust in the belly or groin. Then an expression of anger crossed his features.

The ships were coming in beneath the protection of a cloud-bank, but Colossus spotted them. He flailed a whiplike arm at them as a pettish child might sweep at bothersome flies ... but to no avail. The speedy craft swirled away, but kept their prows pointed at his midriff.

Again Colossus struck at them, and smashed one. Then a new idea struck him. Reaching above his head, by sheer force he tugged from a satellitic course about Titan a rogue rock of tremendous size. A rock which must have been every bit of fifteen hundred feet in diameter, a shard of matter hewn into a perfect sphere by long ages in the Rings of Saturn.

This he clutched and aimed at the spacecraft. Let it be hurled upon them, Rocky knew, and in an instant every spark of life would be dashed from existence as the metal walls of the ships were beaten flat.

But the sphere was not hurled! It was the Colossus who gave way ... not the ships! The cumulative pressure of the repulsor beams caused him to yield, bend, stagger! He tried to regain his balance with a lurching stride forward ... and thus it was that the twin towers, pride of New Boston, were destroyed. Colossus' left foot descended crushingly upon the buildings ... and when it withdrew a moment later, a yawning hole gaped where had been city streets ... a hole partly filled with the crumbled masonry of the once-proud skyscrapers....

But Colossus staggered back one step ... and another ... and still another. Then one foot slipped into the air-*and did not descend*! After it went the other foot. And Colossus *was off the ground*! Off the ground and being pressed farther and farther out into space with every passing moment!

A great cheer ... a cheer which had in it half a sob ... rose from the safeway beside the gunnery-pit. Rocky Russell, glancing up at the hordes who had turned to behold this last-moment salvation, felt a moment of pain strike at his heart.

Saved! A world ... and all these ... saved. But the one most important person in this or any world....

And then he saw her! She had been fighting beside him in this very pit ... weary, disheveled, eyes haggard ... but still, to him, beautiful! And it could not have been mere coincidence that she saw him at the same moment. Their eyes met ... and no longer was there need for words. Both knew what the other was thinking ... both accepted the decisions of their hearts gladly. Without a word she turned and fled into the circle of his arms.

While up above, Bud Mulligan was signaling desperately, "Rocky! CX, Rocky Russell. Dammittahell, where are you? What do we do now? Our beams can't hold this mountain up here forever? What do you want us to—*Great guns of grief!*"

Colossus ... *dwindled*! Like a tinfoil effigy held over a flame, his tremendous bulk began to slough away. It did not fall off in chunks or clots. There was no destruction of his flesh, not horrid streams of blood flowing from open wounds. Colossus simply ... *disappeared*!

A mile-high roaring monster, pinned on invisible repulsor beams ... then a half-mile creature screaming in panic ... then a massive Thing a thousand ... five hundred ... fifty ... five ... two feet tall. Then a small, gray, shapeless wisp hanging like a shredded tatter in space ... a sudden, silent puff of flame ... then nothing....

So found its final resting place the Thing which came from afar. The Thing which, in accordance with the theories of a scientist It had never heard of, had journeyed through black space to spawn on a hospitable world.

So ended another of Nature's blind attempts to convey a life form from one galaxy to another. So ended—Colossus!

CHAPTER X

Afterwards, Bud Mulligan said solemnly, "if you didn't see it very plain from where you was, I ain't going to explain what it looked like. It was ... well, ugly. That's all. What *I want* to know is ... how did you know it would dry up and crumble away if we could lift it off the ground, Rocky?"

Russell grinned. He said, "I suppose you'd be highly chagrined to learn it was really you who gave me the idea?"

"Me?"

"Yes. When you mentioned 'ants'. The word reminded me of a dim thought I had been trying all day to recapture, without success. It reminded me of—Antaeus."

"Aunty *who*?"

"Antaeus. You'll find his story in the folk-tales of our mother planet, Earth. Hercules, while engaged on his famous 'Labors' met this giant in mortal combat. Antaeus was a son of Mother Earth, and from her he derived his tremendous strength. Each time Hercules felled him, he grew larger. At last the hero discovered Antaeus' secret, and overcame him by lifting him completely above his head. Antaeus then dwindled ... as did our own Colossus...."

"Comets!" gaped Bud. "That's exactly what happened? But why?"

"Because," explained his friend, "Colossus devoured not *food*, as we do—but *energy*! Raw, radiant energy. Titan not only fed him ... it gave him a *banquet*! The storage-battery which is this planet—"

"Eh?" interrupted Colonel Graham, startled. "What's that, Captain? Storage-battery?"

"Yes, Colonel. That is the secret of Titan, the secret Grossman learned and hoped to capitalize on after he had frightened or forced all other Earth-men ... including the Space Patrol ... off this globe.

"Titan is not simply a world ... it is a gigantic storage-battery! Its 'acid seas' and 'metallic mountains' are a parallel of the simple voltaic cell. The mysterious 'T-radiation' is nothing more nor less than constantly revers-ing polarity on a gigantic scale. Humans are destroyed by it for the same reason they die in an electric chair. Titanians can endure it because they are endowed with the physical characteristic of being 'poor conductors.'

"Colossus *fed* on this steady stream of current, and in him electrical energy transmuted into matter. How, we do not know ... nor will we ever, now ... unless some day another of Colossus' race is cast by the tides of time upon the shores of one of our solar planets...."

"Which," whispered Bud, "God forbid! Well, it just goes to show you, everything happens for the best, doesn't it? I mean, if you hadn't masquer-aded as a Doctor of Mythology so we could trap Grossman and shove him into clink, like he now is—"

"I might not have guessed," acknowledged Rocky, "the reason for Co-lossus' bulk. Yes, that's right. But speaking of myths—"

He turned to the girl.

"Oh, it's not *you* I want to ask, but your father. I would like to know, Colonel Graham ... have I permission to track down one final 'myth' as 'Dr. Roswell' ... and make her become 'Mrs.' Russell?"

Colonel Graham smiled. "Well, Captain—" he began.

But Bud interrupted him, groaning.

"Migawd, what a terrible pun! You had to stretch that one a mile, Rocky!"

It was then that Lynn Graham proved herself a suitable future wife in all respects. For she smiled gently, and:

"Well, why not, Bud?" she demanded. "According to the old adage ... 'A myth is as good as a mile'...."

DICTATOR OF TIME

Originally published in *Planet Stories*, Spring 1940.

CHAPTER I

Larry Wilson was going to miss his train. He swung from his cab at Philadelphia's Broad Street Station, glanced swiftly at his wrist-watch, tossed a bill in the general direction of the cabby, then dashed for the staircase that led to the train platform. His watch showed exactly 10:59. The New York express was scheduled to leave at eleven sharp.

Behind him, morning traffic made its customary din in the streets of the Quaker City. Automobile horns *whonked* belligerently. Radio loudspeakers blared from the doorways of tiny Market Street shops. A newsboy bellowed headlines on the European war situation. A bus chugged into the station, disgorged its cargo of human freight, lumbered ponderously on down the street. A vendor offered dried lavender; his whine was a thin, discordant note in the hum of a busy city.

But Larry Wilson, intent only on gaining the train platform above, did not notice these things. He brushed by a puffing matron at the foot of the stairs, steamed past a descending red-cap, and noticed with only casual interest as he took the steps three at a time a silken-clad calf before him. He might make it yet, he thought hopefully, if—

Then, suddenly, something was indefinably *wrong*!

Larry had ascended these stairs dozens of times in the past, both leisurely and, as now, at top speed. But at no time had they ever been like this! His stride faltered; then, even as the first, tiny fingers of wonderment plucked at his bewildered brain, he realized that the bright electric lights that limned the staircase had vanished. That in their place was a dull, unearthly, grayish glow that seemed to emanate equally from the walls, the staircase, and from the roof above him.

His foot, reaching for the next step, encountered no support. He staggered, thrown off balance, and stumbled forward to his hands and knees. Yet he was not bruised. As he fell he realized, with numb astonishment, that the steps were no longer there!

Wildly he scrambled to save himself. His shoulder collided with something fragrantly yielding. His outthrust hand clutched warm, firm flesh cased in sheer silk. Then he was falling helplessly, headlong, dizzily, down a dim tunnel of spinning grayness—and he was rolling over and over on a warm, grassy turf. The scent of flower-laden air was in his nostrils.

And a voice was saying indignantly, "Well, really! *If* you don't mind—!"

* * * *

In one hand Larry still clutched his bag. In the other—. He flushed, relaxed his grip in swift embarrassment. The girl was the one whom he had glimpsed before him on the steps of the Broad Street Station. It was her ankle that, in his moment of blind groping, his hand had clutched.

"I—I'm sorry!" gulped Larry. "I didn't mean to be—" Then he stopped, staring about him transfixed. "But what's this? Where the he—I mean, where in blazes are we?"

They were lying on a grassy plain horizoned by a forest of towering trees that reached aimlessly toward a wan and cloudless sky. The girl, her own blue eyes wide in astonishment, forgot her pique in amazement that matched his.

"I don't know. I was running for the train—"

"So was I. I saw you on the steps. Just then the staircase seemed to become strangely gray—"

"And it moved!" added the girl. "I remember now. Something like a *ripple* passed over it—"

"I didn't see that," admitted Larry. "I was too busy running. But—but where are we, anyway?"

A touch of panic flickered in the girl's eyes.

"We—we couldn't be dead?"

Larry shook his head. "I thought of that. But it isn't likely. Not both of us. One of us might have fallen down the steps and broken a neck—but not two, together. And there was no explosion or anything like that. I don't see—"

Suddenly the girl gasped, clutching his arm.

"Look! Over there in the trees!"

Larry looked—and moved swiftly. With a jerk, he ripped open his bag, pawed through its contents, and came up with a snub-nosed automatic.

"Get behind me!" he shouted. "I don't know what's going on here, but—"

"Don't shoot!" The girl's hands tightened swiftly about his wrist, dragged it down as he drew a careful bead on the towering beast that, from the edge of the grassy glen, surveyed the two through tiny, myopic eyes.

An incredible mountain of flesh it was. More than eighty feet long with a rubbery, elephantine hide that draped its ugly carcass in sinewy ripples. Its long neck, surmounted by a ridiculously minute head, twitched nervously from one side to the other as its inadequate nostrils strove to identify this strange, tantalizingly foreign scent.

As Larry watched spellbound, the gigantic monster broke into lumbering motion. Its huge feet created thunder as it crashed blindly through the forest, leaving in its wake a swath of broken young trees and trampled underbrush.

"It won't attack us," explained the girl in answer to Larry's questioning stare. "It's herbivorous. That is, if it's what I think it is. It was probably more frightened than we were. But how it ever got here, in *this* age—"

"For Pete's sake, what was it?"

The girl shook her head. "Unless," she answered slowly, "I've gone completely mad—and I may easily have done so—it was a brontosaurus! An ancient reptile of the Mesozoic Age. *The last one should have died over a hundred million years ago!*"

"Preposterous!" gasped Larry.

"I know it's preposterous. But we saw it. Which means—" The girl turned a puzzled face to him. "Do you know anything about Time?"

"Time?" Larry glanced at his watch. "Why, it's exactly 10:59. Say, that's funny! It was just 10:59 when I was running up those steps."

"I don't mean that kind of time. Though that may have something to do with it. I mean, do you know anything about the scientific theory of Time? For if our experience means anything ... if that really was a brontosaurus we saw ... and if your wrist-watch has stopped at 10:59...."

"Yes?" said Larry.

"Then," said the girl solemnly, "somehow or other you and I have experienced a temporal shift outside the ken of Earthly physics. We are lost in Time!"

"Neatly put, young lady!" said a quiet, approving voice. "Very neatly decided. I should not have expected such quick intelligence from one of your era."

Larry and the girl turned swiftly. Standing near them was a tiny man, no higher than Larry's shoulders. He wore a curious one-piece garment of woven metal fabric, on the belt or harness of which depended a host of studded instruments, pouches, and oddly shaped tools or ornaments.

Upon his overlarge, almost bulbous head was a sort of cap which completely covered his scalp and ears. Strange telescopic glasses, covering his bulging eyes, lent his face an elfin quality. There was a pleased smile on his lips—one which disclosed a pale, double ridge of cartilage in his upper and lower jaws where his teeth should have been. His face was smooth and hairless.

"Who," demanded Larry, "are you? And how did you get here?"

"You were so engrossed in the brontosaurus," said the diminutive stranger, "that you did not notice my approach. Permit me to introduce myself. I am Harg-Ofortu, Chief Archeologist of the Planetary Museum. And you?"

"Larry Wilson. Civil engineer. And this is Miss—Miss—"

"Sandra Day," supplied the girl. "I am—or was—assistant curator of the Philadelphia Museum."

"So?" The little man nodded delightedly. "Don't tell me, now. Let me guess!" He placed a wizened finger on his temple, studied the two carefully. "Those garments ... and that antique firearm ... your early Amerglish speech ... I should judge you to be from that period just preceding the Communal World State. About the year—let me see—the year 2000 A.D. Is that right?"

"You know damned well it's right!" snorted Larry. "This is the year 1940, of course. What's the gag?"

"Gag?" repeated Harg wonderingly. "Oh, yes—gag! A jest; a trick. Why, there is no—er—gag. I was merely attempting to place your position in the world line. You see, *this* is the year M-62. You would call it—" He pondered briefly. "You would call it—25,983 A.D."

"What!" Larry's fingers crept tighter about the butt of his automatic. "Hey, Sandra, let's get out of here! This guy's nuts!"

Harg smiled upon the young engineer benignly, but his hand toyed with one of the metallic studs on his harness. "I shouldn't attempt anything—er—rash, if I were you," he suggested quietly. "I believe the young lady is beginning to comprehend. Am I not right, Miss Day?"

"I—I think so," nodded the girl faintly. "Larry, this really is the two-hundred-and-sixtieth century. Harg is not fooling us. Through some incredible accident ... or maybe by design...."

Harg rubbed his wee hands together triumphantly.

"But by design!" he cried. "Oh, most assuredly by design! *I* brought you here! I, Harg-Ofortu! You are the results of my experiments."

"Experiments?" Larry didn't like the sound of the word. His eyes narrowed.

"Yes. The results of my experiments with the Time warp. Surely you know that Time can be warped? But, yes—of course you do. Even in your unenlightened era men had begun to recognize that fact. Still, it has taken all these intervening millenia for a human brain to unravel the problem of utilizing this knowledge. And I, Harg-Ofortu, have done it! I have brought you here, alive and unharmed, as a living proof of my genius."

"And now that we're here—?" began Sandra.

Harg beamed.

"Ah, the glory that is yours! You most fortunate children of a slumbrous past. From you we shall learn many things, things to fill gaps in our history of mankind. From your infantile brains we can extract racial memories stretching back to the early simian beginnings. From your bodies we can learn the history of man's early structure.

"You have hair! Teeth! Ears! It would not even surprise me to find that you have rudimentary gills. Maybe vermiform appendices! Oh, what marvelous subjects you will make for the dissecting table!"

Sandra's color fled; her breath hissed sharply.

"Dissecting table! But surely you can't mean to use us for—"

Harg silenced her with a tiny gesture. "Come, now. Let us waste no more time in idle chatter. We have delayed long enough, and I am afire with impatience. We will go to the laboratory."

* * * *

Until this morning, Larry had maintained an incredulous silence. But now, with a sudden movement, he stepped before Sandra, his automatic leveled.

"Not us, fella!" he rapped. "I'm not such a keen student of this Time business, but I know when I'm behind the little black ball numbered eight. You got us here, you say? Okay—we've had a nice visit but we don't like the climate. So we'll be toddling off now. Send us back where we belong. And—" He jiggled the gun threateningly. "And get working on it before I make you look like a second-hand punch-board."

"My dear aborigine!" laughed Harg softly. His tiny fingers sought and pressed one of his metal studs. A golden glow diffused about him, forming a radiant mesh of shimmering light about his body. "Certainly you do not think to harm *me* with your elementary weapon of destruction? Now, come, before I am compelled to use force."

"You," said Larry grimly, "asked for it!" And his finger tightened on the trigger. The automatic barked leaden death directly at Harg's breast. The little man of time yet-to-be smiled maddeningly. Before Larry's stupefied gaze, a flattened, shapeless blob of lead *splatted* against the golden haze, fell dully to the ground!

Again Larry fired. This time Harg moved slightly. The bullet glanced off the lustrous force-armor, ricocheted from the ochre web to fly screaming into the woods beyond. Larry flung his impotent weapon away.

"Well, if that won't do it, maybe *this*—" And he stepped toward the smirking scientist, fists clenched. His arms touched the thin mist, then his heaving chest.

And, strangely, his head was aswim with an overwhelming giddiness. His limbs were numb with a creeping impotence that suffused his body, dulled his senses. The gray sky above seemed to recede far, far into the distance. There was mocking laughter in his ears, darkness gathering before his eyes. The last sound he heard as he sank, weak and helpless, into the swirling haze of unconsciousness, was the cry of Sandra Day—

"*Larry!*"

CHAPTER II

First all was blackness, then in that blackness was a spot of light that grew larger and larger and ever larger until the world was filled with roaring light. And now the dim, fluttering sounds began to make sense, and a voice was saying, "I see the young man is awakening. Good. Now we will take a little trip through my laboratories."

This was Larry Wilson's welcome to the incredible surroundings in which he found himself.

He was lying on a small pallet. Or, rather, two small pallets which had been placed end to end to accommodate his six-foot frame. Above him was a silken coverlet, beneath his head a soft pillow cased in the same material. He moved an arm experimentally and discovered that his rough, English tweed business suit was missing, as were his heavy leather brogues. While he had been unconscious, someone had replaced his Twentieth Century garments with those of Harg's era.

A soft and pliable leather harness fitted snugly about his waist—but as he stretched himself up from his cot he saw that his gear lacked the multitude of cryptic studs and instruments with which the scientist's had been decked.

Then, "Larry—you're all right?"

Sandra Day, who had leaped to her feet as Larry stirred, flew across the room. Her clothing, too, had been supplanted by that of the later era. Her harness differed from Larry's only in the addition of a cupped breast-girdle similar to that once worn by Egyptian women. Leather, soft and white and pliant, clung closely to her slim, lithe body. As Larry looked at her, she faltered. A slow flush mantled her cheeks. Harg moved forward, a delighted gleam in his protruding eyes.

"Modesty!" he said in a tone of enchantment. "Sex shame! Imagine! And we had believed that it died out long before the Machine Era. It would be interesting to mate you two young people and—" He stroked his temple thoughtfully. "But we will think of that later. Come, my dear young savages. Let me show you my *other* experiments."

Larry's eyes, smoldering rebellion, sought those of Sandra. The girl's cheeks still flamed with a high pride, but she nodded almost imperceptibly, cautioning him to cause no immediate trouble. He grunted, "Okay, let's go. What is there to see?"

The chamber in which he had awakened was a square box of metal, lighted from above by concealed globes of cold light. No windows or doors marred the smooth luster of the walls. But as Harg stepped forward and touched his fingers to a spot on the wall briefly, a section slid back, exposing a brilliantly lighted corridor beyond.

Silently the three moved into the passage, Larry bringing up the rear. As he passed through the portal, he studied it cautiously. If he could only learn the secret of the operation of that door....

"It would do you," Harg interrupted his scrutiny, "no good, of course. This is but one of many inner chambers. There are many other doors and many guards to pass. Moreover, you cannot return to your Time ever—without my help."

Larry started guiltily. The man was uncanny! He seemed to be able to read thoughts!

"Now, here—" said Harg, "are the results of some of my earlier attempts to bring life-samples through the Time warp."

They had turned a corner and entered into a long chamber walled into sections. In each section there was an animal of some sort. So lifelike were the postures of these beasts that Larry half expected a cacaphony of protest to greet their entrance. But the creatures were stiff, silent. Harg smiled his white-gummed, toothless smile.

"Dead," he said regretfully. "All of them. Their bodies survived the passage through the Time warp. But when they arrived, the spark had gone. We have identified most of them. But some still puzzle us."

He pointed to the motionless figures in the cages as, one by one, they passed them. "A cow," he said, "which I brought through from the Fiftieth Century. Notice the exaggerated udders. The result of centuries of crossbreeding for milk. Somewhat different from the same beast of your day, I presume.

"This next is a pterodactyl from the Jurassic Age. I am glad to say it lived two whole weeks after coming down through the warp. The hardier animals were the only ones to survive at all—until I perfected my process. You have already seen my brontosaurus. A harmless thing. We allow it to roam freely, but we had to destroy the dinosaur that came after it....

"You recognize this sabre-toothed tiger? And the kangaroo? An interesting subject, by the way. I brought it through from the year 12,000. It had reached a high stage of development and could converse in simple phrases. A far cry from man's estate, however."

"You mean," said Sandra, "it could talk?"

"Oh, yes. But then many of the lower animals *do* speak, you know. Of course I use the ancient meaning of the word. I mean they employ the vocal organs. They have not *this*!" He tapped the skull covering which both Larry and the girl had noticed before.

"That?" said Larry wonderingly. "What is it?"

But the little man was wringing his hands in exasperation. "Now, I declare!" he cried. "All this time, you have been opening and closing your mouths while we were communicating, and I thought it was caused by some physical disturbance! *You* use vocal converse, too!"

"But of course," said the girl.

"It is quite unnecessary!" snapped the scientist. "With the *menaudo*, I can understand your thoughts clearly—and communicate my own to you, as well. In the future, both of you will be kind enough to think without speaking!"

"Why?" asked Larry bluntly. "Miss Day and I aren't mind-reading big-brains like you. If we wish to speak to each other—"

For the first time since they had met him, Harg's ever-present smile faded. A trace of his annoying superiority, self-confidence, seeped away. In his eyes there was a groping expression oddly akin to fear.

"There is nothing you need tell her!" he ordered. "I do not care to risk my—" He stopped suddenly, cannily. When he spoke again, it was in a milder tone. "You may, if you wish, converse with your mouths when I am not present. But in my presence I require you to think your conversation."

A sudden suspicion began to form in Larry's mind. He stifled it instantly; thrust it from him lest Harg grasp that faint, half-formed thought. Hastily he changed the subject.

"This other beast—" he began aloud. Then, remembering Harg's warning, he stopped and rephrased the query in his mind. "This other strange beast," he thought. "What is it?"

He knew, then, why Harg had taunted him for his interest in the mechanism of the door. For swift as an arrow the answer formed itself in his brain.

"A phoenix," replied Harg, "of the late Stone Age. A most curious creature; half animal, half bird. Originally it was a native of the planet Mars. It adapted itself to utter cold and airlessness when that planet's atmosphere waned. A few phoenix migrated to Earth, but failed to survive in our heavy atmosphere."

"That explains," cried Sandra, "the legend of the phoenix prevalent in our day. It was believed that the bird destroyed itself in fire to rise again, reborn."

"An amusing misapprehension," nodded Harg. "No doubt it was founded on someone's having seen a phoenix pass unscathed through flame. The creature was quite immune to temperature changes. But not to disease. It was this that, finally, caused its extinction.

"Now, in this next chamber—" He paused, obviously piqued. "I must confess, we have been unable to classify this beast. It is utterly unknown to our science. Apparently it does not breed true, nor can we determine its age—"

Larry and Sandra stared once at the quadruped in the booth, then broke into a duet of long and hearty laughter. Harg stared at them annoyedly. "Well?" he snapped. "Well?"

Larry said solemnly, "Harg, you've caught a rare beast there. There are none left in your day and age except the two-legged variety."

Harg said, "You know it, then? Its name, quickly!"

"We call it," Larry told him, grinning, "the jackass!"

* * * *

The tour of inspection completed, Harg returned his two captives to the cell they shared. When the door closed behind him, Larry turned swiftly to Sandra.

"Now what? I'm not sure I understand just what's going on around here, but whatever it is, it means trouble. Spelled with a capital 'Harg.' That little monkey didn't knock me cold with his yellow fuzz just for the hell of it. He means business."

"I'm afraid," said Sandra seriously, "he intends to do just what he said—and in just as offhand a manner as that in which he mentioned it. To probe our brains for race memories, then dissect us for biological knowledge."

"But why?" demanded Larry. "For Lord's sake, why? We're human beings, the same as he. He couldn't kill us in cold blood, just to—"

"To him," said Sandra, "we are nothing but a pair of savages. He is not being deliberately cruel, no more so than a Twentieth Century scientist who practices vivisection to add to his knowledge. He is proud of us as an acquisition. May even like us in some cold, inhuman fashion, as we like cats and dogs. But we represent a scientific problem to be solved—and there is no thought in his mind of mercy."

"Then," said Larry forcefully, "we've got to pull our freight. Get out of here. But how? That's the rub."

"We're helpless against him," mused the girl, "on all save one point. That is the subject he wanted to avoid. Hearing. Larry—Harg can't hear! Not as we understand the word. His ears have atrophied. Or, perhaps—" A sudden light shone in her eyes. "I have it! His ears are—"

"Wait a minute!" broke in Larry excitedly. "For once I beat you to the draw. I guessed it in the museum. These jaspers of the 260th Century are not only *unable* to hear, they're *afraid* to hear! They wear those leather headgears because they have to. Because something had made them extremely sensitive to percussion."

"And I know," chimed in the girl positively, "what caused it. It was the change!"

"Change?"

"Yes. You've noticed the sky, haven't you? Didn't you see something strange about it?"

Larry thought for a moment. Then, "The sun! There isn't any sun."

"There is a sun," cried the girl, "but you can't see it. It's concealed behind a huge dome of *impervite*—a sort of leaded, polarized glass. Harg told me all about it while you were unconscious.

"In the year 17,000 A.D., or thereabouts, there was a terrible catastrophe on Earth. Man's constant drainage of electrical energy created a rupture in the Heaviside layer, and the layer collapsed. As you know, the Heaviside layer is Earth's only protection against potentials from space, from the undiluted strength of the Milliken rays.

* * * *

"Without that protection, life on Earth was doomed. So large areas were domed over with this sixty-foot-thick layer of *impervite*. And—"

"And in the meantime," interrupted Larry, "intense subjection to cosmic radiation, along with the increasing use of telepathy, turned the human race's hearing apparatus from a useful organ into a vestigial one."

"And one," agreed the girl, "sensitive as the nerve of a tooth. It must be that. It couldn't be anything else. So there is Harg's weakness. Now, if we can only find some way to play upon it—"

Larry said gloomily, "But he still is the only one who can return us to our own time."

Sandra's hand touched his swiftly, confidently.

"We'll find some way to make him," she whispered. "We'll do it, you and I—"

Even under these circumstances Larry Wilson found the touch of that hand thrilling, the confidence of Sandra's voice, with its "you and I," endearing. It was a jest of the gods that this new glory should have come to him at last in such a situation. But the year mattered little. Time or no Time, he knew, and he thought she knew—

"Sandra," he said, "there is one thing—"

"Shhh!" she cautioned suddenly. "Footsteps!"

The metallic doorpane slid back, and once again Harg entered the room, this time accompanied by a pair of diminutive companions garbed in plainer, cruder harness than that of the scientist. Larry made an effort to expunge all thought from his mind, fearful that the man of the future might read his new determination. But Harg smiled easily.

"You will come with me now, Miss Day."

Instantly Larry was on the alert. "Where are you taking her?"

"It is not yours to ask, savage," said Harg curtly. "But reassure yourself. She will come to no harm."

Sandra's eyes pleaded with Larry; silently she let the attendants lead her away. After the door had closed behind them, Larry began to pace the floor angrily. His mind was tumultuous with conflicting thoughts and emotions. Damn them! he thought. If this was the world of the future, it would be better that the future never come! Anyway, he knew he wanted none of it! He wanted to be back in the good old Twentieth Century where men were men, not callous, grinning little sawed-off runts.

But—how to get there?

* * * *

A scraping sound from the farther wall of his cell interrupted his angry reverie. Instantly Larry was again a man of action. On silent feet he tiptoed toward the mysterious sound. The scratching persisted. Larry drew a deep breath, then pounded on the metal with his bare fist.

"Who's there?"

Immediately the noise ended. Larry waited breathlessly. Was this a trap of some kind? Or was it just some experiment of Harg's, designed to test him as laboratory students test the reaction of rats in a maze?

His footsteps deliberately loud, he stomped away from the wall. Then he stole back quietly. After a brief moment of waiting, the gentle, fumbling sound resumed. Larry pressed his ear to the metal wall. He could hear a faint noise as of someone breathing deeply. He leaned closer....

Then, suddenly, the wall before him slid away, and he was catapulted forward against a flesh-and-blood body that grunted under the impact of his weight!

Larry regained his balance; came up with doubled fists. But his fists, like his mouth, dropped open abruptly as he stared in astonishment at his antagonist. This was no puny dwarfling such as he had expected. This was a *man*—a man whose stature was greater even than his own! A mighty, bronzed, strong-thewed giant with a shock of silvery-white hair capped by the *menaudo* of the future folk!

The great one's face was etched with bitter lines of disappointment. But the look faded as his eyes swept up Larry's six foot frame, noted the breadth of shoulder and the lean, hard muscles of arm and thigh. The stranger rose, and his full lips parted in a smile of greeting.

And, "Peace, friend!" he said in a deep, resonant voice, "I, too, am a captive!"

CHAPTER III

Sandra Day, seated in an inner chamber of Harg's laboratories, watched curiously as the little scientist busied himself with cryptic recording devices. Two assistants silently performed the tasks allotted them. Save for these three, the room was innocent of humans. Harg turned to one of the assistants.

"Where is the *menaudo* for our subject?" he snapped.

The man stared stupidly. "In the vaults, Master. I did not know you would want one."

"Fool! You should have known. Let me have yours."

The assistant paled. "No, no, Master! I will get another one quickly. See, I run—"

"You will not be harmed, dolt!" said Harg coldly. "You may get another for yourself immediately—but now I need one for Miss Day. Come, the *menaudo*!"

Reluctantly, fearfully, the assistant stripped the telepathic device from his hairless pate, passed it to Harg. Harg handed it to Sandra. "You will put this on. While my *menaudo* allows us to converse normally, the experiment we are about to try requires complete flux between both minds. This is only possible when each person wears the *menaudo*."

Sandra understood, now, why her innermost thoughts, her conversations with Larry, had not been intercepted. Telepathy was a matter of willed direction. Thought beams, being electrical, radiated only toward a focused object. Harg could only receive the messages she allowed him to get.

Her eyes flickered lightly over the assistant who had already started for the door. Now was the time to test her theory. She scraped one sandalled foot raspingly across the rung of her chair. The noise was a tiny, grating squeak, barely audible—but the assistant's face contorted in swift agony. His eyes bulged with alarm; he clapped his hands to his ears and raced from the chamber.

"Hurry, woman!" Harg was growing impatient. Subduing her smile of triumph with an effort, Sandra buckled on the *menaudo*. As she did so, a wild giddiness assailed her; she grasped the arms of the chair for support. A powerful wave length of forces unsuspected burst through her brain. She caught the faint, amused hauteur of the assistant across the room; felt Harg's keen, scalpel-like mentality probing the depths of her mind. The giddiness passed as she became accustomed to the strange sensation. The turmoil in her brain settled, from its chaos came clear-cut order.

"You must relax now. Clear your mind of all extraneous thought. I wish to learn something of your former existences...."

Strange that Harg's eyes should be so large. They were like a large light glowing deep into the dark recesses of her brain. A light that kept her awake when she was so tired ... so tired....

If she could but rest, now. Sleep for a while and let the dizzy years slip by ... and the strange sounds ... and the strange scenes ... for surely this could not be she? But it was she ... and she was standing by the open fireplace in a medieval castle, facing a knight in full battle-armor.... Her heart was filled with nameless anguish....

* * * *

"Prithee, lass," he was saying, "take this parting not to heart. Ere the moon wanes our work shall be at an end, the king avenged and the foul despoiler wrenched from the arms of his scuttish lady. Mordred hath said—"

"Mordred! Mordred!" she cried bitterly. "Even now it is Mordred you speak of. Yet aforetime didst thou call him a prince's brat and a lickspittle. Pray, Gawaine, my love, forswear this mad fancy and flee now to the defense of our lady Guenevere ere it be too late!"

"Nay, sweet," was his answer. "If Arthur be not shamed of his own cuckolddry, then must the Table Round avenge the pride of Britain for him. But, hark! Gareth calls. I must leave thee, love. Farewell. I return soon."

He strode from the hall, proud and straight in his armor. She wept and could not tell why. "Gawaine, my lord!" she sobbed. "There bodes in me a sense that nevermore shall we twain meet...."

"Go back!" a voice was whispering in Sandra's mind. "Back farther still. To the days of the past...."

The *daryeb* glided, soft as the wing of a moth, upon the smooth blue waters of the Nile. The golden cascade of the sun baked the *sudd* that floated on the water's surface. She raised her finger imperiously and the boatsman obediently turned the light craft to the shore.

As the Nubian reefed the sail, a young man ran down from the portal of the observatory to the edge of the beach. He grasped her hands eagerly. "Belia!" He bent and smothered a kiss in her perfumed hair. She drew away, pouting.

"Now, by Set," she swore prettily, "thou are more ardent than the bulls of Anubis—when the sun shines. But at night where art thou? In there—star-gazing!" She glanced distastefully at the massive pyramid built by the Pharoah Cheops for his astronomers.

Her lover's bronzed face sobered.

"Great things betoken, lovely Belia. Things thou wouldst scarce understand." He pointed to the blinding orb that blazed above them. "Hear, now—ever has man thought that Ra drives his golden chariot about our mother Earth. But now I, silent and alone, have learned a greater truth. It is not the sun that moveth—but *we*! Ra's abode is the hub about which our tiny mote revolveth! This message have I sent, with my proofs thereof, to the great Pharoah. When he has read them, glory and fame will be my lot!"

A swift fang of fear, sharper than the sting of the scorpion, knifed her heart. Her voice was deep and low.

"You speak sacrilege, my love! What have you done? Not fame will be thy lot—but swift death! This thing cannot be so...."

"Into the years beyond," came the whispered command. "Project yourself still further backward, woman from the past. Back ... and back ... and back...."

Dank, steamy rain splattered on her crouched back, plastering the long, coarse hair to her naked body. A tongue of flame ripped from the thunderous vault above and the gods roared in mighty anger. She was Thaa, daughter of Gor, mate of Bab the Hungry One.

Hunkered against the farthest wall of their cave, she shivered with cold and fright as she clutched her mewling newborn to her downy breast. Ten days had the god-tears fallen, now, turning the world into a morass of water. The time of Great Cold approached, when meat was scarce and comfort scarcer. Thaa shivered.

Again the gods hurled a shaft of forked light down the skies. Bab, glowering at the cave mouth, called to her.

"Thaa! See?"

She sidled to him, forgotting her coldness in the strange sight that greeted her eyes. In the plain below was a round and shining ball. A cave stood open in the sides of the ball; from this cave issued creatures. Not men, like themselves, nor animals like Tran the Long-Toothed or Shur the Swinger. But odd creatures dressed in silver hair that glistened. Hastily she swung behind Bab as he clambered down the side of the cliff, intent on plumbing this marvel.

* * * *

Fearlessly they approached the shining ball. One of the creatures raised his voice in strange, fluent, meaningless syllables. Others of the Shining Ones came running. They raised hands in token of friendship. Bab and Thaa responded. Thaa shivered in awe as she watched the strange beings. Were they gods? she thought.

One of the visitors saw her shiver, moved forward.

"Poro methe eus?" he asked.

Thaa gazed at him dumbly; her eyes adoring. The tongue of the gods was not for mortals to know. She bowed. The young visitor turned to one of his elders.

"The creature is cold, but knows not that I have asked her so. What shall I do?"

The elder nodded sadly.

"What matters it? Let them live or die, sad brutes, as you think best.

When I consider the waste, the futility, of our tedious voyage across the emptiness of space to find *these* as our neighbors—" He sighed.

"Yet some day," mused the younger one, "may evolve from these beasts men like ourselves. Who knows? Our world is older than theirs, and wiser. Yet even now our planet is dying. By the time they have become intelligent enough to return this visit, we may be dead, our civilization ended.

"Poor brutes! I am minded to show them kindness. They should live. We can give them at least one comfort—"

From his pocket he drew a glittering toy. As Thaa watched he pressed it. A ruddy, wavering tongue licked from its mouth. "Poro methe eus?" he repeated gently. He handed the tiny cylinder to Bab. Bab's clumsy fingers fumbled with the button, once more the tongue of fire leaped forth. Bab dropped the bauble, howling, and scampered for the refuge of his cave.

But Thaa retrieved the little gift. She too pressed the release, and a pleasure-look passed over her features. Here was warmth! Here was a god-gift against the time of the Great Cold. With this to protect them, their cave would be always comfortable. She raised her eyes gratefully.

"Poro-pro—" Her brute tongue mouthed the god-words awkwardly. "Pro—methe—eus—"

"Back ... back ..." whispered the insistent command. "Back farther still. To the very dawn of life...."

She heard the voice but could not obey. Her mind was a vast sea of swirling blackness, her senses shrieked in rebellion against intolerable pain. "Back—" Mad pictures imaged on her brain, fled howling. There was one brilliant burst of coruscating light—then darkness and peace.

Harg-Ofortu frowned impatiently, fingered his subject's pulse, and snapped off a switch. He motioned to his assistant. "The woman," he said, "has fainted. Take her away. We will continue our experiments later."

* * * *

When Sandra wakened at last, it was to find Larry bending over her, chafing her wrists, looking down into her eyes anxiously. There was a lingering warmth on her lips; short seconds ago might have found his face even closer to hers. He sighed with relief as her eyes opened. The sigh became an oath.

"Damn his rotten little hide! I thought you were out for keeps. What did he do, Sandy? Are you all right?"

She was all right. A little rocky. She discovered that when she tried to rise and her head ached wickedly. But she was all right. She told him her memories of the experiment. "It was like a horrible dream, Larry. But it was more than a dream. It was true. I have lived those scenes before ... some-where ... sometime. They were so clear, so vivid." She shuddered. "But I hate to think of going through that again. I won't be able to stand it. I could feel my brain tottering on the brink of insanity toward the end."

Larry said savagely, "You won't have to go through it again!"

Sandra touched his hand, smiling wanly. "It's no use pretending, Larry. We're caught in a trap, you and I. Fate has destroyed us; thrust us forward into a Time when man is without mercy. Humanity is dead. All that remains is a race of grinning, scientific demons."

"That," interrupted Larry feverishly, "is where you're wrong, youngster! I haven't been sitting around twiddling my thumbs while you were gone. I've had a visitor."

"A—a visitor?"

Larry told her, then, of the silver-haired giant who had forced entrance into the cell. "His name was Sert. He was a man and a friend. He was one of the Underlings."

"The Underlings?" repeated Sandra.

"Yes. This world we are in is not peopled only by cold-blooded creatures like Harg. There are two mutant races of humanity. One tall and strong, as we always dreamed the future-man might be; the other spindling, puny, and viciously intelligent.

"These latter, Harg and his fellows, are the descendants of those men whose brains, for some reason more receptive to the stimulus of ultra-short wave radiation, were spurred to great heights during the period of the Great Catastrophe.

"The cosmic bombardment had three types of result. Either it killed outright—and Sert tells me that millions died—or it damaged the brain and did not harm the body, or it impaired the physique and stimulated the brain. During the era of chaos which preceded the building of the *impervite* domes, the highly activated dwarfs seized the reins of leadership. They have held them ever since. The Underlings are their workers, their slaves, their servants."

Sandra said despairingly, "But I don't see how it can profit us to join forces with dull-witted slaves—"

"Slaves, yes! But they are dull-witted no longer. Generations have erased the madness from the Underlings' brains. The Masters hold them in subjection now only because they have superior armament. The golden force-ray, for one thing.

"But rebellion is stirring amongst the Underlings. Sert is one of the leaders of a secret rebel party. He was stealing through the building, seeking new converts, when he accidentally entered our cell."

Some of Larry's excitement communicated itself to the girl. She said, "But what are we going to do?"

"Sert," Larry told her, "taught me how to open the doors around this joint. It's not hard when you get the hang of it. Every wall has a door-lock. The locks work on a network of selenium cells imbedded in the metal; these are controlled automatically by body-radiation emanating from the fingertips. Ever hear of anything like that before?"

Sandra said dazedly, "Mitogenic radiation!"

"Yes. That's what Sert called it, too. Well, all you have to do is discover the proper way to touch the doors. The right combination and bingo! If your fingers are sensitive, you can do it without much fumbling. I learned easily."

"You still haven't told me what we're going to—"

"We're pulling out of this coop—tonight! In the machine shops, Sert has a gang of a half hundred rebels. We will join them."

"And then?"

"Then," said Larry tightly, "we'll figure out some way to clean out this rat's nest. We're going to give Earth back to the Men again. And I do mean 'men!'"

CHAPTER IV

Larry Wilson tossed a grin over his shoulder to the girl behind him. His fingers moved swiftly, deftly, twisting into strange, unnatural angles as he sought the combination that would open the smooth wall before him.

"Some fun, hey?"

Sandra said anxiously, "How much farther, Larry?"

"We're almost there now. Sert told me there were nine chambers between the one we were in and the machine room. They're all supposed to be unoccupied, too."

"But—if they're not?"

"Then our plans go up the creek. But Sert wouldn't be likely to make a mistake. He has more at stake than we—Ah! There she blows!"

Larry's fingers had finally moved into the right combination. The smooth wall slid back. The pair from the past moved into the next room of the labyrinth of the future. The door closed behind them, and Larry moved immediately to the wall fronting them.

"One more small chamber, and then—"

He stopped, shocked and alarmed. For just as his hand touched the wall, it moved backward and a figure loomed before him. Sandra screamed a little scream of fright. To be so near success, and then—

But the voice that spoke was that of a friend.

"Ah, Larry Wilson! You were long in coming. So I came to find you. But, come! Our council awaits you."

The three entered, then, the final and largest of the chambers. During the working hours of the day it was a machine shop in which Underlings toiled under the harsh supervision of their Master overseers. Now it was deserted save for rather more than twoscore conspirators similar in physique and coloring to the leader, Sert.

Introductions were a brief formality. It was evident that some of the Underlings could not comprehend the anomaly of Sandra and Larry's presence. But what these rebel serfs lacked in intellect they made up for in their lust for freedom. And the two young Americans, hailing from a land that, in its time, had been the bulwark of this precious inheritance, felt a kinship with the suppressed uprisers.

At length Sert said, "—so that is as far as our plans have gone, Larry Wilson. You see how pitifully inadequate they are.

"Not only do the Masters outnumber us, but theirs is the possession of the golden force-ray which no armament can pierce. None, that is, of the feeble type we own. The force of our greater strength ... tools converted into crude swords...."

He looked hopelessly at the massive machinery surrounding them. "Could we but find a way to destroy their protective force-field, we would tear these machines into bits to mold weapons for ourselves. But we cannot."

Larry said, "I've been thinking about that problem. And I've got an idea that may or may not work. Sert, it is only the Masters whose ears are sensitive to sound, isn't it? There's nothing wrong with your hearing?"

"That is right, Larry Wilson."

"Then sound—" began Larry.

Sert shook his head. "Do you forget the *menaudo*, my friends? The Masters wear it at all times. It blocks out the sound waves that would torture them, drive them mad."

"I haven't forgotten it," grunted Larry. "I'm trying to think of a way to pour sound over 'em without making 'em remove the football helmet. And I think I know how to do it. Strangely enough, you have to make them turn on the golden force-ray before it will work!"

"I don't understand," said Sert. Others edged in curiously as Larry explained.

"When the force ray surrounds them," he explained, "their bodies become, in effect, a helical core. Such a core can be made responsive to musical tones by what, in my day, we called C.E.M.F.—counter electromotive force. I suppose you know the method of manufacture of the force ray?"

"Not the details. But the purely mechanical part, yes. We wind the relays in this shop—"

"Then," said Larry crisply, "you've got 'em licked! We'll get to work—*now!*—and build an electrical resonator. One that shoots out plenty of noise on the wave length to which their force-fields are attuned. When this howler gets going, the force-field will act as a conductor, leading the sound directly into their bodies!"

Sert's face broke in a huge grin. "And if they turn off the force-field—" he howled.

"Right! You work out on them with whatever you can lay your hands on." Larry was suddenly all work. "Give me one or two technicians and I'll rig up the electrical siren in jig-time. The rest of you start gathering weapons. This rebellion starts the minute they find out what we're cooking up!"

* * * *

Thus, for the next couple of hours, the room became once more a place of strenuous labor—but this time there was gladness and will in the way the Underling rebels went to work. With ruthless disregard for assigned uses, they tore apart a brace of mighty machines. Bellows sighed, lathes screamed, as rods, bars, balanced shafts became blunt-edged swords, lances and maces.

Meanwhile, in one corner, Larry Wilson cudgeled his brain to remember almost forgotten college physics. Finally his task was done. Before him lay a box some two feet square; within it were two tubes, a slide condenser, and an armature turning on a "howler" disc, pierced with circles of varying diameter. Larry lugged the contraption to Sert's side and crossed his fingers.

"Here it is," he said. "Salvation or the bum's rush in one small package. It'll work as a radio, I know that, but I'm not sure it will pull the trick against the force-field. I've rigged a rheostat control which gives a certain choice of wave-lengths. But if the field blocks 'em all out—"

He shook his head ruefully. But Sert laid a hand on his shoulder. "It will work, my friend," he said. "It will work because—it must! And, now—" He turned to the others gathered about him. "And, now we will strike! For freedom!"

Larry turned to Sandra Day. "This," he said, "is going to be no place for you, darling. Not in a few minutes. So grab yourself a box-seat in the background somewhere and after the fireworks are over I'll—"

The girl said, "L-Larry—what did you say?"

"Beat it. Over in one of the other chambers—"

"No. I mean before that. You called me—" She flushed. That was one thing, Larry discovered, about these clothes of the future. A flush was a real flush, no halfway thing. It started from—

He said, suddenly gentle, "I called you 'darling.' Do you mind—darling?"

"I think," she replied softly, "it's the prettiest word I ever heard." Then she applied that fine feminine attribute for which there is no allowance in man's equations; a woman's logic. "But it is *not* the word to make me get out of here. I stay, Larry. Beside you—where I belong."

Larry protested, "Now, look here, Sandy—"

She merely smiled sweetly. "How," she asked, "do you operate this gadget? I might need to know, later on."

Larry gave up. Grinning, he showed her.

The other Underlings knew their parts in the short play soon to be enacted. It was a play with a simple plot. It required two stooges; two who, daring swift annihilation, would go forth into the frequented parts of the giant building of which this laboratory was but a section, beard the Masters in their dens, and bring them down to this place.

Already such a pair had been selected from the number—the full fifty, it had warmed Larry's heart to notice—who had volunteered. The rest of the men were waiting ... just waiting. Hopefully. Uncertainly. But hopefully.

Sert came to Larry's side.

"They have been gone a full ten minutes. Do you think, Larry Wilson, we should send out others? Perhaps—"

Then he stopped abruptly. There was the sound of a commotion in one of the corridors leading to the chamber, the scrape of running feet, the clash of metal on metal. Larry grinned, his eyes bright, but there was no humor in his grin.

"There's your answer, Sert!" he roared—and bent to his wave-length howler. As he did so, the two messengers came flying into the machine room. One was unharmed, but the other had, Larry noticed with a swift, sickening distaste, lost an arm completely. It had not been cut off. It had just vanished—and there hung from the man's shoulder a short knob of flesh, seared and crisp at the point of cicatrice. So the Masters, Larry thought, had other weapons in their bag? This must be a needle-sharp heat ray—

* * * *

There came a sharp impingement of thought on the brains of Larry and Sandra; a command that was so clear and forceful that for a moment Larry's hand stayed in its journey to the rheostat. "Surrender, rebels! Surrender or you die!"

Then the Masters were racing into the room after their prey. A handful of them at first, then more and more until they were a veritable avalanche of tiny, gnome-like, nervous figures with bulbous heads, curiously shaped guns in their wee, gnarled hands. It must have been a rare thing, indeed, to find two rebellious subjects; the very rarity had drawn a horde of dwarflings in full pursuit.

The Masters burst into the room and stopped stock-still, amazed, to find that the loft harbored not two but a half hundred rebels!

It was this moment of shock that released Larry's hand from its motionlessness. The Masters' thoughts died into confusion, and Larry's brain was free. It would remain so, too, he promised himself. Not again would he relax his vigilance thus.

Then, with a wild cry, "For freedom!" the Underlings, led by their chieftain, Sert, sprang forward on their foes! For a split second the Masters' surprise held; the little men stepped backward in stark fear, and a half dozen went down beneath sledgehammer blows of crude weapons clutched by Underlings.

But this moment passed too swiftly. Wee hands flew to studded belts, and suddenly the room was brilliant with the shimmering glow of the Masters' force-fields. Instantly the tide of battle turned. Here, where some steel lever-handle, converted into a mace, was halfway to a Masters' skull, the rod suddenly flew from its wielder's hands, clanging useless across the floor. There an Underlings, grappling with a Master, suddenly slumped into an inert heap. The retreat ended; the Masters, assured again, and confident, stepped forward vengefully. Sert cast a pleading glance at Larry.

"Swiftly, Larry Wilson, or we all perish!"

But Larry was already twisting the vernier; inside his box the howler disc was spinning one way, the armature another, and from the mouth of the electric siren was shrieking an unearthly wail. It ripped and tore at Larry's own eardrums. Surely it would do the same—and worse—to those delicate organs of the Masters if he could but find—

And suddenly he had it. Sandra gripped his shoulder with fingers that bit and clung. "There, Larry! There!"

He stopped his frantic dialing. For now the menacing advance of the Masters had indeed stopped. As one man, they had raised arms to their heads, were pawing wildly at outraged ears tormented despite the *menaudo*. Weapons fell from unheeding fingers; weapons which the Underlings gathered up eagerly.

And now one Master, eyes bulging, the faint froth of madness whitening his lips, opened his mouth and screamed with vocal cords never before used. It was a piteous mewling sound; the first and the last the man ever uttered. For as he cried out he turned off his force-field—and the nearest Underling split him from crown to navel with one slash of a mighty blade.

Nor was he the only one to die thus. All about the room Masters were stumbling, reeling, falling like men overdrunk with the grape of sonic torment. And wherever one succumbed to the temptation of turning off his force-field current—there was death waiting for him. If he did not turn it off, there was death anyway. Hideous and mind-blasting death from Larry's screaming box.

Reinforcements came, stared once into the bloody chamber of rebellion—and fled, hands clutching their ears. A few scattered remnants of the first retribution party managed to escape the debacle. And finally there came a moment when there were no Masters left alive in the room. The battle was over—and the Underlings had won!

* * * *

Then came Sert to Larry once again, and there was mingled joy and sadness on his face as he held out his hand to the Earthman from long ago.

"The field is ours, Larry Wilson. And it is you who made it so."

Larry said, "Mmm," absently, and turned off the now useless howler. He looked about the room. "How many men did we lose, Sert?"

"Nine dead," replied his friend, "a few injured—but all before you found their force-field's wave-length. A glorious victory, even at such a cost. In the years to come the names of those who died here tonight will be worshipped by a race of free men who were once Underlings."

Larry, brooding thoughtfully, brushed off his final words. "Skip the flag-waving, pal. You sound like a politician back home. This scrap's not over by a damn sight. I think you underestimate the Masters."

Sert said proudly, "And you underestimate our people, Larry Wilson. The news of this battle will spread, and before the next work-period thousands will flock to our standard. We will build more sonic machines, perhaps portable ones, and—"

"Sure. And what are the Masters going to be doing while all this goes on? I'll give even money that right now they're herding in the Underlings from other parts of this city for a little wholesale slaughter. It *is* a city, isn't it?"

"Yes. One large city-state under a single *impervite* dome operated from a control chamber."

"Operated?" repeated Larry.

"But, certainly. It can be opened for fresh air to be admitted, or for the egress and entrance of aircraft—"

"Larry!" It was Sandra who interrupted. "There's our answer, Larry. Life is impossible without the protection of the dome. Whoever possesses the dome control chamber holds the whip hand. We must take that!"

Sert's face brightened. "She is right, Larry Wilson. We must take the dome chamber—"

"Wait a minute!" Larry had been thinking swiftly. "Sandy's got something there. But there are angles. First of all, we've got to seize the control chamber, yes. But we also need more men. If we don't get reserve strength—and good, strong fighting men, at that—sooner or later they'll starve us and our little rebellion right out of our cubby-holes.

"Right now the odds are temporarily balanced. We have fewer men, but our men are more powerful. Theirs are the best weapons, but our single weapon makes theirs useless. They control the dome—a point in their favor. But we are fighting for life and freedom—a point in ours.

"So it's a stalemate. And one that will turn into defeat for us unless we move swiftly. Before they recognize our pitiful weakness." He gazed sharply at Sandra. "Sert is needed here, to rally recruits. So it's up to you and me to get control of the dome chamber. I see one way to win. It's a dangerous way, but—"

And he told them. When he had finished speaking, there was a heavy flush on Sert's forehead. He cried, "But no, Larry Wilson! I will not let you and this girl bear the burden of my oppressed race. We must find another way."

"There is," Larry told him, "no other way. Sandy?"

The girl placed her hand in his. "It is the only way, Larry," she said. "Darling," she added—and smiled.

CHAPTER V

It took but a short time to make their final preparations. Larry taught a half dozen Underlings how to operate his howler, also taught them how to build others like it.

"Now get to work," he told them grimly. "Make as many of these gadgets as you can. And make 'em light and small, portable, so you can carry them around with you."

He turned to Sert. "Well, this is it, pal. Keep your eye peeled for the signal. 'One if by land and two if by sea.'"

Sert said puzzledly, "What's that?"

"Skip it. What I mean is, watch the dome. If you smell something funny, that'll be fresh air, and it'll mean Sandy and I have taken the fort. Attack then. We'll be in a position to crack a whip over the runts." He held out his hand. "Be seein' you, guy! Let's go, Sandy."

Together they made their way through the labyrinth of chambers to their own cell. This time Larry fumbled less with the mitogenic locks that barred their progress; it took them but a few minutes to make the journey.

Yet even at that they barely returned in time. As they came through the chambers, Larry reminded Sandra, "We're banking on the fact that Harg doesn't know we've been out of our coop. That's our story and we're stuck with it. If by any chance he or a guard happened in while we were out, we're sunk, but—"

"It's a chance worth taking," nodded the girl.

"Yes. The big idea is to get to that control chamber. I think we can do it because Harg, big-shot as he may be, has one bad failing. Human vanity. So remember, play up to whatever I say."

"Okay, boss!" said Sandra meekly. But there was a crinkle of laughter in her eyes.

Then they were back in their own cell, the door behind them was sliding closed—and almost immediately the one before them was sliding open to admit Harg-Ofortu and a brace of armed guards!

There was fretfulness on the little scientist's face, fretfulness that turned to swift suspicion as Larry and Sandra started guiltily. His eyes swept the room, returned to Larry. Larry felt the raw demand of Harg's first directed thought, "Can these two—?" then he felt the tenuous fingers of Harg's probing mentality seeking information from his mind. With an effort he forced himself to think of simple, unimportant things. He concentrated on the tag end of an old nonsense rhyme—

> "Oh, do I is? And am I be?
> Or couldn't I have used to be?
> Oh, cruel fate, which was to me; I used to ain't!"

—and chuckled inwardly to catch the shocked repercussion of Harg's amazed, "Incredible! These barbarians are simple minded children!" Then Harg spoke. Or directed a thought to the Twentieth Century couple, his equivalent of speech.

"You will come with me!"

Larry pretended alarm. "Why? We are comfortable here. We don't want to—"

"I am doing," Harg advised him crisply, "that which is best for you. There has been a little—er—disturbance in the city. I am removing you to safer quarters. I will not have my experiments upset by—"

"By—?" prodded Larry.

"That is not your concern. Come!"

* * * *

Harg led the way through the corridors. Larry and Sandra followed docilely. With suspicious alacrity, had the little man but known it. As they walked, Larry deliberately made his thoughts clear that Harg might interpret them. "He can't be anyone important around here. He's just one of the small fry. Obviously, he isn't very intelligent—"

Harg heard—he could not help but hear. And he understood. He could not help but understand. His wizened cheeks gained an unexpected color. He turned to Larry angrily.

"It might interest you to learn, my dear savage," he snapped, "that your thoughts are crystal clear to me. I take it you doubt my importance?"

Larry made a good job of looking embarrassed. So Sandra might know what was going on he mumbled aloud, "Well, I just couldn't help thinking—I mean, I figured you aren't really the big man around these parts. All this talk about a Time warp machine, and all—"

Harg said crisply, "Then you don't believe there is such a thing? Well, you err, barbarian. There is. And it was the genius of Harg-Ofortu that constructed it. I—"

Here Sandra stepped in with a word to Larry.

"It's all nonsense, Larry. Don't believe a word he says. He's done nothing but lie since we've met him. He told me the most impossible tale about a 'dome' and a 'dome control chamber.' Of course such things are absurd!"

"So!" Harg's thought had the crackle of audible sound. "Know, then, my two young innocents, that you choose to mock genius. Genius never lies. Behold!" He turned abruptly from the course they were traveling, led them down a side corridor, fingered open a door and showed them, glistening across a wide expanse of metal flooring, a turret-like structure from which emanated, like the sprawling arms of an octopus, vast cables. From the hemispherical roof of this turret emanated a wide, unwavering cone of light, blinding in its brilliance.

"Behold," mocked Harg, "the dome control chamber in which you presumed to disbelieve. From this heart emanates the life of our city-state—and I am its sole supervisor. Even so, it is a tiny thing compared with the greater invention which was, and is, my own. The Time-warp machine. You still doubt? Let me show you, that you may marvel at the brain of Harg—About, guards! We return to the laboratory!"

One of the guards blinked the thick soft lids of his bulging eyes, said nervously, "But, Master of Masters—"

"We return, I said!" Harg was icy cold, even more nettled because a guard had dared question his decision, determined to exact admiration from his audience.

They turned about, began to retrace their steps. Larry marked carefully the corridor which led to the control turret. He would not forget it, nor how to reach it. And as they walked he caught Sandra's eye for a brief moment. Harg did not see the swift wink that passed between them, nor the way Sandra's hands clenched before her in a delighted gesture of approbation....

But he did see, and gloried in, the amazement mirrored in the eyes of Sandra and Larry when at last they stepped into the chamber which housed the Time-warping machine. It was a huge structure, its inner chamber alone being large enough to house a battalion of men. But its core was small, being an oddly shaped, angular object spinning endlessly on a bar of crystalline material.

Displaying all the vanity Larry had hoped for, the little scientist pointed to the twirling object first, then at a great, banked keyboard like that of some gigantic organ.

"The end product of man's genius," he boasted vaingloriously, "for a thousand millenia! The machine which can span Time. You do not comprehend the object which spins upon the bar, no? I fear it is beyond your puny concept, friends from an unenlightened age. It is a tesseract; the infinite cube of four dimensions. Your eyes see but a cross section of its fullness, which is beyond seeing. Yet I, Harg-Ofortu, conceived and built it!

"These banks control the ages that Have-Been and the ages that are Yet-to-Be. Through their relays are disrupted the world-line of any given thing at any given time. I would demonstrate, but terrific power is expended each time I bring a new object from the past; I would not now waste power to convince such savages as you.

"Yet by pressing a button—so—and deflecting a lever—so!—I can, if I will, bring across the negation or Time-that-Was-Not creatures like yourselves from any period of time. The ages in which I angle are clearly marked here; the position on this sphere called 'Earth' from which I draw my experiments I determine by means of this mapped globe."

He paused, smirking with pride, so blinded with self-glory that he did not even notice the studiousness of Sandra's and Larry's eyes. But when he spoke again, it was to say words that dragged Larry back to earth with a start.

"And it will interest you to know, Sandra Day, that a great tribute is shortly to be paid to you."

Sandra said, "A—a tribute?"

A faint shadow flickered across the diminutive one's face. "A recent disturbance," he proclaimed, "amongst slaves whom we call the 'Underlings' has wakened in us, the Masters, recognition that for too many generations we have allowed our brains to expand whilst our bodies failed in strength.

"We now find this to be an unworthy situation. We have decided to once again become a prolific race—but in so doing we are going to breed in such a way that our children will retain our keen intellects and the perfect bodies of men from the past. After some thought on the matter, and with an enticing example to help solve the question—" Here he fastened a greedily appreciative eye on Sandra, "—we have decided that we shall draw the mothers of our new race from *your* period!"

Sandra gasped.

"But—but you can't do that! They won't want to leave their own age, mate with strangers—"

"What," demanded Harg icily, "are the petty desires of barbarians to the Masters of Earth? Yes, my charming aborigine, soon you will have companionship with many women from your own Time. It will be pleasant company for you, I know." He paused. Then, in an expectant tone, "You may express your thanks, if you wish."

Sandra was speechless. But the words made a sort of sense to Larry; the kind of sense he did not care for. In a grating voice he demanded, "Thanks? Thanks for what?"

The little scientist smiled serenely, arching his brows.

"Because now," he answered, "she will not become a subject for the dissecting table. Her life will be spared. Yet an even greater glory is in store for her. She will not be mated to one of the lesser Masters. She will become the first and favored mate of myself, the great Harg-Ofortu!"

* * * *

For a moment, a vast and terrible rage shook Larry Wilson. Then it evaporated, dissipated before another emotion. His fists unclenched, the frown that had sprung to his brow disappeared in a network of crinkles, and laughter bellowed from his throat, shook him, exhausted him, doubled him.

Sandra laughed, too, hysterically at first, then as completely giving way to amusement as Larry. Harg looked at first one, then the other. He was alternately surprised and startled; then, as the full import of their laughter burst upon him, he became a diminutive phial of wrath.

His goitrous eyes flamed with bitterness, his tiny body stiffened, and his hands jerked toward the studs on his harness. His thought, a maelstrom of vitriolic hatred, became a seething hell that stifled the young couple's mirth.

"You are amused? That is interesting. Perhaps you will be the less so when you lie upon the table beneath the scalpel, screaming, pleading for the boon of death I can give or withhold!" Harg's mouth was twisting with venom. "When that moment comes, O fool, remember that as your life ebbs new life will spring within this woman—Well, what is it?"

He turned and shot the final query to the pair of guards who had appeared in the doorway. The foremost stepped forward, dragging into view a pair of manacled Underlings.

"We found these two rebels skulking about the laboratory, Master. We brought them that you might put them to the question."

"Take them away!" fumed Harg. "I have no time for them now. Destroy them as a lesson to all rebels."

"But, Master, they may know—"

Harg, thoroughly enraged now, stamped his foot in sheer spite. "Destroy them, I told you! Cast them outside the dome!"

Larry and Sandra looked at each other in swift relief. They had seen, if Harg had not, the quick recognition in the captives' eyes as they entered the room; had feared that under the questioning their part in the rebellion would be learned. Then all, indeed, would have been in vain. It was unfortunate that two Underlings must die, but it was better that two should perish than that a plan should fail.

"Well, get along!" Harg told the guards. "Throw them through the Ground Gate—No, wait a minute!" He glared malevolently at Larry. "Take this savage with you; let him behold the agony of their destruction. It will teach him that one does not safely taunt Harg-Ofortu! The woman stays with me."

Sandra's glance stayed Larry's movement. Her lips moved silently but he caught their message. He allowed the guards to lead him, with the two captives, out of the room and down one of the interminable passages of the labyrinth.

Even here he continued to count turnings, memorize passages, so that he might know his way back to the laboratory and—more important still— to the dome control turret. They walked in silence, coming at last to the huge, doubly barred and intricately locked door which was deepset in the *impervite* perimeter of the Dome.

Here, for the first time, the proud hauteur of the captive Underlings broke. Until this time they had maintained their courage; now, as one guard disengaged the locks, a glazed look of fear crept into their eyes. The great door swung open, a tendril of outside air, chill and thin as hoar frost, stirred the fusty atmosphere of the labyrinth. And one of the captives cried out desperately, fell to his knees groveling, pleading, pawing at the guard's spindling shanks with futile hands.

"Down, slave!" came the guard's contemptuous command. But it was not his words that salvaged the blubbering Underling. It was the other Underling who stepped to his comrade's side, laid a firm hand on his shoulder. And—

"Come, Borl!" he said quietly. "Let us die as men should die—that our Cause may live!"

Beneath his touch the other calmed. The febrile terror left his eyes and something new glistened there. He rose, nodded, straightened his shoulders. Then proudly, almost triumphantly, the two exiles strode into the tunneled path to death. They turned there, boldly, and their voices joined in a single cry, "For freedom!"

Then the door clanged shut, and through the adjacent *impervite* transparency Larry Wilson saw two staunch figures march boldly down the tunnel to the barren world beyond.

Beside him one of the guards commented wonderingly to the other, "Remarkable! They are the first I ever saw go through the Ground Gate so gallantly—to death."

Larry asked, "But is it death? The outside atmosphere surrounded them the moment they stepped through the gate. Yet they walked away."

The guard answered tauntingly, "It is death. Make no mistake about that. The ancient archives will tell you that. It was Outside that our ancestors died. No man has yet returned who dared venture beyond the Gate." He stirred himself. "Now let us return this one to the Master Scientist and be about our work. The Underlings still—"

Then Larry stumbled. And as he did so one swiftly outthrust hand caught in the harness of the nearest guard, tugged, ripped. The studded belt snapped at the catch, flew halfway across the corridor.

The man scrambled after it, alarmed. But even as he took his first step, Larry wheeled and threw one hundred and eighty pounds of bone and muscle at his companion's face. Puny jawbones splintered, blood spurted, and the guard went down as if pole-axed. Momentum swept Larry over his prostrate body to the weaponless guard; his fist raised and fell once—and that was all!

He rose, stripped both hairless pates of their precious *menaudos*, slung both studded belts over his shoulder. Armed now, he oriented himself and set off at top speed for the control turret.

Only once was his progress threatened; then but for an instant. The single Master who met him racing down a side corridor had neither time to give alarm, draw his heat-ray pistol, or snap on his force-shield. Larry's reflexes worked at lightning speed, and this was no time for stupid mercy. He sheared a crisp and smoking hole in the Master's breast with a single blast of his gun and sped on toward his goal.

That moment while his fingers sought the mitogenic combination of the turret lock was the longest he had ever lived through. It turned out to be the most elaborate he had yet encountered; ultimately operated on the placement of the fingers of both hands. While he sought the responsive chord he was dangerously exposed to any who might come near.

But Fate, for once, rolled him a natural. He broke into the control turret, stared once wildly, bewilderedly, at the dazzling array of levers and studs therein, then tugged desperately at that which seemed largest, most impressive....

Then sprang to the still open doorway and looked at the leaden-gray roof of *impervites* above him. And as he looked, a great quartered section of the roof slid back, disclosing a bright blue sky in which the sun rode, gold and dazzling!

CHAPTER VI

But only for an instant did he leave open that vent to the treacherous skies above. Harg and Sert had said—nor was there any reason to disbelieve them—that horrible death poured from the heavens in this later age, in the form of intense cosmic radiation. It would be a hollow victory to save a race and destroy a world.

He let the vent remain open but a few seconds, knowing that Sert's army, scattered and ready now, in a thousand secret nooks throughout the domed city-state, would see the signal, know that the dome turret was in friendly hands, and attack the Masters.

And he was right. Even as the *impervite* section slid back into its accustomed position he heard the Underling siren sound from one distant corridor—then another sounded, and another, and another, until from every weaving tunnel of the labyrinth that was this future city Larry heard the ear-splitting tumult that was madness and death to the Masters.

Then a small company of Underlings burst from one tunnel. Larry leaped from the turret, grasped the leader, thrust him into the control room and shouted, "Guard this! I have a little job to take care of!"

Jaw set, eyes hard, he was off toward the laboratory where—if the gods were good to him—he would find the girl he loved and the miserable parody of a man whom he most certainly did not love.

As he ran, his footsteps followed the tempo of an ever-increasing volume of sound. Never before, he thought, since the creation of the world had begun in the high celestial music of the spheres, had mankind ever fought a life-and-death battle with such an accompaniment.

All about him—it seemed from every corridor, out of each vibrant metal wall, through every air duct that fed the gigantic new world labyrinth—came the hideous howling of the electrosonic intensifiers which had been his invention.

His trip was not a short one, and as he sped toward the laboratory he saw many men, both friends and antagonists. The Underlings, straight-shouldered with a confidence born of the up-reaching hope for liberty, were moving ever onward and onward against the foes. Armed with lances, crude swords, whatever tools and instruments they could lay hands on, they were pouring from the recesses of the city-state to charge upon the heart of the city, where dwelt the Masters.

And in the van of each group was one Underling who carried as his weapon a small, square box in which a whirling disc made music of madness.

Larry saw no pitched battles. This was a strange warfare; one in which the Masters possessed superior armaments—but could not use them. Time and again a lone Master would break from some cubicle to face, for a moment, the advancing host of erstwhile slaves. For seconds his heat-ray gun would pour scorching death into their fore, blasting into blackened hulks those who led.

But ever and again the Master, snapping on his golden force-field as protection against the meaner weapons of the Underlings, would fall prey to the ear-bursting delirium of the howler; would stagger, would scream and reach for his *menaudo*, would die in a mist of shrieking madness.

And then, suddenly, Larry was near his goal, and from a side corridor a familiar figure was racing toward him. It was Sert, and the Underling chieftain's face was radiant with joy.

"You have succeeded, Larry Wilson! Soon the day will be ours!"

Larry shouted, "You're driving them back, Sert—but to where? They're not standing and fighting."

"No. They'll concentrate at the central plaza. But our number is growing each minute. Come with us and be in at the death—"

Larry shook his head.

"This," he said, nodding toward the laboratory now in sight, "is where I get off. I've got a private score to settle with a grinning little ape named Harg. Give 'em hell, fella! See you later!"

And alone he burst into the room in which, a short time before, he had left Harg and Sandra.

* * * *

Sandra was there, and in the excitement of the moment it did not seem strange to Larry that at the sight of him she should spring forward to throw her arms about him, drawing his face down to hers; nor did it seem strange that his lips should find hers of their own volition. He knew now, that since first they had met on the grassy plain that outskirted the ultra-world city-state this was inevitable.

Then harsher thoughts dominated him. There was a man's task yet to be accomplished. He drew away from her, demanded, "Harg! Where is he?"

Sandra's face clouded.

"Gone to rally the Masters to a defense. News of the Underling advance came to us here. He alone knew a way to combat—"

Larry laughed grimly. "There is no way. The sonic amplifier is killing the Masters off like flies. Sert's men will soon hold the city."

"But Harg," the girl cried, "has issued orders that all Masters must turn off their force-fields. He guessed the secret of the sonic weapon. With no force-field to act as a conductor, our sound-weapons will be useless. The Masters are gathering in the central plaza. From there they plan to ray into extinction all Underlings who venture near them—at distance too great for hand-to-hand conflict!"

"And they outnumber the Underlings!" This was bad news. Larry saw, now, the one factor that would spell defeat to his friends. There were too many Masters. By holding the Underlings at a distance, destroying them with heat-rays, not permitting a close attack—

"But there is another way, Larry!" Sandra was crying. "I thought of it after Harg left. And—I have already set the machine into operation."

Larry cried desperately, "I don't know what you're talking about, Sandy. There is no other way. We're licked, and only because they outnumber us. I must find Sert, tell him to sound the retreat before all are killed—" He turned, sped for the doorway. Sandra's voice followed him.

"But, Larry, all will be well! I'm—"

"Later!" he shouted back. Then once again he was racing through the tortuous corridors of the domed metropolis. He caught up to Sert's little band on the very edge of the spacious clearing which was the central plaza of the city. That circular area must have been a full mile in diameter, into it fed literally hundreds of corridors. This was the heart of the future-city; the main aorta which fed to the smaller outlying sections.

"Sert!" Larry's cry stopped the Underling leader's upraised arm from falling. "Sert, do not lead an advance!"

Sert turned, wonderingly.

"But why not, Larry Wilson? See, they huddle in the center of their doomed city like kine awaiting the knife. In a few minutes the city will be ours."

"Look again! Do you see their force-shields? No. They've turned them off. They're waiting there for you to attack. If you do—Good Lord!"

Larry stopped, horrified. For as he spoke a group of exhuberant Underlings burst from a tunnel at the other end of the plaza, charged, three dozen strong, down upon the huddled, waiting group of Masters in the center. Their electrosonic machine was shrieking its high note and the Underlings raced forward confidently, expecting to see the dwarflings cringe and fall before the blasts of that potent weapon.

But instead, from the ranks of the Masters came a withering blast of white radiation. The concentrated fury of a thousand heat-ray handguns. There was a brief puff of smoke, the abbreviated scream of agony from Underling throats—then silence! A small untidy heap of charred refuse dotted the spot where gallant men had died instantly.

Sert's face paled. In a shaken voice he said, "It is again a stalemate, Larry Wilson! We lack the man-power to storm that central group."

Larry said hollowly, "Not a stalemate, Sert. Taps! They've beaten us by the oldest of warfare's means—superior numbers."

"You see no hope?"

"I see," Larry shook his head sorrowfully, "no—"

Then, where a temporary awed silence had fallen over the Underlings, there arose a mighty shout that shook the dome overhead! There came strange sounds, the clash of metal upon metal, the sharp bark of musketry, the clatter of shod hoofs, bellowings and trumpetings Larry could not begin to guess the reason for. Stranger still, the sound of crying bugles—and grating commands in tongues harsh and foreign!

And from the corridors to right and left, main arteries of the plaza, spewed an amazing host!

In the fore were a horde of short, dark men garbed in leathern kirtles, with great golden greaves glittering on swart and hairy calves, with burnished shields before them, with broad-swords raised in brandishment as they plunged toward the startled central knot of Masters.

And immediately behind these came, trumpeting and thundrous-hoofed, a dozen elephants in war-trappings of Byzantine splendor! At express-train speed the pachyderms lumbered down upon the shrinking knot before them.

From another corridor spilled yet another incredible host. Four score of men, bearded and moustached, gay-uniformed in the blue and crimson of the *francs-tireurs*, the bitter guerrilla invaders who struck terror into Prussia in 1870. Horse-mounted were these, and their mounts' nostrils quivered with the ancient lust for battle as they hurtled ever forward.

In an endless stream, then, came the man-power that alone could win this battle! And never a stranger host had taken a single field. Here, on swift, hairy ponies, rode a handful of wild-eyed Huns clad in ragged furs. There, from another corridor, burst a clanking foot-legion that rallied beneath the banner of Darius. Behind these, pressing to get through and into the thick of the fray, came a troop of butternut-uniformed musketeers beneath a barred and starred red banner. Their rebel yell sounded shrill and deadly above the tumult.

Sert's face was blank with astonishment, but his fighting heart knew but one thing. That here, by a miracle, were the reinforcements he needed. With a great cry, "For freedom!" he raised his arm—and from their separate tunnels broke forth the Underlings to do battle, shoulder to shoulder, with those who fought their cause!

Not easily was that cause won. After their first instant of shock, the Masters raised their weapons against the diverse foe. Flaming death answered the barks of muskets, colored rays of potency unspeakable poured destruction into the close-pressed ranks of those who stormed the plaza.

But here were a hundred legions, all trained to war and inured to the fact of impending death. Where one man fell another took his place. Spears, arrows, even flaming projectiles filled the air. From somewhere came the biting chatter of a Gatling gun, pouring its slow racket of death into the ranks of the dwarflings.

Force-fields went on—and Masters died as the Underlings' sonic torture burst their brains. Force-fields went off—and Masters died beneath barbaric weapons from ages long forgotten. The metal floor ran red with blood, blood was grit when mingled with charred ashes that had been men.

There could be but one result. It came at last when a cowering Master leader threw both arms skyward, pleading a truce, acknowledging a defeat!

* * * *

Larry found himself in the front rank of the attackers. How he had gained that spot he did not know, nor did he ever afterward remember. He had a confused recollection of having raced forward, Sert on his left side, his right flank guarded by a huge, blond Viking warrior in scarlet casque and birnie; he found that the smoking heat-ray gun in his hand was exhausted. And he knew his eyes were still seeking the one Master on whom he had pledged his personal vengeance. But that one Master, the Master of Masters, Harg-Ofortu, was not to be found.

Perhaps he was one of those headless bodies who had fallen beneath the short-swords of the Carthaginians, or he might have been one of those impaled by the lances of Attila's wayward horde. Possibly even—but Larry hated to remember the typically feminine way in which that tiny band of Amazon allies had treated their foes....

And then Sandra was beside him, sharing with him the triumph of the Masters' surrender. And to her he turned for an answer.

"You did this, Sandra?"

"I tried to tell you, Larry. It was the only thing I could think of. From Harg we learned how to operate the Time-warp machine. I set its dials, brought these warriors through to aid our cause."

"But the language! They speak a thousand tongues!"

Sandra smiled, and for the first time Larry noticed that she, like himself, was now wearing the *menaudo* of the Masters. "And with this, so do I."

Sert was addressing the forlorn leader of the beaten Masters. "A new order rules. From this day henceforth there shall be peace beneath our Dome. No longer will there be Underlings, you Masters. Acknowledge this truth and your fellows will be spared. Together we will build a new civilization to surpass the old."

The Master nodded humbly. "So be it!" he said.

But in the moment of armistice came the last and greatest blow. A droning sounded throughout the vast arena, and the voice of Harg filled the plaza.

"Think you that you have won, barbarian from the past?"

Sandra's eyes filled with alarm. She clutched Larry's arm tensely. "Harg! But where does he speak from?"

As if in answer to her words, Harg spoke again, his voice rage-choked and malevolent.

"Know then, fools, that in a few moment's time the last Master dies—and with him dies the civilization of this accursed planet! When I draw back this lever—"

Larry stiffened.

"The dome control turret! He has taken it again!"

CHAPTER VII

Within arm's reach were a half-dozen riderless mounts of those who had died in battle. To the back of one of these Larry leaped. His nearest companion was an olive-skinned son of antique Persia. He glanced wonderingly at the white-complexioned six-footer beside him, but only for an instant. In this strange meeting place of the ages, existed no lingual difficulties. Larry wore the *menaudo*, and that headgear spoke in the one universal tongue, the language of thought.

Now, succinctly, he broadcast the meaning of this threat to the allies out of time.

"Only the Dome above protects us all from dreadful death. The greatest rogue of all has escaped, and has taken refuge in the chamber that controls that dome. If he pulls the main lever, he can bring it and the world crashing into ruin about us—"

As he thought, he rode, and as he rode a wide path opened before him. Others turned their mounts to follow, and the corridors of the domed city rang with the hoofbeats of a host salvation-bent. There was but one chance—to reach the turret and destroy Harg before he could pull that lever.

Larry was aware that behind him, beside him now, was Sandra. Her thoughts, incoherent, pleading, woman-like, reached him.

"No, Larry! Don't try to storm the turret. We'll take our chances with the Time machine. Try to go back to our own time through *it*—"

"And leave a dead world behind us?" That was his answer. It was enough.

Harg's vainglorious farewell broadcast still went on.

"—Such a little time to live! Breathe deeply of the air, O invaders from another time. Taste its sweetness with longing, for all too soon the Dome will fall, letting in the blasting radiation of the dying universe. Then you, too, with it, will perish—"

Then suddenly his voice altered subtlely.

"But what is this? You approach? You would storm the turret, save your petty skins?"

For already the first of the attacking party was drawing into the final corridor, preparing to break into the great room that housed the control turret.

"*Stop!*"

The command came, clear and incisive. Larry knew it was too late to win now. Harg knew of their coming; a touch of his hand would destroy them all. He raised his arm, halted the pell-mell advance of his diverse army with a gesture. "Let us hear what he has to say!" he ordered.

Harg's bargain reached him clearly. From where he sat, on the very lip of the tunnel that disgorged into the turret room, Larry could see the control chamber, could even glimpse the figure of the tiny scientist standing with one hand poised on a small red lever.

"Larry Wilson, warrior from a savage age, I speak to you, for it is you who led this revolt against my world. I offer you peace or death. It is yours to decide."

Larry's lips were white lines, grim and tight.

"Speak on!"

"First, I demand that the warriors you brought out of the past be returned to their own times."

"Go on!"

"Next, I demand that the Underlings lay down their arms and once more acknowledge fealty to the Masters."

Here a roar of rumbling dissent rose from the ranks of those Underlings who had joined the rescue party. Larry silenced them. "Anything else?"

"And finally," Harg's command bore a snarling vindictiveness, "I require that the woman, Sandra Day, step forward to this turret as hostage until all these other things be accomplished!"

Sandra whisked the thought-revealing *menaudo* from her head, whispered pleadingly, "Yes, Larry! Say yes! It is the only way to save us all. We'll find another time—"

Larry trembled in an agony of indecision. There was truth in Sandra's words. Harg held them all at the edge of a sword now. Later, perhaps—But could he trust the little man's bargain? Might it not be another falsehood?

* * * *

And then, suddenly, the decision was made for him. From the colorful knot on his right burst three riders, gay in blue and crimson. Handsome, perfumed, dashing riders with the eyes of hawks, the hands of falcons, the hearts of gallantry. Men to whom the worship of our lady in domnei was a life-long creed. And—

"Make no bargains," cried one gloriously, "with a shrinking rat! *Comrades! Pour la femme!*"

Before Larry could stay them they had broken past the barrier, were swooping down on the turret chamber. As they rode, their rifles spoke; bullets screamed against the sturdy metal. One pellet found its mark, and Larry glimpsed Harg's body staggering backward, sliding, falling.

Harg's last thought came to them all feebly.

"I die, then. But with me ... dies ... the world...."

Larry shouted then. In a voice of thunder he roared, "Back! Back, everyone! For your very lives!"

For Harg's falling body pressed the fateful lever. Just in time the gallant *francs-tireurs* wheeled their horses, streaked back to the tunnels and safety. Then, with a roar like that of a thousand Niagaras, the broad, conical beam that splayed from the roof of the turret flared into jagged lightning. Earth trembled with the repercussion, up above that blast of pure energy struck the center of the Dome and smashed it into a million bits!

Then came the deluge; the frightful deluge of tons of broken *impervite*, crashing down upon the control room in world-shaking shards, deafening the ears with its tumultuous thunder, burying the tiny turret beneath sixty feet of broken dome. Thus died Harg, Master of Masters....

* * * *

In the outer corridors, Sert sought Larry's side. His face was working bitterly, but he tried to control it. He said in a somber voice, "This is farewell, Larry Wilson. It is good to know that there were once men like you, and it is pitiful to know that so dies a world."

Sandra was crying, her body twisting with great, uncontrollable sobs. "Larry, isn't there anything we can do? Anything?"

He shook his head sadly. "I'm afraid not, Sandy. This is the pay-off. I don't know how long it takes for the radiation to work out on the human body, but I guess, it doesn't take long. We've got a little while, perhaps, and then—"

He stopped. For from the far end of the corridor came a sound strange in that moment of sorrow. The sound of men cheering, laughing, hysterical with joy insurmountable. All turned and looked. There appeared a group of the Underlings, bearing upon their shoulders two men whom Larry recognized and a half dozen others, bearded, clad in rough garments, complete strangers.

Sert stepped forward swiftly.

"What is the meaning of this? Know you not that we are all doomed? Think you this is the moment for such unseemly laughter?"

But one of the Underlings laughed in his face; a carefree laugh of heart-filled happiness.

"Doomed, my leader? We have but *begun* to live! Behold—the two whom the Masters thrust through the Ground Gate five full hours since!"

Larry nodded. It was they, all right. Borl, who had been terrified, and his companion who had cheered him. He said, "Then in five hours the radiation did not destroy them?"

It was Borl who answered.

"In five hours? Nay, not in five years! Behold, my brothers, those have lived on the Outside for these past ten or more years. Remember you Treg ... and Daiv ... and our friend Mundro?"

Sert said dazedly, "I do! It is they. There is no doubt about it. But how—?"

Sandra said, "Don't you see? It is true that the Heaviside layer once broke down under the strain of excess drainage. But that was centuries, millenia, ago. And ever since that time, men have been living beneath the domes. The Heaviside, being nothing but a gigantic field of force, regained its full potential, became once more an efficient shield between Earth and the deadly radiation from beyond.

"But within the domes, the Masters dared not venture outside to discover this thing. They exiled over-bold Underlings to their supposed death— and when the Underlings never returned, they assumed the radiation still existed. Actually, the men were glad to be free—"

The one named Mundro laughed heartily. "But naturally! Why should we return to slavery when we had a wide and beautiful world in which to live?

"There are thousands like us outside. Free men, breathing the fresh air, feeling the mother Earth beneath our feet. Long years have we hoped and prayed that one day we might be strong enough to deliver you, our imprisoned brethren, from slavery. But until today, when these two were exiled, we thought there was no chance.

"Then, when we saw the Dome fall, we knew all was well. We shall rebuild a new world under the clear skies. The clear and beautiful skies. See, brethren, what I mean?"

He pointed skyward toward the gaping rent in the Dome. It was twilight now, and high above their heads shone a single star, white, white, piercing white against the dark sapphire of the heavens. Fighting man though Larry was, he felt something clutch at his heart, and his throat was oddly thick. At his side he felt Sandra's hand steal into his, and heard her whispering, "I know now what he meant—"

"Who, Sandra?"

"Dante," replied the girl softly. "When he returned from the nethermost pits of hell, he had but one greeting for the world he loved. He said,

'Thence we came forth—and saw the stars again—'"

* * * *

It was a silent group that met in the laboratory a short time later. Sert was there, Sandra and Larry, Mundro and the French lieutenant whose gallant defense of Sandra had so unexpectedly turned stalemate to victory. Sert spoke for them all when he asked, "Then you must go, Larry Wilson? Can you not stay here and help us remold a world near to our heart's desire?"

"We must go, Sert," Larry told him simply. "Behind us we left friends, loved ones. It is best that we should return to the Twentieth Century. You others, I suppose, will follow."

He spoke to the *franc-tireur*. But the swaggering horseman shook his head, smiled, his teeth gleaming beneath his waxed mustache.

"Not I, *mon vieux*! This is a world to my liking. Besides, are there not legends on earth of troops of fighting men who disappeared strangely? There are none who returned. I think me this is a natural thing. This new world needs new blood, fighting blood, strong men. And anyway"—he twisted his mustache roguishly—"did you notice those Amazon maidens? Sturdy baggages, but—*aaah, mon cher*, ravissante!"

"Perhaps you're right," acknowledged Larry. And for the last time he gave his hand to Sert. "This is a one-way passage, my friend. We go back to our own time, but—"

"Yes, Larry Wilson?"

Sandra answered for both of them.

"What Larry means to say is—if the occasion ever arises when you should need us, do not hesitate to send for us. Yours is the means of bringing us to your world. And we'll always be ready and waiting."

She paused a moment, then blushed. "It shouldn't be hard to find us," she ventured. "Because I think that we are going to be together—from now on. Isn't that right, Larry?"

"You forgot," said Larry, "the 'darling' part." He led her into the Time-warp field. They waved once more to their friends. Then Sert pressed a button. A shimmering field built up about them, cutting off their view. It was gray and weird, and the passage twisted and curved. Again, as long before, Larry experienced that wild, topsy-turvy sense of bottomlessness ... of falling ... of clutching for some support. His hand found something soft and warm that gripped his own....

* * * *

He opened his eyes to find a black face peering into his; great white eyes staring with fright. A soft hand was under his armpit, raising him; a liquid Negro voice was demanding, "Yo' awright, boss? Yo' hurt yo'se'f?

Ah di'n't see you fall till—boom! Theah you was! Yo' awright?"

Larry said, "Yes, I'm all right." Then he remembered. He turned swiftly. "The girl—where is she? Sandy!"

And Sandra was at his side. Both of them were on the steps in the Broad Street Station in Philadelphia. They were being stared at by curious eyes; a little crowd had gathered. Larry looked swiftly at his wrist-watch. The hands stood at 10:59 on the dot.

He said confusedly, "We—we're back where we started from, Sandy? Everything's the same, only—"

"Only," finished the girl, "everything's different, now." And she stood on tiptoe to kiss him. Somebody in the crowd sniggered. A veteran trainman chuckled and nudged a neighbor.

"Newlyweds?" he said. "You can spot 'em every time. Oh, well—nothin' like bein' young!"

Larry looked at Sandra, and a smile touched his lips. "We're not," he said, "what he thinks. But—it's a damn good idea."

Once more, to the vast amusement of their audience, their lips met. Then, arm in arm, they walked down the steps into the heat and confusion and bustling traffic of the world they knew....

LIGHTER THAN YOU THINK

Originally published in *Fantastic Universe*, August 1957.

Some joker in the dear, dead days now virtually beyond recall won two-bit immortality by declaring that, "What this country needs is a good five-cent cigar."

Which is, of course, Victorian malarkey. What this country *really* needs is a good five-cent nickel. Or perhaps a good cigar-shaped spaceship. There's a fortune waiting somewhere out in space for the man who can go out there and claim it. A fortune! And if you think I'm just talking through my hat, lend an ear ...

Joyce started the whole thing. Or maybe I did when for the umpteenth time I suggested she should marry me. She smiled in a way that showed she didn't disapprove of my persistence, but loosed a salvo of devastating negatives.

"No deal," she crisped decisively. "Know why? No dough!"

"But, sugar," I pleaded, "two can live as cheaply as one—"

"This is true," replied Joyce, "only of guppies. Understand, Don, I don't mind changing my name from Carter to Mallory. In fact, I'd rather like to. But I have no desire whatever to be known to the neighbors as 'that poor little Mrs. Mallory in last year's coat.'

"I'll marry you," she continued firmly, "when, as and if you get a promotion."

Her answer was by no stretch of the imagination a reason for loud cheers, handsprings and cartwheels. Because I'm a Federal employee. The United States Patent Office is my beat. There's one nice thing to be said about working for the bewhiskered old gentleman in the star-spangled stovepipe and striped britches: it's permanent. Once you get your name inscribed on the list of Civil Service employees it takes an act of Congress to blast it off again. And of course I don't have to remind you how long it takes *that* body of vote-happy windbags to act. Terrapins in treacle are greased lightning by comparison.

But advancement is painfully slow in a department where discharges are unheard of and resignations rare. When I started clerking for this madhouse I was assistant to the assistant Chief Clerk's assistant. Now, ten years later, by dint of mighty effort and a cultivated facility for avoiding Senatorial investigations, I've succeeded in losing only one of those redundant adjectives.

Being my secretary, Joyce certainly realized this. But women have a remarkable ability to separate business and pleasure. So:

"A promotion," she insisted. "Or at least a good, substantial raise."

"In case you don't know it," I told her gloomily, "you are displaying a lamentably vulgar interest in one of life's lesser values. Happiness, not money, should be man's chief goal."

"What good is happiness," demanded Joyce, "if you can't buy money with it?"

"Why hoard lucre?" I sniffed. "You can't take it with you."

"In that case," said Joyce flatly, "I'm not going. There's no use arguing, Don. I've made up my mind—"

At this moment our dreary little impasse was ended by a sudden tumult outside my office. There was a squealing shriek, the shuffle of footsteps, the pounding of fists upon my door. And over all the shrill tones of an old, familiar voice high-pitched in triumph.

"Let me in! I've got to see him instantaceously. This time I've got it; I've absolutely *got* it!"

Joyce and I gasped, then broke simultaneously for the door as it flew open to reveal a tableau resembling the Laocoon group *sans* snake and party of the third part. Back to the door and struggling valiantly to defend it stood the receptionist, Miss Thomas. Held briefly but volubly at bay was a red-thatched, buck-toothed individual—and I *do* mean individual!—with a face like the map of Eire, who stopped wrestling as he saw us, and grinned delightedly.

"Hello, Mr. Mallory," he said. "Hi, Miss Joyce."

"Pat!" we both cried at once. "Pat Pending!"

Miss Thomas, a relative newcomer to our bailiwick, seemed baffled by the warmth of our greeting. She entered the office with our visitor, and as Joyce and I pumphandled him enthusiastically she asked, "You—you *know* this gentleman, Mr. Mallory?"

"I should say we do!" I chortled. "Pat, you old naughty word! Where on earth have you been hiding lately?"

"Surely you've heard of the great Patrick Pending, Miss Thomas?" asked Joyce.

"Pending?" faltered Miss Thomas. "I seem to have heard the name. Or seen it somewhere—"

Pat beamed upon her companionably. Stepping to my desk, he up-ended the typewriter and pointed to a legend in tiny letters stamped into the frame: *Reg. U.S. Pat. Off.—Pat. Pending.*

"Here, perhaps?" he suggested. "I invented this. And the airplane, and the automobile, and—oh, ever so many things. You'll find my name inscribed on every one.

"I," he announced modestly, "am Pat Pending—the greatest inventulator of all time."

Miss Thomas stared at me goggle-eyed.

"*Is* he?" she demanded. "I mean—*did* he?"

I nodded solemnly.

"Not only those, but a host of other marvels. The bacular clock, the transmatter, the predictograph—"

Miss Thomas turned on Pat a gaze of fawning admiration. "How wonderful!" she breathed.

"Oh, nothing, really," said Pat, wriggling.

"But it is! Most of the things brought here are so absurd. Automatic hat-tippers, self-defrosting galoshes, punching bags that defend themselves—" Disdainfully she indicated the display collection of screwball items we call our Chamber of Horrors. "It's simply marvelous to meet a man who has invented things really worth while."

Honestly, the look in her eyes was sickening. But was Pat nauseated? Not he! The big goon was lapping it up like a famished feline. His simpering smirk stretched from ear to there as he murmured, "Now, Miss Thomas—"

"Sandra, Mr. Pending," she sighed softly. "To you just plain ... Sandy. Please?"

"Well, Sandy—" Pat gulped.

I said disgustedly, "Look, you two—break it up! Love at first sight is wonderful in books, but in a Federal office I'm pretty sure it's unconstitutional, and it *may* be subversive. Would you mind coming down to earth? Pat, you barged in here squalling about some new invention. Is that correct?"

With an effort Pat wrenched his gaze from his new-found admirer and nodded soberly.

"That's right, Mr. Mallory. And a great one, too. One that will revolutionate the world. Will you give me an applicaceous form, please? I want to file it immediately."

"Not so fast, Pat. You know the routine. What's the nature of this remarkable discovery?"

"You may write it down," said Pat grandiloquently, "as Pat Pending's lightening rod."

I glanced at Joyce, and she at me, then both of us at Pending.

"But, Pat," I exclaimed, "that's ridiculous! Ben Franklin invented the lightning rod two hundred years ago."

"I said *lightening*," retorted my redheaded friend, "not *lightning*. My invention doesn't conduct electricity *to* the ground, but *from* it." He brandished a slim baton which until then I had assumed to be an ordinary walking-stick. "With this," he claimed, "I can make things weigh as much or as little as I please!"

The eyes of Sandy Thomas needed only jet propulsion to become flying saucers.

"Isn't he wonderful, Mr. Mallory?" she gasped.

But her enthusiasm wasn't contagious. I glowered at Pending coldly.

"Oh, come now, Pat!" I scoffed. "You can't really believe that yourself. After all, there *are* such things as basic principles. Weight is not a variable factor. And so far as I know, Congress hasn't repealed the Law of Gravity."

Pat sighed regretfully.

"You're always so hard to convince, Mr. Mallory," he complained. "But—oh, well! Take this."

He handed me the baton. I stared at it curiously. It looked rather like a British swagger stick: slim, dainty, well balanced. But the ornamental gadget at its top was not commonplace. It seemed to be a knob or a dial of some kind, divided into segments scored with vernier markings. I gazed at Pending askance.

"Well, Pat? What now?"

"How much do you weigh, Mr. Mallory?"

"One sixty-five," I answered.

"You're sure of that?"

"I'm not. But my bathroom scales appeared to be. This morning. Why?"

"Do you think Miss Joyce could lift you?"

I said thoughtfully, "Well, that's an idea. But I doubt it. She won't even let me try to support *her*."

"I'm serious, Mr. Mallory. Do you think she could lift you with one hand?"

"Don't be silly! Of course not. Nor could you."

"There's where you're wrong," said Pending firmly. "She can—and will."

He reached forward suddenly and twisted the metal cap on the stick in my hands. As he did so, I loosed a cry of alarm and almost dropped the baton. For instantaneously I experienced a startling, flighty giddiness, a sudden loss of weight that made me feel as if my soles were treading on sponge rubber, my shoulders sprouting wings.

"Hold on to it!" cried Pat. Then to Joyce, "Lift him, Miss Joyce."

Joyce faltered, "How? Like th-this?" and touched a finger to my midriff. Immediately my feet left the floor. I started flailing futilely to trample six inches of ozone back to the solid floorboards. To no avail. With no effort whatever Joyce raised me high above her head until my dazed dome was shedding dandruff on the ceiling!

"Well, Mr. Mallory," said Pat, "do you believe me now?"

"Get me down out of here!" I howled. "You *know* I can't stand high places!"

"You now weigh less than ten pounds—"

"Never mind the statistics. I feel like a circus balloon. How do I get down again?"

"Turn the knob on the cane," advised Pat, "to your normal weight. Careful, now! *Not so fast!*"

His warning came too late. I hit the deck with a resounding thud, and the cane came clattering after. Pat retrieved it hurriedly, inspected it to make sure it was not damaged. I glared at him as I picked myself off the floor.

"You might show some interest in *me*," I grumbled. "I doubt if that stick will need a liniment rubdown tonight. Okay, Pat. You're right and I'm wrong, as you usually are. That modern variation of a witch's broomstick *does* operate. Only—how?"

"That dial at the top governs weight," explained Pat. "When you turn it—"

"Skip that. I know how it is operated. I want to know what makes it work?"

"Well," explained Pat, "I'm not certain I can make it clear, but it's all tied in with the elemental scientific problems of mass, weight, gravity and electric energy. What *is* electricity, for example—"

"I used to know," I frowned. "But I forget."

Joyce shook her head sorrowfully.

"Friends," she intoned, "let us all bow our heads. This is a moment of great tragedy. The only man in the world who ever knew what electricity is—and he has forgotten!"

"That's the whole point," agreed Pending. "No one knows what electricity really is. All we know is how to use it. Einstein has demonstrated that the force of gravity and electrical energy are kindred; perhaps different aspects of a common phenomenon. That was my starting point."

"So this rod, which enables you to defy the law of gravity, is electrical?"

"Electricaceous," corrected Pat. "You see, I have transmogrified the polarifity of certain ingredular cellulations. A series of disentrigulated helicosities, activated by hypermagnetation, set up a disruptular wave motion which results in—counter-gravity!"

And there you are! Ninety-nine percent of the time Pat Pending talks like a normal human being. But ask him to explain the mechanism of one of his inventions and linguistic hell breaks loose. He begins jabbering like a schizophrenic parrot reading a Sanskrit dictionary backward! I sighed and surrendered all hope of ever actually learning *how* his great new discovery worked. I turned my thoughts to more important matters.

"Okay, Pat. We'll dismiss the details as trivial and get down to brass tacks. What is your invention used for?"

"Eh?" said the redhead.

"It's not enough that an idea is practicable," I pointed out. "It must also be practical to be of any value in this frenzied modern era. What good is your invention?"

"What good," demanded Joyce, "is a newborn baby?"

"Don't change the subject," I suggested. "Or come to think of it, maybe you should. At the diaper level, life is just one damp thing after another. But how to turn Pat's brainchild into cold, hard cash—that's the question before the board now.

"Individual flight *a la* Superman? No dice. I can testify from personal experience that once you get up there you're completely out of control. And I can't see any sense in humans trying to fly with jet flames scorching their base of operations.

"Elevators? Derricks? Building cranes? Possible. But lifting a couple hundred pounds is one thing. Lifting a few tons is a horse of a different color.

"No, Pat," I continued, "I don't see just how—"

Sandy Thomas squeaked suddenly and grasped my arm.

"That's it, Mr. Mallory!" she cried. "That's it!"

"Huh? What's what?"

"You wanted to know how Pat could make money from his invention. You've just answered your own question."

"I have?"

"Horses! Horse racing, to be exact. You've heard of handicaps, haven't you?"

"I'm overwhelmed with them," I nodded wearily. "A secretary who repulses my honorable advances, a receptionist who squeals in my ear—"

"Listen, Mr. Mallory, what's the last thing horses do before they go to the post?"

"Check the tote board," I said promptly, "to find out if I've got any money on them. Horses hate me. They've formed an equine conspiracy to prove to me the ancient adage that a fool and his money are soon parted."

"Wait a minute!" chimed in Joyce thoughtfully. "I know what Sandy means. They weigh in. Is that right?"

"Exactly! The more weight a horse is bearing, the slower it runs. That's the purpose of handicapping. But if a horse that was supposed to be carrying more than a hundred pounds was actually only carrying *ten*—Well, you see?"

Sandy paused, breathless. I stared at her with a gathering respect.

"Never underestimate the power of a woman," I said, "when it comes to devising new and ingenious methods of perpetrating petty larceny. There's only one small fly in the ointment, so far as I can see. How do we convince some racehorse owner he should become a party to this gentle felony?"

"Oh, you don't have to," smiled Sandy cheerfully. "I'm already convinced."

"You? You own a horse?"

"Yes. Haven't you ever heard of Tapwater?"

"Oh, sure! That drip's running all the time!"

Joyce tossed me a reproving glance.

"This is a matter of gravity, Donald," she stated, "and you keep treating it with levity. Sandy, do you *really* own Tapwater? He's the colt who won the Monmouth Futurity, isn't he?"

"That's right. And four other starts this season. That's been our big trouble. He shows such promise that the judges have placed him under a terrific weight handicap. To run in next week's Gold Stakes, for instance, he would have to carry 124 pounds. I was hesitant to enter him because of that. But with Pat's new invention—" She turned to Pat, eyes glowing— "he could enter and win!"

Pat said uncertainly, "I don't know. I don't like gambling. And it doesn't seem quite ethical, somehow—"

I asked Sandy, "Suppose he ran carrying 124. What would be the probable odds?"

"High," she replied, "*Very* high. Perhaps as high as forty to one."

"In that case," I decided, "it's not only ethical, it's a moral obligation. If you're opposed to gambling, Pat, what better way can you think of to put the parimutuels out of business?"

"And besides," Sandy pointed out, "this would be a wonderful opportunity to display your new discovery before an audience of thousands. Well, Pat? What do you say?"

Pat hesitated, caught a glimpse of Sandy's pleading eyes, and was lost.

"Very well," he said. "We'll do it. Mr. Mallory, enter Tapwater in the Gold Stakes. We'll put on the most spectaceous exhibition in the history of gambilizing!"

* * * *

Thus it was that approximately one week later our piratical little crew was assembled once again, this time in the paddock at Laurel. In case you're an inland aborigine, let me explain that Laurel race track (from the township of the same name) is where horse fanciers from the District of Columbia go to abandon their Capitol and capital on weekends.

We were briefing our jockey—a scrawny youth with a pair of oversized ears—on the use of Pat's lightening rod. Being short on gray matter as well as on stature, he wasn't getting it at all.

"You mean," he said for the third or thirty-third time, "you don't want I should *hit* the nag with this bat?"

"Heavens, no!" gasped Pat, blanching. "It's much too delicate for that."

"Don't fool yourself, mister. Horses can stand a lot of leather."

"Not the horse, stupid," I said. "The bat. This is the only riding crop of its kind in the world. We don't want it damaged. All you have to do is *carry* it. We'll do the rest."

"How about setting the dial, Don?" asked Joyce.

"Pat will do that just before the horses move onto the track. Now let's get going. It's weigh-in time."

We moved to the scales with our rider. He stepped aboard the platform, complete with silks and saddle, and the spinner leaped to a staggering 102, whereupon the officials started gravely handing him little leather sacks.

"What's this?" I whispered to Sandy. "Prizes for malnutrition? He must have won all the blackjacks east of the Mississippi."

"The handicap," she whispered back. "Lead weights at one pound each."

"If he starts to lose," I ruminated, "they'd make wonderful ammunition—"

"One hundred and twenty-four," announced the chief weigher-inner. "Next entry!"

We returned to Tapwater. The jockey fastened the weights to his gear, saddled up and mounted. From the track came the traditional bugle call. Sandy nodded to Pat.

"All right, Pat. Now!"

Pending twisted the knob on his lightening rod and handed the stick to the jockey. The little horseman gasped, rose three inches in his stirrups, and almost let go of the baton.

"H-hey!" he exclaimed. "I feel funny. I feel—"

"Never mind that," I told him. "Just you hold on to that rod until the race is over. And when you come back, give it to Pat immediately. Understand?"

"Yes. But I feel so—so lightheaded—"

"That's because you're featherbrained," I advised him. "Now, get going. Giddyap, Dobbin!"

I patted Tapwater's flank, and so help me Newton, I think that one gentle tap pushed the colt half way to the starting gate! He pattered across the turf with a curious bouncing gait as if he were running on tiptoe. We hastened to our seats in the grandstand.

"Did you get all the bets down?" asked Joyce.

I nodded and displayed a deck of ducats. "It may not have occurred to you, my sweet," I announced gleefully, "but these pasteboards are transferrable on demand to rice and old shoes, the sweet strains of *Oh, Promise Me!* and the scent of orange blossoms. You insisted I should have a nest egg before you would murmur, 'I do'? Well, after this race these tickets will be worth—" I cast a swift last glance at the tote board's closing odds, quoting Tapwater at 35 to 1—"approximately seventy thousand dollars!"

"Donald!" gasped Joyce. "You didn't bet all your savings?"

"Every cent," I told her cheerfully. "Why not?"

"But if something should go wrong! If Tapwater should lose!"

"He won't. See what I mean?"

For even as we were talking, the bell jangled, the crowd roared, and the horses were off. Eight entries surged from the starting gate. And already one full length out in front pranced the weight-free, lightfoot Tapwater!

At the quarter post our colt had stretched his lead to three lengths, and I shouted in Pending's ear, "How much does that jockey weigh, anyway?"

"About six pounds," said Pat. "I turned the knob to cancel one eighteen."

At the half, all the other horses could glimpse of Tapwater was heels. At the three-quarter post he was so far ahead that the jockey must have been lonely. As he rounded into the stretch I caught a binocular view of his face, and he looked dazed and a little frightened. He wasn't actually *riding* Tapwater. The colt was simply skimming home, and he was holding on for dear life to make sure he didn't blow off the horse's back. The result was a foregone conclusion, of course. Tapwater crossed the finish line nine lengths ahead, setting a new track record.

The crowd went wild. Over the hubbub I clutched Pat's arm and bawled, "I'll go collect our winnings. Hurry down to the track and swap that lightening rod for the real bat we brought along. He'll have to weigh out again, you know. Scoot!"

The others vanished paddockward as I went for the big payoff. It was dreary at the totalizer windows. I was one of a scant handful who had bet on Tapwater, so it took no time at all to scoop into the valise I had brought along the seventy thousand bucks in crisp, green lettuce which an awed teller passed across the counter. Then I hurried back to join the others in the winner's circle, where bedlam was not only reigning but pouring. Flashbulbs were popping all over the place, cameramen were screaming for just one more of the jockey, the owner, the fabulous Tapwater. The officials were vainly striving to quiet the tumult so they could award the prize. I found Pending worming his way out of the heart of the crowd.

"Did you get it?" I demanded.

He nodded, thrust the knobbed baton into my hand.

"You substituted the normal one?"

Again he nodded. Hastily I thrust the lightening rod out of sight into my valise, and we elbowed forward to share the triumphant moment. It was a great experience. I felt giddy with joy; I was walking on little pink clouds of happiness. Security was mine at last. And Joyce, as well.

"Ladies and gentlemen!" cried the chief official. "Your attention, please! Today we have witnessed a truly spectacular feat: the setting of a new track record by a champion racing under a tremendous handicap. I give you a magnificent racehorse—*Tapwater*!"

"That's right, folks!" I bawled, carried away by the excitement. "Give this little horse a great big hand!"

Setting the example, I laid down the bag, started clapping vigorously. From a distance I heard Pat Pending's agonized scream.

"Mr. Mallory—the suitcase! Grab it!"

I glanced down, belatedly aware of the danger of theft. But too late. The bag had disappeared.

"Hey!" I yelled. "Who swiped my bag? Police!"

"Up there, Mr. Mallory!" bawled Pat. "Jump!"

I glanced skyward. Three feet above my head and rising swiftly was the valise in which I had cached not only our winnings but Pat's gravity-defying rod! I leaped—but in vain. I was *still* making feeble, futile efforts to make like the moon-hurdling nursery rhyme cow when quite a while later two strong young men in white jackets came and jabbed me with a sedative ...

* * * *

Later, when time and barbiturates had dulled the biting edge of my despair, we assembled once again in my office and I made my apologies to my friends.

"It was all my fault," I acknowledged. "I should have realized Pat hadn't readjusted the rod when I placed it in my bag. It felt lighter. But I was so excited—"

"It was *my* fault," mourned Pat, "for not changing it immediately. But I was afraid someone might see me."

"Perhaps if we hired an airplane—?" I suggested.

Pat shook his head.

"No, Mr. Mallory. The rod was set to cancel 118 pounds. The bag weighed less than twenty. It will go miles beyond the reach of any airplane before it settles into an orbit around earth."

"Well, there goes my dreamed-of fortune," I said sadly. "Accompanied by the fading strains of an unplayed wedding march. I'm sorry, Joyce."

"Isn't there one thing you folks are overlooking?" asked Sandy Thomas. "My goodness, you'd think we had lost our last cent just because that little old bag flew away!"

"For your information," I told her, "that is precisely what happened to me. My entire bank account vanished into the wild blue yonder. And some of Pat's money, too."

"But have you forgotten," she insisted, "that we *won* the race? Of course the track officials were a wee bit suspicious when your suitcase took off. But they couldn't prove anything. So they paid me the Gold Stakes prize. If we split it four ways, we all make a nice little profit.

"Or," she added, "if you and Joyce want to make yours a double share, we could split it three ways.

"Or," she continued hopefully, "if Pat wants to, we could make *two* double shares, and split it fifty-fifty?"

From the look in Pat's eyes I knew he was stunned by this possibility. And from the look in hers, I felt she was going to make every effort to take advantage of his bewilderment.

So, as I said before, what this country needs is a good cigar-shaped spaceship. There's a fortune waiting somewhere out in space for the man who can go out there and claim it. Seventy thousand bucks in cold, hard cash.

Indubitatiously!

REVOLT ON IO

Originally published in *Planet Stories*, Spring 1941.

The ship's clock bonged drowsily three times. Bud Chandler, the junior watch, glared at it languidly. "Thus," he yawned, "endeth the lobster patrol. Three bells, my fine bucko—and the soft, warm hay for you. Or—" There was a hopeful note in his voice. "Or would you like to finish out my trick for me? I'll stand double for *you* some night."

Dan Mallory said, "Comets to you, sailor!" And he rose, stretching the kinks out of weary muscles. His collar was open at the throat, his back ached from five solid hours in the bucket-shaped control chair. His eyes were strained. That was from peering alternately at glowing panels, through a *perilens* plate into the murky, blue-black space before the void-hurtling *Libra*, and back to the panels again. "There's a little thing called sleep which I'm going to grab some of. As soon as Norton shows up. Where the pink Cepheids—?"

"Tell you what. Finish my trick tonight, Dan, and I'll double for you *twice*. That's fair enough, isn't it?"

"Fair enough," said Mallory, "but not sufficiently enticing. Like an albino on a desert planetoid. Ah, here's our hero now! Welcome, Sir Relief! Dump it into the basket and let poppa go seek the arms of Morpheus."

"Who's she?" growled Rick Norton, Third Mate. His eyes were puffy; he squinted and glared at the bright lights of the control turret. "Hell's howling acres, I'm tired! I just about got to sleep when—Oh, well. Log in order?"

"Directly." Mallory shot a curious glance at Norton. "Just got to sleep? How come? What were you doing up so late?"

"It wasn't official business," answered the junior officer curtly, "so it's none of yours. Let's have your log sheet." He slumped into the control chair, squinted through the *perilens* and made a few tiny course corrections. Across the room, Bud Chandler's shoulders shrugged a reply to Dan's swift lift of the eyebrows. The Second Mate's lips formed a word. "Sore-head!" Mallory nodded. Norton *was* a surly son-of-a-spacewrangler.

But that wasn't any skin off his nose. He went to the chart table. Footsteps clattered up the Jacob's ladder, the door flew open and the Old Man stomped onto the bridge. He snapped, "'Zuwere!" and glowered over Mallory's shoulder, shrewd, space-faded eyes reading sense into the senior lieutenant's neat, precise columns. He jabbed a horny finger at one line of figures. "Sure o' that, Mallory? Velocity that high?"

Mallory said respectfully, "Yes, sir. All figures have been checked and double checked. We're point oh-oh-one on course. Forced speed, point thirty-nine above normal."

"Checked and double checked," said Captain Algase, "is good enough most of the time. But this trip is special. And vitally important. Forty thousand innocent lives depend on our reaching Io damn soon! Remember that, Mallory. All of you remember that."

The stern lines of his face eased a trifle. "It's been a hard shuttle, I know. A brutal, punishing trip. And we've all been under a terrific strain. But our difficulties are nothing compared to those of the garrison and the honest colonists of New Fresno. They're looking to us for aid, and we're bringing them aid.

"That is, someone aboard this ship is. I honestly don't know who that person is. No one knows except the man himself, the commander of the SSP Intelligence Department on Earth, and maybe someone at New Fresno. But he *is* on board, either an officer, sailor or passenger, and he *is* carrying to Io the plans for the new ray weapon recently perfected by the SSP Ordnance Bureau.

"Those plans will enable our New Fresno garrison to subdue this mysterious uprising on Io. That's why the *Libra* is traveling at forced speed. That's why we must redouble every normal precaution to insure our reaching the Io colony. That's why, too, we must keep our eyes open; watch even each other. What's the matter with you, Norton?"

Norton had started suddenly. Now he muttered, red-faced, "Sorry, sir. Sudden light in the visiplate. It looked like a meteoride."

"There's nothing there now," said the skipper.

But Chandler repeated, "Watch each other, Captain? I don't get it. We're all pledged and trusted members of the Solar Space Patrol, aren't we? We all live by the SSP motto. I don't see—" He fingered his breast insignia, that tiny, golden rocket emblazoned with the words, *Order out of Chaos*. "I don't see why we should—"

"Because," explained the skipper grimly, "wherever there's an uprising there are converts to the new cause, traitors to the old. Where there are plans, there are spies to steal them. That's not a warning from H.Q.; that's plain, old-fashioned horse-sense. I fought through the Rollie Rebellion, you know. After the Grantland massacre I discovered that one of my own messmates was in the pay of the Mercurians.

"I won't say for sure that there is a spy aboard the *Libra*. But if there is, we must give him no opportunity to learn anything. Weary or not, we must remain on the alert at all times. But I needn't say any more. Finished, Mallory?"

"Yes, sir. Log in order, sir."

"Very good. You may retire. Chandler, you seem to be fagged."

Bud said, "One more yawn and I'll be a zombie."

"A gabby zombie?" sniffed the Old Man. "I'll finish your trick for you. Go get some rest." Still glowering, he plumped himself into the seat vacated by Chandler, cut in the intercommunications board, audioed the radio turret. "Is that you, Sparks? Wake up, you lazy scut! Any news from the Earth? Or Mars Central?"

The radioman's voice clacked metallically, "No, sir. I can't get through to any station. The rebel forces at New Fresno are still jamming the ether with static interference on all wave bands."

"Well, keep trying. Let me know if you get through. Well?" The skipper glanced back over his shoulder. "Well, I thought you two were tired? What are you waiting for? Want to stand another trick apiece?"

"No, sir!" said both men hastily. "We're leaving, sir!" They fled.

"Ain't he a whipper, though?" asked Chandler affectionately. "He growls like a terrier pup, but he's got no more bite than a cup custard. 'Scuse me!" A gigantic yawn split his grin in two. "Must have been something I et!"

"The hell of it is," said Mallory ruefully, "now I'm off duty, I'm not a bit tired. I wasn't tired at all, really. Just had hardening of the panties from squatting in that seat so long. Got a cigarette?"

Chandler tossed him a package. "And don't swipe the coupon, either. Six thousand more and I get an electronic microscope. Well, you can do what you like. I'm going bye-bye and try to forget the waffles that bucket-seat has pressed into my hip pockets. 'Night, pal!"

His footsteps rang sharp little echoes on the metal flooring, echoes that hollowed as he disappeared down a corridor leading to the sleeping quarters and Mallory turned toward the observation deck.

wildsidepress.comThe tall First Mate leaned against the heavy quartzite pane staring into the depths of space through which the *Libra* scudded. The sight was no novelty to him, but as ever it wakened in his heart a sense of awe, a feeling of weird instability, a sort of pride in Man that he, of all the many, strange life-forms experimenting nature had devised, should so far be the only one whose imagination was so great, whose curiosity was so strong, that he had found a way to fling himself at blinding speed across the broad, unfathomable reaches of the void.

It was disheartening to realize that even though he had attained the stars, Man had not yet sloughed off the instincts and habits of the ape from which he sprang. Man's genius had blazed a path across the spaceways, Man's bravery had established new colonies from scorching Mercury to frozen Uranus. SSP lightships bridged the chasms between and beyond; even now the concentrated rays of faraway Sol were steaming the rimy crust off Pluto that Earth's miners might extract the valuable ores revealed by the spectroscope. But with the growth of the colonies, Man's ever latent cupidity had come into play. This past half century, thought Dan Mallory with a sort of savage anger, had been nothing but one long, bloody era of warfare between the forces of law and the outlawry of the greedy.

Now there was this uprising on the first satellite of Jupiter; Io. A charming little world. A pleasant Earth-like orb, spinning quietly about its gigantic parent. Up to this time, its natives had never been troublesome. Squat, muscular creatures, more or less anthropoid, except for the fact that their complexions had a pale, greenish cast and their eyes were double-lidded like those of snakes. They had an intelligence of .63 on the Solar Constant scale. Within a century or so the control board meant to award them autonomy; toward this end educators had been working ever since Io had been removed from the British Imperial Protectorate in 2221.

Trouble had sprung, both literally and figuratively, like a bolt from the blue. A cosmic *blitzkrieg*. One moment there had been peace and sweet content on Io; the next came a frantic, garbled message about "a rebel army ... natives ... led by...." The rest had been drowned in an ear-drum blasting burst of electronic static that had rendered all further communication impossible.

"Kreuther!" said Mallory thoughtfully. The affair sounded like one of Kreuther's moves. That power-mad genius, exiled from Earth after the thwarted Lunar Campaign of 2234, was accustomed to strike in just this fashion. He alone, of all avowed SSP enemies, had the persuasive ability to win to his cause a horde of normally contented Ionians, the wealth with which to set into motion war's red machinery, the genius with which to disrupt interplanetary communications.

"But if it is Kreuther," thought Mallory consolingly, "this time he's bitten off more than he can chew. That new weapon—" He wondered, briefly, which officer, sailor, passenger, had been entrusted with the secret of the new ray gun's construction. Then he cast the thought from his mind. It was none of his business. It were better he didn't know.

It was at that stage of his reverie that a sudden byplay of movement captured his attention. In an instant he had cupped his cigarette into his palm, stepped into a dark patch of shadow. A figure had glided from the passageway that led to the sleeping quarters, was now peering uncertainly into the observation deck. It was David Wilmot, one of the six passengers aboard the *Libra*.

Wilmot's thin face was pinched with nervousness; he coughed, a thin little hacking sound in the muted quiet, then put the back of his hand to his mouth. Dan stood motionless, his dark uniform blending perfectly with the drapes that concealed him. As he waited, watching, the door at the far end of the deck opened, a short, plump man in night-robe entered. Wilmot sprang forward eagerly. His whisper carried to Dan's keen ears. "Have you got them, Doctor?"

"Quiet, you fool!" Dr. Bonetti's forehead creased angrily; his eyeglasses reflected a subdued light owlishly. He fumbled in his pocket, passed something white to the other man. "Here! But not a word, about this, mind you!"

"I know. I know." Wilmot seized the papers avidly, turned and fled down the corridor whence he had emerged. The doctor stared after him for a moment, shook his head regretfully, then disappeared. The door closed behind him softly.

"That's why, too, we must keep our eyes open—."

The skipper's words echoed in Dan Mallory's memory as he stepped from his hiding place, brow furrowed. What the devil was going on here? Could Bonetti have been the bearer of the secret plans; could Wilmot have been the spy? Had he just witnessed the sell-out of a traitor?

But before he could get his jumbled thoughts into order, a voice addressed him from behind, gravely, quietly.

"Rather confusing, eh, Lieutenant?"

Dan whirled to look into the face of Garland Smith, another of the *Libra's* passengers. He said, half pettishly, "You, Captain? What are *you* doing up at this time of night?"

The one-time officer of the SSP, now on the retired list, shot a swift glance at the glittering panorama visible through the quartzite plates.

"Night, Lieutenant? Night and day are nothing but quirks of speech out here, sleep a matter of habit. When you have lifted gravs as many years as *I* have—" He sighed. "I was restless. And perhaps it is just as well. I witnessed the same thing you did. And strange things are going on aboard the *Libra.*"

Mallory said cautiously, "Perhaps you're too apprehensive, Captain. Just because two passengers are sleepless like yourself, meet in the observation chamber—"

"They're not the only two who are still awake. The whole slumbering ship stirs with movement, my boy. A moment or so before you arrived I saw Albert Lemming stealing down the No. 2 corridor—and 'stealing' is the only word that describes his progress. Before that, Mrs. Wilmot had a secret rendezvous with some one in the smoking room; I don't know who her companion was. And Lady Alice has not been in her cabin all night."

The older man's eyes sought Mallory's, his gaze was piercing.

"My boy, I realize that I no longer rank you. But not so long ago, I was your senior. Once a Patrolman, always a Patrolman, you know. I feel we are in the midst of an intrigue too weighty for one man to solve. Perhaps the experience of an old officer may help. Tell me, is it true what I have heard? That someone aboard this vessel is carrying to the New Fresno garrison the secret of Earth's new ray weapon? If so, the mysterious actions we've witnessed may be espionage, agents of the Kreuther forces—"

Mallory said respectfully, "I'm very sorry, sir. I am not permitted to say anything. But I would suggest that in the morning you speak to Captain Algase. I'm sure he'll welcome your offer of assistance." His face clouded. Slowly he said, "Lady Alice. Where did you see her last?"

"In the reading room."

Mallory saluted, turned and went to the ship's library. As he walked he found himself hoping, why, he did not try to explain to himself, that he would find the room empty. But it was not. A single lamp was lighted inside. As Mallory pressed open the door, shadows danced on the farther wall; the wavering, unidimensional symbol of an upright figure spun and made swift, jabbing motions, dropped. There was a sound of paper rustling, the rough scrape of calfskin on buckram. Then he was in the room, and Lady Alice was seated beside the refectory table, ostensibly reading a book. She glanced up with a little movement of surprise.

"Why, Lieutenant, what a pleasant surprise!"

Mallory stifled the impulse to say, "Pleasant?" He stared at the girl curiously, reminding himself for the hundredth time since she had come aboard this ship, six days ago, that as man and woman they had no common meeting ground, they lived on planes inordinately diverse. He was Dan Mallory, a Lieutenant of the Solar Space Patrol, a respectable, if underpaid, watchdog of law and order in man's widening circle of influence. Moreover, he was a *young* lieutenant. It would be years before he earned a major brevet, became an acceptable social figure. Even if a miracle were to happen, if he were to be selected into the envied corps of Lensmen, he would only be a super-cop. While she....

She was Lady Alice Charwell, possessor of a name and title respected for more than eight hundred years. Of course the title was now one of courtesy only; there was no Duchy of Io since the cession of that satellite to the World Council. But once her father had been manor lord of the entire globe; in the *Almanach de Gotha* her family name and crest still figured prominently.

All of which had little to do with the fact that her eyes were blue as the morning mists of Venus, that her limbs were white and straight and supple, softly feminine despite the mannish slack and shirt ensemble she affected, that her hair was a seine of sunlight gold that snared Dan Mallory's heart and quickened his breath.

He forced his voice to calmness. He said, "Lady Alice, don't you think it would be better if you were to go to bed? This—this staying up at night—"

Her laughter was warm and delicious.

"But, Lieutenant! Surely there's no harm in my reading myself to sleep?"

"Not a bit," agreed Mallory. He bit his lip. "I might suggest, though, that unless you're reading a book in the Lower Venusian language, it would be easier to read if the book were right side up. And—" He walked past her, swiftly, stared at the book which, hastily thrust back into the bookcase, still jutted out beyond its fellows. "And you might find more interesting reading matter than a tactical survey of Ionian military resources."

The girl's face was scarlet. She came to her feet indignantly. "Really, Lieutenant, you go too far! I don't see that it is any of your business."

"Lady Alice," said Mallory pleadingly, "a state of war exists on Io. Strange things are happening aboard the *Libra*, things the exact nature of which I am not at liberty to explain. If you will try to forget, for a moment, that I am a space officer—just think of me as a man—will you allow me to make the suggestion that you do absolutely nothing to lay your actions, your motives, open to any sort of suspicion?

"I realize that as one who inherited a claim to the title, 'Duchess of Io,' you are deeply interested in current affairs on that colony. Others may read another meaning into your actions, though. At least one person has already hinted that you—"

Lady Alice's breathing was swift. "Who?" she demanded. "Who is this person?"

"I'm sorry. I can't say. But will you do as I suggest?"

There was a moment of silence. Then the girl shut the book on her lap, laid it on the table, rose. "Very well, Lieutenant. I'm a rather poor deceiver, aren't I? Nevertheless, I thank you for your well-meant advice." She moved toward the doorway, grace and poise in her every stride. And she turned there to smile back at him, her voice soft and unamused. "Lieutenant," she said, "you should lay aside your shoulder-straps more often. The man beneath is most—interesting."

Then she was gone, leaving behind her a red-faced, speechless, utterly chaotic Dan Mallory.

* * * *

At breakfast, Mallory presided at the head of the table. Bud Chandler, arriving a few minutes late, stared at his comrade surprisedly.

"Why, Skipper!" he said, "What this trip is doing for your complexion! You look thirty years younger. Where did you get them pretty pink cheeks?"

Mallory growled, "Sit down, pal, and shut up. The Old Man's grabbing forty, and he deserves 'em. He and Norton ran into a loft-bound vacuole last night, had a hell of a time pulling out. Didn't you hear the commotion?"

"All I heard," complained Bud, "was somebody in my room snoring. It woke me up once, and what made me maddest was when I found out it was me." He nodded to the assembled passengers, sat down and made wry faces over his grapefruit juice.

Albert Lemming, the swarthy-skinned jewel merchant en route to his company's headquarters in New Fresno, stared at the acting-Captain curiously.

"A vacuole, Lieutenant? What's that?"

"A hole in space. Something like an air-pocket in the ether. They aren't particularly dangerous, but the one we ran into was whirling in the wrong direction; if Captain Algase hadn't pulled us out, we'd have lost time on our trip to Io."

Mrs. Wilmot looked up. She was not, thought Mallory, a bad looking dame—if you went for that sharp, peaked sort of beauty. But there was a touch of cruelty to the cut of her lips, a pinched look about the nostrils, he didn't go for. And her eyes were too close together. She said, "That would be unfortunate, wouldn't it, Lieutenant? Losing time, I mean?"

There was a touch of some subtler meaning behind her words; Mallory couldn't decide just what it was. Maybe it was sarcasm, maybe it was fear, maybe it was mockery. He said, "I think we all share the desire to reach New Fresno as soon as possible, don't we?"

Her answer was unexpectedly sharp.

"I don't care if we never reach there. I'd rather die peacefully in space than—"

"*Susan!*" Her husband's voice sheared the end of the sentence into silence. Her eyes glared defiance at him for a moment, then she returned to the business of eating. Lemming looked embarrassed. Dr. Bonetti shook his head. Captain Smith coughed, suggested mildly, "Captain Algase must be an excellent astronavigator, Lieutenant. I didn't notice a single jarring motion. In *my* day, escape from a vacuole was a tedious, ship-wracking process. Of course—" His eyes wandered about the table querulously, "Of course there are so many new inventions nowadays. Improvements in all lines. Spacecraft, air-modifiers, armament—"

Mallory rose suddenly. He was half angry with the ex-space officer. Smith wasn't being very subtle in his effort to help matters. No doubt the old duck meant well, but—

He said, "If you'll excuse me, ladies and gentlemen, I must go to the bridge. Ready, Bud?"

Bud Chandler gulped, "Ssswllwmcffy! Ulp!"

"What?"

"I said, 'As soon as I swallow my coffee!'" repeated the Second Mate aggrievedly. "Can't you understand English? Let's go."

Lemming intercepted them as they passed his end of the table. He asked, "Lieutenant, I've been wanting to ask for several days—might I be permitted to visit the bridge? This is my first spaceflight, you know. I've always wanted to see how the controls are operated."

"Speak to Captain Algase," suggested Dan. "That's not within my power—Yes, Billy?"

The mess-boy had just raced in from the outer deck, trayless, almost breathless. "Y're wanted on the bridge immejitely, Lootenant! Cap'n orders!" His eyes were as big as saucers. "Sparks just got a message through. A message from New Fresno!"

Dan had just time to notice, out of the corner of one eye, how this bald pronouncement affected the passengers. He saw the concerted motion that dragged them all to their feet as if they were puppets on a single string; saw the sudden gleam in Wilmot's eye, the worried frown that creased Bonetti's forehead, heard the swift, startled gasp from Lady Alice and intercepted Captain Smith's darting glances from one to another of the listeners. Lemming's voice quavered, "A—a message from New Fresno!" and Susan Wilmot laughed, a short, strident, triumphant burst of sound.

Then Dan Mallory saw no more. For with Chandler at his heels, he was pounding through the corridors to the Jacob's ladder that fed the control turret.

* * * *

Captain Algase was no beauty even when garbed in his officer's blues; in pajamas and slippers he was something out of a nightmare. His bare legs were like cylindrical hair mattresses, his pajama slacks bulged at the equator as if he were concealing there a half watermelon. His eyes were red and gummy, his temper like something that could be poured out of a cruet. As Dan and Bud entered the control turret he was battering the bewildered radioman's defenses into oblivion with a salvo of verbal thermite.

"Message!" he was howling. "You call this thing a message! I'll have you stewed in slow gravy for waking me up like this, Sparks! Of all the damn, dumb—" He saw his two lieutenants. "Never mind, you two. Go back and finish your breakfast. False alarm."

"We've finished, Skipper," said Dan. "What's all the commotion?"

"This &![oe])$$[oe]09!—" began Algase.

Sparks said miserably, "But it was Marlowe's hand on the keys, Cap'n!

I swear it was. I know the message don't make sense, but you can't fool a bug-pounder. Every radioman has a distinctive sending style. Ask anybody. Even one of them wise-cracking Donovan boys. They'll tell you. And this was Marlowe's hand—"

"Let's see," said Mallory. He took the flimsy from his senior's fingers, frowned as he ran an eye over the cryptic symbols. "Numerals! All numerals. Sparks—?"

"It was like this. The static interference is still going on. The audio wouldn't bring in voice at all. But as I was twisting the dials, I got this power wave from Lunar III, Joe Marlowe's station. It had a—a sort of cadence. I began putting down the things it sounded like, and—and that's what come out."

Chandler, peering over his comrade's shoulder, said,

"Well, hell's bells, are you all nuts? It must be a code of some sort. Sparks, we use several numerical codes, don't we?"

"Yes." Meekly. "But that ain't one of them, Lieutenant. That don't fit no code in the reg book."

Mallory continued to stare at the message. It was long, and undeniably confusing. It read:

83.7-152-232.12-167.64-31.02-16-184-167.64-9.02-1-126.92-
144.27-186.31-50.95-16-175-47.9-16-14.008-4.002-39.944-
50.95-173.04-19-16-10.25-69.87-14.008-16-184-232.12-186.31-
39.944-127.61-14.008-20.183-184-19-186.31-118.70-16-1-74.91-
127.61-14.008-74.91-28.06-32.06-181.4-14.008-140.13-138-92-
20.183-184-39.944-222.-32.06-138.92-162.46-26.97-126.92-
140.13-40.08-10.82-26.97-32.06-31.02-88.92-14.008-16-184-16-
14.008-6.94-79.916-39.944-40.08-195.23-39.944-114.76-150.43-
126.92-232.12-114.76-127.61-14.008-32.06-126.92-19-88.92-
140.92-16-127.61-12-47.9-16-14.008-16-19-20.183-184-78.96-
52.01-16.721-225.97-88.92—

"—and there it began all over again," said Sparks. "The same sequence. I agree, it's a code. But what good is a code when we ain't got the key to it. It ain't a simple word substitution cryptogram or a five-by-five. I studied them in the Academy, and tried them all before I brought this to the Captain. In other words, it ain't no good to us unless we've got the clue—and we ain't got the clue!"

Mallory said, "Billy said this was a message from New Fresno?"

"Well, he was wrong, as usual." Determinedly. "It come from Earth's moon. I know Joe Marlowe's fingers when I hear 'em. Damn, we was classmates for three years. Before I got crazy and gave up chemistry for key-pushing—"

"Chemistry!" Mallory started. "Did you say chemistry? Did you and Marlowe study chemistry together?"

"Yeah. Why?"

"Why! Because that's the answer. Marlowe is nobody's fool. He knew you were the radioman aboard the *Libra*, prepared a special code, the key to which would lie in your brain as the 'memory of auld lang syne'—Bud, look at these figures again. You notice the number '16' appearing over and over? Even in that thick skull of yours, '16' suggests—?"

"Oxygen," declared Chandler promptly. "The atomic weight of oxygen."

"And eighty-three point seven? Forty-seven, nine?"

"Krypton. And—let's see—titanium?"

"Right! Grab a pencil, pal! I think we've got a solution here. Jot these down—krypton, europium, thorium, erbium—Hold it!" He looked at his companion disgustedly. "Just the symbols, you dope! Don't you see? The symbols of the various elements employ every letter in the English language except 'j' and 'q'—and those are the two least commonly used, anyway. Start over. Krypton—"

"Kr," said Bud.

"Europium—"

"Eu."

"Thorium. Erbium—"

"'Kreuther'!" howled Bud. "That's it, Dan! Keep going!"

The message slowly scrawled its way onto paper. A word appeared, another, another. Then:

"Ten point twenty-five!" said Mallory. "Followed by 69.87! What the hell are they?"

Bud said, "Maybe he made a mistake? Boron's 10.82. Lithium's 6.94—"

"No. That's not it," said Mallory. He frowned. Captain Algase had long since wakened completely, was listening to his two juniors with glowing pride. Now he cut the Gordian knot.

"Chromium," he suggested, "is fifty-two point one, Dan. The reverse of the number that stumps you."

"Right! That's it, Skipper! And the meaning must be that the symbol is to be written in reverse. 'Rc' instead of 'Cr.' There aren't enough combinations to spell every word in the language unless you use some subterfuges like that."

"Which makes the word," said Bud, "'forces.' Go on, pal...."

Mallory plunged into the heart of the coded letter. "39.944—"

"Argon," said Bud, "'A.'"

"114.76. Indium. 150.43—"

"Samarium. 'Sa.' Next?"

"Iodine."

"'I.'"

The message was finished. Bud handed it to Captain Algase. Mallory's curiosity was at fever pitch. He had not been able to piece the letters together as he went along; he had gained but a smattering here and there. He waited. The skipper read slowly, breaking the message up into coherent sentences.

"'Kreuther power behind revolution. Heavy forces now threatening New Fresno—'"

"Kreuther, huh?" growled Bud. "I thought so."

"'Hasten assistance. Lane warns—'" The captain stopped, stared a moment, glanced swiftly at Mallory. There was a tight note in his voice. "'Lane warns Lady Alice, cabal spy, now in *Libra*—'"

"Lady Alice!" blurted Mallory. The warmth of the control turret suddenly weighed down upon him; his brow felt hot, oppressed, as if some gigantic hand had descended upon his temples.

"'Captain saith,'" continued Algase, "'intensify protection of new secret ray.'" He crumpled the paper. "And that is all, gentlemen. Mallory—"

"Yes, sir?"

"Our fears were justified. There *is* a spy on the *Libra*. We must take no chances. You will arrest Lady Alice Charwell, place her under lock and key for the duration of the voyage."

Bud Chandler muttered, "Where does Marlowe get that Old English stuff? 'Saith!' Why didn't he say, 'Says'?"

"Because," Mallory answered mechanically, "there is no 'ys' combination in the elemental vocabulary. He had to say it that way." The recollection of his unpleasant duty flooded back on him; with it came protest. "But it can't be true, Captain! There must be some mistake. Surely Lady Alice wouldn't be—"

"On the contrary, Daniel," Algase's voice was unusually gentle, "she would be. Once her family owned all of Io. It is more than likely that she should want to see the globe freed of Board control; regain her lost property. She could well be in league with Kreuther to overthrow the present government. According to this, she *is*."

"Yes, sir," acknowledged Dan dully. He was thinking of Captain Smith's warning. Of the book Lady Alice had been reading, the book on military tactics. "Shall I make the—the arrest now, sir?"

"Yes, Lieutenant."

"Very good, sir!" He turned and left the room. His jaw was white and rigid; a dull hurt was behind his eyes....

* * * *

A strained assemblage awaited his return to the mess hall. As he entered the room all conversation ended abruptly; an almost audible silence fell upon the group of passengers. Lemming half rose from his seat, opened his mouth as though to say something, closed it again, his lips a white slit against the green pallor of his cheeks. Lady Alice's eyes were tense, expectant. Captain Smith moved forward to meet him. The ex-space officer's heavy frame was poised and ready; there was a note of subdued eagerness in his voice. He said stridently, "Well, Lieutenant—?"

Dan Mallory's patience with the older man was quite exhausted. He said curtly, but in a voice that did not reach the ears of the others, "Captain, I must remind you that you have no authority whatsoever on this ship! I appreciate your willingness to help, but—" Angrily. "For God's sake, man, stop acting like the hero of a Twenty-second century dime novel! Stop fingering your needle-gun, and—"

Smith looked embarrassed. His heavy shoulders sagged, and swift contrition swept over Mallory as the one-time officer said, "I—I'm sorry, Lieutenant."

Lemming had found words at last. He asked, shakily, "The—the message, Lieutenant? Was it—?"

He had to arrest Lady Alice, thought Dan Mallory. But he didn't have to humiliate her. To brand her eternally as a traitor in the eyes of her associates. And he still held doggedly to the hope that somehow, somewhere, had been made a dreadful mistake. He said, "The message was a routine transmission, Mr. Lemming. Of no great importance. Now, will you all be kind enough to disband, quietly?"

No one moved. Mallory, glancing at the faces about him, felt again that conviction that an interwoven webbing of intrigue entangled these passengers. He said, firmly, "That is not a request, but a command! You will all retire to the observation deck at once!"

The little group stirred. Mallory sought the side of Lady Alice, said, "I've been wanting to show you the ship, Lady Alice. Wouldn't you like to see it now?"

Her look of pleased surprise burned him. She said, "Why, Lieutenant, how nice! I would enjoy it."

They moved in a direction opposite that of the rest of the passengers. Even so, they did not escape unnoticed. From the corner of his eye Dan Mallory caught the glitter of Dr. Bonetti's spectacles, realized that the dumpy man was watching them shrewdly. And for a moment his eye met that of Captain Garland Smith; the old officer's head was nodding in mused speculation. He, too, had guessed Mallory's concealed purpose.

Only the girl herself seemed unaware that this was not merely a pleasantry. Her shoulder brushed that of Mallory as they pressed through a narrow doorway; the soft, feminine warmth of her heaped reproach on the young lieutenant, as did her words.

"Lieutenant, I see you can take advice as well as give it. I had no idea, last night, when I suggested that you reveal the man beneath the uniform more often, that you would actually—"

They were alone now. And Mallory turned to face her, his voice purposely hard and impersonal.

"If you please, Lady Alice! It is my painful duty to inform you that you are under arrest!"

"Under ar—!" Her gasp ended in a burst of light laughter. She brought her hand to her forehead in mock salute. "Aye, Lieutenant! Brig, ho! But if I'm not too inquisitive, what charges are preferred against me? Murder? Of course, I *do* kill time most horribly, but these long trips—or could it be theft? I'm sure I've stolen nothing. Unless you mean—" She paused in sudden confusion; her eyes lifted to his; there was something written there, something breathtaking. Mallory had to hold tight.

"The charge," he said tersely, "is—treason! That message was from Lunar III, Lady Alice. It bore a warning from the commander of the Intelligence Division there, advising us that you had been discovered to be a member of Igor Kreuther's organization!"

The light died from the girl's eyes, the smile on her lips turned to ice. Her slim body stiffened, straightened. And for an instant Dan Mallory saw, with swift prescience, that this girl was not all charm and allure; that beneath her tempting softness there was a core, steel-strong, of strength and daring.

"Treason! Treason, you—you blind fool!" she spat. "You dare accuse *me*, Lady Alice Charwell, Grand Duchess of Io, Lady of the Rocket and Globe, Maid of the Golden Crest, of—of treason! Sir! My family ruled Io when that dominion was first discovered. For almost three hundred years the Charwell crest has—"

"Please, Lady Alice!" pleaded Mallory. "I know how you feel about it. To your mind, your actions were not treasonable. But Io is no longer yours; it is under the guardianship of the Control Board. And you mustn't talk this way. I will be called to testify against you; anything you say will be convicting evidence—" He touched her shoulder as though the warmth of his hand might melt its icy stiffness.

She shrugged herself loose disdainfully.

"I think we can dispense with the amenities, Lieutenant. The smile on the lips ... the gracious invitation to 'see the ship' ... the friendly hand of comfort...." There was scorn, anger, pain in her eyes. "It is my right to demand the privilege of communicating with my accusers, is it not? Those on Earth who—?"

"I'm sorry. No audio transmission is possible because of the blanket-static. The message came through in a code."

"I see. I must wait, then, until we reach New Fresno. Never mind, Lieutenant Mallory. You have said enough. I presume you are placing me under guard? Where—in my own quarters? Very well. If you will be kind enough to escort me there!" She laughed brittlely. "But, of course, you will. You couldn't let a traitor out of your sight, could you?"

In throbbing, bitter silence they moved down the corridors to Lady Alice's stateroom. There she spoke for the last time.

"The message that accused me, Lieutenant. Might I be permitted to hear the damning evidence? What did it say?"

There was no harm, thought Mallory miserably, in telling her that. The words were like acid, etched into his brain. He repeated them. She listened intently, frowned—and then a new, curious look stole into her eyes. She said, "But—"

"Yes?" said Mallory. "Yes?"

The look faded. She laughed scornfully.

"Hoping to hear more 'convicting evidence,' Lieutenant? I'm so sorry to disappoint you. Now, will you lock the door after me, please?"

Dan Mallory made a last try. It would cost him his rocket if anyone heard his words, but—

"Lady Alice," he pleaded, "I'm honestly sorry about this. I don't believe you are guilty. If you'll trust me, tell me your side of the story, I'll do everything in my power to—"

"You have done," said the girl tightly, "more than enough right now. Guard me well, Lieutenant!" With a short, mocking laugh she slipped through the door, Mallory waited a long minute, then turned the key in the lock. Its grate was a taunting sneer. He returned to the bridge....

* * * *

He couldn't help overhearing the end of that conversation. The runway that fed the control turret was narrow and metal-walled; it formed a perfect soundbox. Moreover, the door was ajar. The voice was Captain Algase reached his ears perfectly as he approached the room.

"—don't want to have to remind you again, Norton, that it is highly unethical for a space officer to become involved with a woman passenger. Especially with a married woman."

And the surly voice of Third Mate Rick Norton saying, "Very well, sir!" Then footsteps approaching the door, a figure confronting his squarely, Norton flushing, snarling, "Getting an earful, Mallory?"

Dan was in no mood for bickering. He said, "Don't mind me, Norton. I've known for months you were a skirt-chaser. I don't consider it any of my business."

Norton's cheeks flamed. He said insultingly, "And I suppose you stand behind your stripes as you say that?"

"Forget the stripes." Mallory looked at his fists. "I stand behind these."

"Good!" Norton swung. He was a well-built man, a strong man. His blow packed dynamite—but it needed a target to set off the percussion cap. It found no target but a moving one. Mallory ducked, rolled with the punch, came up inside the Third Mate's guard to land a short, jabbing left to the midsection, a blasting right to the point of Norton's jaw. Norton gasped and collapsed soggily. Arms behind him reached out to support his falling weight; other lips behind Mallory whistled softly as Bud Chandler, coming up to serve his trick, witnessed the swift, decisive exchange of blows. And Captain Algase, releasing Norton's inert form, glared at Mallory.

"Well! Well, Lieutenant, I think you know we have rules against brawling?"

"Aye, sir!"

"But—" Captain Algase stroked his jaw speculatively, "In this case—Chandler, get him below! It served him right. Maybe he'll spend this rest period sleeping, instead of stirring up trouble amongst the passengers. Dan, my boy—"

He led the way back into the turret, completed the log record for the previous trick, handed it to Mallory, who had slipped into the control bucket.

"Twenty-four more Earth hours and we'll be there," he said. "And, believe me, I'll be glad when this trip ends. Trouble. Nothing but trouble from beginning to end. Long tricks and short tempers. Norton getting mixed up with that Wilmot dame—a damn' hussy if I ever saw one, and her husband a neurotic wreck. Smith bothering the blistering Hades out of me, wanting to 'help' catch spies and a thousand other—" He glanced at Mallory, who had stiffened at the word. His glance was sympathetic. "I'm sorry I had to ask you to arrest her, Daniel. But it's experiences like that that make strong men out of space officers.

"You have to be hard in this business. Crime hides beneath strange disguises. The sweetest smiles, the friendliest hand-shakes, the most honeyed words, may conceal—"

"If you please, sir!" said Dan Mallory, white-lipped.

"I know, lad. I've seen the way you looked at her. But remember—forty thousand innocent lives! Had she learned the secret of that new weapon, our voyage might have been disastrous. From this distance she could have made a flight to Io in one of the auxiliary safety rockets, given the plans to

Kreuther's forces. The very weapon we look to for salvation would have been used against us. Io might have become a nest of rebellion, instead of a peaceful member of the solar family. Now that we've snared our spy, the messenger—whoever he is—will be safe."

On the visiplate it was a glowing red spark, but in the *perilens* before him it was a gigantic orb dominating the heavens through which the *Libra* hurtled. Jupiter; monster of Sol's scattered brood, untamed sphere of writhing gases and vague mystery, itself a pseudo-parent emanating enough heat to make its far-flung satellites livable worlds. Soon they would fling themselves, they aboard the *Libra*, halfway around that gigantic orb, settle to the small body now wanly visible as a silver crescent.

* * * *

Dan Mallory punched a control-key savagely, felt the *Libra* shake itself into a slightly changed curve, turned to his superior.

"I'm not so sure of that, sir. Oh, I'm not trying to defend Lady Alice. Earth's Intelligence officers don't make mistakes—not mistakes of that magnitude, anyway. But there are other passengers I don't trust. Lemming. Wilmot. Dr. Bonetti. Why are they aboard the *Libra*? Why were they so excited when they heard we'd received a message from Lunar III? Suppose one of them is also a spy?"

"Or suppose," said the skipper, "one of them bears the secret of the new ray weapon. Wouldn't that one naturally be excited?"

"But the others?" Mallory inquired.

"I don't know. You may have something there, Daniel. I'm still taking no chances. I've put Aiken on guard at Lady Alice's door. If anyone tries to liberate her—What *is* it, Sparks?"

He snapped the query at the intercommunications box which was spluttering and growling. The radioman's tone was weary. "It's Mr. Wilmot again, sir. He insists on talking to you."

"Tell Mr. Wilmot I will see him at midday mess."

Sparks was stubborn about it.

"But he insists his message is important, sir. He demands to see you at once. Says—"

"*Demands!*" The skipper's jowls reddened. "Please tell Mr. Wilmot passengers do not *demand* favors of spaceship officers. I will see him at mess. That is all!" And he cut the communications board; turned to Mallory angrily. "That's why I didn't put you on report for slugging Norton. Wilmot's mad as a hornet and I don't blame him. Norton catting around after his wife—"

Chandler appeared, grinning. He said to Mallory, "What a sock, pal, what a sock! If that guy counts sheep in his sleep, he's going to wake up allergic to mutton. Wish I had done it. He's a grouchy son-of-a— What's biting you?"

Mallory said, "That's just it, damn it! I don't quite know. It just came upon me like a flash that someone said something funny ... something that didn't ring true ... but I can't remember what it was. If I could—"

"See, Skipper? It's got him, too. We're all going to be candidates for the straitjacket squad when we finish this trip."

Algase smiled sourly. "Well, don't lift gravs for the next twenty-four hours, that's all I ask. See you later, boys." He turned to leave; was interrupted by the buzz of the intercommunications box. "What, again! Yes, Sparks—what is it this time? If it's Wilmot again, tell him to go beat his brains out with a rusty bar! I'll see him at—"

Sparks' voice was harsh with excitement.

"It is Wilmot, sir! But I can't tell him anything. He's dead, sir! Murdered!"

Chandler said, "Murdered? Mi-god!" Captain Algase said a more effective and less printable thing which ended in, "Come on!" And he and Chandler pounded down the runway, their footsteps ringing on the Jacob's-ladder, disappearing in the distance.

Dan Mallory, his thoughts chaotic, sat chained to his bucket seat by the obligation of guiding the spaceship through the treacherous void. His fingers played over the control keys automatically; slowly the chaos left his brain and cold, clear, reasoning thought took its place.

Wilmot dead. Why? The first thought that suggested itself was Norton. Motive—jealousy. The desire to get Susan Wilmot's husband out of the way so—

But that was illogical. Norton was a skirt-chaser and a quixotic fool, but he wasn't a criminal. Murder was not in his line. Why else, then?

Because Wilmot had been the bearer of the formula? Had he been slain by a spy? And if so, by whom? Lady Alice was in her cabin, or at least— with a swift constriction of the throat—Dan hoped she was. He pressed the intercommunications button hurriedly; Sparks' face appeared before him on the visiplate. "Get me the M-13 plate, Sparks! The one in the stateroom passageway!"

The scene shifted. Aiken, a space gob, looked up as the audio before him glowed into life, touched his forelock respectfully. "Lieutenant Mallory?"

"The prisoner is in her stateroom?"

"Aye, sir."

"She hasn't been out?"

"Not for a moment, sir." The sailor added, "Might I ask the lootenant what the h—I mean, what's going on?"

"Plenty!" snapped Dan. "That's all, sailor. Carry on!"

The glow faded. Mallory shook his head. No dice on that hunch. Then what else—?

The thought came so suddenly, so breathtakingly, that it literally lifted him out of his chair. There was but one possible answer! The reverse of his former theory. Wilmot was neither the bearer of the precious secret nor a spy. He was the "innocent bystander"; the traditional victim who, from time immemorial, has always been the one to get bopped. Somehow the nervous, jittery little man had learned *who* the spy was. He had attempted to communicate his knowledge to Captain Algase; the petulance of his own nature had rendered this impossible. And the spy, knowing that Wilmot had learned his secret, had—

Again he pressed the button. This time Sparks said, "Lieutenant Mallory? Have you seen Mr. Lemming? The captain wants to question him, but he can't be found anywhere—"

"Never mind that!" rapped Mallory. "Sparks, I want to know this. How was Wilmot killed?"

"Rayed, sir. Needled."

"I thought as much. And who was the first to find him?"

"Dr. Bonetti, sir. He's being held under suspicion. He confesses to having supplied Wilmot with drugs, sir. *Teklin-root*, sir. (That would be, thought Mallory swiftly, the package surreptitiously exchanged in the observation room.) But he claims he didn't kill Wilmot—"

"Quick, man! Was Captain Smith anywhere around the radio turret when this happened?"

"Why—why, he *had* been, sir. But he left before Mr. Wilmot did—"

Captain Algase's face appeared in the visiplate beside that of Sparks. "Daniel, my boy, keep your eye peeled for Lemming. He's disappeared. Susan Wilmot has told us he isn't a jewel merchant at all; he's a jewel thief! Fleeing Earth to gain settler's amnesty on Io. Wilmot knew his secret, tried to blackmail him. Lemming threatened—"

"You're after the wrong man!" screamed Dan Mallory. "Captain, I see it all, now! The whole story. These other things have confused us. Sparks, swiftly—get me that M-13 plate again!"

* * * *

The scene spun, changed dizzily. Once again Mallory was gazing down the corridor where Aiken had stood guard. But Aiken no longer stood before Lady Alice Charwell's door. He lay there, limp, still forever. A smoking hole charred his broad chest, crimson stirred sluggishly from the needle-ray's telltale trail. The door of the stateroom was open.

A hoarse bellow told Dan that the captain was seeing the same scene.

"*She* did it! She killed him and escaped!"

"No!" roared Mallory. "*Smith* did it! The man we should have suspected all the time; the man who *admitted* his guilt, but I was too blind to see it. Kreuther's spy. The renegade space officer—Captain, did you feel that?"

His space-trained senses had felt the swift, tiny moment of jarring repercussion that meant only one thing—that from one of the escape ports a life-skiff, an auxiliary safety rocket, had slipped from its base on the *Libra*, taken off into space!

"He's escaping! He's kidnaped her and taken off in a life-skiff. Bud! Take over! I'm lifting gravs!"

And for the first time in his career as an officer of the SSP, Lieutenant Daniel Mallory violated, deliberately, a rule of the Space Patrol handbook. He rammed the *Libra's* controls into the robot hands of the Iron Mike, and abandoned his post in mid-flight!

* * * *

It was not that he considered himself more capable than his captain or the second mate. His move was dominated by only one thing, the urgent need for haste. Safety rockets are, as everyone knows, blindingly fast. Much faster than the heavier, sturdier, cruising vessels that bear them like so many unfledged wallabies in a pouch. Give Smith a flying start and he would never be apprehended. And *he*, Dan Mallory, was much nearer a life-skiff port than the other officers up in the loft of the radio turret.

Slipping, skidding, stumbling in his haste, he raced to the nearest port, flung open the control-bar, threw himself into the small, tear-shaped vehicle lying there. There were regulations demanding that air, food, water supplies be ascertained before flight in one of these was attempted. But there was no time for such nonsense now. Each second seemed an hour as Mallory warmed the hypatomic motors of the skiff, rammed the button that opened the *Libra's* outer shell, struck another that catapulted the safety-rocket away from its parent craft.

Then the dark of the womblike casing was gone, and he was blasting, under his own power, through space illumined with the candle-gleams of a trillion galactic motes. He set his range-finder and attractor—but even as their needles found their objective, his searching eyes located it. A tiny, silvery gleam against the tawny night ahead—a gleam from the stern of which flared burst upon flaming burst of superheated light.

The rockets of Smith's skiff, hell-bent for Io!

Minutes *had* been precious! Vitally so. Already the little craft was countless thousands of miles before him. It was a wide margin that separated him; and in that margin lay the difference between freedom and peonage for forty thousand Earth-men, millions of Ionians, the difference between life and death for the girl Smith had kidnaped, the difference between victory and defeat for the Solar Patrolmen.

There was only one way to catch Smith. Recognizing the fact, Dan Mallory bit his lip, set his jaw stubbornly. Acceleration! Acceleration great enough to fling him across the yawning void, enable him to snare his quarry in tensiles....

And he was not strapped! No safety corset to hold tight the straining cords of his viscera, no yards of gauze padding to keep his wracked body from literally flinging itself to shreds. No—

He glanced about him hurriedly. There were piles of cushions, soft, plump, airy, scattered about the metallic cockpit. He jammed a dozen of these behind him, under him, about him. There was an oxy-helmet in its container beside him; he thrust this over his head. Its rubberoid halter settled about his chest, his shoulders. At least his straining eyes would not bulge from their sockets; by adjustment—if he could raise a hand—he could compensate accelerative force with pressure.

He drew a deep breath. Then, recklessly, wrenched the dial of the motor to full acceleration!

* * * *

It was as though ten thousand fiery demons tore at his body with claws of flame. A weight, massive, imponderable, kicked the breath out of his lungs, forced it from his gaping mouth and flared nostrils into the helmet he wore. He gulped and strangled, fighting to draw into a shrunken chest a breach of fleeing life. One hand moved—or tried to—to his throat in an instinctive gesture of distress. The hand moved a half inch from his knee, flung itself back into his stomach like a leaden weight.

The quick burst of nausea saved his life, because tortured ductless glands released a stream of adrenalin into his churning blood-stream, the miraculously adaptable body of Man rose once again above its normal limitations. Air crept into his lungs, his heart's tumultuous pounding no longer throbbed a threnody in his eardrums.

Still he could move with only the greatest of effort—but he could move! And his eyes, no longer blinded by the red mist that had drowned their sockets, saw the rocket-flares before him seem to literally stop in midflight, race back toward him!

A great exultation seized him. He was hardly aware that bright blood had burst from his nostrils, and that as he opened his lips to shout hoarsely the corners of his mouth drooled red. The craft he pursued whirled fiercely toward him; like flame-riding charioteers they jockeyed across the cosmic wastes. Smith knew he was there. Must know. But—Mallory's grin was the grimace of a gargoyle—he didn't have the guts to duplicate the young lieutenant's mad burst of speed.

He was depending on other weapons. Even as Mallory experienced the thought, a stabbing beam spat backward from the other rocket, a coruscating ray of silver that bore sudden death.

But Mallory had anticipated the move; his slow hand had been straining for seconds to forestall it. He pressed a lever—the ship slid into a dive. Another and the terrible pressure lifted from his limbs, his body felt suddenly light and buoyant, strength surged back to him with singing sweetness.

Again that stabbing ray searched for him. But Dan Mallory was no novice at the art of space warfare. He spun his craft into a cycloid Laegland arc, the lethal ray spent itself on indestructible space, and when Mallory came out of his maneuver he was within scant miles of his objective.

Grinning savagely, his hand sought the button that would smash Smith's ship into oblivion—then stayed! Lady Alice! He could not destroy her with Smith. Because now he knew, certainly and surely, two things. One of which was that she must be the bearer of the secret ray formula to Io. In no other way could you account for the fact that Smith had dared everything to kidnap her. She carried the secret, not in papers, but in her mind.

Were she to die—and might the gods of space forbid that his hand should destroy her loveliness!—Kreuther would still be the victor. For with her would perish the final hope of the besieged New Fresno garrison.

The other thing he realized was—

But there was no time for that now. His fingers spurned the ray button; found another. A jolt shivered the space-skiff from fore-quartz to rocket as his tensile beam reached across the closing miles, fastened its grip on Smith's craft.

Mallory's grin tightened. He cut motors. His tensile beam would contract like a rubber band, drawing the two ships together. Smith, feeling that beam upon him, unable to sheer it off, would not be able to turn a lethal radiation upon him now. For the tensile beam was a perfect conduction ray. To destroy one ship meant to destroy both.

There was a groan behind him. Shocked, he turned. From the storage bin, bleeding from nose, ears, mouth, body twisted as though wrung through some gigantic mangler, crawled the missing jewel thief—Albert Lemming!

Mallory choked, sickened. "Lord, man! How did you get aboard here? Why—"

Liquid breath gurgled in Lemming's throat. Glaze filmed his eyeballs. "Tried to—" he panted, "—stow away. Wilmot dead—knew suspect me—hid—"

His head fell forward to the floor. Dan fingered his pulse, found there not the feeblest stir of life. Lemming, fleeing the dreaded breath of suspicion, had lost the more important breath of life. The miracle was that he had survived, even so long, the tremendous acceleration that had taxed all Mallory's space-trained, protected faculties.

And the two space-skiffs closed inexorably the gap between them. Mallory's quick brain leaped to the final problem. But before he could solve it, the small skiff audio burst into speech.

"Well done, whoever you are!" said the voice from the other skiff. "But you realize it won't do you any good?"

Mallory rasped, "I'm coming alongside in a minute, Smith. Stand by to surrender peaceably, or—"

"Or?" mocked the ex-space officer. "So it's you, Lieutenant? I might have guessed it. Your valor is exceeded only by your lack of foresight. I repeat, your hectic pursuit has done you no good."

"Never mind the talk. Stand by. This is the end," said Mallory. "This is checkmate, Smith."

"Not checkmate, my gallant young friend," corrected Smith. "*Stalemate.* True, you hold me captive in your beam. But to what end? You can't hope to take me alive. Whenever I choose, I can blast you and myself into atoms. And with us goes—" he paused significantly—"Lady Alice! Ah, you are silent, Lieutenant? I thought you would be. Of course, I'm an old man. These youthful romancings no longer interest me. But—bless us, she's much too beautiful to die, isn't she, Lieutenant?"

Lady Alice's voice interrupted.

"Take him, Dan! Don't think about me. I'm not afraid to—"

"You hear, Lieutenant? The girl's gallantry is a fit match for your own. But by this time, surely, you have realized that if she dies, the secret of the new ray weapon dies with her. I think my leader's forces will have taken New Fresno before a second messenger reaches Io."

It was the truth. Knowing that, Dan Mallory groaned. This was a deadlock; one that neither force could break. He said slowly, "Well, Captain? What is your price for Lady Alice's safety?"

"My own," replied the renegade spaceman promptly, "and the secret she bears. I'm not an unreasonable man, Lieutenant. Even though—" bitterness edged his words—"even though the Solar Space Patrol did take the best years of my life, squeeze the heart out of me, throw my aging body into the discard like a dried pulp. No, I'm not unreasonable—"

So that was it. The self-pity of an aging man, perhaps a man gone off his gravs from the letdown after active years. That was why Smith had renounced his SSP pledge, gone over to the other side. Captain Algase's words rang in Dan's memory. "Where there are new causes, there are traitors to the old—" Even a spaceman was not exempt from human weakness.

"If Lady Alice will surrender her secret to me," the renegade captain was continuing, "with convincing proof that the formula she gives me is no lie, I will permit you both to live. I will allow you to keep one of these ships, return to safety—"

Mallory thought feverishly. It was against his every scruple to parley thus with the other man. But he could gain nothing by destroying himself and Lady Alice. Alive, there was always a chance they might win through to the New Fresno fort, carry their message, howsoever belated. If they died, Kreuther and his hirelings would surely win.

He said, "Very well, Smith. I accept. Give him the formula, Lady Alice."

Her answer was tense, vivid.

"No! No, Dan, don't trust him! He won't keep his promise. I know he won't!"

"We must take that chance." Grimly. "Tell him!"

* * * *

The audio went dead. Mallory waited impatiently. Somewhere, lost in the immensity that engulfed them, the *Libra* surged through space on a mission now in the hands of the deadlocked three. So near that it was more sunlike than Sol, Jupiter swung in its titanic orbit about Man's luminary. The endless night was spangled with an infinitude of stars. The stars toward which Man, yearning, groped—while Man's feet still stumbled through the muck and mire of deceit....

And the audio woke to life again. Smith's voice was triumphant. "Very well, Lieutenant. I am satisfied. I have finished the demolition of power and arms units in this ship. Its radio, however, still operates. I think it will sustain life for you until your friends arrive. I am ready to board your ship."

Lady Alice's cry broke in, "Be careful, Dan! He'll kill you! He—" There was the sound of flesh upon flesh, a silence. Then, "Well, Lieutenant?"

Dan said, "Come ahead."

"You will take your place," said Smith, "in the pilot's seat where I can see you from the moment I enter the lock. Put your hands above your head. Do not move or turn as I enter. If you do—"

"Come ahead," repeated Dan. The audio disconnected.

Dan sprang into motion. He believed Lady Alice's warning. And he was prepared to meet subtlety with subtlety; deceit with deceit. Not yet had Smith won. He bent and lifted the broken body of Albert Lemming. Hurriedly he jammed the oxy-helmet down over the dead man's bloody features. He grunted, "Sorry, pal!" as he hoisted Lemming into the pilot's chair, forced stiffening arms back and up in token of surrender. The high back of the chair, the padded cushions made the form hold its position.

He finished just in time. There was a scraping at the airlock. The two ships had drifted side to side now, and entry was a simple matter. Mallory ducked back into the compartment from which Lemming had emerged. His needle gun was in his hand, poised, ready....

Smith entered quietly. He glanced once at the figure in the pilot's chair, said, "Don't move, Lieutenant—" and his arm raised. The girl's warning had been all too true. There was rankest treachery in the leveling of that gun, in the fiery needle dart that hurled across the chamber, burying itself in Lemming's defenseless head. The stench of charred flesh filled the room. The dead body wobbled, lurched to the floor. And—

"Now, *you* stand still, Smith!" gritted Mallory.

Smith whirled, his jaw dropping open. In his eyes dawned horror, disappointment, rage. He cried out once, raised his gun.

That was how he died. With his traitorous fingers lifted for the last time against a man who wore the uniform he had once worn ... and had disgraced....

* * * *

Afterward, as they stood in the control turret of the *Libra*, watching a sober-faced Rick Norton plot the landing that would bring new life to the Ionian colonists, swift retribution to the fomenters of the uprising, Bud Chandler whaled his comrade's back enthusiastically.

"Guy," he said, "in words of one syllable, you're terrific!"

"That's not one syllable," grinned Mallory.

"All right, then, you're a lallapalooza! But how the blue asteroids did you get onto the fact Smith was the guy?"

Dan said, "It came to me almost too late. It had been worrying me subconsciously ever since I had to—" here he flushed—"had to arrest Lady Alice. I knew that someone had, in conversation with me, said something that didn't ring true. And when Wilmot was killed for having discovered the truth about Smith, I suddenly remembered what it was.

"The night before we got the message from Lunar III, assuring us that Kreuther was behind the revolution, Smith had mentioned to me, quite casually, that he suspected there were on the *Libra* 'espionage agents of the Kreuther forces.' What he was attempting to do, of course, was ally himself with us in order to divert suspicion. But he tipped his hand by that little slip of the tongue."

Lady Alice smiled. She said, "Well, you're not awfully smart. Any of you. I knew he was the spy as soon as I heard the message from Earth."

Captain Algase interrupted, "Yeah, that message! I'm going to raise an assortment of hell about that. Causing us to arrest the one person on board we could really trust."

"And all," smiled the girl, "because of one, small, chemical symbol that you misread. Oh, yes, I understand now. I've seen the original. Bud—you went to the Academy, didn't you?"

"Why—why, yes."

"Your professor there must have been quite an old man. I mean your chemistry prof."

"He was. Ancient. But what has that got to do with it?"

"Everything. He taught you the old, the original chemical symbol for the element samarium. 'Sa.' The more common symbol, the generally accepted one, is 'Sm.' Now you see what a great difference that one little error makes in the meaning of the message. You read it:

"'Lane warns Lady Alice, cabal spy, now on *Libra*. Captain saith intensify protection of new secret ray.'"

"And it should have been read," broke in Dan Mallory, understanding at last, "'Lane warns Lady Alice cabal spy now on *Libra*—Captain Smith! Intensify protection—' and so on. It was a warning *to* you, not about you!"

"Exactly. Naturally, I was—well, indignant when I was placed under arrest. Afterward, I began to think it a good idea. Confined to my quarters, guarded, I would be completely safe. But unfortunately Captain Smith guessed, when I was arrested, that *I* was the bearer of the formula. So he killed my guard, seized the skiff, and kidnaped me."

"Saith!" grunted Bud Chandler disgustedly. "I told you that word was phony. Joe Marlowe never used good English in his life when a cuss-word would do just as well. Hey! Where are you two going?"

It is doubtful whether Dan Mallory heard the question. There was one other little matter that needed clearing up—but soon! That was the way Lady Alice Charwell, in the moment of their mutual peril, had hurdled the amenities of speech, addressed him not as "Lieutenant," or even as plain "Mallory," but as—

"Dan," he said. "You called me 'Dan.' It's not right, Lady Alice. You shouldn't do things like that unless you mean them. And I—"

"Suppose," she asked, "I like that part of your name best. It is a nice name, you know."

Dan Mallory's big hands pawed futilely at the blue of his uniform. "So," he croaked, "is Mallory. And—and I guess I'm completely crazy. I couldn't ask you to share a name like that. I'm just a space cop. And you're a Lady. A titled Lady."

She said softly, "A Lady, Dan? There is no Duchy of Io any more. That's a thing of the past, and my title is only a courtesy. And, oh—I'm so tired of courtesies. I'm a space cop, too, now. There's nothing in the rules to keep two cops from teaming up, is there? Oh, you big, damn, dumb idiot—!"

Her face, smiling up at his, was inclined at just the right angle. They told him afterward that Rick Norton made a swell landing. He didn't believe it. For it seemed to Dan Mallory that the whole cosmos was swirling and dancing and twisting upside down in a delirium of delight....

THE BALLAD OF VENUS NELL

Originally published in *Planet Stories*, Spring 1942.

Oh, the science of Man has narrowed the span
Between the near and the far,
With thunderous roar the great ships soar
From Earth to the dimmest star;
But though in their lust for gold they thrust
From planet to asteroid
The Will of the Great Astronomer still
Is the Will of the cosmic void.
And from Earth's own Sol to the ebon hole
Of the Coalsack's gaping maw
Though Man may jet, he is subject yet
To the Universal Law.
For whoever shall plot for another's lot,
Be he brother or foe or friend
Who seeks his gain of a fellowman's pain
Has a price to pay in the end.

I

Now, Dougal MacNeer was a pioneer.
Just one of a million such
Who labor and toil in unmapped soil
With shovel and pick and hutch.
He was six-foot-two, and a man whom few
Would care to engage in a fight,
With shoulders as firm as a pachyderm;
A tower of granite might.
He had eyes of gray, and a quiet way
Of minding his own affairs;
He never came down to a commerce town
Save for fueling or ship repairs.
Thus it was that he roused the *whys?* and *hows?*

In the minds of the spaceport clique
When he landed at Krull [2] with his tanks half full
And rented a berth for a week.
The cradle-monk [3] stared, then boldly dared,
"By golly, you've struck it rich!
I always knew some day you'd come through,
You lucky son-of-a———"
"Which,"
Asked Doug MacNeer with a smile sincere,
"Is the best joy-joint in Krull?
I've lived alone till my mind's ingrown;
This prospecting life is dull.
"I want to go play from the dusk of day
Till I waken to morning bells."
The attendant said, with a nod of the head,
"You amble to Venus Nell's.
It's the hottest place in this end of space,
Just a couple of minutes' jaunt;
Nell's got music and games, and likker and dames
—And anything else you want!"
"Thanks, that sounds great!" said Mac. But, "Wait!"
Begged the other, "Gimme a break!
Help me out of this rut, MacNeer, and cut
Me in on a share of the take?"
"The take?" asked Doug with a little shrug,
"But *I* haven't made any find!"
And he strolled away with a whistle gay
While the monkey glowered behind.
In a moment or two, Doug wandered through
The gaudily-neoned door
Of a feverish-gay, bright cabaret;
Below, on the mirrored floor
Of the dancehall swayed a cavalcade
Of every breed and race
Whose daughters and sons defy the suns
To journey the ways of space.
A miner from Mars, pockmarked with scars
Pressed close to a woman from Io,
A Jovian baby drawled lazily, "Maybe—"

2   *Krull, a mining town in N. Campbell Terr., Mars. 84 m. SW of Sand*
City; pop. 3,587.
3   *Cradle-monkey; spaceport attendant.*

To pleas of a tar from Ohio;
A vicious-mouthed slattern from faraway Saturn
Sang ditties to make the hair curl.
And then—curtains parted, and Doug MacNeer started
To see such a beautiful girl!

II

Venus Nell was no saint, any preacher would paint
A bad ending for her at a peek.
But her worst enemy would be forced to agree
There was nothing wrong with her physique.
She was flat where it flattered, and curved where it mattered,
A creature of streamline and bubbles;
She had bright yaller hair, and a definite flair
For taking men's minds off their troubles.
She never had known the cap or the gown
Of grammar- or high-school or college,
Which didn't mean she couldn't win her A.B.
In a certain and specialized knowledge.
She had lure and illusion; creating confusion
'Mongst men was but one of her tricks.
Doug's eyes opened wide when she strolled to his side
—And he fell like a cargo of bricks!
She drawled, "Howdy, sailor!" and Dougal turned paler,
"H-howdy!" he managed to answer.
Then, in sudden alarm, "Are you one of the charm-
Gals?" he questioned, "Or only a dancer?"
Now, why an admission of her true position
Nell should at that moment decide
To conceal is a mystery buried in history;
Whatever the reason, she lied.
In fashion designed to make any man blind
She lowered her lashes and blushed.
(Which was no mean achievement itself.) "Oh, believe
Me! I'm no—entertainer," she gushed.
"I sell cigarettes, and I sometimes take bets
On the rocketship races—" MacNeer
Slowly nodded his head as he quietly said
"A girl like you shouldn't be here!
"I think we'd do well to get out of this hell
Of evil and vice," he decided.

Nell had to sit still and bite her lips till
Her inner amusement subsided.
This curious sucker, it suddenly struck her,
Meant business! His motives were pure.
To lead on the calf should be good for a laugh ...
She smiled at him, shy and demure.
"Oh, I cannot do that," she replied, "but a chat
In a quieter spot—?" And she led
Dougal out of the blare to a cool garden square
With the stars burning high overhead.
She gave orders by sign that a beaker of wine
Be served in their shady retreat,
And wondered how long it would be ere this strong,
Handsome stranger acknowledged defeat.
But strangest to tell, it was Doug and not Nell
Who emerged from that contest the victor.
It was nothing he did, but a loneliness hid
In her bosom that finally tricked her.
For Doug spoke of the night, and the glorious flight
Of ships through the reaches of Space;
Of his hopes and his schemes—and his words wakened dreams
That softened the lines of Nell's face.

III

He was just on the verge of confessing the urge
That brought him back out of the void
When a servant discreet appeared in their retreat
And Nell faced the fellow, annoyed.
"Well?" she icily said. The man bobbed his head.
"A visiphone call on the rack."
Nell sighed as she rose. "Some friend, I suppose.
Wait, Dougal; I'll hurry right back."
An expression surprisingly soft in her eyes,
She answered the visiphone.
Her caller, however (the cradle-monk), never
Detected her altered tone.
"Hey, Nell, there's a chump on his way to your dump,
A big, quiet sort of a lout
By name of MacNeer—" Nell told him, "He's here;
What's all the commotion about?"
A hungry grimace of greed mottled the face of

The vengeful space-harbor assistant.
"Do I get my percent for a tip on the gent?"
He parried in accents insistent.
"You mean—?" whispered Nell. And, "Surer than hell!"
The answer came back, swift and eager,
"I've just seen his log, and he's in from the Bog
With a claim-stake the size of Omega!"
Now, for those who don't know their A. L. & O. [4]
The "Bog" is a treacherous sector
Of planetoids legion, a tightly-packed region
Avoided by every prospector.
None but the most daring do any space-faring
In those lethal, whirlagig niches,
But spacemen all claim that the Bog is aflame
With infinite, fabulous riches.
'Twas thence that the crew of the L-32
Returned with a cargo of ore
That assayed ninety-one and a half to the ton
—Or maybe a little bit more.
It was out of the Bog that old space-weasel Scrogg
Withdrew on his gravity-tractor
The rock 4-Omega, which brought such a figure
Scrogg set himself up as a Factor.
So it's easily seen why Nell's new, serene
Complaisance should disappear rudely.
She gasped and she started; her crimson lips parted;
Her eyes narrowed sharply and shrewdly.
"You're positive?" Slyly responded the spy,
"Why else would he put into Krull
With motors O.Q., and flame-jets brand-new,
And fuel-chambers more than half-full?"

IV

Now, though Nelly was young, as has often been sung,
Her chosen profession was old.
Both instinct and habit advised her to *"Grab it!"*
Whenever she heard the word "gold."
She broke the connection, her vivid complexion
More flushed, and with movements exotic

---

4   A. L. & O.—Astrogational Loci and Orbits, the space mariner's
handbook.

Returned to the glade in which Dougal had stayed,
Her inner emotions chaotic.
She studied MacNeer as she slowly drew near,
Appraising him in a new light.
Nell trusted her spy; he would not tell a lie—
But somehow it didn't seem right!
MacNeer didn't act like a man who had cracked
A cache of asteroid dough,
And yet—Venus Nell smiled tightly—Ah, well,
She'd know in a minute or so.
With a cute little shrug she curled on the rug
And smiled into Doug's sober face.
"Go on!" she implored, "and tell me some more
About your adventures in Space.
Have you ever struck gold in the terrible cold?"
Her voice was a query and taunt.
Doug grinned at her there as he fondled her hair.
"I've found all the gold that *I* want!"
Nell's eyes opened wide. "You have?" she replied,
And suddenly somewhere within her
A duel transpired 'tween the Nell who admired
This miner and Nelly the sinner.
Which would have won out is a matter of doubt
But Dougal MacNeer, growing bolder,
At that moment tossed dice with Fate—and he lost!
—By placing a hand on her shoulder.
He bent to her ear, and, "Nelly, my dear,"
He whispered, "Come lift gravs with me
To the skyways above ... I'll teach you to love ...
How wonderfully happy we'll be...."
And—that was a story to Nell old and hoary;
Nell shrugged with a gesture resigned;
A lustful and bestial man, just like the rest
Of his sex....
And she made up her mind.
Averting her face, she escaped his embrace
And whispered, "Wait here for a minute—"
A prearranged sign brought a fresh jug of wine
To Doug—with a sleeping drug in it.
Dougal, gleaming of eye, the glass lifted high
And drank it down, swiftly and deep;
In no time at all, he lay there asprawl

In impotent, stertorous sleep.

V

A pungent aroma jarred Doug from his coma
Much later. He lifted his head
To find he was not in the cool, shady grot
But in some sort of workshop, instead.
His senses were blurry, his tongue thick and furry;
He gagged at the odor and choked.
Then, head still awhirl, he noticed the girl,
And, "Nelly, where are we?" he croaked.
But the girl standing there with the bright yaller hair
Was hardly the girl of his dreams.
She was distant and cold, her manner was bold,
Her eyes glistened brightly with schemes.
With icy élan she spoke to the man
At Dougal's side, "Very well, Gurk,
He's come to his senses, let's drop the pretenses;
Its time we got down to our work."
"Work, Nell?" Dougal gasped, and confusedly clasped
His hammering head in his hands.
He learned, then, that he was bound, foot and knee,
To his seat by unbreakable bands.
Nell said with a numb, deadly smile, "Don't play dumb!
Be smart and you'll shorten this visit.
We know from your log you struck gold in the Bog;
Now, come clean and tell us—where is it?"
"G-gold?" gulped MacNeer. "Th-there's some mistake here!"
He grinned, "Aw, you're kidding me, honey!
Now, be a good sport—" The girl cut him short,
"I don't think this matter is funny!
I gave you a chance to go into your dance;
If you won't, why—" She shifted her eyes
To her white-coated aide. "Well, Gurk, I'm afraid
He must talk through the *menavise*."
As Doug MacNeer's eyes opened wide in surprise
Gurk drew from a nearby cask
A shimmering, fiery helmet of wire;
A sinister sort of mask.
Doug never had seen the fantastic machine
Before, but he'd oftentimes heard

Of the dreaded and hated device that translated
Men's thoughts into spoken words!
With a terrible cry of anger, on high
He lifted his brawny fists,
But an instrument clicked, and manacles snicked!
Like vises about his wrists.
"Well, *now* will you tell us?" persisted Nell.
"There's nothing to tell!" he said.
Nell's warm lips drew fine, and she made a brief sign ...
And the helmet dropped over his head!

VI

It was Nell who depressed the stud that expressed
In flaming, electric flood
The current that boils its way through the coils
Of a menavisal hood.
There was silence at first, then the silence burst
In a moment of horror fraught,
As Doug MacNeer's voice babbled clear
In fragments of tortured thought.
"*I don't understand ... I can't move a hand ...
head aches, and my brain is on fire....
Stars ... Nelly ... Oh, Lord!*" Thus Dougal's thoughts poured
In words through the webwork of wire.
"*Must be a mistake ... I can't be awake
The orbit of Ceres is reckoned
"At three-oh-oh-ten....*" Nell stepped forward then.
"O.Q., Gurk—let up for a second!"
The shimmering died, and to Dougal she cried,
"MacNeer, all we want to know
Is: *Where is the gold?* As soon as you've told
We promise to let you go."
"I've told you already," gasped Doug, unsteady,
"You're wrong if you think I'm rich—"
Nell's scarlet mouth curled. "Fool! Liar!" she snarled;
She viciously closed the switch.
Once again sallow flame trembled hot through the frame
Of the *menavise*; once again
Electrical stresses probed deep the recesses
Of Dougal's tormented brain.
"*The torments of hell—but I never can tell ...*

A man must fight to the end ...
My eyes—I've gone blind ... my head ... and my mind ...
If I only ... could only ... bend...."
It is better to not reveal just what
Things Dougal said and did
In the hour or more that followed, for
Such secrets are better hid.
He babbled of dreams, and hopes and schemes,
And names long lost in the past;
He spoke of flight through the endless night,
And of cosmic reaches vast.
But never he told of wealth or gold,
Though now he was growing weak;
Till finally the girl turned to her churl
Lips set, and as marble bleak.
"He's stalled long enough!" she rasped. "He's tough,
And he's held out for more than an hour;
But I'm going to get that secret yet,
If I have to turn on full power!"
Gurk shook his head, and warningly said,
"I wouldn't attempt it, Nell!
'Twould be of no use, an ounce more juice
Would blister his mind to hell.
He's weak as a cat; if you try that—"
He frowned—"After all that he's had,
Another degree of power would be
Sufficient to drive him mad!"
"That's up to him!" cried Nell, and grim
Of eye she approached the side
Of Doug MacNeer, and, "Listen here,
You obstinate fool!" she cried,
As she pressed the key to the last degree,
"You know very well you told
Me you'd found all the gold that a man could want
—Now, answer: *Where is that gold?*"
The *menavise* flamed, the battered and maimed
Hulk standing before them jerked
As the blistering pain seared Dougal's brain,
MacNeer's lips horribly worked....
And across the tomblike expanse of the room
His feeble answer carried:
"*... lonely as hell ... must ask sweet Nell ...*

It's time I was getting married...."
"I think that she ... and I could be ...
So happy ... a golden prize....
But ... Oh, the pain!" And he screamed again,
The light died out of his eyes.
And Nell stood aghast, to have seen at last
The terrible answer bare:
The gold of his dream was the glorious stream
Of her own bright yaller hair!

VII

So, stranger, if you should happen to
Drop jets in the City of Krull
By chance you may meet on a quiet street
A man who with movements dull
Roams up and down through the little town
Like someone bewitched by a spell;
And the one at his side, his companion and guide
Is the lady once known as Nell.
For the woman who made of love a trade
And discovered true love too late
Has paid at last for the sins of her past
With Dougal MacNeer as her mate.
Her hair, that was gold, is streaked now with cold
White tendrils, but still she sighs
And she waits and she prays, through long, endless days,
For the light to return to his eyes.
For—Man in his lust for raw gold may thrust
From planet to asteroid,
But the will of the Great Astronomer still
Is the Will of the cosmic void.
And whoever shall plot for another's lot,
Be he brother or foe or friend,
Who seeks his gain of a fellowman's pain
Must pay a price in the end.

THE CASTAWAY

Originally published in *Planet Stories,* Winter 1940.

There was an ad in the classified columns of this week's *Spaceways Weekly*. It asked for information concerning the whereabouts of one "Paul Moran, last known to have taken off from Long Island Spaceport for parts unlogged." Captain McNeally drew the notice to my attention. He said, "Look at this, Brait. Wasn't Moran the chap we picked up in the asteroids? It seems to me I remember—"

"You should," I told him. "You see his name twice every shuttle, engraved on cold steel. And you can be thankful for that. But I don't think he'll answer this ad. I don't think they'll ever hear from him."

"That," scoffed the Shipper, "is nonsense! Do you realize what this means, Brait? This ad was inserted by the Government Patent Office. There's a fortune waiting for Mr. Moran back on Earth, when he sees this—"

"A fortune waiting," I said softly, "when and if he ever sees it. But I wonder, Skipper. I wonder."

* * * *

We were about three thousand miles north, west and loft of Ceres when we first sighted him. I remember that well, because I was on the Bridge, and our Sparks, Toby Frisch, had just handed me a free clearance report from the space commander of that planetoid.

I read it and chuckled. I said, "Sparks, this bit of transcription is a masterpiece. Nobody expects a radioman to be good-looking or have brains, but blue space above, man, your spelling and grammar—"

"Leave my relatives," said Sparks stiffly, "out of this. Is the message O.Q. or ain't it?"

"Yes," I told him, "with a light sprinkling of no. Sometimes I wish we had a good operator aboard the *Antigone*. Like one of those Donovan brothers, for instance."

"Them guys!" sniffed Sparks. "Too wise for their britches, both of 'em. I'm a bug-pounder, not a joke-book. If it's smart cracks you want, why don't you buy an audio?"

It was at this point that Lt. Russ Bartlett, First Mate of our ship, who had been shooting the azimuth through the perilens, turned and waved to me excitedly.

"Brait, take a look! Quick! There's a man down below! On one of the minor asteroids!"

I said, "A joke, Bartlett? You'd better check the alignment of that perilens. That's the Man in the Moon you see."

Gunner McCoy, Bartlett's staunchest friend and admirer, looked up from the rotor port, wrinkled his leathery, space-toughed cheeks into a frown, and squirted mekel-juice at a distant gobboon.

"Mebbe you better look, Mr. Brait," he said. "If Russ says there's a man there, then there's a man there."

So I looked. And to look was to act. I cut in my intercommunicating unit and bawled a stop hypo order to Chief Lester in the engine room below. Bartlett was right. There was a single, bulger-clad figure sprawled on the craggy rock of a tiny asteroid hurtling beneath us. A man who lay there quietly, did not rise, did not wave, gave no sign of noticing our approach even when I dropped the *Antigone* down toward the spatial island.

Bartlett, peering through the duplicate lens, said, "Dead, Brait. He must have cracked up. He's not moving."

But there was no wrecked spaceship anywhere around. I said, "We'll know in a few minutes." And then the Skipper burst into the bridge, startled and curious. "Something haywire, boys? Here, I'll take over."

He was a good man, Cap McNeally. A hardened spacehound, canny and wise to the ways of the void, always on deck in moments of emergency. That's why the IPS, the Corporation for which we work, had placed him in command of the *Antigone*, finest and fastest ship in the fleet.

But I calmed his rotors. "Everything O.Q., sir," I told him. "We're standing by to take on a space-wrecked sailor. I think."

My guess was right. A few minutes later we threw out a grapple, space-anchored the *Aunty*, and a rescue party landed on the asteroid. They brought back with them a sad looking specimen of the genus *Homo sapiens*. His cheeks were drained and sunken beneath a bristling, unkempt beard; his skin was blistered frightfully from long exposure to solars and cosmics; his limbs were so feeble that he couldn't walk unaided. He had to be carried.

Someone unscrewed his face-port for him. He drew a long, deep breath of the pure *Antigone* air. His wan eyes lighted dimly and he spoke in a voice that was a thin husk of sound.

"Thank you, gentlemen. I had hoped that at last I might—But you meant well, I suppose."

Which was, I thought at the time, a damned strange speech of gratitude. But I had no time to answer. For his knees suddenly buckled beneath him, his eyes closed. Had it not been for the friendly hands that supported him, he would have pitched forward on his face.

Cap McNeally snapped, "Sick-bay! Snap it up, you lubbers! The man's in bad shape. Out on his feet, cold!"

Sparks whispered, "Gosh, he looks like a corpus!" as the sailors bore our unexpected passenger away. I stared at him disgustedly.

"Corpse." I said.

"Huh?" said Sparks.

"Corpse!" I repeated. "Corpse!"

"You," suggested Sparks, "oughta take somethin' for that indigestion, Lootenant. My sister had it. It made her a physical reek."

It's against the rules for a Second Mate to punch a radioman. So I kicked him. There are limits.

* * * *

That was our first meeting with the mysterious Paul Moran. We didn't know his name then, of course. We learned that several days later. After Doc Jurnegan, our medico, had coaxed, bulldozed and sulfanilamided him back off the brink of the dark and nasty.

Doc was the first to tag Moran with the adjective we all, eventually, accepted.

"It's the damnedest thing," he told me, "I've ever seen. Brait, I'll swear on a pile of prescriptions that he didn't have one chance in a million of pulling through. But he's still alive!

"By rights, he should have been dead two weeks before we found him. Do you know he was on that asteroid five solid weeks? Without food. With only one container of water. With the oxygen reserve in his tank practically exhausted!

"And his condition—" Jurnegan shook his head uncomprehendingly. "Deplorable! He was dessicated, undernourished, fouled from weeks in a bulger. Acute cyanosis alone should have killed him. But—"

I said, "The will-to-live, Doc. It's the determining factor in many a borderline case. I've heard of men with holes in their heads you could drive a stratoplane through who simply refused to—"

"That's just it," said Jurnegan. "He *wants* to die! He refused to take food. I had to feed him intravenously and force him to drink. But in spite of his physical and mental condition, he still lives. It—it's mysterious, Brait!"

So I went in to visit our strange passenger.

He wasn't a bad looking chap, now that his whiskers had been plowed. Thin, of course; hollow of cheek and eye. His skin was sallow, faintly olive; the contours of his head long and narrow, short-indexed. He was a typical Mediterannean, if what my profs taught me is right. Medium stature, small-boned, thin, tapering fingers. Crisp, oily hair, black as space.

I said, "Well, you look like a new man!"—which he did, and, "You're looking fine!" I said—which he wasn't.

He turned his head slowly, studied me with grave, questioning eyes. His voice was faint, but low and pleasing.

"You are Mr. Brait, the Second Mate? I believe I have you to thank for having rescued me?"

"That's all right," I told him.

"Why," he interrupted gently, "did you do it?"

I said, "Oh, come now! You've got to perk up! You get a little flesh on your bones and you'll feel better."

But he went on, as though not hearing my words, "It was a chance. The best chance I've had for years—a thousand years—and you took it from me. Out there I might have found peace at last. The power cannot—it *must* not—extend into the depths of space."

His voice had risen; there was a light of madness, of strange, savage intensity in his eyes. I felt the little hairs on the back of my neck pringling. I knew, now, that the man had not come unscathed through his experience. He was space crazy. Wildly, desperately so. I said, in what I hoped was a soothing voice,

"Now, take it easy, Mr.—er—Moran, isn't it?"

The ghost of a smile touched his lips, and his body became less tense. He said wearily, "Moran—yes. Or Ader. Or Cart—Oh, anything you choose. It hardly seems important any more. I've had so many, many names."

That wasn't exactly encouraging. But at least he was quieter now. And I had to know a few things about him to put in the ship's log. I asked, "How did you get on that asteroid, Moran? Were you space-wrecked? If so, what was the name of your craft? The authorities will want to know."

He answered, almost mockingly, "I was marooned."

"Marooned! But—but that's criminal! Who did it? We'll have them picked up and punished!"

"You'll do nothing of the sort. They marooned me on that asteroid because I deserved it and I respect and thank them for it!" His voice was rising again; higher, shriller. "I thank them, do you hear? I bless them, a hundred, thousand, million times. Though their effort was in vain. I was, and am, a Jonah. A Jonah, Jonah, *Jonah*!"

He sat bolt upright in bed, screaming the word defiantly. Doc Jurnegan raced in, glanced at me reproachfully and took his patient in hand. "You'd better go, Brait," he suggested.

So I left. The sweat on my forehead was damp and cold. I needed a drink.

When I told Cap McNeally of my experience, he nodded soberly.

"I know, Brait. I saw him before you did. And he acted just as loony toward me. Warned me he was a Jonah—"

"I'm not superstitious," I interrupted, "but there *are* such things as Jonahs. Men whose very presence aboard a spaceship seems to cause trouble, dissention, disaster. You remember that Venusian blaster on the *Goddard III*? The survivors always swore he caused the crack-up."

"Moran's case," frowned the skipper, "is more than just superstition. He told me that he never wanted to see Earth again. When I told him that was too bad, that we were headed for Earth right now, he warned me solemnly that he'd do everything in his power to prevent our getting there. So what do you think of that?"

"I think," I said glumly, "he's nuts! And if we pay any attention to him, we'll all be nuts, too. Well, I've got to go, Cap. I've got to check the shield generators before we go busting into Earth's H-layer."

And I left.

* * * *

Well, I was busy for the next four days on my job. It was a plenty important job, and had to be done carefully. The H-layer of the planets— the Kennelly-Heaviside layer—is a supertensioned field of force similar in composition to the corona of a star. A wide swath of ionized gas with high potential, serving as a shield against the murderous Q- and ultra-violet rays that emanate from solar bodies.

But the H-layer is a barrier as well as a shield. The first space-flight experimenters learned that, and the knowledge cost them their lives. For their craft hit the H-layer unguarded; and where had been a glistening ship, now was pitted, blackened metal; where had been life, now there was charred carbon.

Now all spaceships were equipped with shield generators. They were "generators" by courtesy only; actually they were huge condensers fed by cable lines tied at intervals to the hull plates. The theory was that as the craft plunged into and through the H-layer, these condensers would absorb the excess potential, thus allowing the ship to pass through unharmed.

And it worked swell, most of the time. Oh, every year a few ships would get theirs—would blow out in a blue wreath of coruscating flame— but for the most part the trip was safe enough. Except, of course, when a condenser was in bad condition. Which was why I was giving ours a check and double check.

Still, I could never rid myself of a queasy moment when we hit that blanket of spark-happy ionization. Particularly when a planet was at aphelion as Earth was now. Because at such times the H-layer was more highly activated than usual.

And to tell the truth, I wasn't satisfied with the way my work was going. First I hit my thumb with a monkey-wrench. It didn't hurt the wrench, but the thumb turned pale mauve and throbbed like a sixteen-year-old kid's pulse on his first hayride.

Then I lost a brass collar off the hull-brace, and since we didn't carry a reserve stock I had to ask Chief Lester to make me one. By the time that was ready, I'd busted a .44 coil cable lock, and had to jerry-rig a substitute.

Oh, it was a headache! But I wasn't the only guy on board the *Aunty* who was having troubles. Slops raised a howl to high heaven because his stove went on the squeegee. Gunner McCoy stalked into the officer's mess one afternoon demanding what such-and-such so-and-so had stripped the gears of his pet rotor-gun. Sparks burned out three vacuum tubes in one day, breaking contact with all transmitting stations and almost causing us to crack up on a rogue asteroid. Even Cap McNeally was visited by the plague. He came wailing to me, on the bridge, that the refrigeration units in the No. 3 storage bin had broken down.

"—and we've lost a whole binfull of *clab*, Brait! Worth at least six thousand credits on Earth. The Corporation will be mad as hell."

"That's tough," I said, "but there's nothing we can do about it. It wasn't your fault."

He eyed me curiously. "Brait—" he said.

"Yes, Cap?"

"I've been wondering—do you think there could be anything in what Moran said? About him being a—a—"

"Jonah?" I'd been thinking the same thing myself. "I don't know, Skipper. I wouldn't say yes, and I wouldn't say no. But there's no doubt about it, things have been going haywire ever since we picked him up. I'll be glad when he lifts gravs off the *Aunty*."

Cap said petulantly, "Of course it's just nonsense. Bad luck doesn't hang around one man like that. It's against the law of averages. Still, I wish you'd sort of keep an eye on him for the next three days, Brait. Till we land on Earth. I've got a notion—"

"So has Earth," I grinned. "Five of 'em. Atlantic, Pacific, Indian and the two Etceteras. What's yours?"

"It might," frowned the skipper. "Be sabotage. He said he'd do everything in his power to prevent our reaching Earth. And he's up and around now."

"If you think that," I suggested, "why don't you shove him in the clink, just to make sure?"

"Can't do it. Because I've no *proof* he's responsible for these occurrences, and besides, a rescued passenger is entitled to the courtesy of the ship."

* * * *

So that's how I assumed, in addition to the rest of my duties, the job of watch-dogging the mysterious Paul Moran. As Cap McNeally had said, Moran was up and about now. He had made what Doc Jurnegan claimed was the swiftest recovery in the annals of medicine. He still looked like a skeleton in search of a square meal. But there was sanity in his eyes. If not always in his speech. Like that afternoon in Sparks' radio turret, for instance.

We had been talking, Sparks and I, about space-flight. What a great thing it was. How, only in its infancy, it was already changing man's outlook, widening the borders of man's domain, creating a newer, greater universe.

"We got," Sparks said, "reason to be proud of ourselves. Gee, I was readin' in the library—"

"You," I interrupted wonderingly, "can read?"

"Comets to you, Lootenant!" sniffed Sparks. "As I was sayin' before I was so rudely ruptured, I was readin' in the library some old books from the Twentieth Century. Just about a hundred an' fifty years old, mind you! They had the craziest ideas about what men would find on other planets, if an' when they ever got there. Flame-men, an' robots, an' all sorts of things.

"Nothin' like what we actually found. 'Course, we shouldn't laugh at 'em too much. They had no way of knowin'. We're the first people ever traveled in space."

"No!" said Moran.

Sparks said patiently, "Well, I didn't mean us here in this room. Of course we ain't. But I mean the people of our time."

"And I still say," said Moran gravely, "no! Man in all ages is a creature of conceit, self-pride, self-glorification. There was space-flight long before you lived, Sparks. A race, long dead now, from a neighbor planet."

I said gently, "You're thinking of those pyramids found on Venus and Mars, Moran? I know that's a puzzler to modern science. And I've read several theories regarding their builders. But most authorities agree that their mere presence does not necessarily imply the existence of a single race of engineers. The pyramid is a fundamental structural form. Any intelligent race—"

"Man," said Moran almost sadly. "Man the dreamer; Man the doubter. No, Lieutenant, I am not speaking of theories, now. I am speaking of tales I've heard; accounts I've read in archives long molded into dust. At least three times in the past have civilized races spanned the void. It was the dying Martian race that first achieved space-flight. They found Venus a rank and stinking jungle, but on Earth certain of them set up their new abode."

He smiled quietly. "And reverted to savagery, as is always the case when civilized men, removed from the source of their culture, find themselves face to face with stark reality.

"Then it was the Moon-creatures who fled their airless world, spanned the distance to nearby earth."

I said, "That's an interesting thought, Moran. It explains the coloration of the races of man, doesn't it? I'd like to read that book you mentioned. Where can I get it?"

He shook his head sadly.

"You can't, Lt. Brait. The last copy of it was destroyed more than twelve centuries ago. Simon Magnus was the last man to read it as I remember. I loaned it to him—"

He stopped abruptly. But Sparks' eyes were plate-sized and incredulous. "—you loaned it to him?"

I spun on Sparks, angry. Jurnegan had told us to humor Moran, help him to a complete recovery. I didn't approve of this, not a little bit. I snapped, "That'll do, Sparks! Good Lord, man—What's the matter, Moran?"

For suddenly his face had paled, his eyes widened in horror, and he was backing away from me. He thrust out a trembling hand, gasped hoarsely, "Have a care, Brait! 'Thou shalt not take the name of the Lord, thy God, in vain—'!"

Then he fled; his running footsteps clattered down the ramp, and the echoes were strangely disturbing. Sparks stared after him, then made a circular motion at his temple.

"Nuts!" he said. "Crazy as a loon, Lootenant."

* * * *

Oh, he was an odd one, that Moran. Those next days are somehow garbled in my mind. They were so full of incident that now, looking back upon them, I can hardly distinguish between that which actually *was*, and that which an active imagination conjured for me out of fancy.

This I do know—it was the worst trip I've ever experienced in the *Antigone* or any other ship. Something was always wrong. Lt. Russ Bartlett, whose mind is as accurate as the cogs of a computing machine, discovered to his dismay that he had made an error in calculation; that at our present rate of speed we would miss Earth entirely and plunge Sunward at a rate that would destroy us all. He discovered that by sheer accident, and just in time to scream a hasty, "Cut hypos!" to the engine room, else I wouldn't be here to tell it. Then there was that mysterious occurrence in the galley. Our cook had a pet cat, and if it weren't for his habit of feeding the pussy before he fed the crew, half of us would be stiff now. Because the cat slopped up its dinner and forthwith proceeded to give up all nine of its lives simultaneously. Ptomaine, from faulty food tins. The first time such a thing had happened in more than forty years!

You couldn't say Moran was behind either of these near-disasters. For I was dogging his footsteps; I'll take my oath he was not involved. Physically, that is. But they say a Jonah's curse works even though the Jonah takes no actual part.

Oh, he was an odd one, that Moran. For instance, the time Sparks' selenium plate blew out. It was Moran who got permission to use the machine shop, construct a substitute out of a uranoid-steel atmochamber. We used that freak audio throughout the trip, then replaced it with a standard one when we reached Earth. Like dopes! Because two years later that screwball First Mate of the *Saturn* "invented" a uranium time-speech-trap exactly like the one Moran made us. He earned a quarter million credits from it. Imagine!

Then there was the time, as we were approaching the Lunar outpost, that our calculating machine jammed. Lieutenant Bartlett and Cap McNeally were in a dither trying to figure the approach velocity. It's a fifteen-minute job for the machine; a six-hour job for a man's brain. But Moran, who happened by, glanced casually at the declension chart, said, "Cut to forty-three at 3.05 Earth Standard, Captain. Maintain full speed for point three five parsecs, alter declension to north one, loft seven, fire fore jets twice—"

Having no better idea, McNeally did as Moran suggested. And we warped past the Moon oh-oh-oh on trajectory!

Which put us within scant hours of Earth's H-layer. And which also roused in me the realization that the mysterious Paul Moran was more than the ordinary space-sailor he pretended to be. Maybe I'm snoopy, I don't know. Anyway, I went to the radio room. I told Sparks grimly, "You and I are going to find out just who or what this Moran guy is. Send a message, Sparks. To Fred Bender, at Long Island Spaceport. Tell him to find out if there's a scientist missing who answers to this description. Five feet, seven and a half inches; a hundred and twenty-five pounds, dark hair, brown eyes—"

The relay of that description and the subsequent reply took longer than I had anticipated. That's why Sparks and I were among the last to learn of the new trouble. We didn't learn until, excited, we burst onto the bridge, confronted the skipper with our information.

"Look, Skipper!" I yelled. "No wonder 'Moran' was able to fix Sparks' radio and set your course! Do you—"

And the Captain raised haggard eyes to me.

"Brait, where have you been? I've been audioing all over the ship for you."

"In Sparks' cabin. Listen, though. Moran is—"

"I don't care," said the skipper wearily, "who he is. And in a little while, nobody else will, either. Your check-up, Mr. Brait, was a miserable failure! We are only an hour and a half out of the H-layer—and the shield generators refuse to function!"

I just stared at him for a minute. When I caught my breath, there was only enough of it for one word.

"Impossible!"

"Impossible, maybe," acknowledged the First Mate, "but unfortunately, Don, the Captain's right. Three lead-in cables are broken, the stripping is off the condenser."

"But—but everything was in perfect order an hour ago! I don't understand! Yes, I do! Moran! He said he'd destroy us all if he got a chance! Skipper, there's the answer. He's done it. The madman—"

Then there was a mirthful chuckle in the doorway, and Moran was standing there looking at us, his thin lips wide in a smile.

"You're right, Brait. I *did* do it. But I'm not a madman. I'm a happy man. The happiest man who ever lived!" His eyes lighted triumphantly; he stretched his arms above his head in a great, yearning gesture. "Soon will come freedom! The great, everlasting freedom of death."

"Get him!" said the Skipper succinctly. Gunner McCoy lumbered forward, his long, hairy arms encircled Moran's body. The Skipper pawed his graying thatch. "This is no time for reproaches, Mr. Brait. I told you to guard this man; for some reason you failed to do so. But now our problem is to repair the damage he has done. Or else—"

His pause was significant. But Moran's quiet, mocking laughter persisted.

"It is useless, Captain. Not in hours, no, not in weeks, will you repair the damage. Don't you see—" There was a feverish light in his eyes, a shuddering vibrancy in his voice. "Don't you see that I bring you the greatest of all boons known to man?

"Death! Wonderful, blissful death! Death that I have sought so long ... so hopelessly."

Those were the last words I heard for some time. I dashed from the room, Bartlett, Sparks and McCoy at my heels. We picked up the Chief Engineer. We covered the *Antigone* from stern to stern. And our worst fears were realized. It was no use. The damage Moran had done was irreparable.

Russ Bartlett said, "There's only one way out. We mustn't try to penetrate the Heaviside layer. We must shift trajectory, pass Earth and remain in space until we get the shield generator operating again."

And Chief Lester said somberly, "Have you forgotten the trajectory you planned, Lieutenant Bartlett?"

"The trajectory?"

"I thought it was unusual," rumbled the engineer, "when you called it down to me. It's paper-thin, balanced on a knife-edge between counter-gravitations. If we try to shift course now, we'll tear the ship into shreds!"

I knew, now, why Moran had come up with such a ready answer when the computer failed. He had planned well. He had deliberately forced us into this trajectory from which there was no escape.

* * * *

Back on the bridge, we found Captain McNeally pacing the deck like a caged cat. Moran was silent, watchful intent, with an unholy gleam of justification lighting his curious eyes. The skipper looked up hopefully as we entered.

"Well, gentlemen?"

Bartlett shook his head.

McNeally was silent for a long moment. His glance roved the smart, glistening interior of the *Antigone's* control room. I knew exactly what he was thinking. It was too bad that this smooth perfection, this finest ship built by master craftsmen, should become a brief, winking flame in the atmospheric borders of Earth.

And it was tough that we must all go out together like this. Through no fault of our own. Through the machinations of a space-mad castaway. He turned to me. "Lieutenant Brait, you and Sparks will go to the radio turret. Send a complete report to the Earth authorities. Tell them—" He gulped. "Tell them why the—the *Antigone* will not come in."

I said, "Aye, aye, sir!" mechanically, and started for the door. But Sparks stopped me.

"Ain't you gonna tell 'em what we learned?"

"Eh?"

"About *him*?"

He jerked his head toward 'Moran'.

"It doesn't really make any difference now," I said. "But—" I suppose my voice was scornful. There was scorn and bitterness in my heart. "They might as well know that the man who has condemned us all to death is—or was—one of Earth's greatest scientists. Had he not become a raving lunatic his genius could have stemmed this disaster."

McNeally said, "What's that, Lieutenant? What do you mean?"

"I mean this man's name is not 'Paul Moran'—"

"Names," murmured Moran gently. "What difference does a name make? When one has had thousands of names."

"His name," I continued, "is John Cartaphilus!"

Bartlett said, "Cartaphilus!" In a leap he was at our strange guest's side, his voice eager. "Then he will—he *must*—help us!

"Cartaphilus, listen to me! Of all men, only you have the genius to devise some way of escaping this peril! You've been mad, sir! Insane from your privations! But now I beg that you cast aside this madness, come to our rescue!"

Moran—or Cartaphilus—brushed his hand aside. A dreamy look was in his eyes.

"Death at last!" he whispered. "Oh, sweet boon of mankind—death! I who have suffered so long, waited such a long time—"

"Can't you hear me, man? Snap out of it! Time is growing short. In a half hour, maybe less, we'll nose into the H-layer. And then—Please, sir!"

But there was no reply. Captain McNeally looked at me uncertainly. "Are you sure, Brait?"

"Positive. I forwarded a description to Bender at L.I. He said Cartaphilus has been missing for a year and a half. He fled Earth because of a scandal. It seems—"

"Never mind that now." McNeally confronted the insane scientist. "Mr. Cartaphilus, you must help us out of this jam! We're not thinking only of ourselves, but of the mothers and children waiting for us on Earth. And of the future of space-travel. If the *Antigone*, the finest ship ever built, blows out in the H-layer, it will strike a heavy blow at all astronavigation. Help us, sir! For Heaven's sake—"

Cartaphilus spoke suddenly, sharply.

"Don't say that!"

"Only Heaven can save us now," said McNeally simply, "if you won't. It's our only hope. May the Lord help us if you—"

"Don't!" The strange, thin man screamed the word. Suddenly he buried his face in his hands, and his words were an incoherent babble of torment. "Don't you see what you're doing? Man, have you no pity?"

He raised wide, tortured eyes. "The endlessness of time—" he whispered. "But I thought that, free of Earth, lost in the depths of space, I might at last find peace. But now you call upon me to save you in His name.

"I won't do it! I won't! The power cannot force me, here in the void. Two thousand years.... No! No!

McNeally stepped back, torn between dread and doubt. He shook his head at us. "It's no use. He's completely mad."

Then Russ Bartlett cried, "Wait! *Listen!*"

For Cartaphilus, his face worn and aged, had bowed his head as though surrendering to forces greater than his will-to-die. And he was droning in a drab, lack-lustre voice, "Tell the engineer to reverse the polarity of the alternate hypatomic motors. Transmit the counter electromotive force helically through the forward coils. Use full power. Keep all motors running at top speed. Cut out the intercommunicating and lighting systems; there must be no D.C. current in operation anywhere on the ship. The cross-currents will—"

Chief Engineer Lester's face was a masque of blank dismay. He husked, "A hysteresis bloc! It might work. Nobody ever thought of it before."

"What do you mean?" That was Cap McNeally.

"His suggestion. Heterodyning the web-coils, so we'll counter the H-layer radiation with an alternating current of our own. It's just about one chance in a million!"

"Then take that chance!" cried the skipper. "Try it! Do as he says. And, for God's sake, man, *hurry*!"

Cartaphilus, his eyes drained of all expression, rose sluggishly. Once more he spoke, faintly. "It will work," he said. "It will work, and I have failed again. And all because I would not let Him rest...."

His voice broke in a great, wrenching sob. Then he lurched from the control room like a broken thing.

I never saw him again. No one aboard the *Antigone* ever saw him again. For the next hour we were in a turmoil, rearranging the electrical units of the ship as Cartaphilus had told us. We finished our task just in time; scant seconds after we had thrown on the power we nosed into the web-like field of force which is the H-layer.

It was a breathless moment. Despite our efforts, there was not a man of us but expected a brief, brilliant instant of horror—then oblivion. But we were as wrong as Cartaphilus had been right. There was a jolt as our forcefield met that of Earth's shield; the permalloy hull of the ship sang and hummed and glowed cherry-red under the impact of that terrific electromotive strain, but we slipped through the barrier with greater ease than ever had any ship using the old style shield generators.

In our jubilation we quite forgot the mad scientist whose strange, last-minute change of mind had saved our lives. We landed. And sometime between the moment of landing and the moment when we remembered our passenger, he fled. Disappeared completely from the ship and from our lives.

Cap McNeally was nothing if not a square-shooter. He refused to take credit for the invention that had brought us through the H-layer. The patent rights were taken out in the name of our deranged passenger. The "Moran H-penetrant" it is called. All spaceships used it until just recently; until Cap Hawkins of the *Andromeda* and the Venusian scientist, Jar Farges, discovered Ampies could be used as H-layer shields.

But afterward, Cap McNeally came to me, wondering.

"Why should he have wanted to die, Brait? I can't understand it. A man like John Cartaphilus; wealthy, intelligent, respected—was he really mad, do you think?"

I hesitated. I, too, had been wondering about that. I had gone so far as to look up the life history of the mad scientist. I had found several curious things. No man knew when, or where, John Cartaphilus had been born. All agreed that he was "remarkably youthful" in appearance. It was rumored that he had outlived a wife married in youth; that she had been an elderly woman when she died.

I said, "I told you there had been a scandal in his life, recently, Skipper. It concerned a friend of his, a worker in one of his shops.

"Cartaphilus was, and is, a genius, but he has a reputation for driving his men too hard. They say that on this occasion, seeking the answer to some problem that evaded him, he forced this assistant to labor for weeks, begrudging him even a few hours sleep each night.

"On the eve of the solution of the problem, this worker came to him, nervous, ragged, exhausted, begging for a brief respite. Claiming he was sick with overwork and fatigue. But John Cartaphilus insisted, impatiently, there was no time for rest. He ordered the man to get about his work.

"The job was completed. But the friend died. The doctors said it was a pure case of exhaustion. When he heard this, Cartaphilus' brain snapped. He blamed himself for the man's death, fled Earth. He became—or so we may believe—the wandering spaceman we found in the asteroids."

Cap McNeally frowned.

"Do you believe that story, Brait?"

I started to say no. I started to tell the skipper something else I had discovered while probing into the life history of John Cartaphilus. Something that, to my mind at least, more fully explained the oddness of our erstwhile passenger.   .

It was an old legend I had run across. The queer story of a man with many names ("I have had so many names," Moran had said) who wandered endlessly about the Earth, perhaps the universe now, simply because he had not let another rest for a moment on his doorsill.

Sometimes this man had been known as Cartaphilus. He had also been known as Juan Espera en Dios, as Ahasverus, and as Butta Deus. The Parisian gazette, "Turkish Spy," had in 1644 A.D. reported his presence in that city traveling under the name of "Paul Marrane." But men in general knew him by a more descriptive name. The Wandering Jew. The Eternal Jew....

But I did not tell Cap McNeally this. After all, it was a fanciful thought. And surely Moran—or Marrane, or Cartaphilus—was mad when he claimed to have met and talked with Simon Magnus twelve hundred years ago?

Anyway, when we saw that ad in the classified columns of this week's *Spaceways Weekly*, and McNeally claimed Moran would return to claim his reward, it raised again the question in my mind.

Will he return? Or will he find, at last, whatever peace awaits him out there? In the vast emptiness of space, where the power cannot—must not—extend? I wonder....

THE ULTIMATE SALIENT

Originally published in *Planet Stories*, Fall 1940.

CHAPTER I

I thought at first he was the census-snoop, returning to poke his proboscis into whatever few stray facts he might have overlooked the first time. My wife was out, and when I saw him coming up the walk, that bulky folder under his arm, I answered the door myself—something I seldom do—sensing a sort of reluctant duty toward the minions of Uncle Sam.

He was a neat and quiet person. One of those drab, utterly commonplace men who defy description. Neither young nor old, tall nor short, stout nor slender. He had only one outstanding characteristic. An eager intensity, a *piercingness* of gaze that made you feel, somehow, as if his ice-blue eyes stared ever into strange and fathomless depths.

He said, "Mr. Clinton?" and I nodded. "*Eben* Clinton?" he asked. Then, a trifle breathlessly I thought, "Mr. Clinton, I have here something that I know will prove of the greatest interest to you—"

I got it then. I shook my head. "Sorry, pal. But we don't need some." I started to close the door.

"I—I beg your pardon?" he stammered. "Some?"

"Shoelaces," I told him firmly, "patent can-openers or fancy soaps. Weather-vanes, life insurance or magazines." I grinned at him. "I don't *read* the damned things, buddy, I just write for them."

And again I tried to do things to the door. But he beat me to it. There was apology in the way he shrugged his way into the house, but determination in his eyes.

"I know," he said. "That is, I *didn't* know until I read this, but—" He touched the brown envelope, concluded lamely, "it—it's a manuscript—"

Well, that's one of the headaches of being a story-teller. Strange things creep out of the cracks and crevices—most of them bringing with them the Great American Novel. It was spring in Roanoke, and spring fever had claimed me as a victim. I didn't feel like working, anyway. No, not even in my garden. Especially in the turnip patch. Hank Cleaver isn't the only guy who has trouble with his turnips.

I sighed and led the way into my work-room. I said, "Okay, friend. Let's have a look at the masterpiece...."

His first words, after we had settled into comfortable chairs, made me feel like a dope. I suppose I'm a sort of stuffed shirt, anyway, suffering from a bad case of expansion of the hatband. And I'd been treating my visitor as if he were some peculiar type of bipedal worm. It took all the wind out of my sails when he said, by way of preamble, "If I may introduce myself, Mr. Clinton, I'm Dr. Edgar Winslow of the Psychology Department of—"

He mentioned one of our oldest and most influential Southern universities. I said, "Omigawd!" and broke into an orgy of apologies. But he didn't seem to be listening to me; he was preoccupied with his own explanation.

"I came to you," he said, "because I understand you write stories of—er—pseudo-science?"

I winced.

"Science-*fiction*," I corrected him. "There's quite a difference, you know."

"Is there?" He frowned. "Oh, yes. I see. Please forgive me. Well, Clinton—" The professorial stamp was upon him; quite unconsciously he addressed me as if I were one of his students. "Well, Clinton, I came to ask a favor of you. I want you to transmit a message to a certain man. I want you to write the message in such a form that it will not be lost—in the form of a fictional narrative."

It takes all kinds to make a world. I gazed at him thoughtfully. I said, "Don't look now, but isn't that doing it the hard way? I'll be glad to help you out. But putting a simple message into story form is—well, why not just let me *tell* the guy? By word of mouth?"

"I'm afraid," he said soberly, "that is impossible. You see, the person to whom this message must go will not be born until the year 1942."

"Nineteen—!" It worked. It threw me off balance for a minute. Then came the dawn. It *was* a gag, after all. My pal Ross being funny from out Chicago way, maybe? Or Palmer, deserting Tark long enough to joyride me over the well-known hurdles? I chuckled. I said, "That's all right, Professor. I'm young; I can wait. Just tell me the name of this unsprouted seedling, and I'll stick around till he gets old enough to talk to. Only the good die young; I expect to live to a ripe old age."

He glanced at me slowly, and a bit sadly, I thought. "I'm sorry, Clinton," he said, "but that won't do. It won't do at all. It will have to be written. You see—you won't be here then...."

* * * *

You know, it should have been funny. Uproariously, screamingly funny. I should have laughed my crazy head off, given my obviously screwy visitor a smoke and a drink and a clap on the back and said, "Okay, pal. You win the marbles. Come clean, now. Who put you up to this crystal ball stuff? What's the payoff?"

But I didn't, because somehow it wasn't funny after all. There was a deadly seriousness to my visitor's manner; the knuckles of his hands were white upon his knees, his icy blue eyes burned with a tortured regret that was like a dash of water to my mirth.

"I'm sorry, Clinton," he said. "I'm really dreadfully sorry."

I lit a cigarette carefully. In as even a voice as I could muster, I said, "Perhaps you'd like to tell me more? Perhaps you'd better start from the beginning?"

"Yes," he said. "Yes, I think that would be best." He fingered the thick brown envelope nervously. "The story begins," he said, "and ends—with this manuscript...."

"As I have already told you," said Dr. Winslow, "my profession is teaching. Psychology is my field. Recently I have given much of my time to research into the lesser-known faculties of the human mind. Experimental psychical research such as that investigated by Prof. J. B. Rhine of Duke. You are undoubtedly familiar with his work?"

"Extra-sensory perception?" I nodded. "Yes. Most fascinating. The results are far from satisfactory, though. And some of his conclusions—"

"You make a common error," said my visitor gravely. "Dr. Rhine has not assumed to draw any conclusions—as yet. He offers only a few, and completely logical, presumptions.

"Dr. Rhine's studies to date, however, have been in the field of extra-sensory perception only. There are other fields of psychical research quite as untouched, and, I have reason to believe, even more important and—fruitful.

"It is in one of these companion fields that I have been laboring. I have been investigating the phenomenon you may know as 'telaesthesia.'"

"You mean," I asked, "telepathy?"

"There is a difference between the two. Telepathy, as defined by Myers in 1882, is 'the communication of impressions of any kind from one mind to another, independently of the recognized channels of sense.' It implies a deliberate, recognized contact between two minds existent at one time.

"Telaesthesia is a more complex meeting of entities. If A, let us say, reaches out and helps himself to the contents of B's mind *without* the knowledge or assistance of B, that process will be called 'telaesthesia.' Unlike telepathy, it knows no barriers of Time. There are hundreds of recorded case histories from which we learn of men of our time who have established telaesthetic contact with former forgotten eras.

"And of days to come, as well!" Here Winslow's eyes literally gripped me. "But never, until now, has anyone succeeded in gaining more than a fleeting glimpse into the Time stream of the future. Never before has a man established a contact so deep, so strong, that he could read not one sentence or one paragraph of that which is to be—but an entire chapter, decades long...!"

* * * *

It was spring in Roanoke. Outside, warm April sunshine poured down luxuriant gold upon the faint, green buds. My place, *Sans Sou*, lies in a quiet fold between two rolling hills. There was nothing to disturb that quiet now save the boastful warble of a redbird, "Purty! Purty!" and the petulant complaint of a chipmunk in the sycamore.

The sky was a pale, soft blue, cloudless and serene. There were no clouds, and even the delicate fronds of the weeping willow drooped motionless. So it could not have been a storm I heard. Yet as he spoke, a dark shadow seemed to scud across the sky, veiling the sunlight, and the gods made portent in the swell of distant thunder. I felt the short hairs stiffen on my neck, and despite the warmth I shivered.

I said, and why I spoke in a whisper I cannot tell, "Never before ... until ... *now*?"

"Until now!" he repeated. And suddenly his fingers were swift with eagerness, he fumbled with the flap of the envelope while words raced from his lips. "Several months ago I began to experiment with automatic writing, one of the means by which telaesthetic contact is authenticated.

"At first the results were—as might be expected—faulty. From the autohypnotic syncopes into which I was able to project myself, I woke to find nothing on the sheets before me but meaningless scribbles.

"And then, suddenly, I woke one day to find that in my period of subliminal usurpation I had achieved a definite result. I—or someone—had written four full pages. The first four pages of this manuscript!"

Here he handed the manuscript to me. I had time to notice that the writing was full-bodied, flowing. Then Dr. Winslow's words claimed my attention again.

"That was but the beginning. Once having established contact, it was as though I became the *alter ego* of this mysterious correspondent. From that time on my experiments were graced with success. Whenever I resumed contact, pages were added to the manuscript. By the periodicity of these, I am led to believe that Brian O'Shea is a diarist, and that through some inexplicable phenomenon, it is given to me to be able to set down, telaesthetically, the very words he writes in his diary—"

"You said," I interrupted, "Brian—?"

"O'Shea," nodded Winslow. "Brian O'Shea. A soldier in the army of the Americas, Clinton—in the year 1963 A.D.! His diary is a history of the things to come!"

* * * *

What I would have said then, I do not know. Maybe I would have said something bitingly scurrilous—which I most certainly would have regretted later. Or perhaps, as is most likely, I was momentarily stunned into speechlessness. But I was spared the necessity of speaking. Dr. Winslow had risen; eyes glowing strangely, he touched my shoulder.

"I am going to leave you now, so you may read this manuscript in peace. When you have finished, you will understand why I came, and know that which must be done.

"You will find that the manuscript begins abruptly at the moment when first I 'contacted' O'Shea. It ends with equal abruptness. There are fragments missing; these may be filled in or rounded out as you consider necessary for the purpose of story-telling. I have made a few slight changes in spelling. Whether O'Shea was—or should I say 'will be?'—a poor scholar, I do not know. The spelling of some words may have changed over a period of trouble-swept decades....

"But whatever surprises lie in store for you, whatever conclusions you draw from the manuscript you are about to read, I beg of you that you play the game of caution. If you end by doubting O'Shea's story, *still* you must convey to him the message the manuscript demands. It is the only way. We must take no chances. I will leave my address—" Here he scribbled a few words on his card; I noted subconsciously that his own handwriting was tiny, crabbed, angular. "When you have finished reading, get in touch with me. No, don't get up!"

For a long moment I stared after him. Is there any way I can tell you how I felt? I, who have written fantasies woven of thin air, now thus to be suddenly thrust into a fantasy beyond my own wildest imaginings? Even more important, is there a way I can make you believe that this is not merely another amusing tale, to be read today and forgotten soon?

The structure of this narrative is mine. I supplied the story form. But is there any way I can convince you that the words which follow are not my own? *I did not write this story!* It is the story of a man who is not yet born, who will not live these happenings for twenty years.

Here is the story of Brian O'Shea, soldier....

CHAPTER II

—Stumbled and pitched to his knees. I ran to his side and would have carried him, but he shook me off.

"It's too late, O'Shea," he said. "My number's up. Take over. And—" He hiccoughed convulsively and his lips drooled red. "And for Lord's sake, Brian, get the men out of this trap!"

His eyes glazed, then, and his head dropped forward to his chest. Someone tugged at my shoulder. It was Ronnie St. Cloud; he was screaming, above the splatter of shrapnel, "The hills, O'Shea! They've cut us off from the river. The hills are our only way out!"

Danny Wilson was beside him, and Knudsen, and a few more. About us milled a shrieking, terrified throng; it was impossible to tell soldier from civilian. Our uniforms were anything but uniform. We wore whatever serviceable garments we could salvage. I still had—though I suppose it was unrecognizable beneath a layer of caked sweat and mud—an old khaki campaign shirt, but my breeches were a corduroy pair I had found in a demolished farm house near Sistersville. St. Cloud wore the horizon-blue jacket of a *poilu* beside whom he had fought in Belgium. Knudsen looked least military of all in whipcord riding breeches commandeered from the tack rooms of the Greenbriar Inn at White Sulphur.

St. Cloud was right, of course; we might have known from the beginning we couldn't hold Huntington. It was open to the west, and that entire sector, from Chicago to Detroit and spearheading southward to Akron, Cincinnati, Zanesville, was occupied by von Schuler's Death's Head Brigade.

But Captain Elmon, who had whipped our tiny company into some semblance of order after the debacle at Pittsburgh and had brought us safely down the river through Parkersburg and Gallipolis, had believed we might be able to defend this West Virginia river town until reinforcements could reach us from the Fort Knox garrison.

There was a school here, a Marshall College, with a layout ideal for our purposes. The buildings were more than a hundred years old, sturdily built; there were dormitories, kitchens, private power plants for heat and light. The campus was encircled by a waist-high brick wall which, sandbagged, made a perfect first-line defense against infantry.

The rugged, mountainous terrain made it impossible for the Toties to bring up mechanized units. Nor could they bring pressure to bear from the Ohio River which, here, was not only shallow but bedded with rubble from the locks and dams we had blown up.

But—the old, old story. They got us from the air. Their Messerschmitts and Junkers descended on us like a host of locusts, bombed the town ruthlessly; small pursuit planes strafed the fleeing populace with merciless persistence. We couldn't do anything about that, of course. Captain Elmon told me once—he saw volunteer service in Sweden before our country got into it—that in the early days of the war, aircraft confined its operations to military objectives. But I laughed; I knew he was just leading me on. He was a great one for joking, was the captain, even in the darkest hour.

Now Elmon lay dead at my feet; his final command had been that I take over. Get the men out of this trap. There was no time to waste in bootless grieving. Already the sharp bite of sidearms augmented the scream of shellfire ... which meant the Toties were up to their old trick of parachuting an army of occupation into the beleaguered town.

I shouted swift orders to the others, bade them pass the word around to "take to the hills." There were viaducts under the railroad at 16th and 20th Streets; we used these as our ports of egress. It wasn't a matter of minutes. We gave ground slowly, fighting off the enemy advance from street to street, alley to alley, house to house.

By the old football stadium, now an ammunition dump, I found Bruce MacGregor, the Canadian, and the roly-poly Hollander, Rudy Van Huys. They had impressed the services of a dozen scared civilians, were loading trucks, vans, anything with our meager store of ammunition. MacGregor glanced at me sharply.

"Where's the Old Man, O'Shea?"

"Dead," I told him. "We're on our own. Mac, do you think you can handle this job alone?"

"Why?"

"I want Van Huys to forage. We're retreating to the hills. Use the 20th Street underpass, cut south to the Big Sandy, then west at Louisa. Rudy, get all the food-stuffs you can lay hands on. We're heading for hungry country."

They grunted understanding and I went on. They were two good men. The chubby Dutchman could smell out provisions like a beagle. Our men wouldn't starve immediately, anyway.

That moment's delay was the only thing that saved my life. I was but a half block away from the underpass when a Totie bomber spotted the stream of refugees flooding out of the city through that viaduct. My ears sang to the screaming whine of his power dive, concussion threw me to the pavement as he loosed his entire rack full of bombs into the heart of the fleeing throng.

They never had a chance. Those who did not die instantly in the explosion were buried a split-second later in the tons of twisted steel and concrete that cascaded down upon them. There was one moment of dreadful cacaphony, hoarse screams of fear mingling with the thunderous roar of the explosion—then a dull, unearthly silence, punctuated only by the muted whimper of a few charred bodies that could not die and the grating slither of broken masonry filling the chinks of the funereal mound.

I rose, shaken, nauseated. Others had come up behind me; among them was Devereaux. There were tears in the young Frenchman's eyes. He lifted his head blindly toward the sky, shook an impotent fist.

"*Les sales cochons!* Will it never end, O'Shea, the triumph of these devils? Are honor and mercy dead? Is God dead? My country ... all of Europe ... now yours...."

"They haven't taken America," I told him savagely, "yet! Come on. We're leaving town through the 20th Street viaduct. Is that you, Ronnie? What's the news?"

"They've consolidated position along Fifth Avenue, thrown a defense line from Four Pole Creek to the river, infantry advancing north along the river bank to the college. Thompson and a foray squad are trapped in the First National, no use trying to save them. We blew the Toties' brains out, though." St. Cloud grinned ghoulishly. "We had City Hall plaza ground-mined. They chose that spot to set up general headquarters."

"Where's Frazier?"

"Dead. Blue Cross."

"Janowsky?"

"Same thing."

"Wilson?"

"He's all right. Or was. He went back toward the college. Said something about having an ace up his sleeve, whatever that means."

I didn't tell him. I didn't have to, for at that moment Danny came racing toward us. He waved his hand at me in a sort of vague salute or greeting, yelled, "If you're ready to get goin', *git*! There'll never be a better time."

"Why?"

"Because the Toties are goin' to have their hands full in a minute. With something too hot to handle. I just happened to remember that college we were bunked in had its own heating plant. A natural gas pipe-line. Since it was the Toties' objective, I thought maybe I'd warm house before they got there. Hold your hats, folks! There she goes!"

There came a sudden, terrific blast of sound. Even at that distance we felt the shuddering repercussion, felt a breath of superheated air fan our cheeks as the natural well Danny had set off let go with a thunderous detonation. Into the gathering dusk shot a writhing spiral of white-hot flame ... the jagged outlines of oft-bombed houses looked black and ugly against the searing screen.

The flames leaped higher, higher, spread. An oily pall blotted the dying rays of the sun; from afar came to us the crackling agony of a city destroying itself. I watched, spellbound for a moment, then turned to the others.

"Danny is right. This is our chance. Let's go!"

* * * *

MacCregor and Rudy Van Huys were waiting for us in the hills beyond the city. We paused to take stock of equipment, count noses, and plan our next move. Of our company—which had numbered six hundred before Pittsburgh, and had been one hundred and sixty-odd at yesterday evening's rollcall—now there remained but fifty-seven men. Twelve recruits joined us from the clamoring mob of civilian refugees. These were, of course, either graybeards, striplings, or men of dubious value as soldiers. All men of fighting age and caliber had long ago been called to the colors by wave upon wave of government drafts.

We were a pitiful collection, poorly fed, inadequately armed, raggedly clad. Even so, the civilians were loud in their demand that we remain with them to "protect" them. But this I could not agree to do.

"You'll be safer," I told them, "hiding here in the hills than marching with us. We'll try to contact Preston's brigade at Fort Knox. You have food, water, radios, medical supplies. Hide out, keep living and—keep hoping!"

And so we left them. They must have numbered three thousand, mostly women and children. A few tried to follow, but I quickened the pace. The last weeping woman abandoned the pursuit after five miles; I saw her fall to earth, beating the insensate soil with weary, hopeless fists.

Beside me marched Danny Wilson. He was a reckless, devil-may-care lad, was Danny. Even in the thick of battle his ruddy features were habitually wreathed in a grin. But it had deserted him now. He said soberly, "Maybe we should have stayed with them, Brian, boy. It's a hard row to hoe."

"We can't fight a war in small detachments," I told him grimly. "You know that. Mexico tried it, and now their country is under Totie rule. Nova Scotia tried it, and now the swastika flies there. Our only hope is to concentrate, meet them somewhere in one decisive battle."

"I suppose you're right. We go to join Preston?"

"Yes. It's the general concentration point. Elmon got instructions by radio just before he went west. Jackson is bringing up his army from the Gulf, Davies is marching in from Springfield. They say three flights are taking off from Fort Sill; we'll have a small air force. If we can beat the Toties off at Louisville, we'll cut their communications line from Pittsburgh to Cincinnati, hold the Ohio."

That night we slept along the Big Sandy. Before we bivouacked I broke our little company into six squads, each of eleven men, each headed by a veteran on whom I knew I could depend. I appointed Danny Wilson and Ronnie St. Cloud as my lieutenants. In arranging the squads, I tried to place the men according to nationality under one of their own race.

Raoul Devereaux led one of the French squads, while Anatole LeBrun the other. That would have been funny a few years ago, when the army was still organized under the caste basis, because Devereaux used to be a captain and LeBrun a common private. But that old "officer and gentleman by Act of Congress" stuff had gone overboard a long time ago. Now we picked our leaders by their leadership ability.

Ian Pelham-Jones, the Britisher, and Bruce MacGregor headed two English-speaking squads; Rudy Van Huys commanded a group of Dutch and Belgians; the tall Norwegian, Ingolf Knudsen, led a collection of assorted Scandinavians. Norwegians, Swedes, Finns, Danes—Lord, there was a tough outfit!

And so we hit the trail. There's not much use telling about the days that followed. We marched and slept and ate and marched again. We were spotted once by a Totie spyplane; he came down to do a little plain and fancy strafing but we had the advantage of broken terrain. We took to cover and turned his crate into a colander before he decided he'd had enough. Lars Frynge, the Swedish sharpshooter, claims he punctured the pilot as well as the plane, but I wouldn't know about that. Though it's true that he did wobble as he flew away.

* * * *

We avoided Lexington, cutting south through Campton and Irvine. We picked up a railroad at Lancaster. Joe Sanders, a native of these parts, said it was a part of the old Louisville & Nashville. If it were in operation, he said, it would take us right to our destination. But that was like saying if we had wings we could fly. The rails were twisted ribbons of steel; in some places the roadbed had been so completely eradicated you would never know it had been there.

We saw people from time to time, but mostly in the small towns. They came out to cheer us as we marched through, offered us what little they had in the way of fresh water, barley bread, clothing that would never be used, now, by sons, husbands, brothers, who had fought their final battle. I got a fine new sweater in one village. In another we had an odd experience. A white-haired granddame insisted we accept a flag she had sewn for us. A funny-looking red flag with blue diagonal cross-bars and thirteen white stars. We used it later to bury Johnny Grant. He died of a delayed gas hemorrhage.

The larger towns were deserted. We saw only one man in Danville. A scrawny, long-haired weasel skulking through the ruins of what had once been an A & P supermarket. Bruce MacGregor took a shot at him, but I knocked his rifle up. The bullet whistled over the man's head, and he scurried away like a sick, desperate rabbit. I knew there was a G.O. to shoot all looters on sight, but the time had passed, I told Mac, to concern ourselves with such trivialities. Ammunition was too precious.

And, anyway, if he didn't find the buried provisions, maybe the enemy would.

The seventh night out, we camped in the woods north of Bardstown, just a few yards off what had once been a main highway. I was beginning to smell smoke. Tomorrow we would join the main garrison, get fresh clothing and equipment and be assigned our duties in the projected offensive. That is, I suppose, why I was sleepless.

We had stumbled across a deserted tobacco shed the day before. The brown leaves were old, parched, crumbling, but it was better than the hay-and-alfalfa mixture they had given us up North. I rolled myself a cigarette and was sitting by the side of the road when suddenly I heard it. The sound of an approaching automobile.

A moment later moonlight glinted on metal; I saw it picking its slow, lightless way over the cracked asphalt. My heart leaped. This must be a car from Louisville. I ran down to the road, stood waiting eagerly. It approached at a snail's pace, but in the gloom the driver must have had all he could do to watch the road without keeping an eye peeled for vagabond troops, for when, as it came beside me, I cried a greeting and reached for the door, there came a startled sound from within, the motor roared stridently, and the car leaped forward, almost wrenching my arm from its socket.

Somehow I managed to hold on, though the automobile bounced and jarred crazily as it struck deep ruts in the roadbed. My head glanced metal and I saw whirling stars. "Hey!" I yelled. "What the almighty hell are you trying to do! Take it easy!"

Brakes squealed; the car jolted to a stop. And from the interior a voice, high-pitched with relief, cried:

"You—you're an American! Thank Heaven!"

Then a slim form collapsed suddenly over the wheel. I yanked the door open, dragging the unconscious driver from the cab. He must be, I thought, wounded. He must be—

But it wasn't a "he" at all. As the body fell back limply over my arm, a campaign hat tumbled earthward. Soft brown hair cascaded from beneath it. The driver was a girl!

I had ammonia tubes in my first-aid kit. I snapped one beneath her nose, jolted her back to awareness. And she proved her femininity by coming out of it with a question on her lips.

"Who—who are you?"

"O'Shea," I said, "commanding a detachment from the Army of the Upper Ohio. Marching to join Preston's brigade at Louisville. But never mind that. Who are *you*? Where do you think you're going?"

She said, "Louisville!" In the darkness her face was a white blur, drab, expressionless, but there was a touch of hysteria to her voice. "Louisville! But haven't you got a radio? Didn't you know—"

We hadn't. It didn't make sense. As she faltered, I snapped, "Know what? Go on!"

"Louisville has fallen. The Toties have taken Fort Knox. Our troops are destroyed, the government has fled, and the Army of the Democracies is in utter rout!"

I stared at her numbly. In the black of the woods a nightjar screamed a single, discordant taunt....

CHAPTER III

The commotion had roused most of the others. Quiet forms in the midnight, they had drifted to the road. Wilson spoke now. He said, "That's the end, then. If she's right, Brian, the war is over. And we've lost."

I said to the girl, "How about it?"

She shook her head.

"I'm afraid so. The last reports I heard, they had seized the Mississippi, cut all contact between our Eastern and Western armies. The Japs control California and Nevada. There was a terrific battle being waged at Albuquerque. The Russian navy holds the Great Lakes. Everywhere you hear the same story."

Pelham-Jones demanded harshly, "St. Louis? Did you hear anything about—?"

"Wiped out to a man. It was caught in a vise. The Germans from the east, the Italians from the north."

Pelham-Jones said, "I see," quietly. He turned away. His shoulders looked heavy. He had a younger brother at St. Louis. Van Huys looked at the girl suspiciously.

"How do we know she's telling the truth, O'Shea? It may be more lies. She may be a Totie spy."

I said, "You have your dent?"

She nodded and handed it to me. I flashed my light on it. It was authentic, all right. The picture on the tiny metal identification tag was an image of her; the name beneath was *Maureen Joyce*. She was tagged as a WAIF, a member of the Women's Auxiliary Intelligence Force. I gave it back to her.

"Very good, Miss Joyce. Sorry. We can't afford to take chances, though. You understand, I'm sure. But—" My curiosity made me exceed my authority. "But what are you doing here? Surely you wouldn't be attempting to escape the Toties in this direction? If they hold the east?"

She hesitated for a moment. Then, carefully, "I am acting under orders, Captain O'Shea. They were supposed to be *secret* orders. But in view of what has happened—" She made up her mind. "It would be better for more than one to know. In case—in case anything should happen to me.

"You've heard of Dr. Mallory?"

"Thomas Mallory?" I said. "The physicist? The one who pestered the daylights out of the government about some crack-brained invention during the early days of the war? Is he the one you mean?"

"Yes. The government isn't too sure, now, that it acted wisely in refusing to listen to his plan. But you know how it was for a while. Miracle men flooded the War Department with fantastic ideas for 'smashing the enemy.'

"Only, in this last extremity, the War Department decided to investigate Mallory's claim. As a last resort. I was commissioned to find him, bring him to Louisville. But now—" Uncertainly. "Now I don't know just what I ought to do. Even if he has a plan, and a good one, there is no one to whom we can communicate it."

* * * *

Surprisingly, it was Danny Wilson who interrupted.

"Except," he said suddenly, "us!" He turned to me. "Brian, it would be suicide for us to go on to Louisville—and there's no place else to go. We might as well make this our job. We have everything to gain, nothing to lose."

"Do you," I asked the girl, "know where Mallory is?"

"Only roughly. Somewhere in the hills of the upper Cumberland. I plan to comb the neighborhood—"

The Kentuckian, Joe Sanders, edged forward.

"Don't need to do no combin'," he drawled. "Reckon I c'n help. This yere Mall'ry—he a big man? White hair? Red complected?"

"Why—why, yes. I believe so."

"Mmm. Figgered it'd be the same one. I know him. Usta fish near his place when I was a colt. He come there in the summertime, big house in Cleft Canyon on Mount Rydell. I 'member we usta call him the 'devil Doc,' 'count of there was alluz queer goin's-on at his place. Well, Cap'n?"

He squinted at me. I weighed the chances briefly. It was probably a wild goose chase. On the other hand, it was useless, as Danny had pointed out, to throw our little force against the might of the Toties who now held Fort Knox. And there was a faint, insane possibility that Dr. Mallory had a 'plan'—an invention, maybe—that would enable us to form the nucleus of a new army that, reorganized, would sweep the invaders from our land....

"We'll do it!" I said. "We'll march at dawn!"

We had to leave the car there on the road and strike out across country. It was the shortest and safest way to Cleft Canyon. Now that the Toties had made a clean sweep of the East, the roads were no longer open to us. As in Mexico five years ago, as in Ontario, the Maritimes, the New England States year before last, as in Illinois last year, floods of Totie scavengers were pouring through the conquered land in a series of "mop up" operations.

Time and again aircraft droning over our heads sent us scurrying to cover. Once a flight surprised us in an open field. That's when we lost Johnny Grant and three other men. Nearby woods saved the rest of us.

Before we abandoned the car, I had the men strip it of everything we could possibly use. Upholstery, tires, all electrical accessories, including the televise. It was this last that kept us going, kept our spirits aflame with determination, even when the trail was hardest. Wherever we spun the dial we found the ether crackling with the boasts of the enemy; each scene pictured on the plate was one calculated to tighten the already grim jaws of my men.

The Totie banner floated everywhere. It was a blood-red flag; in the center was a quartered circle. In each of these segments was a symbol of one of the four totalitarian states that had welded to form the Totie army. Swastika and crimson sun, side by side with the Italian fasces and Soviet hammer-and-sickle. The Big Four that, irresistibly combined, had ground the principles of democracy under foot.

It made me bitter, but it made me heart-sick, too. I could not help wondering how, or why, my father and those of his generation had been so blind as not to see the shadow of the inevitable creeping toward them.

Surely they must have known, as early as 1940, that Sweden would not be the last neutral to be drawn into the conflict? Even then there must have been rumblings in the Balkans, on the Mediterranean? Did they not guess that Italy and Russia were just waiting until the hour was ripe, that Japan's leisurely conquest of China was a mere military exercise to keep Nippon warmed up until the day should arrive for a blow at the Pacific Islands?

My own country was perhaps the worst offender. Had it not been told by a wise man, centuries before that, "In Union there is Strength?" Yet America, like Switzerland and Portugal, Greece and Egypt, played ostrich. Hoping against all sane hope that each succeeding conquest would so weaken the Toties that the few actively fighting democracies could win out in the end.

I remember, as a child, the gleeful shouting in the streets of America when news reached us across the Atlantic that Hitler had been assassinated. I remember my father saying to a neighbor, "That's the last of the mad dogs. Stalin and Mussolini are gone; now Hitler. There'll be an armistice within a month. After that—"

I wonder if Dad ever thought of that when he fought with his regiment at Buffalo. The true facts must have come to him as a series of staggering blows. The sudden collapse of the Franco-British union when Russia and Italy, selecting their moment with diabolic accuracy of timing, threw their support to Germany. The three mad dogs were dead, yes, but four younger, madder dogs took their place. Himmler, Ciano, Molotov, and Kashatuku. The crushing of India, the rape of Africa, the shadow of the crimson banner stretching across the Atlantic Ocean to touch Brazil.

It was too late then to evoke the Monroe Doctrine. Too late to throw defenses about our own shore line. Canada owned but a shell of its former man power, Mexico was a hotbed of Totie sympathizers. Our militia was unready, theirs fired for twelve years in the flaming crucible of war.

These were not pleasant memories I had as our small band marched toward Mallory's hide-out in the hills. But I could not escape them. I, myself, had witnessed the siege of New York, had seen Philadelphia blown to shards by the mighty Armada that swept up the Delaware, had heard the last, defiant cry of the defenders of Los Angeles—

* * * *

Unfortunately, here a portion of the manuscript is missing. To Brian O'Shea the events mentioned must have been so commonly known as to render unnecessary the mentioning of specific dates. Dr. Winslow places the probable date of the invasion of the United States at 1959, but this may vary as much as two years, one way or the other.

"—low!" warned Sanders. "I don't think he's seen us!"

Danny's eyes had widened; he was pointing eastward.

"He's not looking for us! There's what he's waiting for. Look! An American plane!"

I was soaked to the skin, cold and miserable. The damned Totie scout might, I found myself thinking unreasonably, have waited just five more minutes before sneaking up over the horizon. Five more minutes and we would have finished fording this stream, would be up the rise and through the tangle of elm that Joe Sanders claimed concealed the place that was our destination.

Beside me, Maureen sneezed. The poor kid was wet, bedraggled. I don't know how she contrived to still appear beautiful under such circumstances. Somewhere behind me, I heard the snick of a breech-bolt. I turned in time to find LeBrun raising his rifle. I slapped it down.

"No, you idiot!"

He looked sulky.

"He's low, O'Shea. I can lay one in his gas tank."

"And if you miss," I hissed, "you'll have the whole damned Totie army down around our ears. We've come this far without being caught. We'll take no risks now."

Still, I knew how he felt. It was rotten to crouch there, knee-deep in icy mountain water, concealed by a vault of foliage, watching one of our planes—one of what must be a very, very few of our planes—drive blindly into the path of a hedge-hopping Totie fighter that had spotted its prey and was now waiting for it.

Then, suddenly, there was the roar of motors. The American plane had come within range. The Totie plane broke from concealment, spun skyward in a swift, dizzying burst of motion. White puffs broke from its nose seconds before our ears caught the spiteful chatter of machine-gun fire.

It caught the American flyer off guard. Something broke from his left wing, flapped crazily in the wind, as he jammed his plane—more by instinct than anything else—into a dive. The Totie was on his tail in an instant. And we stood there, helpless, watching a sweet, if one-sided, air battle.

The Totie plane was superior, of course. But our pilot was a master. Time and again he wriggled out from under the other's nose just as it seemed he would be riddled into fragments. Once he managed to climb high enough to try a few shots of his own, but the Totie Immelmanned, was back on his tail before he could even get his sights trained.

It ended as suddenly as it had begun. One minute they were spiraling for position, whirling around each other like a pair of strange, snarling dogs. The next there came a thin streamer of smoke from the tail of the American plane; a streamer that thickened to a cloud as we watched, became flame-shot black, choking, menacing.

The Totie fired a final burst into the damaged plane. It went into a spin. Something dark appeared from a gap over the fuselage, it was the pilot climbing free. For what seemed an endless moment he poised there, then he was a brown chip on the blue breast of the sky, a chip that hurtled headlong to earth. Beside me Maureen gasped; I felt her shoulder tense against mine.

Then a white mushroom blossomed suddenly; I choked a word of profanity that somehow I didn't mean to be profane. The parachute, bloated with air, zigzagged languidly to the ground. The pilot was halfway down when his plane crashed. Flames leaped in a wooded thicket across the rise. The Totie airman circled several times. Then, apparently content, he gunned his ship, disappeared northward.

MacGregor frowned. "They must be confident. First Totie I ever saw who didn't gun a parachuter."

* * * *

We left our hiding place, then; broke into the open where the caterpillar could see us. He was a good flyer. He sighted us, played his cords expertly, and landed less than an eighth of a mile from where we had gathered. A couple of our men helped him fight down the still-struggling 'chute; he kicked himself loose from the straps and approached me.

"Won't have any more use for that," he said ruefully. "You're the leader here? My name's Krassner. Jake Krassner. Fourth Aerial Combat."

I introduced him around. Danny Wilson said eagerly, "Did you say the Fourth? I knew a guy flew with them. Name of Tommy Bryce. From Hoboken. You know him?"

Krassner shook his head. He had hard, black eyes, a little close. Crisp hair. Broad shoulders. He was a good-looking chap. A little haughty, maybe. But airmen are like that, especially to ground-huggers.

"I'm sorry. Our personnel has changed a lot. Lately," he added grimly. He looked at me. "I seem to have picked a hell of a place to get shot down, Captain. What on earth are you doing in this desolate spot?"

Van Huys chuckled, and Joe Sanders grinned.

"Don't look like much from topside, eh, Krassner? I figgered it wouldn't. The old man's a fox. He spent more than twenty years givin' this hide-out the damnedest coat of natch'ral camouflage you ever seen."

"Old man?" said Krassner curiously. "Camouflage?"

Maureen touched my arm. She whispered, "Maybe you had better not tell him, Brian. It's our secret—"

I started to tell her what the hell. He was one of us, and there were mighty few of us left. We needed all the men we could get. And Krassner looked like a man. I didn't get a chance to say any of this, though. For as we talked, we had continued to follow Sanders. Joe was now picking his way confidently through an opening in the tangle of foliage.

Sunlight dimmed as we entered a huge, cleared space entirely roofed by an interwoven network of boughs. In this space was a wide, rambling, one-story house, adjoined by a number of inexplicable sheds. And on the veranda of the house stood a man I recognized instantly. It was Dr. Thomas Mallory.

CHAPTER IV

Mallory made us welcome. More than that, he seemed positively delighted that we had come. He showed anxiety on only one point.

"No one saw you come here, Captain? You're sure of that?"

"Positive," I told him.

"Good!" He called, and assistants came from inside to lead my men to quarters. I was surprised, as well as a little shocked and disappointed, to discover the number of women attached to Dr. Mallory's household. There were a few men, but for the most part he seemed to have surrounded himself with girls. Not only that, but with young and pretty girls!

But this was no time to sit in judgment on a man's morality. We had an important mission. Maureen broached the subject as soon as we three were rid of the others.

"You must know why we're here, Dr. Mallory. We did not find this place by chance. We came because you are the last hope of our country. Too late, the government realizes it needs the invention you offered it five years ago."

Mallory shook his head sadly.

"I'm sorry, my child—"

"You can't refuse, Doctor!" I broke in. "Don't you understand? The Toties overrun all the Americas. Democracy is dead unless—"

He raised a weary hand.

"Then democracy is dead, O'Shea. Not even I can restore its life. I can say only one thing; I am glad from the bottom of my heart that the government refused to listen to me when first I approached the War Department with my plan."

"Glad? Why?"

"Because I was guilty of that which a scientist must ever dread. I jumped to a hasty conclusion, based on insufficient evidence. My conclusion was wrong, my plan—" He sighed, turned toward a door. "But come. I will show you."

* * * *

He led the way from his office into an adjoining room; a laboratory, spotless, white-gleaming. About the walls of the laboratory were a number of cages. In some of these were small animals; I saw monkeys, guinea pigs, a squirrel, rabbits. Some were active, eating, shuffling about, looking at us with bright, inquisitive eyes. Others lay apparently asleep.

But these I noticed with some remote part of my mind. For the focal point of attention was a glass-walled case in the center of the room; a topless case in which lay the body of a man. Maureen started. She said, "Dead, Doctor?"

"He is not dead," replied Mallory somberly. "He is the result of my dreadful error of judgment. These others—" He nodded toward the cages. "—were the experiments that misled me. This man, one of my assistants who trusted me and was daring enough to become my first human experiment, sleeps. How long he will continue to sleep, I cannot guess. But it may be for one, two, or even more decades!"

"Sleeps!" I said. But Maureen, with a flash of that swift intuition I had seen before, guessed the answer. She said, "Anaesthesia! That was your plan, Dr. Mallory!"

"Yes, my child. That was my plan. I am a scientist, but five years ago I was sociologist enough to recognize that the United States could not match the power of the Totalitarians. I realized, even then, that the ending we have seen come to pass was inevitable. I set myself the task of finding a way to meet the impending menace.

"I found the answer in a new form of anaesthetic. I will not tell you its formula. It is a dismal failure—but that I did not know. I thought it was a great success. When I permitted small animals—those you see before you—to inhale some of the delicate granules—"

"Granules, Doctor?"

"Yes. It was a revolutionary means of inducing unconsciousness. When I permitted the animals to inhale these granules, they fell into a soft, deep, harmless slumber. I timed their periods of sleep carefully, discovered the anaesthetic rendered them senseless over periods ranging from one to two weeks.

"It was then, heady with success, I offered my plan to the government. It was, I thought, so simple. Our planes would scatter the granules over enemy terrain—" He laughed shortly, mirthlessly. "—and the enemy would fall into deep slumber. While they were thus incapacitated, our men, garbed in specially constructed suits, wearing protective masks, could walk amongst them, disarm them, imprison them. The war would be ended bloodlessly—"

I stared at him incredulously. I said, "But—but if it really works that way, Dr. Mallory, that is the weapon we need!"

"Yes, my boy. But it doesn't work that way. I have told you I made an error in judgment. I assumed that Man, being a higher animal than those on which I experimented, would experience the same, or a slightly less drastic reaction than that experienced by the animals. I did not take into consideration the fact that Man is also a more highly integrated animal. That he is weaker, in some respects.

"When Williamson, here, volunteered to become a human guinea pig, I accepted his offer. I exposed him to the granules. He breathed deeply, fell asleep—" Dr. Mallory shook his head. "And that was more than four years ago. He still sleeps!"

I said, "I understand now, Doctor, why you consider your plan a failure. But you speak as a scientist and a humanitarian who would shudder at seeing thousands of men sleep for a decade. I am a soldier. I have met War face to face, and have learned, by bitter experience, that there is no weapon too dreadful to use if the results are satisfactory.

"What if your granules *do* put the Toties to sleep for years instead of days? Isn't that better than seeing our countrymen die beneath the sword of the aggressor? Unless we act swiftly, this war is over. Freedom, liberty, equality of men, all the things we believe in, are doomed. But there is yet time to equip a few of our troops with the suits and masks you speak of, turn loose your slumber-granules to the winds.

"Even though thousands of our own men share the sleep of the enemy, we can go through with the disarmament program you planned. When our foes awaken, a decade hence, they will have lost their leaders and their war. When our friends waken we will take them, triumphantly, to the homes and cities we have rebuilt while they slumbered."

Dr. Mallory said, "I wish it were as simple as that, O'Shea. But there is one other thing you do not know. The granules that are my anaesthetic are more than mere granules. They are spores. Worse—they are self-propagating spores!"

He pointed to a trebly barred and locked door opening on one wall of the laboratory. For the first time there was nervousness in his voice.

"There is a storeroom beyond that door, O'Shea. In that storeroom, quiescent in sterile containers, lie spores. Countless thousands, millions of them. They are the granules I made for the government before I discovered their real nature. There lies beyond that door a weapon potent enough to end this war immediately—"

He paused suddenly. We had all heard it, the squeak of a worn hinge, the shuffle of a footstep. I motioned Mallory to silence, tiptoed to the office door and flung it open.

The aviator, Krassner, stood there. He was smiling. He said, "Ah, there you are, Captain! I was looking for you. I wanted to ask if—"

"How long have you been here?" I asked angrily.

"How long? Why—just a minute or so. I—"

"Were you listening to our conversation?"

He stiffened; a flush highlighted his cheek bones.

"I beg your pardon, sir!" he said.

"Because, if you were—" Dr. Mallory was beside me, his hand was on my arm. I hesitated. There was no sense in being so violently suspicious. I said, "Well, never mind. Go back to your quarters, Krassner. I'll be with you shortly."

"Very good, sir!" He saluted, turned and stalked from the office, a picture of affronted honor and dignity. I felt somewhat ashamed of myself.

Mallory said, "It really doesn't matter whether he heard us or not, O'Shea. What I was about to say is, there lies beyond that door a weapon potent enough to end the war immediately—but it must never be used. For once loosed to the winds, those abominable spores would not only end this war, they would still all animal life on the face of Earth. I have said they were self-propagating. Each new generation of spores would deepen the slumber into which mankind had been soothed by the first—"

I said, "But why keep them, Doctor?"

"I don't quite know, O'Shea. Perhaps I have done so because I am, at heart, more emotional than a true scientist should be. Perhaps I have a secret fear that there may come a day when I shall be forced to play God, give mankind its release from the chains of the tyrant."

Maureen shuddered.

"No, Doctor! You mustn't even think of that. Things look black now, but they can't go on like this forever. Right and truth and liberty will prevail in the end. There must be some other way to escape—"

"There is," said Dr. Mallory quietly. "There is another way. A plan I have been working on ever since the failure of my first. There is one last refuge to which they cannot follow us."

I said, "I don't understand, Doctor. Do you mean Antarctica?"

His grave eyes captured, held mine.

"No," he said. "A place more remote than even that. I mean, O'Shea— the moon!"

I knew, then, suddenly and with a great, overwhelming despair, that our journey to Cleft Canyon had been a vain one. As a last resort we had sought the hidden laboratory of one who had been a great scientist. We had found a madman.

I said, "Maureen—" and I suppose there was regret in my voice.

But Mallory stopped me. "A moment, O'Shea. I'm not insane. Nor is my plan—as you undoubtedly think—impossible. Did you ever hear the name of Frazier Wrenn?"

The name was vaguely familiar, but I couldn't place it. Maureen could, and did. She said, curiously, "Isn't he the traitor who disappeared from Earth with a group of followers? Years ago? From a laboratory out west somewhere?"

"Yes, my dear. In 1939. From Arizona. But whether he and his tiny band were traitors is something future generations must decide. Wrenn hated war; foresaw what must come of Earth's second Armageddon. He fled Earth, his destination was the planet Venus, his purpose to maintain, on that wild colony, a vestige of culture and civilization until Earth's feverish self-destruction should end."

Mallory sighed. "We do not know what has become of Wrenn's expedition. There has been no remotest sign, no signal—"

I said, "Venus! But, Doctor, that means *spaceflight*!"

"Yes, Brian. I was to have been a member of that gallant party. But I was delayed in reaching their Arizona rendezvous, and their departure was hastened by an unexpected attack. They left without me. But, fortunately, Wrenn had confided in me the plans for his spaceship. For years, now, with what scraps of metal I could steal from a war-ridden, metal-hungry humanity, I have been secretly building a small duplicate of the *Goddard*.

"You wonder where it is hidden? Our Kentucky hills conceal great caverns, Brian. There is one beneath the hill on which this house stands. Below us—as I will show you shortly—is a gigantic cave. In it is my almost completed craft."

I had not noticed that Maureen's hand was in mine until I felt its soft whiteness tense within my grasp. She cried, "But why the moon, Dr. Mallory? Why not follow the Wrenn expedition—?"

"You ignore a major factor, my dear. Celestial mechanics. Wrenn's flight was planned for a time when Venus and Earth were in conjunction. Such is not the case now. Earth approaches the Sun, while Venus is at aphelion. And my craft is, as I have said, but a small copy of Wrenn's. Moreover, I have been able to collect only a small amount of fuel.

"There is only one body within our cruising range—Earth's moon. It is my dream that we shall go there—"

I had been listening silently, stunned. Now I came to my senses.

"No, Doctor! I can listen to no more. You forget I am a soldier of the United States army."

"The government has fallen; the last of the democracies is crushed beneath the conqueror's heel, Brian, lad."

"It will rise again. In the hinterlands—"

"—are Totalitarian troops."

"There are still eighty million Americans—"

"And a hundred million aggressors!" He put a hand on my shoulder. "Don't you see, Brian, this is how you can best serve your country? Make this flight with me. We will take your men and my followers—two score men and the women you have already seen—and form a colony on the Moon.

"We will return, then, secretly, for more Americans. And more, and more. We will transfer our democracy to a new soil, there grow in strength and power and wisdom until some day we can reclaim our heritage."

Despite my training, I could not help but be convinced. I said, shaken, "But astronomers tell us the Moon is a barren, lifeless world?"

"For the most part, it is. But the Caltech telescope indicates that air still lingers in the depths of the hollow craters. And in underground caverns. Water can be synthesized. It will be no easy existence, but it will be—"

"The ultimate salient!" breathed Maureen at my side. "The last line of defense for freedom's children! Brian, Dr. Mallory is right! We must do this thing!"

He looked at me hopefully. "Well, Brian O'Shea?"

I took a deep breath. "When does our flight depart?"

CHAPTER V

At Dr. Mallory's suggestion, I did not tell my men too much about our plans. "With so much at stake, O'Shea," he said, "the less they know the better it will be."

But they did not ask to know much. They were good men; they trusted me. And if they chafed a little at the enforced idleness of the next week, the rest must have been a welcome surcease from months of fighting. Only one man failed to share their calm acceptance of my orders. Krassner. He told me, sulkily, "There's something going on around here, O'Shea. And, damn it, I have a right to know what it is. As a fellow officer—"

"I respect your brevet, Krassner," I told him somewhat curtly, "but for the present I must ask you to remember that you are attached to this division through courtesy only, and have no authority. In a few more days, now, I will be at liberty to explain everything."

He had to be satisfied with that. Though it was the nature of the man to be snoopy; several times he was observed prowling around the grounds, searching some clue as to Doctor Mallory's well-concealed secret.

He was chasing a will-o'-the-wisp, of course. A man might have searched for months without finding the entrance to Mallory's underground workshops. Mallory admitted Wilson and St. Cloud, my lieutenants, to his confidence. He took us to the cavern wherein was being constructed the spaceship.

The gateway to the depths was that which appeared to be a photographer's dark-room. Once inside, Mallory pressed certain carved ornaments, the entire farther wall slid back, and there stretched before us a smooth, well-lighted passage leading downward at a gentle incline.

We must have followed this more than a half mile before we debouched into the main cavern; a mighty, vaulted chamber, a huge bubble of emptiness blown in the solid mountain centuries ago when Earth was in the travail of making.

But it was not this natural wonder that made me gasp. I had seen others; I had, indeed, once taken refuge for four weeks with the Ninth Artillery in Luray. That which brought an exclamation to my lips was the shimmering monster braced on an exoskeleton of girders in the middle of the chamber. A gigantic, tear-shaped rocketship, stern jets lifted some feet off the ground, streamlined nose pointing at the roof of the cave.

About it, in and around it, sweating men fretted, worried, labored, like so many restless bees. Here the brief chatter of a riveting machine woke snarling echoes as a final plate was welded into place; there a master electrician wove an intricate network of wires into some obscure purpose. In still another place, a strong-thewed gang trundled seemingly endless trains of supplies into the ship's capacious holds.

Dr. Mallory smiled at the expressions on our faces, and there was pardonable pride in his smile.

"There, my friends," he said quietly, "is the *Jefferson*."

"*Jefferson?*" repeated Maureen wonderingly.

"Named for him who, in our country's infancy, wrote down in blazing words the principles on which all democracy is based. The inherent right of men to enjoy life, liberty, and the pursuit of happiness. Once his words showed us the way. Now his name shall lead us to a new civilization."

"Amen!" said Danny Wilson piously. Then, "Now can we have a look at her? I mean *him*, Doctor?"

Knowing every nook and cranny, berth and hold, turret and gun-chamber of the *Jefferson* as I do now, it is hard to remember my feelings on that day when first I strode her permalloy decks. Even so, I can recall the vast wonder that engulfed me as Dr. Mallory led us through the ship, pointing out the engines, the control-rooms, the Spartan simplicity of the living quarters, the well-equipped kitchen and compact storage bins. There was much I did not understand until long afterward. Permalloy itself was a novelty to me. The metal had been invented, Mallory said, by a German scientist. One of the old school. A Doktor Eric von Adlund.

"I do not know what has become of him. Perhaps he, like the other peace-loving great of his race, has long since been liquidated by the Totalitarians."

* * * *

So said Dr. Mallory sadly. And he tried to explain the operation of the small, inconceivably powerful, atomic motors, the invention of Frazier Wrenn. It was a concept so novel, yet so simple, that it staggered us all. But I could see how, without first having a knowledge of the heretofore unknown element *inektron (the spelling of this important word seems to have confused Brian O'Shea. In the manuscript it is incomprehensibly scribbled. Dr. Winslow suggests the philological similarity of such words as* "inertron" *and* "inactron"*? NSB*) man might never have discovered the long-sought power of the atom.

St. Cloud, frankly at sea as regarded scientific matters, was delighted with the military efficiency of the ship. I could see his fingers yearning for the lanyard of one of the rotor-guns installed in the fore and aft turrets. He liked, too, the foreman who came over to meet us.

"How many men have you working here below?" he asked.

Myers, the supervisor, told him twenty-three. "And there are twenty women topside," he grinned. "Doc says we're going to a brutal frontier. But if the women can stand it, we can. A man can do lots of impossible things with his wife at his side."

I understood, then, the number of girls I had seen above ground, and regretted my hasty judgment of Dr. Mallory's character. I might have realized that he did nothing without purpose. He had seen—as I saw now—that without something, some*one*, to fight for, the men of our little colony-to-be could easily lose heart. He was assuring our venture against all eventualities.

I was glad, suddenly, that Maureen was beside me. I wondered if she felt the same way.

Danny Wilson voiced a problem that had puzzled me.

"But this cavern, Doctor? Aren't you like the man who, in his spare time, built a yacht in his cellar? How are we ever going to get this monster out of here?"

Mallory said placidly, "When the hour comes, we will burst from this cavern like a moth from its chrysalis. You have not yet witnessed the power of our atomic beams.

"One thrust of blinding energy from the forward jets and we will shear an exit through the tons of solid rock and earth that now conceal us. Before we leave—" He looked at me significantly. "—we will destroy the buildings above ground. Including that one, sealed chamber that no man must ever open.

"The Totalitarians will have no way of guessing who we were, what we did here, or where we have gone. And even if they should guess, they would be powerless to follow us."

His voice was low, vibrant, anticipatory.

"Your men and mine, Brian O'Shea, we hundred odd will establish the first base on Luna. Then there will be other trips to Earth, gathering more converts to our cause. The day will come when we will match our conquerors in strength. And then—"

I said thoughtfully, "One more thing, Doctor. The *Jefferson* is supplied with water and provisions, yes. But if our number grows, we will need our own farms and granaries. How are we to grow food in the lightless grottoes of the moon?"

He nodded sagely.

"All that has been provided for, Brian, lad. I have overlooked nothing. Chemical culture is possible. Trust me to take care of that problem when it arises."

Danny Wilson coughed apologetically. He said, "We do, Doc. But—but I think I know what's in the back of Brian's mind. Suppose something should—I mean—if anything might happen to you—?"

"That, too, I have considered. There is a complete scientific library in the aft turret. Science is no secret to the man who can read and think."

Danny's face lighted. He said beautifully, "A library! Golly! Books! I haven't seen a book for nigh onto fifteen years. Except Field Code manuals. There hasn't been much time for reading lately."

"And that," said Mallory darkly, "is perhaps the greatest catastrophe of this war. Reading men, thinking men, are happy men. They are not concerned with the lust for conquest of anything save the unknown. Yes, Wilson, there are books. And for those who seek light entertainment there are even volumes of fiction. Magazines for amusement."

"Magazines?" I said, puzzled. "Magazines for amusement? I don't see anything funny in an armament warehouse."

Mallory sighed.

"Forgive me, O'Shea. I had forgotten your youth. There was a time, when you were a toddling child, when 'magazines' were not always ammunition bins. Publishers used to issue monthly periodicals, printed on paper, bound in bright jackets, filled with stories. Exciting adventures in sports, the West, tales of crime and its detection, fictionized hazards as to the future of the world—

"Ah, but that was long ago. That was when paper was cheap and common. When the vast mills of Norway and Denmark and Canada poured endless rolls of pulp into our country."

Danny said eagerly, "I'd like to see some of these here 'magazines,' Doc. Could I?"

"You may. Myers will help you select some from the storage bin, Wilson. And now, my friends, if you are ready to return to the surface—?"

* * * *

That, as I recall, was on the 29th day of July, 1963. Yes, I know it was that day, because that was the date of the fall of Santa Fé. We watched that battle through our televises; it was triumphantly broadcast—a braggart deed in keeping with their boastful ways—by the Toties.

Albuquerque having fallen, General Bornot, commander of the Army of the West, had withdrawn his forces to the old capital of New Mexico, there to make a last, desperate stand.

It was a valiant, but doomed, defense. The very fact that intimate details of the battle were televised shows how vastly superior the Totie forces were; their airplanes could fly without hindrance over our lines, spying out resources, reserves, and the pitifully weak remnants of our Army.

Like our own demolished Eastern army, the westerners were a motley crew. I saw French, English, Scandinavian and Canadian uniforms; loyal Sikhs from India fighting shoulder-to-shoulder with kilted Scots; swarthy refugees from Totie Mexico and Guatemala defending futile breaches beside blonde, fair-skinned Icelanders.

The main body of attackers stormed up from captive Albuquerque to the south; these were the trained warriors of Japan, the yellow horde that had ravaged California, Arizona and Utah and pressed eastward to meet Kievinovski's command. The Russians came down from the north, cutting off any avenue of escape through Taos. ("Once," Dr. Mallory told us sadly, "Taos was the artistic center of the United States. Now but one pigment flows there; the red of blood.") And Schneider's Army of the Mississippi had swept westward through Arkansas and Oklahoma, leaving nothing but waste and desolation behind them, to meet the other armies at this last defense post of democratic gallantry.

It was no battle at all, really; it was a slaughter. Our army had refortified old Fort Marcy, earthworks built by General Kearny more than a hundred years ago. Two divisions were quartered in the Garita, the old Spanish headquarters. Thus they lay, more than four thousand Democratic troops—waiting behind breastworks of earth and 'dobe for the attack of armies whose artillery was built to blast steel and concrete pill-boxes out of existence.

Even so, the gallantry of their defense turned the blood in my veins to electricity. They did not wait for the Toties to attack; they carried the fight to the enemy. With the first, tentative shot from the besiegers there came an answering blast from the besiezed. Then the bedlam was on.

Stream upon endless stream, the Toties flooded into the city. As they did so, we—and the enemy—discovered that the spying televise had not told the whole story. Windows opened to expose spitting, snarling machine guns. Doorways gaped to expose light fieldpieces that poured fiery death into the Toties. Fake walls split miraculously, from them charged concealed troops of Americans, faces grim, guns flaming, roaring, bayonets flashing.

Guerrilla warfare became the order of the day. At street barricades powder and flame were forgotten as men met face to face, looked with stark eyes upon dripping steel. Americans and their allies fell, but for each of them fell two, three, a half dozen of the invaders. The scream of explosives was deafening, the street pictured on the metallic screen before us was a shambles of blood; bodies lay asprawl like the forgotten toys of a careless child.

And—the televise screen went blank!

Danny Wilson loosed a great cry of joy. "They're licked!" he roared. "The dog-whelped cowards are licked! I never knew of them to turn off a televised victory—"

For five glorious minutes we shared his hope. Then the broadcast was resumed, after a murmured comment about a "technical difficulty in transmission"—and when again our eyes looked upon the streets of Santa Fé, the picture had changed.

Once more it was aircraft that had won the day. In the face of impending disaster, the Toties had loosed the full power of their air armada against the beleaguered forces. It did not matter to them that their thermite bombs fell amongst their men as well as ours; that was a hazard their hirelings had been trained to accept. Burst after flaming burst rocked the streets of old Santa Fé, broken bodies were flung brutally against shattered walls, doorways and windows emptied—and there were no more defenders. Only fresh, unending troops of Toties filling the gaps left by their fellows.

I saw the Garita fall, a flaming shambles; I saw an airplane swoop low over breastworks hastily flung up at the *Puenta de Los Hidalgos* and wipe out a company of Americans. I heard the biting rasp of machine gun fire, the staccato bark of anti-aircraft; once the visiplate before us whirled giddily for an instant as the plane in which our broadcaster rode narrowly escaped disaster.

I saw the last great moment of Fort Marcy; the fall of the gates and the horde of snarling Toties that rushed in, bayonetting all before them; I saw the bayonet wielded that slashed the rope holding the American flag to the flagpost. I saw the man who turned and raced to that flagpost, grasped the ropes and held them taut as, for a moment longer, the tattered ensign whipped out through the smoke and flame.

Then I saw the bullet that found this unknown hero's breast; saw him cough and loose his grasp, slip earthward as the flag above him tumbled to the dirt. There was a look of hurt surprise in his eyes. Then I saw no more, because my eyes were wet. And Dr. Mallory said, "There is nothing more to see—"

And turned off the televise.

* * * *

Yes, that was the 29th day of July, 1963. I remember it well. For it was after that I asked Mallory, "Do we go now? There is no reason to delay."

And he said, "We will leave in five days. By that time all will be in readiness. And the third of August will be a day of good omen. It was on that day, centuries ago, that a humble Portuguese sailorman with a great dream sailed westward to the Indies and found a new world.

"Like Chistofero Colon, we will select that date to set our course for New America—"

Maureen's hand tightened on mine. Krassner, who had been watching the televise silently, gaped at us.

"New course? Go? Go where?"

"Skip it—!" I began. But Dr. Mallory stopped me. "No, I think it is well the men should be told now, O'Shea. My helpers know. Your men, who must be the fighters of our party, should be told where they are going."

And he told them. It came as a stunning blow. Some of them looked frightened; some, to be quite truthful, simply did not understand. Others were openly incredulous. Among these was Krassner. He epostulated, "But—but, O'Shea, this old fool must be insane! Flight to the Moon! Absurd!"

His eyes narrowed.

"There's more to it than that. This is a trick of some kind I'll bet it's tied up with that mysterious invention you've got hidden in your closet—"

I grasped him by the shoulder, whirled him about.

"Then you *did* hear us that day?"

"Sure. I heard you. Is there anything wrong in that? I couldn't help hearing you say you had a weapon that would end the war. If that's what you've got, trot it out! That's a lot better than dying like rats on a fool's expedition to the *Moon*!

"Luna! Pah! I, for one, won't have anything to do with it—"

I said hotly, "You damned fool, we can't open that closet. Don't you realize—?"

"Brian!" snapped Dr. Mallory.

I shut up suddenly. Krassner looked at me, then at the old man suspiciously. He snarled, "You reminded me once that I had no authority over your command, O'Shea. Well, now I remind you that you have no authority over me. I'm pulling out of here. I've had enough of this insane secrecy and—"

He started for the door. I said only one word.

"Lars!"

Lars Frynge, the towering Swede, had his revolver at Krassner's mid-section. He said amiably, "Ay tank maybe you batter lissen to Captain, hey?"

Krassner's face purpled. He bellowed, "This is the last straw, O'Shea. Insulting an officer and an equal! By the gods, I'll—"

He was right. He was an officer and an equal. But I was determined of one thing. Go with us he would, whether he liked it or not. But in the meanwhile—

"All right, Lars," I said. "Krassner, I'm sorry. I wasn't just trying to throw my weight around. But think it over carefully, man. This means a lot to all of us. You're at liberty to do what you will."

He snorted and strode from the room. Danny Wilson cocked an eyebrow at me; I nodded. Danny followed him. Maureen said nervously, "He's a trouble-maker, Brian. I don't think we should trust him out of our sight."

"That's why Danny left us," I grinned.

"And when we go, we should leave without him."

"That," said Mallory, "is impossible. When we go, there must remain no one behind to know where we have gone."

* * * *

And there were five days left in which to finish all that had to be done before our departure. Those were days of feverish excitement and activity for all of us. Having been let into the secret, my men were shown the way to the underground cavern. There they labored, side by side with Mallory's helpers, to load the cargo, put the last finishing touches on the *Jefferson*.

We stripped the house; we gathered all forage from the barns and silos and bins. We rolled cask upon cask of fresh spring water into the holds. We locked and sealed the holds, one by one.

Danny raised a fuss about that. He had found something new and wonderful—something I meant to investigate myself as soon as the opportunity permitted. The joy of reading fiction.

"It—it's swell, Brian!" he told me. "Boy, I wish I'd lived in them days when magazines was common. You ought to read some of them stories. Sports and detective stories and—" He looked sort of sheepish. "The ones I like best are science stories. Gosh, you'd be surprised, Brian. Them old writers guessed sometimes pretty near what was going to happen.

"There was a guy named Bender, or Binder, or something like that, who guessed 'way back in '40, at the start of this war, that we'd get into it. And there was another guy named Clinton who said the same thing—he was nuts, though. He said the women would bust loose from the men and set up their own government.

"And those others, they predicted things like the spaceship we'll soon be riding in. And television, and—"

I said, "Those magazines must be plenty old."

"They are. Ancient. But they're still fun. Brian, can't I sneak a few of them into my berth instead of sealing them up in the library? Do you think Doc would mind?"

"I guess not," I told him. So he did just that. By the time he'd finished robbing the library, it looked moth-eaten and there was scarcely enough room in his berth for him to turn around in....

Those were full days and exciting ones, but pleasant. It is hard to realize that we were living on the bright edge of grave calamity. Nor did we know it until the eve of the day on which we were to take off.

It started with a thin, high droning to the north. The familiar drone of aircraft. As always, under these circumstances, Dr. Mallory sounded the "Take cover!" signal, and everyone scurried to the shelter of the camouflaged grove, there to wait until the danger should pass.

But it did not pass. The droning came nearer, deepened in tone. And we saw, through the leafy veil that concealed us, that it was not a single plane that was approaching, nor a single flight—but a solid phalanx of enemy aircraft!

Even then we did not guess the dreadful truth. It was not until they had come directly over us, swung into an involute loop and began concentrating upon us, that we knew what was happening. Then we saw something dark and ominous loose itself from the rack of one bomber; a thin screaming filled the air—and in the woods to our right there came a frightful blast!

Earth shook beneath us, Maureen screamed needless words in my ear. "They're bombing *us*, Brian! They've found our refuge!"

CHAPTER VI

There was only one thing that spared all of us in those next few minutes. That was the fact that the Toties did not know *exactly* where we were. Somehow they had learned the approximate location of Dr. Mallory's mountain hide-away, but not in vain had the aged scientist spent twenty years nurturing plant life to form a perfect barricade of concealment about the dim, squat buildings. From above, the wooded dell that hid his laboratory must have looked like one of thousands such.

Therefore they scattered their shots. One bomb exploded a quarter mile from Mallory's house; I learned afterward that it killed two workmen who had been laying in cordwood. Others exploded as far as five miles away as the hive of lethal wasps eddied back and forth, bombing the entire countryside with abandon.

A thousand questions seethed through my brain, but there was no time now to ponder the answers. No time to ask why, or how, the Toties had learned of this place. I seized Maureen's elbow, half-led, half-dragged her toward the laboratory. Above the crashing din I howled in her ear, "To the cavern! That's the only safe—"

The rest was lost in an ear-splitting thunderbolt. But she knew what I meant.

We were not the only ones who fled to the security of the house. The lab was the lodestone toward which all we tiny, helpless motes gravitated. By the time we reached it, the shaking walls were jammed with soldiers, workers, women, who had sought refuge there.

A few of these were itching for action. Such a one was Danny Wilson. He was pleading with Mallory, "How about it, Doc? Just one of them anticraft guns? We can get it up here in no time."

"No. They don't know just where we are, Wilson. A shot would locate us definitely. We must remain silent and take our chances against a lucky placement."

Krassner, his handsome face oddly pale, clutched at Mallory's arm.

"This cavern you were talking about, Mallory. Take us there! We'll all be blown to bits—"

Joe Sanders' nose wrinkled, he looked at the airman disgustedly, and spat. Mingled with my own contemptuous reaction to Krassner's demand,

I felt a warming glow of pride in my men. Each of them had realized, as had Maureen and I, that the only safe place was the underground shelter. But each of them had wanted, before we took to that refuge, at least one vengeful poke at the enemy. Quivering capitulation like this rubbed them the wrong way.

But Mallory, serene as ever, had already led the way to the secret entrance. He pressed the knobs, the door swung open. I was beside Krassner as he did so; I saw the look of surprise on the aviator's face as he saw the long tunnel that fed to the depths beneath. I couldn't restrain the taunt.

"Thought Mallory was insane, eh, Krassner? Does this look like the work of a madman?"

He muttered something incoherent. Then Pelham-Jones, whose squad had been quartered farthest from the main house, burst into the room excitedly.

"They're landing foray parties, Brian! How long will it take to get everyone out of here?"

I glanced at Mallory. He said, "Fifteen or twenty minutes, at least."

"And to get the *Jefferson's* motors started?"

"Another ten."

"Then," I snapped, "you'll need protection for a half hour. That's what we're here for. Bruce, Rudy, Raoul, split your squads. Send half below; have the others throw a cordon about the laboratory. If they're dropping infantry, they'll have to stop bombing. By the time they find us, the others will be below. Then we'll take to the cavern—"

"Very good, sir!" They sprang into action.

* * * *

The women continued to file singly into the small dark-room, pass through the doorway into the tunnel. Maureen clutched my arm.

"Brian, you don't have to stay up here. You're too important. You're the leader. You've got to—"

"—to stay with my men!" I told her quietly. And I did what I had been wanting to do, but had never before dared. I took her, unresisting, into my arms; kissed her. Her lips were warm against mine. Then I pushed her toward the doorway. "Get down there. Don't worry about us. If we hold our fire it will take them a long time to locate us. Danny, where did Krassner go?"

Danny grimaced.

"That yellow mutt? Don't ask me. He's probably down there by now, hugging a stalactite."

"Well, to hell with him. Let's get going. And don't forget—don't fire a shot unless they actually see us. We don't want to give our position away."

Mallory said quietly, "I'll herd them below as fast as I can, Brian. When you hear the signal, bring your men on the double. But before you leave the laboratory, you know what must be done?" He nodded significantly toward the inner room, toward the trebly-barred door that contained a world's fate. I nodded.

"I know."

The steady evacuation continued. I went outside again. As Pelham-Jones had reported, the Tories were parachuting infantry to the ground. More planes had reached the scene; the sky swarmed with them. And a mass occupation was in progress; from each transport rumbled a steady stream of dark figures that, like strange, winged insects, plunged out of their humming cocoons, hurtled headlong toward Earth for a moment—then suddenly grew filmy, white umbrellas that lowered them gently to the ground.

It was a random, haphazard occupation for the Toties *still* had not solved the secret of our exact location. But many—too many—were dropping near our sheltered grove. It would not take them long, I knew, to find us.

Happily, the aerial bombardment had ceased with the dropping of the infantry. That was good. No chance explosion would find the heart of our refuge, destroy the lab and cut us off from the underground cavern.

Approximately twenty of us remained above ground as defenders. I told MacGregor, "Encircle the house. Defend it at all costs until you hear Mallory's call—then hightail it for the tunnel. I've got something to do inside."

I went back to the door beyond which were concealed the lethal anaesthetic spores. There were two barrels of oil there; we had placed them there for the purpose I now carried out. I broke them open, spilled their contents every which way. Now a single match would set the house ablaze, destroy forever the danger Mallory had feared. I would strike that match just before ducking into the tunnel myself—

A single, explosive crack sounded outside! A rifle had spoken!

That ripped it! With that shot there came a moment of macabre silence; then the air was alive with an answering volley from the hills and woods surrounding us. I raced out of the house, found Rudy Van Huys. I roared angrily, "Who fired! Why? Good God, man, don't you realize—"

His pink, chubby cheeks shook with anger to match my own. He said, "I don't know, Brian. They hadn't spotted us until then. But now—"

He didn't need to point to the forest; I could see the grey-green uniforms sifting through the trees, closing in on us. The *spang!* of a Wentzler shrilled in my ears, spent lead splattered against the wall behind me. All about us, now, rifle fire rasped and spat; I saw an advancing Totie soldier stop short in his tracks, stagger, spin, and fall, clutching his stomach with red hands that clawed. I heard a grunt from one of the men beside me, saw his mouth form an astonished O and an ugly, purple-black third eye appear magically in the middle of his forehead. The back of his head....

Then came a welcome sound, a cry from Mallory.

"All clear, O'Shea! Bring your men!"

They came on the double. Not all of them. Half of them, maybe. Those few minutes of gunfire, raking our fearfully exposed position, had cost us. MacGregor, huge bear of a man, staggered around an ell of the house carrying a still figure. Danny Wilson. I cried, "Mac, is he—?"

"Bad, Brian! Mighty bad." MacGregor lumbered into the house with his burden; the rest of the men followed him, lingering to throw last shots into the advancing force before they disappeared.

There remained, still, my most important task. Now the Toties had apparently brought up several pieces of light artillery, for mingled with the snap of musketry I heard the familiar coughing bark of ordnance. Once the house shuddered and quaked, concussion deafened my ear drums as a shell found us. But I sped down the empty corridors toward the lab. Time was precious. All too soon the Toties would close in on the house; before that I must toss my flame, race back to the tunnel entrance.

I burst into the room, at last, and—

—and stood aghast! I had only presence of mind to throw a shielding arm across my face, hold my breath. For no longer was the closet sealed. The bars had been smashed inward, the lock was a shard of broken metal, the door a heap of splinters. The gods of chance had tossed a die for our enemies. That shell I had heard—had found its way into the granary of death!

I had a momentary glimpse of the inside of the closet. I saw grey, fungoid granules sifting through the broken door; a cloud whirled and eddied toward me. To breathe that cloud meant oblivion. Beating at my clothes, my hair, with suddenly frenzied fingers, I turned and fled from the room.

In the hallway I stopped, ignited the box of matches I carried, tossed the blazing brand onto the oil-soaked floor. Flame licked hungrily along those stained boards; the bright fire-flower grew before my eyes. Even so, I knew my effort was in vain. The shell had entered through the walls of the house, and even now I could see those spores of slumber sifting out to float with the winds.

An agonized cry brought me to my senses. Mallory's voice, "Brian! Brian, lad—where are you!"

I turned and fled toward the secret portal. I made it just in time. The aged doctor and I were the last to enter the tunnel as the first Totie set foot in the laboratory. Stumbling, panting, we raced down that smooth slope to where the *Jefferson* awaited us. A dull throbbing wakened echoes in the hollow depths; eager hands helped us into the air-lock.

I heard Mallory gasp, "Take off! *Now!*" The humming deepened to a frightful roar, the Niagara of powers beyond comprehension. I was dimly aware of a cascade of broken rock smashing down about the *Jefferson's* permalloy casing, of an unearthly sheet of flame mirrored through quartzite windows. Then a tremendous tug pulled me to my knees, my lungs strained for precious air, blood danced before my eyes and there was agony in my bones....

CHAPTER VII

Earth was a tremendous disc, swaddled in lacy veils of gleaming white, when next I looked upon it from the control turret of the *Jefferson*. I did not look for long. I had, when I turned my gaze upon it, some vague idea of being able to determine (if nothing else) broad continental outlines of the sphere from which we were roaring at a speed which Mallory had told me was approximately 25,000 miles per hour.

But the sheen was so terrifically blinding that I had to shut my eyes. Dr. Mallory, no longer so intent over his instruments now that he had checked his course and found it satisfactory, noticed the movement, reached over and turned the pane through which I had been looking a quarter-turn in its grooved frame. Immediately the burning radiance dimmed into murky grayness.

"Earth-shine, Brian," he answered my unspoken query. "Our mother planet is a great reflecting body. At this distance it is even more painful to look upon with the naked eye than is the sun."

Maureen said, "But the moon, Doctor? We don't seem to be moving toward it?"

"We aren't. It's moving toward us. Or perhaps I should say both it and we are moving toward a mutual point in space where our paths will intersect in—" He glanced at a chronometer and at his calculations. "In a little less than eight and a half hours.

"Before that, however. Brian," he turned to me seriously, "there will be a few minutes that I am afraid will be rather uncomfortable for our party. The period of absolute weightlessness when we reach the 'dead spot'; the spot where the gravitational forces of Earth and its moon are completely nullified by each other.

"You might go below and warn everyone that this is to be expected. Bid them not to be alarmed."

Someone coughed apologetically at the turret door. It was St. Cloud. His face was granitelike, but his eyes were haggard. He said, "Brian—"

"Yes?"

"It's Danny."

"Danny? Is he—?"

He nodded. "I'm afraid so. He'd like to see you."

* * * *

I followed him swiftly down the ramp, through the corridors, and into the sick bay. There were a half dozen of the men in there receiving first aid treatment from one of Dr. Mallory's assistants. Wilson was in one of the private wards off the main hospital room.

He turned his head slowly as I entered, essayed a grin that froze, suddenly, as a spasm shook him. But he said, in a low, husky voice, "Hyah, Cap!"

I said, "Hayah, yourself, soldier!" and motioned the others to get out. The door closed softly behind them. "Got a blighty one, did you?" I said.

He said laboriously, "You wouldn't kid a guy, would you, Brian? I got a west one this time." His hands plucked at the sheet covering him, drew it down. Even the bandages had not been able to staunch that slow, staining seepage. I drew the cover back again.

"You're tough, Irish," I told him. "You'll get over that one before breakfast."

But I had a hard time saying it; the words rang false from my lips. I was lying, and he knew it as well as I. He shook his head.

"I don't much give a damn, Brian. I got the guy who done it, and a couple others for good measure. There's only one thing I'm sorry about."

"Yes, Irish?"

"That story. It was about a guy named Kinniston. A Lensman. He was in a hell of a jam. I'd like to have known if he got out." He said plaintively, "I can't lift my hands, Brian, boy. They're so damned weak...."

I said, "One of those magazines? Where is it?" He nodded to the chair beside his bed. I picked the thing up, found the place where he'd left off. I started reading to him the story that had captured his fancy. It wasn't easy. I hadn't read much of anything since I left military training school at the age of thirteen. A lot of the words were unfamiliar, and I guess I made pretty heavy weather of it.

But he seemed to be enjoying it. He lay back on the pillows, breathing hard, so intent on the adventures of this "Gray Lensman," printed in an old and yellowed fiction book, that he almost forgot the icy fingers closing in upon him.

He only interrupted me once. That was to say suddenly, "Brian—it was Krassner, you know."

"What?"

"He fired ... the shot."

The shot that had betrayed us! I was reminded, forcibly, that I hadn't seen Krassner aboard ship. I didn't know whether he'd made it or not. But if he had—

"Go on ... Brian. Get him out of trouble before...."

So I read on. It was weirdly strange, sitting there reading a story of spaceflight adventure written twenty years ago. While we, ourselves, soared the void in a craft bound for Earth's satelite. But I read on. And it must have been ten minutes before I sensed something wrong. At first I couldn't figure what it was. Then, suddenly, I realized. It was the fact that Danny's breathing no longer rasped beside me....

I rose and closed the magazine. I hope that somehow he knows, now, how the Lensman fought his way out of that jam.

* * * *

I went back to the turret, then. But on the way I sought out Ronnie and Mac and Rudy. I asked them about Krassner. They hadn't seen him.

"But we will! If he's aboard this ship, we'll dig him out!"

They were gathering their squads into search parties as I left. In the control room, Dr. Mallory had just completed another check-up and minor course revision. He was jubilant because the *Jefferson* was reacting so beautifully. "Another six hours, Brian, and we'll be there. I've been teaching Maureen to operate the ship. She's an apt pupil."

Maureen flushed with pleasure. Mallory continued, "I'm glad we have another pilot. Now she can make the next trip back to earth, pick up more colonists while we build our Lunar colony—"

I started, and looked at him swiftly. Then he didn't know! I said, "Doctor—those spores. How swiftly do they propogate?"

"With drastic swiftness, Brian, lad. That's why I kept them in a sealed, sterile chamber. Had they ever been loosed, within two month's time all Earth would have succumbed to their somnivorous power. But why do you ask—?" A sudden look of fear swept his features; his voice rose.

"Brian! You destroyed the spores? I saw flames leaping before you entered the tunnel—"

And then I told him.

It took him a good while to speak again. And when he spoke, his voice was deep with sorrow. He glanced at the dim shadow of earth outlined on the polaroid window, and his hands made a yearning gesture.

"That which I feared most has come to pass. We are powerless to prevent it. We might have time for two, three, a half dozen trips to Earth to save a few refugees from the sleep to come—but even that is unsafe. Were a single spore to get into the ship, be borne back to Luna, our colony, too, would be stilled in centuries, aeons of slumber. You're *sure* the spores escaped, Brian?"

"I'm sure."

"Then soon we will be the last of Earth's waking children. Our responsibility is graver than ever. Now must we not only keep alive the spirit of liberty, but all man's dreamed-of future is in our hands."

Maureen cried desperately, "But the responsibility is too great, Dr. Mallory. Surely you, who invented the spores, know some way to counteract their action? Isn't there some way to effectively destroy them?"

"None, my dear. None ... except ..." His eyes dimmed uncertainly. "I don't know. Maybe. There's a faint, far possibility. Once, as I was experimenting, I happened to expose certain of the spore-plasm to synthetic chlorophyll. A reaction took place, a sloughing of the spore cell. I was not interested in that at the time, so I didn't pursue the experiment. But it is remotely possible...."

"We must try, then," I told him. "As soon as we get to Luna, you must try that experiment again. Try it on your sleeping assistant, Williamson. Better he should die now than slumber on forever in his glass coffin.

"And if the antidote works, we'll be in a position to reclaim Earth. Sweep away the plague, and while doing so, end the war in the very fashion you once planned."

"I'll do it!" he cried excitedly. "Chlorophyll must be the answer! As soon as we reach—"

He stopped abruptly. Footsteps were pounding up the runway; breathless men were tumbling into the room. Big Mac was at their head, his brow was red with unbridled rage. He yelled at me, "Brian! We've found him! We've found the dirty, skulking rat!"

"Krassner, you mean?" I thought again of Danny, and of those others who had died because of Krassner's revealing gun shot. My anger flared to match MacGregor's. "Where is he? Bring him in!"

"We've got to take him. He's barricaded himself in the aft storage compartment and threatens to blow the ship to hell if we make a move!"

CHAPTER VIII

For a moment, everything before my eyes was outlined in crimson. As from afar I heard my own voice gritting, "Get your men together! Follow me—"

Then Dr. Mallory's sharp command, "No, Brian! Don't move hastily. He has the upper hand. He can do just what he threatens. Those aft storage bins are loaded with explosive, inflammable substances. Maybe we can reason with him—" He turned to Maureen. "Hold the ship to its course, my dear. I will be back in a few minutes."

We moved aft. Mallory and myself, MacGregor and Ian Pelham-Jones,

Devereaux. We passed through the bulkhead that sealed the forward from the aft portion of the ship, hurried down a long corridor, and came to the carriage lock beyond which lay the storage bins, the engineers' berths, the recreation room and the library.

This door was closed; before it, tense, nervous, uncertain, hovered a dozen of my men. Van Huys headed them; he looked up at me, his pale blue eyes troubled.

"He's in there, Brian. I think the man's gone mad!"

Mallory raised his voice, called mildly, "Krassner?"

There was a shuffling sound from behind the lock. A moment's silence, then Krassner, suspiciously, "Well?"

"What's the matter, my friend? You mustn't act like this. What is it you want?"

"Turn the ship back to Earth!"

"But we can't do that." Mallory's voice was soothing, persuasive. "We've set our course. We can't return."

"You must, damn you!"

I couldn't restrain myself any longer. I brushed by Mallory, cried, "Krassner, you're acting like an idiot! Come out of there immediately!"

Again there was a brief instant of stillness. Then Krassner's tone altered subtlely, became half-mocking. "Is that you, O'Shea?"

"Yes."

"The gallant captain of a drag-tailed company. You want to save your command, don't you, Captain? Then make the old fool turn this ship back, and do it *now*!"

Wrath inflamed me; I stepped forward and hammered on the metal door. There came the sound of swift, frightened movements inside. Krassner yelled sharply, incisively, "Don't try to come in here, O'Shea. I can blast this ship to shards, and by the Banner, I'll—"

He stopped abruptly, aware that in his excitement he had finally given himself away. But if he was startled, I was even more so. Suddenly, now, it all made sense. I wondered why I had not guessed the truth before. But I am not a clever man; I am just a soldier. And we had met Krassner under circumstances that favored his deceit.

I said slowly, "So you're not one of us, after all, Krassner? You're one of them?"

He had recovered his aplomb. He laughed stridently. In my mind's eye I could see his face, thin lips drawn in a tight smile, those too-close eyes lifted at the corners with mockery. His voice was a taunt.

"Congratulations, O'Shea, on having played the dupe so long and so excellently. Allow me to introduce myself in my proper character. Captain Jacob Krassner of the Imperial German Army—at your service!"

It was all too clear, now. I remembered the day we had met Krassner, seen him "shot down" by an enemy plane. I remembered MacGregor's comment at the time. "Damned funny. First Totie I ever saw who didn't gun a parachuter."

And that day I had caught him listening to us from Mallory's outer office. His restless wanderings around the laboratory grounds; now I knew he had been seeking the hide-away of the *Jefferson*. And the betraying rifle-shot—

"You Americans are a naïve race," Krassner was saying amusedly. "It never occurred to you, did it, O'Shea, that I might have concealed on me a portable transmitter? It was I who exposed the location of the laboratory to our gallant forces. We had suspected for some time that strange things were brewing near Cleft Canyon. That is why I—shall we say 'dropped into the picture'? To learn the meaning of certain things that puzzled us."

He was a braggart, like the rest of them. Now that he had given himself away—only Toties swore "by the Banner"—he was gloating triumphantly. And he held the upper hand. We could not even tell him that which we knew; that Earth was doomed, that already hundreds of thousands of his compatriots as well as ours by quiescent in dreadful, sleeping undeath. If he discovered the Totie cause was lost—well, they were ever ones for the heroic, the vainglorious gesture. And his hand controlled forces that would blast us all into nothingness.

* * * *

I glanced about me nervously. The faces of the men mirrored my anxiety, Mallory's brow was heavy with fear, Van Huys gnawed his full lower lip savagely. Only the gleaming metalwork of the corridor was impassive; that and the heavy door that barred us from a traitor and an enemy. A grilled square, high in the walls of the corridor, was like a great, fanged, laughing mouth. I stared at it.

"Mallory!" I whispered the name. "What is that?"

"Eh?" He followed my glance. "Oh—that? Part of the ventilation system. But, why—?" Then he grasped the reason for my sudden eagerness. "Yes, Brian. It feeds into every chamber. We'll give you a hand. Bruce—"

Krassner's voice came to us, suspicious. "What are you whispering about out there? I warn you, don't attempt to enter this room. If you do, we'll all die together!"

Mallory somehow managed to keep his tone steady.

"Krassner, you're an intelligent man. Listen—"

"Keep him talking, Doctor!" I whispered. I nodded to MacGregor; his huge hands cupped to give me a hand-up to the grill. My fingers tore at the four studs that bolted it into position. One came out. Another. All eyes were upon me as I lifted the heavy grill from its position, lowered it into the outstretched hands. Only Mallory continued talking, pleading, arguing, reassuring. Stalling for precious time.

I nodded, MacGregor's shoulders heaved, and I was scrambling into the smooth bore of the ventilating system. It was narrow, but not too narrow; the air was cool, clean-smelling. I crept from the opening, was lost in darkness.

A native sense of direction, keen-edged by years of guerrilla warfare, aided me in threading that black labyrinth. How long the creeping journey took, I had no way of knowing. It seemed endless, for I moved slowly, cautiously, dreading the revelatory scrape of clothing upon metal, the sound that might send Krassner suddenly into action.

A turn, a rise, a descent, and another turn. Then before me loomed a networked square of light. And the sound of Krassner's voice was no longer muffled; it reached my ears loudly. "—fine organization, O'Shea, where the soldiers address their 'captain' by his first name. But we will teach you obedience, you Yankee up-starts! We—"

I was at the grill. There was no way to unscrew it from the inside. What could be done must be done—and in a single, sure move—from here.

Krassner stood a few yards from the barred and bolted door. He had not been bluffing. He had prepared the way for the destruction of the *Jefferson* in the event his demands were refused, his scheme went awry. The end of a coiled fuse lay beside him, he toyed nervously with an electro-lighter as he talked. But now his patience was wearing thin. He said, "But enough of this conversation! Are you, or are you not, going to turn about? Your answer now, or by the Banner—"

Mallory answered reluctantly, "Krassner, once more I beg of you to listen to reason."

"The time for reason is past. I want action. You, O'Shea! Speak to me! Are you going to turn the ship?"

Silence. I eased my revolver from its bolster with infinite slowness. I saw a puzzled look appear on Krassner's features, turn to a look of sudden doubt.

"O'Shea! Where are you? Speak to me!"

My gun spoke for me.

* * * *

Krassner never suffered for the misery he brought on others. He never knew what struck him. My shot crashed into his brain like a Jovian bolt. Without a word, a whimper, a groan, he collapsed where he stood, his lips still parted in the question he had been hurling at the door upon which, now my comrades were battering.

But even in death, Krassner was destined to throw a last blow amongst us. My cavernous eyrie echoed with a roaring blast; when my deafened ears could hear again they heard a sizzling crackle. The stench of burning powder stung my nostrils.

I craned to look down through the grill; saw there that which damped my forehead coldly. Krassner's weapon had been the hand flame-thrower of our enemy. The stricken convulsion of his fist had shot a withering blast of flame upon the fuse. Now a charred line of fire was racing to the charge Krassner had prepared.

In frantic haste I screamed this knowledge to those beyond the door. "You've got to get in somehow! Stop that fuse!" Their efforts redoubled. I heard the ringing crash of metal upon metal which meant they had brought up a pry, then came a hissing sound, and at the doorjamb, by the hinges, metal warmed, turned orange, glowed cherry red. A blowtorch!

I could do no good behind this grill. It was the act of a contortionist to turn in that meager space, but somehow I accomplished it, scrambled desperately toward the corridor grill through which I had entered the air-duct.

It was just as I gained the opening that the hinges of the lock finally gave way, the door burst open. Even I was not prepared for that which appeared through the frame. The entire aperture was one solid sheet of flame. Despite their eagerness, no one could blame my men for falling back, horrified, from the scorching fingers that leaped out to grasp them.

All but one! And that one was Dr. Thomas Mallory. Perhaps it was because he alone realized the vital necessity of jerking that fuse from its charge before everything ended in one coruscant moment. Arms locked before his face, head lowered, he dashed recklessly into that flaming hell!

I fell—or dropped, I know not which—from my outlet, found myself on my feet, heard myself bellowing, "Water! We've got to stop that fire before—"

But they knew that. Already someone had raced to the jets, another was tugging desperately at a reel of fire hose. I suppose what I did next was heroic. Either that or damned, blind foolishness. It could not have been deliberate heroism, for there was no time to measure the chances, weigh the consequences. I leaped through the doorway, followed Dr. Mallory. And even so, there was another figure at my side. That of burly Bruce MacGregor.

We found him at the same time. He lay face down on the floor, arms outstretched before him. But in one blistered hand was—the end of the fuse. Scant inches from its charred end stood piled boxes of Triple-X, most deadly of all explosives. The flames had not yet quite reached it, but in another moment—

Then the water came! Like a solid fist it caught me in the middle of the back, shot me, sprawling, forward. The breath shot from my lungs before that impact—but never had I been more grateful for a bruising blow.

MacGregor, a sorry sight with his blistered cheeks, scorched hair, spark-charred garments, bent his brute strength against the flood, roared directions.

"Here! On these boxes first! Soak them, ruin them! We can fight the fire later...."

* * * *

We got Dr. Mallory out of that furnace. How long we battled the fire after that is hard to say. At least an hour. Krassner had planned his coup with deadly Teutonic thoroughness. Not only had he arranged the fuse and explosive charge; he had also soaked walls, drapes, furniture, with gasoline.

Against this, our water was useless. We had no sand. Men labored to drag the lethal crates of explosive out of the danger zone; after that we went back at the ever-spreading fire. Chemicals did the trick finally. The last blaze succumbed to the stifling blanket of carbon dioxide, a clean-up crew methodically swept up the last of the charred débris.

Thus died Krassner—but at what a cost! Ten of my men in the hospital, at least two of them seriously burned. Three whole bins of provisions gone forever, devoured by the hungriest of all foes. A binful of linens, clothing, blankets, burned to cinders. And every other room that had been in that aft section of the ship gutted!

All these disasters paled into insignificance when, bandaged, cleaned, reclad, I went to visit Dr. Mallory. One look at his face and I knew that here was the heaviest price we were to pay for the destruction of our last mortal foe. Only Mallory's eyes were visible under the swaddling mask of bandage, and these were raw and bloodshot. But the ghost of a smile lighted these fine old eyes, and his voice, sieved through a layer of gauze, said weakly:

"I ... reached there in time ... Brian, lad."

"You did that," I told him huskily. "You saved us all, Doctor."

"Not only us, but ... mankind. We *had* to live, Brian. You must lead ... our people ... out of the wilderness."

I said, "Not I, Doctor. *You.* You are the only man who can save us, reclaim the sleeping world—"

He said, as though not hearing me, "It's a good ... thing I showed Maureen ... how to run the ship. Isn't it? Now she can take us to Luna.

"Brian, boy ... find the notes ... in my desk. They'll help you. I believe ... you'll find the crater of Copernicus ... the best place to land. There will be air there. Thin, maybe. But air. In the underground grottoes ... should be ... water...."

A spasm shook him; his eyes closed for a moment in pain, then opened again. They were febrilely bright.

"Most important of all ... Brian ... the spores. You must find a way ... to destroy them. Go back to Earth ... and awaken man ... to a new, a peaceful, world."

He was silent so long that I cried out, "Doctor!" I couldn't say more.

But he spoke again, and for the last time. "I am sure now ... Brian ... you will find the answer ... in chlorophyll. Keep after it. The fate of all ... mankind ... is in only your...."

And that was all. His eyes closed, then, as if they had finally found peace. I turned away. Maureen covered his face tenderly. She came to my side, and her voice was soft.

"He was right, Brian. You are our leader now. It is up to you to find the antidote for Earth's illness."

I stared at her long and bitterly. My voice must have been harsh.

"I! I, Maureen? Tell me—do you know the formula for chlorophyll? Do I? Does anyone aboard this ship, now *he* is gone?"

"Don't be upset, Brian. No, we don't—but there's no cause for despair. It, and everything else you need know, is at our disposal. That's why he went to such pains to provide a scientific library for the ship. All man's knowledge lies there, waiting for us to seek it out."

I took a deep breath. I said, "That's just it, Maureen. I couldn't bring myself to tell him. But—"

"But, Brian—?"

"The library is gone! The books that meant life or death for mankind are a pile of crumbled ashes!"

* * * *

I suppose I should be grateful that we are here. I should be thankful that Maureen's quick intelligence made it possible for us to land here at the crater of Copernicus. I look from the window of my little shack. I see shanties like my own arranged in a crude circle here at the base of towering mountains.

Dr. Mallory was right. We have air here, and water. We have enough provisions to last us for years. By the time those are exhausted, we will be independent of our Earthly supplies, for already Sanders and Van Huys have set soil into cultivation; they claim, gleefully, that this thick, rich, Lunar soil flowers like a desert when watered. And we have set up plants for the synthesis of water.

Strange how quickly we have adapted ourselves. We even laugh sometimes, nowadays. There have been marriages; I suppose that means that in a little while there will be births. Imagine that! The first Earth child to be born on the Moon.

I, too, should be happy. At times I am—comparatively. For I have Maureen beside me; our love is a great, sustaining force in a desperate existence.

But I cannot be completely happy, for night or day I am reminded of the great, impossible burden that weighs my shoulders low. The Earth, a massive, glowing globe, lights our sky. Occasionally I think I can glimpse the gleaming ocean waters of Earth; once, on a clear night, the familiar outline of our lost homeland, America, was crystal clear to our eyes.

Yet all life on that nearby mother planet is, must be, now deep in everlasting sleep. Everlasting because I am powerless to interrupt it. Because Mallory's library is no more; because I am a stupid soldier, not a clever man.

Only recently there came a wan ray of hope. It was as we were transferring the last pieces of furniture from the *Jefferson* to our shacks. In the berth that had been Danny Wilson's—gay, laughing Danny!—I found pile upon pile of those amusing, colorful "magazines" that Danny loved.

They are old and ragged; many of them are coverless. But most of them—for such was Danny's preference—are the kind which Mallory once called "science fiction." Dreams of the world-to-be, pathetic in the face of that which now confronts us.

But it is my only ray of hope, these magazines. I brought them to my shack. I am culling them carefully, one by one. There is a faint, and oh! so faint, chance that....

Yet I fear it is a hopeless search. There is so much of fancy in these little books, so little simple fact. Had but *one* of those imaginative writers of years ago thought to include in one of his stories that which must have been, to him, a commonplace formula—that for chlorophyll—I could yet do that which Mallory demanded of me. Here we are rich with ores, the soil teems with every element known to man. We have a well-equipped laboratory, we could synthesize *anything*. But we cannot create this "chlorophyll" because we do not know what it is, nor what elements combine to form it.

Hope dwindles as I read. There remains but one more slim pile of magazines before me. If the answer is not in one of them, then we must perish. I turn pleading eyes to the past, to the year 1940, before I was born. But there is no one to hear my plea. Unless, in one of these remaining—

(Here the manuscript ends.)

POSTSCRIPT

Common sense tells me there can be little doubt but that this "manuscript," purported to be written by one Brian O'Shea, a soldier in the Army of the Democracies in the year 1963, A.D., is a deliberate and painstaking hoax.

Who is responsible for it, I cannot begin to guess. Somehow I can't bring myself to believe that Dr. Edgar Winslow (whom I have investigated and found to be exactly what he claimed, a fellow in the psychology department of one of our nearby Southern universities) would lend himself to such a fantastic trick.

But it is hard to believe, also, that Winslow could and did achieve the perfect telaesthetic rapport evidenced by the foregoing pages.

But—there was an earnestness about Winslow that stirred me strangely. He did not have the air of a man perpetrating a fraud. He asked me, you will remember, to "play the game of caution," even if I did not believe that which I found in the manuscript.

I should, perhaps, dismiss the whole thing with a shrug; heave the "story" back at Winslow with the advice that if he wants to become a science-fiction writer he should do so honestly, not try to insinuate his way into print on the byline of another.

Yet—it is a queer manuscript. It is quiet here in Roanoke today. As I write, I look from my office windows to see the rolling hills, now sweet-breasted with fresh green, misted with the soft white of dogwood. The sky is blue and clear, the sun a warm beneficence. Still, the morning papers tell of the desperate plight of the Allies. Again they have lost ground to a grim, mechanized Totalitarian army. Finland, Norway, Belgium, Holland,—the list grows.

Mussolini has sent his restless legions to battle; Japan makes overt gestures toward the Indies. Russia, the patient bear, crouches in the north, watches ... and waits....

I don't know. I honestly don't know. The manuscript is probably a hoax. And yet ... and yet....

Anyway, here it is, Brian O'Shea. Here is what you asked for. You'll find it on the cover of this magazine. If this magazine is one of those through which you still have to search, the world you mourn may yet blossom anew.

And because covers, like man's freedom and dreams and hopes, too often crumble into dust, the formula you want is printed here again, man of the future.

$C_{55}H_{70}O_6N_4Mg$ is the empirical formula for chlorophyll, Brian O'Shea!

$C_{55}H_{70}O_6N_4Mg$!

THE BALLAD OF BLASTER BILL

Originally published in *Planet Stories*, Summer 1941.

When you're hurtling 'round the Sun
  On the perihelion run
  Through the asteroids from Jupiter to Mars,
  You may chance to see a light
  In the everlasting night,
  An unwinking beacon, sister to the stars.
  Then each member of the crew
  From the lowest wiper to
  The Skipper on the bridge, a moment will
  Drop all work and gravely, mute,
  Raise his arm in full salute
  To the final resting place of Blaster Bill.
  Afterward, if you are not
  Just a nosey rankey-pot, [5]
  And the thing that ticks within you isn't stone,
  You may learn from spacemens' lips
  Tales of ancient days and ships,
  And why Bill the Blaster lies there all alone.

II

Surly Jonathan McNeer
Was the Master Engineer
On the wallowing old freighter, Dotty Sue.
He was gruff, uncouth, unclean,
And his language was obscene,
But a better grease-pot never sheared the blue.
He had nerves of tempered steel,
And without a squawk or squeal
He would plot a course to Hades for a thrill;
But his temper was like fire

---

5   *rankey-pot*—Earthlubber; from the Venusian "*renqui-pth*"

And the man who drew his ire,
Who tried his patience most, was—Blaster Bill.
Bill the Blaster was a lazy,
Good-for-nothing (some said crazy),
Guy who didn't have a gray cell in his head.
He had muscle in his shoulders,
And his forearms were like boulders,
But his cranium and can were filled with lead.
Without ever even trying
He could make McNeer start crying
Down the wrath of Baal upon his hapless dome.
He and awkwardness were cousins,
He broke things by scores and dozens
Just one look at him and tubes sang, "Ohm, sweet Ohm!"
On the Dotty Sue, *his duty*
Was to keep all tutti-frutti
The rocket-blasts, the motors and the rest
Of the intricate equipment
Which insures a speedy shipment
To the planets that are buttons on Sol's vest.
But McNeer's deserved objection
Was—Bill practiced vivisection
Every time he placed his thumbs (which numbered five)
On a section of machinery.
"He'd be better in a beanery!"
Was McNeer's complaint. "I'll skin the guy alive!"
"Now, there, Jonathan!" the Skipper
Used to say, "Don't be a yipper.
I'm sure Bill does the best he can." But grief
Etched gray, fretful lines and horrid
On McNeer's space-weathered forehead.
"The best is none too good!" complained the Chief.

III

Two months out of Io City
Everything was running pretty,
The asteroids were thirty hours away,
When McNeer, to whom perfection
Was a sort of predilection,
Said, "Bill, we'll take the hypos down today."
Well, the hypatomic motors

Are the energy-plus rotors
That control a spaceship's motion in the void.
When the ship is once free-wheeling
'Neath the vast celestial ceiling,
Then's the time to clean the grit with which they're cloyed.
So Bill said, "Yup. Okey-dokey!"
And with movements slow and pokey
Dismounted Number one and got to work.
"Do a perfect job, you globaar! [6]
Or I'll crown you with a crow-bar!"
Warned McNeer—and then he vanished with a smirk.
It was some two hours later
As, upon his "sweet pertater"
The Chief Engineer was tootling Venus Nell,
That the Second Mate, half witless,
Out of breath and frightened spitless,
Burst in crying, "Chief, we're on our way to hell!"
"What, already?" drawled McNeer
But the mate, pale green with fear,
Bawled, "Go get the hypos working, without fail!
And go do it on the double,
'Cause we're in a peck of trouble!
A rogue asteroid is riding on our tail!"

IV

Now, in case you don't remember,
A "rogue asteroid's" a member
Of the minor planet group that's slipped its cogs.
Wrenched by gravitational forces,
It careens about its courses
In an orbit not computable by logs.
Tons on tons of granite, metaled,
By the tug of Jove unsettled,
Weaving in, about, below its normal belt;
Is it any wonder why a
Spaceman fears this mad pariah?
Dreads the moment when its power may be felt?
With a single, sharp, explosive
Word that acted as corrosive
On the mate's embarrassed eardrums, raced McNeer

---

6   *globaar*—shiftless person; Ionian term of reproach

To the engine-room where, peaceful,
Happy, busy, very grease-full,
Labored Blaster Bill, with grins from ear to ear.
"Bill!" McNeer cried, voice all blurry,
"Get that hypo in a hurry—"
Then his order strangled as he stared, aghast.
"What is this?" he faltered weakly,
"What is this?" And Bill, quite meekly,
Said, "I thought I'd melt it down for a recast!"
His imagination racing
The Chief gazed upon the casing
Of the hypatomic motor Number Three,
Now a pool of molten metal
Bubbling gently in a kettle.
"Goddlemighty!" yelled McNeer. "This thing can't be!"
Bill asked, "Why the mad commotion?"
Then they glimpsed a sudden motion
And the Skipper's face was in the televise.
"Got the motors fixed, McNeer?"
And the Chief said, low and clear,
"No. Does someone know a prayer amongst you guys?"
"Why?" the Skipper roared, distrait;
The Chief let him have it straight.
"The hypatomic's melted into wax!
But before that rogue gets near,
I've a twelve pound hammer here
To warp across my blaster's parallax!"
"Wait!" the Captain cried, "Not yet!
We must cover every bet.
I'm commander of this freighter while she rolls.
We must somehow make a turn,
Shake that damn rogue off our stern.
Suppose you try the manual controls?"
McNeer sadly shook his head
As he saw the rusty red
Of the long neglected manuals, but yelled,
"Hop to it, Bill, you dope!
It's our last and only hope—"
And then he stopped and gulped, "Well, I'll be helled!"
With his back arched neck to heel,
Bill was straining at the wheel;
The year-old rust was breaking off in flakes.

McNeer's eyes lit with joy,
He shouted, "Bill, my boy!
See, there, lad? She gives! She shakes!"
And true enough, the screw
Of the gallant Dotty Sue
Was turning 'neath the blaster's mighty brawn.
The C. E.'s voice was thunder,
"We're getting out from under!
Just hold 'er, Bill; the danger will be gone!"
A moment, still as death,
While Bill the Blaster's breath
Rasped through the rocking room in tortured sobs,
Then from the bridge rang out
The Skipper's warning shout,
"Too late! Abandon ship, Chief! Don your lobs!"
McNeer said, "Too bad, Bill,
Just hold 'er there until
I get the lobs, and then we'll pull our freight."
With firm, untrembling hands
He took down from their stands
Two spacesuits, worn and old and out of date.
But Bill the Blaster stood
As motionless as wood;
His arms like knotted oak in cords of strain.
He slowly shook his head
And to the Chief he said,
"If all break ship, we'll not see Earth again."
"I know—" began McNeer,
But Bill roared out, "Stand clear!"
His arms upon the wheel were like a vise.
"Break ship and wait outside,
I'll make this baby ride!
I'll hold 'er till the devil skates on ice!"
Then in the visiplate
Appeared the Second Mate,
"All out below? Did you break ship, McNeer?"
McNeer said, "Right away!
Come on, Bill, don't delay!"
But Bill the Blaster panted, "Chief, stand clear!"
"You fool, you're courting death!"
Bill answered, "Save your breath,"
And grinned, "You'll need that oxygen outside!"

And stood like frozen steel
Beside that bucking wheel,
McNeer, reluctant, hovered at his side....
Till Bill cried, "You damn fool!"
And grabbed a handy tool
And slashed it 'cross his headpiece like a mace.
There came a crashing roar,
McNeer knew nothing more
Until he woke to find himself in space.

V

About him, staff and crew
Of the ill-starred Dotty Sue
Were huddled, bitter, grim, but unafraid.
A quarter mile away
The last scene of the fray
Tween Man and Asteroid was being played.
Her stern jets flaming white
Against the endless night
The bobbing ship was fighting, bolt and nail,
To curve from underneath
Those looming tons of death
That poised above her like a cosmic flail.
McNeer cried, "No, Bill! No!"
And then his audio
Clacked with the Skipper's thin, metallic voice,
"There's nothing we can do
But hope he pulls her through.
He made his choice, McNeer; a hero's choice."
As they watched tensely, all,
The spaceship seemed to crawl
An inch, a foot, a yard, another yard....
Meanwhile, the massive rock
Raced blindly toward the shock
With vast, colossal, cosmic disregard.
And nearer yet they drew,
To their strange rendezvous
In space; Fate's balance hovered fine and thin.
And then, "The Lord be praised!"
The crew a paean raised;
McNeer's white lips cracked in a nerveless grin.

Imponderable mass
And spaceship seemed to pass
Each other with a hair 'twixt hull and face;
But then, as every voice
Roused in a loud rejoice,
A single boulder slashed through empty space—
The spaceship buckled, bent;
A gaping, white-fanged rent
Split stern plates, and McNeer's voice cracked with fear.
"Board ship, all hands!" he cried!
"Bill's dying there inside!"
The wan sun watched the killer disappear.
McNeer was first to kneel
Beside the shattered wheel
And Bill's pale, silent figure; gray with grief
He cried, "He's breathing yet!
Here, Skipper! Help me get—"
But Bill said, "No—don't try to lift me, Chief."
"I look all right on top
But ... better get ... a mop....
My underneath part's not so good...." A chill
Ran through his broken frame,
But, to the last ditch game,
"I held 'er to 'er course—" said Blaster Bill.

VI

So—hurtling 'round the Sun
On the perihelion run
Through the asteroids from Jupiter to Mars,
You may chance to see a light
In the everlasting night,
An unwinking beacon, sister to the stars.
And then, if you are not
A lousy rankey-pot,
With the instincts of the back end of a horse,
You'll stand a moment, mute,
Arm raised in full salute
To Blaster Bill—who held 'er to 'er course.